Ashes
and
Angel wings

World of Darkness Fiction from White Wolf

More Demon Fiction!
Lucifer's Shadow: Tales of Fallen Angels,
edited by Philippe Boulle

The Victorian Age Vampire Trilogy
Vampire: A Morbid Initiation by Philippe Boulle
Vampire: The Madness of Priests by Philippe Boulle
Vampire: The Wounded King by Philippe Boulle

The Dark Ages Clan Novel Series
Dark Ages: Nosferatu by Gherbod Fleming
Dark Ages: Assamite by Stefan Petrucha
Dark Ages: Cappadocian by Andrew Bates
Dark Ages: Setite by Kathleen Ryan
Dark Ages: Lasombra by David Niall Wilson

The Werewolf Tribe Novel Series
Tribe Novels: Shadow Lords & Get of Fenris
by Gherbod Fleming & Eric Griffin
Tribe Novels: Silent Striders & Black Furies
by Carl Bowen & Gherbod Fleming
Tribe Novels: Red Talons & Fianna
by Philippe Boulle & Eric Griffin
Tribe Novels: Bone Gnawers & Stargazers
by Justin Achilli & Bill Bridges
Tribe Novels: Children of Gaia & Uktena
by Richard Lee Byers & Stefan Petrucha
Tribe Novels: Silver Fangs & Glass Walkers
by Carl Bowen & Tim Dedopulos
Tribe Novels: Black Spiral Dancers & Wendigo
by Eric Griffin & Bill Bridges

FOR ALL THESE TITLES AND MORE, VISIT

WWW.WHITE-WOLF.COM/FICTION

Ashes and Angel Wings

Greg Stolze

Book One of the Trilogy of the Fallen

Cover art by Steve Ellis. Graphic design by Kieran Yanner. Art direction by Richard Thomas. Copyedited by Carl Bowen.

ISBN 1-58846-805-4
First Edition: March 2003
Printed in Canada

White Wolf Publishing
1554 Litton Drive
Stone Mountain, GA 30083
www.white-wolf.com/fiction

Dedicated to Paul N. Stolze, 1939–1988

One fatal Tree there stands of Knowledge call'd,
Forbidden them to taste
—Milton, *Paradise Lost*, Book IV

PROLOGUE

In the darkness, there was a mind.

The mind was alone in the darkness, because the darkness was, itself, almost perfect loneliness. The mind had no body. It had no eyes with which to see that there was nothing around it to see. It had no mouth to scream and no hands to claw pointlessly for release.

It was thought and memory, alone, without even the distraction of physical agony.

Time was meaningless in the darkness. For the first span of time, the mind raged against its imprisonment. It did not know how long it raged. It could have been five minutes. It could have been five thousand years.

After its rage was exhausted, the mind grieved. Once it had lived in a world of sunshine and apples and bright-colored birds. Fish had darted, trees had grown, clouds had carved poetry in skies lit by sunrise. The mind had been named Hasmed. He had served with honor and distinction; he had loved his duties and rejoiced to

perform them. He had possessed a body, he'd had friends, and he'd known love.

Now he had nothing. Not even pain or hope. For all Hasmed knew, the world was as lost, as broken, as annihilated as himself.

After grieving, Hasmed despaired. He wondered if this void, this torment, was what the Maker of All had felt before Creation. Surely no other suffering could lead a perfect being to create a flawed world. But the maddening silence—silence that was not merely the loss of sound, but its impossibility—surely that, and the dark beyond darkness, and the crushing, numbing terror of being all there was, of being a universe unto oneself... that could drive even an infinite entity mad.

And for an infinite entity, any madness would be infinite as well.

These fears filled Hasmed's mind, which was all that remained of him. The cosmos was doomed from the start. All of it—the glory, the corruption, the hope, the horror, the pride of defiance and the brutality of War on Earth as in Heaven—all had been preordained. The ending was cut in stone before the first word was breathed.

Hasmed was mired in this despair when he heard the voice.

The voice was one he knew, one from the world. In ages past (or perhaps, only moments), that voice had belonged to Vodantu, a being like Hasmed. Like Hasmed, Vodantu had been condemned. Like Hasmed, Vodantu was trapped in a private nullity. But unlike Hasmed, Vodantu was still strong enough to communicate.

Beings of their type—once called Elohim—had been the rulers of Creation, and their essence was infused in every far corner of the cosmos. Even the void in which they were confined touched upon something other than itself, some space that was not nothing. Even though they were fallen, some were strong enough to shake their cages with thought alone, sending vibrations of their will

coursing out to make faint, reedy contact with their fellows.

Hasmed, said Vodantu's voice. *Attend*.

Hasmed ignored it.

I have need of you, Hasmed. I have a task.

Still, the imprisoned Elohim did not reply.

Then Vodantu spoke the true language of reality, and Hasmed could not ignore it—for the word Vodantu spoke was Hasmed himself, written on the book of existence. Vodantu knew Hasmed's True Name, and by this Hasmed was compelled.

What would you have of me? Hasmed sullenly asked.

The walls of our isolation are cracking, Vodantu replied. *Already some of our lesser fellows slip through and return to the physical realm.*

And you think I could escape as well?

Though once mighty, I know you were greatly reduced in the War. You might escape. I bid you try.

To what end? Our cause was doomed when the world was young. Now the cosmos is surely aged and decayed, broken by the curse of The Ancient of Days. What can we gain by escape?

Ask not what we can gain, but what we can lose, Vodantu replied. *By working our will on the world of men, we can hasten the world's demise. Is that not what cursed Ahrimal foresaw so long ago? And with the world destroyed, what can keep us sealed? Without a boundary of existence, our realm of void collapses. With even the void destroyed, with no place to hold us, no field in which we can be contained, surely the curse of our consciousness will fall as well. When creation is annulled, we will be annulled as well. We can finally cease to exist. We can finally be free of the burden of ourselves.*

I don't believe it. The Allmaker is too spiteful. The One Above would find some way to torture us still, even past the end of the world.

I DO NOT ASK YOUR OPINION, HASMED. I COMPEL YOUR OBEDIENCE.

Send someone else. Send Joriel. Send Rabbadün. Send someone who still cares enough about the world to destroy it.

THEY ARE SENT, AND NOW YOU ARE SENT AS WELL.

Hasmed fought, but against the call of his own true nature, he could not win. Silently screaming, damned Hasmed was torn from his lightless prison and flung once more into the storm of existence.

chapter
one

Mikey Diamond had a headache.

If it was a normal headache, Mikey would have taken a couple aspirin, maybe a shot of whiskey—done, no problem. But this wasn't a normal headache.

He'd had them before, and he'd discreetly asked a doctor about them. The doctor said they sounded like classic migraines, and he prescribed a drug called Cafergot. Sometimes the Cafergot worked; sometimes it didn't.

Today, it didn't.

Today, Mikey Diamond had gotten the funny feeling that something was wrong when his vision started to gray out. This was common for migraines—the doctor called it a "visual aura." Pressure built up on the optic nerve, causing a growing patch of his eyesight to simply disappear.

The visual aura was, in Mikey's opinion, pretty goddamn creepy. It didn't black out like you'd think it would, the missing space just kind of got ignored. Like his mind wallpapered over it or swept it under a rug. It could take him a while to notice that something was wrong, that there was a place where, if he looked at things... those things weren't there. It was never dead center, never what he was *looking at*. It was stuff around the edges. If he was reading a paper, the ads on the side would vanish. Driving along the street, he'd suddenly have no rearview mirror. But then he'd look—actually turn his eyes and face to

look—and the mirror or the ad or his own hand would be there, right where it was supposed to be.

The doctor had tried to explain it. He'd said that everyone always has a blind spot. It's natural—the place where the optic nerve connects to the eyeball or to the brain or something. So your brain had wiring in place to just ignore little holes in what you see. Or, in the case of a migraine aura, *big* holes.

The aura would come and get bigger until he couldn't miss it anymore—until his legs were vanishing unless he looked down, or until everything on his right side was simply unseeable—and then it would fade out.

That was pretty unpleasant.

In fact, the first time Mikey ever got a migraine, when he was in grade school, he'd been so upset by the aura that the school nurse sent him home—even though there didn't seem to be anything wrong with him. Young Mikey had been truly terrified. He'd thought he was going blind. When his sight came back, it was a huge relief. He even believed the headache afterward was just stress from worrying about his vision.

That first headache hadn't been so bad.

Now, at age twenty-nine, the headaches were really fucking bad. They got bad enough to make him cry, then got worse until he couldn't cry. They started out painful and got worse. They became so agonizing that he'd think it was the worst pain he'd ever experienced. Then it got worse again until he remembered the last migraine, which had been just as bad.

In the course of his life, Mikey Diamond had once been hit on the back of the head with a pool cue. It had sent a feeling like an electric shock all the way down his body and into his toes, it had nearly knocked him clean out, but it hadn't been this bad. On one memorable occasion, he'd been hit in the crotch with a police officer's nightstick. He'd puked that time, and he'd gone along quietly, and he'd been hospitalized when his right nut swelled up to the size of a small apple. Nonetheless, it hadn't hurt as bad as a migraine.

Migraines had taught Mikey that there were three levels of pain. The first level was just pain—everything from a paper cut to a sock in the jaw. No fun, but just what

it was. Next there was *serious* pain—pain where you're actually afraid you're going to die. The pool cue, the nightstick—those were the real deal.

Only migraines were level three. The level where you're terrified that you're *not* going to die, that you're somehow going to live on and on for years, suffering and miserable, unable to think, but somehow not dying. Migraines were the reason he kept his guns locked up and the reason he kept a syringe and some fine brown heroin hidden under the gun cabinet.

Most people just take a sick day and head home when their vision fails and they're suffering enough that suicide seems perfectly reasonable. Most people work traditional jobs, but not Mikey Diamond. His job had no sick days, no paid vacation, no dental plan. On the plus side, he didn't have to deal with FICA or Social Security taxes either.

Mikey was a gangster—a made man, a mobster—and he didn't think the guys in his crew would have much sympathy if he slacked his duties because of a headache.

Rather than pick up a nickname like "Mikey Headache" or "Migraine Mike," he kept his condition to himself. It had never really gotten in the way. He only had one migraine a year, generally. They were infrequent. Really, he was lucky. But on the days they came, he never felt lucky.

The day Mikey Diamond got his last migraine ever, he was on the job. It wasn't even supposed to be a very difficult job. He'd spent the morning and early afternoon rumbling deadbeats. Now he had to find Harvey Ciullo and request that Mr. Ciullo pay up the cash he owed Dennis Porter. When Harv couldn't do it (and Diamond was sure he couldn't—he knew Harvey), Mikey would request the vig. When Harv started in with his lame excuses about why he couldn't even meet the vigorish (that is, the interest on the loan he'd taken out to cover his gambling debts), Mikey would probably have to hurt him some. Nothing permanent yet. After all, there was still a *chance*, that with his knees and thumbs intact, he might be able to make Dennis's money back—or, at least, keep up his vig payments.

Mikey Diamond wasn't optimistic. Privately, he was hoping Harvey would give him the slip so that he could do a half-assed search then go home and hit the icepack.

As he parked in front of Ed's Tap—Harvey's home away from home—Mikey's vision cleared. He was just entering the second stage of pain.

Naturally, Harvey was there. Didn't even have the sense to hide. Mikey sighed and asked him to come along for a drive and a talk. Everyone else in Ed's got real quiet. Harv stammered and stuttered and tried to weasel out, but Mikey was good at his job, and he got Harvey into the car.

"So, Mikey, eh... How's it going, huh?"

Even when he didn't have a headache, dealing with Ciullo could give him one. It was a nearly unanimous opinion in the circles Harvey moved through that he was just about freakin' worthless. He had a body like a potato—round, lumpy and gray. He had a face like a potato's eye—ugly and discolored. It somehow looked like it had been pushed out of his neck unwillingly. His eyes had watery brown pupils, centered in an eggy white, where bloodshot pink and sickly pale yellow fought to be the secondary tone. His unruly thatch of brown hair was shot through with the gray of a dirty scouring pad, as were the wires of beard stubble that sprang from the fold between his first and second chin. He was wearing a cheap brown suit and a green and blue tie. There was food on the tie. It was an improvement.

His voice was like his face: something you'd rather not have in your car. It was low, dopey and nasal, and when he pronounced sounds like *ch* or *sh*, there was a phlegmy gurgling that made you think of your last bad cold. Even worse, when he whined—which was often—it rose in pitch and warbled.

"Look, Mikey, I know what this is about," Harvey said. "Really, I do."

"That's good, Harv. That saves me time. So, should we just swing by your house and get it?"

"Get...?"

"The money. You know, the money you owe? You remember that money, right?" The pain was waltzing through stage two at a good clip, and Mikey was driving Harvey out of town to an abandoned fuel refinery next to a sewage treatment center.

"Oh, I remember, Mikey. I couldn't forget! I wouldn't, wouldn't do that to you guys. But here's the thing…"

"The thing."

"The thing is… I ain't got it."

"Yeah, well, I'm not surprised."

Harvey paused. In the silence, Diamond thought he could feel his skull creaking. He reached up under his sunglasses to wipe away a tear. He really did not need this.

"Uh…"

"I mean, that Series bet was just fuckin' stupid, you know?"

The landscape was artificial ugly. Huge pipes and tubes, rusty metal walls and broken-in windows. The ground was dust. Every plant but the most stupid-stubborn weeds had given up.

"I thought they were due."

"An' I asked myself. I said, 'Mikey,' I said, 'is a guy stupid enough to make that bet going to be smart enough to make a lot of money fast?' An' you know what, Harvey?" They'd pulled up by a chained-up fence, but the hasp on the padlock hadn't been pushed in all the way. Mikey knew this.

"What, Mikey?"

"The answer was obviously no. Get outta the car and open the gate, a'right?"

Harvey obeyed. Mike Diamond got out behind him and pointed. They walked.

"Look, Mikey…"

"It's not a big deal, Harv."

"Eh?"

"Could you fuckin' listen? What did I *just fuckin' say*?"

"That it's… it's not a big deal."

"What do you think that means?"

Harvey's oily eyes darted back and forth. Even with eyes blurred by pain, Mike could read him like a book. Harvey had large-type expressions. Harvey's brain was stuck—stuck between Mikey telling him the money was no big deal and his dead-certain knowledge that owing money to Dennis Porter and his friends was a very big deal indeed.

"I don' know, Mikey."

"Jesus Christ. Get on your knees."

"Mikey, I—"

Out came Mikey's gun, which was (for today's job) a small Beretta semi-automatic. A little bigger than a good wallet. Harvey knelt.

"Mikey, please, dear God, please, Mikey…"

The sun was starting to set. It was absolutely beautiful.

"Let's talk vig, Harvey."

"Oh Jesus, Mikey, you can't, you gotta, I mean, come on…"

"The vig, Harvey. The vigorish on your bet. You got *that*, right?"

"Please, Mikey. I'm, I'm beggin' you. I'm beggin' and praying. I'm *praying* to you, Mikey. Please, don't kill me, please don't, I got, I got a *little girl*, Mikey, I got a…"

The third stage of pain had begun, and Mikey was seriously considering putting the gun in his own mouth. He was also nauseated. It wasn't Harvey's groveling—if he hadn't had the migraine, Diamond probably would have been laughing out loud—it was the feeling of pressure in his head, spreading through his whole body. His last migraine had brought nausea too. It had snuck up on him in the middle of the night, and he'd wound up crouched over the toilet, trying, really *trying* to puke. But he hadn't been able to. He'd known it wouldn't help, but he'd hoped it *might* help, so he'd tried it.

Now he felt like puking again.

"Harvey, you cunt. Shut up and answer the question."

"Mikey, you, you can't do this. You're a good Catholic, right? I seen you, coming out of church on Sunday. You can't just go and, and whack a guy over a little money? I mean, a *little* money. You probably go through money like this in a weekend. You could save my life with just this little, *tiny* piece of money, save me and my daughter."

"Harvey, you ain't got a daughter."

"No one knows about her…. Shit, up until last year *I* didn't know about her. But, ah Christ, Mikey, she's an angel, a fuckin' *angel* and her mama died. It's horrible; it's a fuckin' tragedy. I'm all she's—"

"And you can't make the vig. Right?" Mike pointed the gun. Harvey pressed his hands together.

"Mikey, please, you gotta listen, you could... you could tell 'em you couldn't find—"

Mikey pulled the trigger.

He didn't even think about it. He didn't mean to do it, not really. It was like his finger did it all by itself. If he'd thought about it, he'd have considered how many people saw him leave with Harvey, how much evidence there was pointing to him. Mikey Diamond had done hits before and you didn't do 'em like this. You did 'em clean and smart. He'd brought Harvey out here to put a scare in him, but he just got fed up.

The gunshot was painfully loud to his headache-tightened ears.

Harvey dropped with a hole right in the middle of his forehead, a meaty tunnel boring down through his brain. With a wet sound, one of his eyes loosened and dangled a couple millimeters out of its socket.

There was no exit wound.

He dropped.

"Ah *shit*," Mikey groaned as he went to try to throw up.

❖ ❖ ❖

A storm raged in the dim depths outside space. It raged through the world of the dead and the forgotten, scream-winds slithering through the ghosts of torn-down buildings, shaking the leaves of burned trees, rending the souls of dead children. It was a wind of woe and a rain of regret.

When he squeezed and pushed and broke free of his confinement, the storm was what Hasmed found. He was buffeted and shaken, torn and tortured, but at least he was something.

Ages before, Hasmed had been a protector. His duties had given him an instinct for fear, and that instinct was still strong. Even warped by his battles and imprisonment, he could still hear the call of a soul gripped by terror. Driven by some strange new urge, he fought toward the fear.

In the dim of the deadspace, Hasmed could vaguely perceive two men. One was hardly visible at all—just a suggestion of form, standing, pointing some object at the other. Hasmed suspected the object was a weapon, because

it was much easier to see than the man himself. The other man was much clearer, brightened and clarified by the fright that filled him.

There was a sudden, blinding flash—a crack of daylight in the night world's rainy murk—and Hasmed plunged toward the opening, toward the physical, toward the real.

He could see the fearful man topple backward, and he could see the man's soul. It was a small, weak soul, but it was fighting fiercely. The weapon was killing him—somehow scrambling the brain in which the mind lived—but the soul was fighting, trying to stay alive, trying to stay coherent. It was fighting for this more than it had ever fought for anything, but it was losing.

The soul reached out in that moment, desperate for anything that would help it live.

It found something just as desperate and battered. It found Hasmed.

For a moment, the two spirits—one from the world and one from beyond it—were fully exposed to each other.

"Tina!" the mortal soul shrieked. "Tina! Help her! Help Tina! Help Tina!"

Then Harvey Ciullo was gone, a lost signal, a pattern shattered. But Hasmed had climbed through him into the physical world.

❦　❦　❦

Mikey Diamond had turned his back on Harvey, so he didn't see the bullet-holed body sit up.

As for Hasmed, he was pretty confused. Going from the infinite quiet of annihilation to a New Jersey sunset within the span of a few minutes was enough of a shock. Showing up in a body with a hole in its face was another problem. But the worst was probably the scrambled brain.

Mikey had shot Harvey with a small-caliber round. It had entered his brainpan, but it had lacked the force to exit again, so it had ricocheted inside until it hit a weak spot—the thin plate between Harvey's brain and his sinuses. Cracking the sinus had released the pressure that kept his left eye in place. The slug had entered his nasal passage and stuck there.

Hasmed's first act upon returning to the physical realm was to put a finger in his nose and search for the

bullet. When he couldn't reach it, he hooked the finger and thumb behind his eyelid, pushing the eye aside to grope in the socket.

When he pulled out the bloody shell, he sat up and began trying to put Harvey's wrecked head back together. He was about halfway done when he spotted Mikey.

Diamond finally noticed something when Harvey's body lurched to its feet. He was crouching, trying fruitlessly to throw up, wishing he had more Cafergot (or his heroin needle) when he heard the sounds of movement behind him.

He turned, not really expecting anything. Maybe Harv was still twitching. You got that sometimes with headers. He didn't expect to see Harvey shambling toward him, looking unusually focused for a dead man.

Disbelieving, Mikey raised the gun to shoot again, but Harvey lunged forward and grabbed his hand—grabbed it with more strength than he'd expected from Ciullo, even alive.

What he expected even less was for the dead man to bite through his wrist.

Mikey wasn't screaming—his migraine had built to the point where it could eclipse even a severed hand—but he did raise the stump and stare at it dumbly before Harvey punched him in the gut.

Mikey was solid, but this was a hell of a slug, and he bent forward, just as Hasmed had expected. It had been centuries since Hasmed fought, but old habits die hard, even in a body without trained reflexes or much muscle. Hasmed grabbed Mikey's head by the chin and the base of the skull, stomped on the back corner of Mikey's knee to drop him forward onto the ground, then put his hips and shoulders into a hard twisting movement until Diamond's neck broke.

Hasmed dropped him into the dust. The sunset was purple, turning to charcoal gray. He felt surprisingly good. He'd enjoyed killing Mikey. It was good to have hands once more, to have a body and senses.

As the dark thickened, he wiped his face on his jacket then flung the garment to the ground. The buzz of leftover thoughts and memories in Harvey's brain was thick and

confusing, but there was one thought, one image that dominated.

It was a little girl with brown eyes and thick, blond, ringlet hair.

Tina.

❖ ❖ ❖

As he drove back toward the city, Hasmed's happiness proved brief. The body he'd gotten was clearly weak and sickly. He was able to seal over most of the damage in its forehead, but the eye was resisting his attempts to force it back into health.

Beyond those obvious problems, the body was wreathed in a thick layer of needless fat. The teeth were loose and pitted, set in gums that were withered and weak. As he drove, his tongue probed two sockets. The teeth had come out when he bit Mikey's wrist.

The tongue itself was sluggish and dull of sensation. It seemed to have a coating on it, which Harvey's battered brain associated with nicotine. That was also (it seemed) the explanation for the thick clinging slime in his nose and throat, the weakness of his lungs and the craving he felt through his blood and his bones.

There was a packet of cigarettes in the car's cup holder. Harvey's body cried out for one. Hasmed threw them out the window.

There were two courses of thought going through Hasmed's mind. One traced the mortal concerns left over in Harvey's brain, and the other catalogued the immortal goals of the creature who was now running the show.

Harvey's brain was chattering and disorganized, thinking about fingerprints on Diamond's body, blood, DNA, the car, all the people who saw… It was terrified of the cops and the Mafia and above all, terrified of what would happen to Tina if he got locked up or murdered.

Hasmed was trying to think how it could establish some sort of power base in the mortal world—something that would protect him from threats and eventually amass enough strength to summon Vodantu.

Slowly, as the spirit and the brain became acclimated to one another, the two streams merged. The problems

spun out by Harvey's rabbity nerves were considered by Hasmed's chill reason.

First, Mikey Diamond. The major pieces of evidence included Harvey's bloodied jacket, Diamond's body, Diamond's car and the witnesses at the bar.

The body and jacket were in a distant, obscure place. It was unlikely that anyone would find them immediately. He could go back later, bury the body and burn the jacket. No problem. Better yet, stuff the body in an oil drum and then bury it. He'd need an oil drum, a hammer and a shovel.

The car was not particularly flashy. If he pried off the VIN plaque, got rid of the registration and stripped off the plates, he could drive it into New York, sell it to Juan in Harlem and rely on it being chopped into parts by next Sunday.

The witnesses were more troublesome, but they wouldn't talk to the cops. Even if they did, the cops knew Harvey and Mikey. They'd never believe Harvey did it, especially if they didn't find a body.

The Mafia was far more likely to get them to talk, but even they wouldn't believe he did Diamond. He'd lie, and they'd believe it.

So much for Harvey's priorities. They were pressing, but hardly unmanageable.

Summoning Vodantu would be much more of a problem. Hasmed could feel that his powers, which once shook clouds and sundered mountains, were weak. He was a ghost of his old self, and he didn't know how to recover his former strength.

Parking Mikey's car in front of a nondescript row of small apartment buildings, Hasmed softly said "Vodantu. Vodantu. Hear me, my lord. Your servant would speak."

He listened intently, but there was nothing. No connection. Whatever gulfs lay between him and his master's prison, they were too far for him to span.

Yet.

Shrugging, he left the car and went up the steps into his apartment, where he was struck in the face with the edge of a cast-iron frying pan.

❖   ❖   ❖

The frying pan was in the hands of Helena Schirokauer, Harvey's half-sister, and she later felt just horrible about it. But it all happened so fast—she just reacted.

Tina was in the living room, watching *Sesame Street*, and Helena was in the kitchen, making a Spanish omelet. She'd heard the door open, and she'd been a little puzzled—Harvey wasn't due back for a couple of hours. He was supposedly down at the bar with his worthless "friends," trying to find some "angle" to make the money he owed. Still, he might have come back early.

Helena heard Tina ask something, but she couldn't make out exactly what it was. Then she heard Tina running toward her, and she heard heavy footsteps following.

Helena knew Harvey, and that wasn't his tread. She didn't think this consciously, but at some low, animal level, she knew. She couldn't have explained why she got scared, but something made her grip the handle tighter.

Then Tina had come around the corner of the doorway, and Helena had only had a moment to gauge the little girl's expression. A moment was enough. Tina was scared and upset.

A half-second later, a huge man with blood all over his face and shirt had come around the corner only a step behind the little girl.

Helena had done what any quick-thinking woman would. She screamed and hit him between the eyes as hard as she could.

For the second time in two hours, Harvey Ciullo's body dropped hard.

Tina just stared, then threw her arms around her father's body.

"*Daddy!*" she screamed. "*Daddy! Daddy!*"

Helena gaped, and, after a moment, she recognized her half-brother's shoes.

chapter
two

Hasmed was not the only spirit to escape durance within the Abyss. While Helena was making a hysterical call to 911, another freed spirit was in Miami making a sandwich.

The body had originally been named Christina Vadrudakis, and Christina's memories were still present within it. A new tenant was in the house, but it still had the old owner's furniture—for the time being. (Christina was in there too, but, to continue the metaphor, she'd been locked in the basement and had no say about anything.)

Her current driver's license read "Angela Meyerhoff." The spirit within was named Sabriel.

The sandwich was ham and Swiss on rye. To Christina Vadrudakis, that's all it would have been—ham, Swiss cheese, rye bread and some ranch dressing to tart it up. On one level, that was how Sabriel experienced the sandwich.

But on another level, she was aware that the ham was dead animal flesh, shredded and processed and embalmed in some sort of oleaginous mixture of hog fat and chemicals. The cheese was animal squeezings mixed with germs and left to harden and bubble before the requisite chemicals were used to preserve it. The bread was more chemicals, mixed with drowned and pulverized wheat. As for the dressing, the less said about that suspension of sour milk and desiccated vegetables, the better.

Sabriel ate the sandwich because she was hungry and Christina's body wanted it. Sabriel hated it.

Nosing around in the refrigerator, she found something called "Nutella," which Christina's body also remembered enjoying. Sabriel pried up the lid, stuck her finger in and sucked off a thick brown glob. Chocolate and hazelnut.

Still holding the Nutella, she wandered into the living room, where a plain man was making beautiful music.

The music was a piano concerto by Beethoven, and the plain man was Nathaniel Kowalski, guest pianist for the Miami Symphony Orchestra. Nate was scheduled to play that evening and was very nervous.

Sabriel came right up behind him, close enough that Nate could feel the warmth of her body, even though Sabriel—or "Angela"—had the soft tread of a kitten.

"It sounds fine," Sabriel said.

"I'm glad you think so." Nate's voice was quiet, and he didn't stop playing. Sabriel nudged him in the back with a hip.

"You're going to wear your fingers out."

"I need to practice before tonight," Nate said, biting his lip. He'd met "Angela" two weeks earlier.

I won't look up at her. I won't turn around, Nate thought to himself. He looked.

Angela was lovely. Not in a distant, alienating, centerfold way. She was short and slender, with just a little outward curve beneath her bellybutton, like a tiny roll of baby fat. Her limbs were lithe and soft without the taut harshness of a gym regimen. She had perky breasts. But her real glory was her face, a sweet, dimpled, gentle face. Her complexion was peaches and cream—it really stood out in the ocean of tanned Miami cheeks with Botox-treated eyes and bulging, liposculpted lips. Angela looked like a baking powder ad from the 1950s, except for the hair. The hair was modern, a dyed carroty orange with thick streaks of ashy blond. It was never orderly, and it always looked fantastic.

As Nate watched, Angela gave him a level glance, stuck a slim fingertip in the Nutella and then gave the finger a deliberate sucking.

Nate had only had one lover before Angela, and that woman had been, like Nathaniel himself, very plain. The only thing people remembered about her was her buck teeth.

Sabriel had initially used the "supermodel" approach when she designed a new appearance for herself, but she had quickly learned that most people were distant and a little confused around such perfect representations of the current beauty standard. When they'd looked at her, they'd almost expected her to start selling them dish soap or vacation cruises or magazine subscriptions. It was much better, she learned, to be close to perfect but have a few flaws. Just enough to seem reachable. Just enough to be real.

Sabriel was now an expert at making people love her. She hated it.

"Do you know the piece?" Sabriel asked.

"Of course I know it! I've been playing this since I was twelve."

"But you still need to practice? You must be a slow learner." She said it with a teasing tone and sat down next to Nate on the piano bench.

Unconsciously, Nate shifted away from the contact of Angela's thigh on his own. Not because he disliked it, but because he liked it too much.

Sabriel felt the contact too, and hated it. She shifted her weight so that it resumed.

"You don't understand," Nate said weakly.

Angela shifted away, and the pianist bit his lip again, wishing she was still touching him.

"Oh, well, I'm no *artist*. I'm sure the deep, profound, *magical* rapport you have with the music is something a simple woman like me could never comprehend."

"Angela…"

"I guess that I can only stand outside with my nose pressed against the glass…"

"It's not that!"

"...while you with your, your *superior artist's soul* commune with, with God and nature and music."

"Please, please don't! I have to practice! I... I don't think I'm better than you. But *you* know... Hal Guelder's going to be in the audience. And I need to be, you know, really good for the conductor, too. Miami took a chance on me! I can't let them down."

They were quiet for a moment.

"Hal Guelder's the guy from Sony Classic, right?" Angela asked.

"He might get me a *record*, Angela."

Angela nodded. "I'm sorry," she said. "I just... I never had anything I did so well. You know? Anything I cared about like you care about this. And I get jealous."

"Sometimes I'm not sure if being... being 'talented' is a blessing or a curse," Nate said.

He was lying. He'd never thought being talented was a curse. But he thought it might play well with Angela. He knew everyone expected musicians to be temperamental and high-strung, expected them to suffer for their art.

Sabriel knew Nate was lying, but she didn't let on. "I just worry that you're going to overdo it," she said softly.

"Well..." Nathaniel looked at Angela and saw confusion, shame and doubt.

With a perfect body, Sabriel never could have so perfectly portrayed doubt, shame and confusion. Nate reached over and stroked Angela's hair.

Sabriel hated it.

"I... I do overwork sometimes."

"I just worry that..."

"What?"

"I worry that music will always mean more to you. That's what I mean by 'jealous.' Not that I want what you have, but that I..."

"Oh Angela." Nate turned on the bench and embraced her. He kissed her then, and it was tender and passionate, full of trust and vulnerability. It was intensely human.

Sabriel hated it. She put her hands under Nate's shirt and stroked the bare skin of his back and hated it. She put her face to the side of Nate's neck and nuzzled behind his

ear and hated it. She hated Nate's small sigh, and the way his grip tightened, and the way the young man's body pressed close to her, yearning for her.

They made love, and Sabriel hated it.

She hated how much she loved it.

❖   ❖   ❖

In New York City, a woman with red hair and green eyes was playing four games of chess simultaneously against three opponents.

The four players were in the basement of a local YMCA. The chess sets were identical—old lacquered wood cases that folded open to reveal the black and white squares. The pieces inside were cheap pine and cedar, lathed into shape by mass production. The only exceptions were a rook, three pawns and a bishop. Those few pieces were plastic, put into the wood sets to fill in for the casualties of years of use.

The woman's first opponent was a young boy, maybe ten years old. He'd picked black and, as she opened with the pawn in front of her king, her other opponents smiled a little and exchanged a look.

Her second opponent was the boy's grandfather, a portly gent in his sixties. He chose white and started what would (eventually) become a textbook Larsen/Nimzovich opening. She pushed a pawn immediately and moved to the third game.

Her next challenger was a handsome man with dark hair and dark eyes. He could have been anywhere between twenty and forty. His hair had no white and his face had no wrinkles, but there was an austerity and maturity to his bearing that gave the impression of age. He picked black and made a quick but conservative response to her aggressive Bird variant attack.

Interestingly, she took the longest pause before the fourth board. She stared and chewed her lips, then pushed a white pawn. Immediately, she reached across that same board and moved a black knight.

Then she was back to the first game, where her opponent had already responded. She brought out a bishop without seeming to consider his move, then went on to

engage his grandfather. Then on to the third man, ending with unhesitating moves on both sides of the final board.

By her fourth move, she'd checkmated the young boy. The two older men nodded knowingly.

"It's called the Scholar's Mate," the woman said kindly. Her face was covered with thick clouds of freckles, and her smile was straight out of Norman Rockwell.

"I've warned you about that before," the grandfather (whose name was Samuel) said. "You've got to keep an eye on that weak F7 pawn."

"Did you see how I did it?" the woman asked.

"Uh huh," said the boy, eyes downcast.

"So you won't fall for it again, right?"

"Nuh uh."

"Okay then."

"Grandpa, I'm gonna go play shuffleboard, okay?"

"Sure," said the old man. "Just stay where I can see you." He looked up at the woman. "Don't think you'll get me that easy."

"I know I won't. Are you rated?"

He shrugged. "I've got an eleven hundred in the USCF."

"Plenty of time to push it."

"Yourself?"

"Never bothered."

As they spoke, she made two more orbits of the games.

It did take her longer to beat Sam—long enough for the grandson to grow bored of shuffleboard and pinball and checkers with a young girl, and to start whining a little. In the end, though, she pinned his king with a rather pedestrian two-rook pincers movement.

"Good game," he said, shaking his head.

"I enjoyed it," she replied.

He took his grandson's hand, and they wandered off.

This left her opposed only by the dark-haired man—and herself.

"Interesting strategy you used on him," her final opponent said.

"Despite the pushy opening, he was a very conservative player at heart," she replied. "Very reluctant to lose any

piece, even a pawn. So I had to keep my pieces too, to prevent him from simply outgunning me."

"But at the end, you won with fewer pieces," the man said.

"Well, I outmaneuvered him. Once I moved the attention of the game into a smaller area, the rest of his pieces didn't matter. They were isolated."

"Mm-hm." He contemplated his next move while she did two more plays in her solitaire game. "I'm Max, by the way. Max Hirniesen."

"Penelope," she replied. She didn't look up from the board.

"You were much more aggressive with me," he noted.

She shrugged. "It's good to play different people different ways. Keeps you sharp. Versatile."

"The body count on our game is certainly higher."

"That's the natural progression, isn't it? You start out with a lot of pieces and pare down to the essentials."

"Making room on the board for wider maneuvers as you do." He made a move. "Check."

She moved out, then took more steps with her personal game.

"I knew a man in Vienna," she said, "who believed that the way you play chess reveals your personality."

Max chuckled. "Another reason to practice different styles? Check."

She countered. "He would have said Sam was insecure, or maybe afraid. He's had losses in his life, and his fear of loss is reflected in his defensive play."

"That's rather a killjoy way to look at it. Check."

She escaped again, and several turns were played in silence as she fought her way free of his area of control. All the while, she stayed in the rhythm of playing one move against him, then one move on each side of her other game.

Max pressed harder. They were closely matched, and both were battling hard to control the center of the board.

"What about the little boy?" he asked. "What's his personality?"

"In a four-move game, he didn't get a chance to show much."

"Like life, I suppose."

"Mm?"

"Chess is like life. You start out with a great store of years and, as you approach death, inescapably have fewer and fewer of them." Although he didn't show it, Max was slightly annoyed that Penelope kept splitting her attention between him and her other game.

"I wouldn't know," Penelope said. "I've never run out."

"But surely as we age, the years we have become more precious—since we ourselves are wiser, more mature and more experienced? Like a rook—not much use in the early game, but often crucial in the end."

"You could just as easily argue that the remaining years are like an endgame knight—hobbled by poor mobility, eccentric and often irrelevant."

"All things run down, I suppose."

"You'd think so, wouldn't you? But look at the boy's game. It didn't run down. It got chopped off suddenly. Checkmate."

Max blinked, then squinted down at the board.

"Impressive," he said, and tipped over his king.

Penelope shifted over to the side of the remaining board and began making increasingly rapid moves.

"So," Max said. "What did the game show about my personality?"

"You're generally extremely confident, almost cocky, but something has happened recently that shook your certainty. I think you lost some sort of mentor figure? Or perhaps just misjudged something, misjudged it badly."

Max raised an eyebrow. She was frighteningly correct. He turned his head and rubbed beneath his nose to cover his confusion.

"Done!" she said brightly, looking up from the board. He inspected it.

"Neither king is checkmated," he said. No pieces had been removed from the board, but they were locked together in an intricate, spiral entanglement.

"Correct. Look closer. It's stalemate. A *perfect* stalemate. Neither player can move any piece without going into check."

He looked at it silently for five full minutes. "Wow," he said at last. "You're right." He looked up at her again. "And you're not ranked?"

"Doesn't seem important."

"You were toying with me, weren't you? That series of checks I got."

"I wanted to frustrate you so that you'd be even more aggressive later in the game."

"And it worked."

She shrugged. "That's a very interesting ring you have," she said.

Max narrowed his eyes. He'd suspected there was something unusual about this woman. Now he was certain.

"Yes. It's an antique."

"Is it silver or platinum? Or something else?"

"I don't really know." He turned the dark metal band around his finger a couple times.

"I used to know someone with a ring just like it," she said, looking directly in his eyes. Suddenly, Max's mouth was dry.

"Really." He fought to keep his voice calm.

"It was a long, long time ago."

"Still, I've always been curious about the... provenance of this one."

"Then you should go to Toronto and look up Clive Keene. That's 'Keene' with an E at the end."

"I see. Maybe I'll do that. What does Mr. Keene do?"

"I'm not sure what he's doing now. As I said, it was a long, long time ago. But you two will find something to talk about, I'm sure. You could talk about... the weather."

With that, she stood and swept the pieces off the board.

"Wait," Max said.

But Penelope, who was much better known by a different name, didn't wait.

In the desert, inside her ages-old prison, the demon Avitu slept. She did not dream.

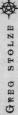

chapter
three

Hasmed's spirit was suspended once more between the worlds of life and death. Once more, he was battered and shaken by the howl of a storm that stirred nothing mortal, nothing living, nothing tangible. Like the lost memories and dead feelings around him, Hasmed was gripped by a hellish wind of souls.

He retained a tenuous connection to Harvey Ciullo, but it was weakening fast. The world had once been Hasmed's to command, but now the act of forcing his will upon it was arduous and exhausting. Saving Harvey from death had weakened him. Doing it again, so soon… he wasn't sure he could. He wasn't sure if he should even bother.

From the realm of the dead, he could still vaguely see what was happening to Harvey. They'd taken him to some room of white and silver and bright moonlike lights. They had cut him and drugged him and tried to use chemicals and tools to do what Hasmed could do with a whisper and a wish. But their science was weak, and Harvey's body was badly broken.

As Hasmed watched, the body's last flicker of vitality winked out.

What of it? Perhaps now Hasmed would be pulled back to the Pit, back to the nothingness that had been his fate for so long undisturbed. Perhaps it was just as well to be there, with no power and no hope and no future. The world he'd found, Harvey's world, had wearied and disgusted him. Given a

planet of glories, the humans had clearly worked hard to insulate themselves from everything natural and pure and important, creating a world of their own—a world shabby, small and sad. Let them go. Let them fester. Let them be the gangrene in the wound they themselves had inflicted.

And yet...

Outside the white and silver room, Hasmed could see a figure waiting in a drab gray chamber. A figure burning with life. Unspoiled and innocent, golden and pure.

Tina.

More than seeing her, he could feel her. He could feel her tears as they trickled down her cheeks. He did not hear her whimper, "I want Daddy," he felt it. He felt the push of unbroken, unconditional love that circumstance had yet to stress and weaken—love uncomplicated and untried.

To this little girl, her father was perfect. He was everything. She needed him. Hasmed felt it the way a flower feels the rising sun.

Perhaps he had the strength after all.

Nurse Schwabbe had seen it all. That's what he thought, anyhow. He'd seen gunshots and stabs and falls and car crashes. He'd seen strangling and poisoning and overdoses on just about any drug you could name, including aspirin. He'd seen the many ways people could come to grief and, without thinking deeply about it, he'd decided that he'd seen all there was to see about the human body.

Checking Harvey Ciullo in post-op, he changed his mind.

One moment Harvey was out cold; the next his eyes popped open—instantly alert, completely focused. Schwabbe hadn't seen that before. People came out of total anesthesia one of two ways: gradual and fuzzy, or shaking and disoriented. But not Harvey.

"I wanna talk to Danae Sieferson," he said.

Another first. People emerging from a sedative fog made plenty of weird statements and odd requests—lots of times it was just gibberish. Even when they said something coherent, it was usually "What happened?" or "I want to speak to my doctor" or "Did you get all the tumor?"

They almost never asked for a hospital administrator.

"Mr. Ciullo? Are you, uh... How do you feel?"

"I feel like makin' love. Crap, how do you *think* I feel? Look, just get Danae."

"I think the first person you should talk to is Dr. Lipowicz."

"Great. Can he check me outta this dump?"

"She, actually. And I think you'd better get used to the idea of a long stay."

"A male nurse and a lady doctor. Go figure. A'right, send 'er in."

Dr. Lipowicz, a portly and maternal woman, came quick and looked at him with frank curiosity.

"Mr. Ciullo? You're awake?"

"Nah, I'm sleeping with my eyes open and my gums flappin'. Can you get Danae for me?"

Lipowicz smiled and made a note on his chart next to the time: *Conscious, alert, capable of humor!*

"I'd like to ask you some questions first. Yours is a very... interesting case."

"Yeah? That gonna get me a discount?"

"Now's not the time to worry about that."

"So says the woman with the salary. You're what, a brain surgeon?"

"Neurosurgeon, yes."

"What do you pull down? Never mind, I don' wanna know. What I wanna know is how soon I can get out of here."

She leaned down and looked in his eyes with a flashlight, making another note as she spoke. "That depends on many factors, but there are a lot of tests I'd like to run."

"What do you need to know? I'm awake, I'm fine, and I wanna go home. You can keep me against my will?"

"I'd be neglecting my duties if I let you go in a risky condition. I'll be the first to admit you've made a *remarkable* recovery. Nearly unprecedented. But I'd still like to do a CAT scan and an MRI to fully evaluate the extent of your injuries and their nature."

At that moment, the door opened once more, revealing a hesitant Helena and a jubilant Tina.

"Daddy!" the little girl shouted. "Daddy Daddy Daddy!"

"Shh," Helena said, finger to lips. "Daddy's tired, honey. Daddy's very sick." She pulled at Tina's shoulders, but the little girl squirmed free and ran across the room.

"It's a'right," Harvey said, as Tina climbed up onto his bed.

"What are those?" she asked, pointing at his various tubes.

"Beats me." He looked up at the doctor.

"Honey, you can visit your father for a little while, but not long, okay?"

"I want my *daddy!*" Tina said, locking her arms around Harvey's stomach.

"Let her stay," Harvey said, and some hard tone in his voice made Dr. Lipowicz uneasy for a moment. She turned to Helena on the way out and quietly said, "Five minutes."

Helena shuffled in and stared at her half-brother.

"I am… *so* sorry," she started.

"Yeah, well." Harvey shrugged.

"I mean… Jesus, I could have *killed* you."

"You did, didn't you? I mean, I died on the table, right?"

"How'd you know about that?"

"I knew." Helena bit her lip. "Look, Helena, it's okay. Honest. A'right? I mean, I accept your apology."

"It was just that… I didn't know it was you. You didn't *look* like you."

"You thought you were protecting Tina?" Helena nodded. "Then I wouldn't change a thing."

"You mean it?"

He nodded.

"Well…" She shuffled her feet. "Is there anything I can do? I mean, anything I can… I don' know, get you or something?"

"You can get me Danae Sieferson."

Eventually, with some tears and tantrum, Tina was persuaded to leave. After much more of his insistence, Danae Sieferson appeared. She was the executive Harvey had talked to three months earlier when he'd brought Tina in after a bad fall onto the sidewalk. Danae had been trying to get him to pay, just two days before Mike Diamond took him on a ride.

"Mr. Ciullo. I hope you're feeling better." She said it like she didn't particularly mean it.

Harvey was already sitting up in bed making phone calls and checking the TV news. As she entered, he turned off the television.

"Let's cut to the chase, 'kay? You don't want me here, and I don't wanna be here. Surely we can work something out."

"I'm sorry?" she said.

"I can't pay for treatment. You *know* this. You been riding my ass about Tina's stitches an' I'm guessing this shit costs a *lot* more. So why not cut me loose?"

"It's not that simple."

He shrugged. "Okay, if you're gonna force me to stay and get scans and tests and pokes and prods, that's your business, but I ain't gonna pay for 'em, I'll tell you that right now. I ain't signing nothin' unless it gets me outta here."

"We have a duty to our patients."

"Why not do your duty to your *other* patients, huh? Dr. Lipowicz thinks I'm an 'interesting case,' which means she's gonna soak you and ignore everyone else. I ain't interested in being interesting."

"You can't be released until she okays it. She's the physician in charge."

"Ah." He raised his hands. "*Now* we're making progress."

Harvey was released early the next morning after Danae (over Dr. Lipowicz's objections) asked the Chief of Surgery to transfer Harvey from Dr. Lipowicz to Dr. Lyons. Dr. Lyons, the trauma specialist who'd been on ER duty when Harvey came in, was more than happy to let Ciullo go. He had plenty of other patients to worry about.

Helena came to get him and was startled to see him picking at his bandages even on the elevator down.

"Leave that alone," she said.

"Don't tell me what to do," Harvey replied.

She frowned. There it was again. He didn't seem like the old Harvey. The old Harvey was (frankly) a bit of a hypochondriac. Or maybe not that. Maybe he just enjoyed the sympathy when he was sick. Certainly he was never… *impatient* with illness. Not like now.

He got the last of the bandages off in Helena's car and examined himself in the makeup mirror.

"Crap, what a mess," he said. "I look like Jethro Tull should be writing a song about me." Helena glanced over and nearly ran the car off the road.

"Harvey! How did they let you *go* like that?"

"Relax, it looks lots worse than it is."

In the middle of his forehead there was a thick knot of black surgical stitching and angry pink scab tissue. The scab spread stubby starfish arms out from its deep crimson center, radiating from the hole that had been punched into his brain.

In a contest of ugliness, however, his right eye was a likely contender. Where its white had once been bloodshot, it was now simply bloody, crisscrossed with broken veins and brownish clots.

Harvey rubbed his cheek. "I got bum fluff, too." Then he ran his hand up the back of his scalp, which had been shaved so that they could drain and suture the contusion the floor had left when he'd fallen back after Helena's blow.

"Listen," he said to her. "Did you tell anyone about this? That you clocked me, I mean?"

"Tell anyone? Well, I... I called Mom down in Florida."

"That's okay. Anybody else?"

"No."

"Good, that's good. Call Ma back and tell her to keep quiet about it, a'right?"

"Why?"

"It'll help me out. Now if you'll excuse me..." They were in front of his building.

"What are you going to do?"

"Go in and take a nap, what do you think? Trust me, I ain't about to, y'know, rearrange the furniture. Tina's with Doris, right?" Doris was Helena's neighbor—she'd watched Tina before.

Helena nodded.

"You got Tina all day?"

"If that's what you want."

"It'll really help me out. I'll come by this evenin', we'll eat."

"Are you sure you should be driving?"

He opened his mouth and closed it again. "Mm, good point. You wanna pick me up?"

"I think it's best."

"Okay. Six o'clock? Or how 'bout six-thirty?" When she nodded, he said, "Thanks Helena."

"Well, you know... I'm just, I really feel awful about this."

"Don't let it eat at you."

"Get some rest, now."

"Yes ma'am."

After she left, Harvey paused only long enough to shave his entire head. When he'd dried off his newly bald pate, he put on a hat and sunglasses and went to his car.

❖   ❖   ❖

Valley Garden Mall wasn't too far from Harvey's apartment, but it was far enough. He parked his car there and started walking down the rows of mini-vans and sports-utes and station wagons, discretely peeking in the windows and looking for unlocked doors. After about ten minutes, he found one on a dark blue Xterra.

Figures, Harvey thought. *People who ain't got much will beat your brains in to protect it, and people with good stuff leave it unlocked.*

Hasmed blinked. He hadn't banked on more trouble from the individual consciousness called "Harvey Ciullo"—he'd expected death and a scrambled mind to leave Harvey pretty quiet. But the brain had habits, and they made Hasmed uneasy. Still, there was no cure but to ignore it. He shook off his concern and got in the car.

Harvey's memories contained all the knowledge needed to hotwire a car, but Harvey had never really been a car thief. He'd stolen a few cars in his day, most often "borrowing" from friends without permission, but he didn't really have the cool nerves needed to do it consistently and well. In fact, Harvey really hadn't done much of *anything* consistently or well.

Hasmed, of course, did not have such psychological limitations. He stripped the steering wheel and jammed a cheap screwdriver into the ignition. In a minute and a half, he was underway.

He drove to the parking structure of a nearby office building and looked for an Xterra near the doors. He figured that's where the employees would park, leaving the farther spots for their clients. The first building yielded nothing, but after a couple more tries, he spotted a dark green one. Close enough.

Hasmed double-parked and hopped out with a high-torque electric screwdriver and a can of WD-40. Swapping the plates was actually much riskier than stealing the car in the first place: It took more time and was more obviously suspi-

cious to the casual observer. But he thought it was worth it. If he carried it off, he could probably count on a whole afternoon without police hassles.

Leaving the garage, he double-parked in front of a convenience store and got a bottle of Evian. He pulled the tips off some weeds from the sidewalk and added it to the water. Then he got in his stolen car and paid a visit to Roscoe Paum—better known as "Roscoe Shakes."

❖ ❖ ❖

If Roscoe Paum's life had gone according to plan, he would have eked out a living doing small-purse prizefighting. His actual *plan* was to be heavyweight champion of the world, but that was never a realistic option. For one thing, genetics doomed him to a top fighting weight of 160 pounds. For another, he wasn't a world-class boxer. Roscoe had a flash jab and was a weird sort of genius with crushing body blows, but he couldn't go the distance. His punishing gut shots were wonderful for wearing people down in the long term, but to use that strategy, a fighter has to be in it for the long term himself—and Roscoe wasn't a withstander. Lacking a deal-closing roundhouse or uppercut, he was exiled to the bad side of the bookie odds. He wasn't worthless in the ring—not by any means—but he wasn't a contender.

It was frustrating, and Roscoe wound up with a reputation as a dirty fighter. It turned out that skill at low shots worked just as well for tangling people up and smashing their elbow joints, but league officials tended to look askance at that sort of tactic. He landed more than his share of groin punches, too.

Like most Jersey boxers, Roscoe made acquaintances in the mob. After delicate inquiries, he let it be known that his repugnance toward taking a fall wasn't completely implacable. He didn't take a *lot* of falls—you don't get good odds if you fail too often—but he took enough. He even did a little muscle work for them a couple times, though he didn't have a taste for it. He never did anything permanent.

Between the purses he legitimately won and the cuts he got under the table for sacking out in the ring, Roscoe was doing all right.

Then he fell apart.

He claimed it was Muscular Dystrophy, but everyone figured it was too much booze.

When he opened the door to his apartment, Hasmed could instantly see that Roscoe had been telling the truth all along. He smiled.

"Hawvey Ciullo," Roscoe said. "You look like shit. What you do to your head?" His tremors were mild today, but visible.

"Good mornin' to you too, Shakes."

"Don' you fuckin' call me that."

"A'right, a'right. Just bustin' your chops. How's it goin'?"

"Shitty." Roscoe made no move to let him in. "What you want?"

"What do I always want when I come see you?"

"You wan' me to do you a favor." Shakes looked disgusted, but Harvey had always known that Roscoe secretly liked having someone ask him for help. It annoyed him, but it also encouraged him to know there was someone even more pathetic than himself.

"Uh huh. Unless you got a hot date?"

Roscoe's eyes flashed and he started to close the door. "Fuck you, Ciullo. I gotta take a lot of shit, but I ain't gotta take shit from *you*."

"Before you kick me out, drink this." He held out the Evian bottle.

Shakes glared at it with distrust. "What is it?"

Hasmed shrugged.

Roscoe gave him a hard glance, and there was something… maybe it was just the shaved head and that new knot in his forehead, but the man before him suddenly looked like someone to take serious.

Roscoe took a drink.

As he did, Hasmed breathed out, but not just with his body. He breathed out with his spirit.

Thousands of years ago, Hasmed had been an angel of healing and protection, and some small sliver of him still was. Weakened and twisted, his power could still flow forth like a warm spring breeze, rolling out and over and into Roscoe's wracked frame.

Hasmed exhaled. The boxer drank, and his tremors stopped.

Roscoe blinked. He looked down at the hand holding the bottle and turned slightly right and left.

"What did you do?" he whispered.

Hasmed said nothing.

"What did you *do?*"

"Feeling better?"

"What is this stuff?"

Hasmed gave him a dry little smile.

Roscoe lunged forward and grabbed Harvey's shirtfront. Though enfeebled, he still had a strong grasp. He drew back his left hand, still clutching the bottle, and aimed a blow at Harvey's head.

"You'll spill it."

Roscoe froze in place.

"Now, if you wanna hit me, I guess I can't stop you. But listen, Shakes. I just had *brain surgery* yesterday. So you punch me in the head, you might just have a murder rap on your hands. Not to mention that, if you beat my brains out, there's no way I can make more of your miracle cure."

Roscoe's breath started to come fast and uneven. He wasn't sobbing, but he seemed to be panting, hyperventilating. He didn't know what to do. He was panicking.

"Now why don't you let go?" Hasmed said, and his voice was ice.

Roscoe obeyed.

"Let's go for a ride."

"A'right." Shakes was subdued, staring at the bottle in his hands. "W-whatever you say."

"Mm, and you better get some gloves for in the car."

"Is it that cold out?"

"The weather ain't cold, so much as the car is hot."

"Ah."

It took about an hour for Roscoe's quivering to return. In that time, he and Hasmed grabbed a couple of shovels from a construction site, along with an empty fifty-gallon drum. They didn't talk much. Shakes was simply stunned. Hasmed didn't see much point in talking until the other man was receptive.

"What's goin' on, Hawv?" Roscoe finally asked it as they started out of town.

"Well, some weird shit, Roscoe. Some real weird shit. You know Mikey Diamond?"

"Uh huh."

"Yesterday he killed me."

Roscoe jerked his head around. At that moment, his body began to tremble once more. He took a drink from the bottle and, as Hasmed sighed, he felt better again.

"You mean he…?"

"He put a bullet in my brain, Ros. We were fighting for his gun an' it went off. I guess I must've fallen on top of him though, 'cause when I came around, he was on the ground dead. I drove myself back into town an' went to the hospital."

"So you… you came back to life?"

"Well, I didn't die right away. The bullet knocked me out, or somethin'. You've had that, right? You get knocked out but come back quick?" The boxer nodded. "So I wasn't dead then. I died on the operating table, last night. But I came back."

"Shit."

"Just wait. It gets weirder." He frowned, watching the road, not looking at his passenger. "I saw stuff while I was dead," he said at last.

"Saw stuff? You mean… like, your life before your eyes? Or the, whatsit, the tunnel of light?"

"Nothin' like that. I saw everything from the outside, Paum. I could see the whole world." He chewed his lip for a moment. "It ain't nothing like you think."

"Yeah?"

"The world is fuckin' weirder than you can possibly imagine. There's all kinds of… of secret connections. It's all fate. It's like, a guy in the Bronx decides to wipe his forehead with a beer, right? Like, on a hot day?"

"A'right…" Roscoe's brow furrowed.

"And because he did that… that little movement… it might affect, just a little, how the grass grows in Central Park. And that grass growing, it affects people jogging past it. And those people make all kinds of tiny changes too, that spread out all over the world, until that one guy in the Bronx has affected *everything*. Y'see? It's all hooked together."

"I guess."

"That's how I fixed your shakes. I could see stuff they were hooked to. That stuff I gave you, it doesn't work for any *reason*. No reason a scientist could find. They'd say it's a coincidence, right? But coincidence *is* a reason, if you see it right."

"So this stuff is... what, magic?"

"Pah, magic nothin'. Magic is cups and balls and linked rings. It's some faggot in a tux at your kid's birthday party. No, this is... it's always been there. It's real. It's just hard to see when you're inside it. But I see it now."

"Shit, Hawv, I don' know..."

"Look, you're superstitious, right? I mean, I've seen you throw salt over your shoulder an' stuff."

"Well... yeah, I mean, everyone's a little superstitious, I guess..."

"Same thing man. Just one level higher."

They pulled in by the old fuel refinery.

"That ain't all there is to it," Hasmed said quietly. "I see the connections. I see other stuff too. There's stuff that's not... not exactly real? Things that think. They see the hookups too. They can do stuff, even though they ain't exactly here or there."

There was a pause.

"I ain't sure I follow you," Roscoe said as they got out of the sports-ute. "But I guess I can't argue with results, y'know?"

"That's smart thinkin'. I can trust you, right?"

"What do you mean?"

"I mean..." Hasmed did another sigh. He wasn't even sure why he was doing it. He was following leads in Harvey's memories, notions Harvey had about how Roscoe would react. "I mean I'm the only one with your cure, right? I don' wanna put it this way, I really don't but... that's a hold over you, right?"

Roscoe looked down, uncomfortable.

"Yeah," he muttered.

"That's okay, though, 'cause I'm gonna give you a hold over me. Then we can trust one another."

"Mikey Diamond."

"I need your help, Roscoe."

Hasmed pulled the lock and opened the gates.

"I guess I need yours, too," the boxer replied.

Hasmed dragged the oil drum while Roscoe carried the shovels.

IV
chapter
four

Hasmed and Roscoe left the shovels in a ditch and abandoned the Xterra a couple blocks from a bus stop. They didn't talk much on the bus ride. They were both exhausted.

"I gotta get in shape," Hasmed said at last. Roscoe gave him a sideways glance. His tremors were back, and the water was gone.

"You got a shape," he said automatically. "Round."

Neither laughed.

"Nah, I mean it," Hasmed said. "This is disgusting." He mopped his neck and forehead with a dirty handkerchief. "Look at me. I'm wheezing, I'm sore, I'm weak… and *this*." He grabbed a double handful of his belly and shook it up and down. "Look at that! That's so nasty I don't even know where to start."

"Well, you did just get out of the hospital," Shakes replied.

"I won't have that excuse forever. You were an athlete. Tell me how I get in shape."

Shakes gave a little bark of laughter. "It's not like there's some fuckin' mysterious secret, Hawv. You exercise. You just, y'know, get your sweat pants on and go running and jump rope and do sit-ups. Pump some iron. Get a medicine ball."

"What was your old boxing gym?"

"I trained at Conley's," Roscoe said. He gave a moody frown and looked out the window.

"Would you go back?"

"Quit it."

"I'm serious, Ros! If you got cured for good, would you go back in the ring?"

"You think that could happen?"

"Anything's possible, I guess." Hasmed tipped back his hat to reveal a little more of the scar that glared like an angry third eye from the middle of his forehead. "I'm getting the hang of… stuff. I think I can see it. See a way."

Roscoe Paum shifted in his seat. "Cut it out, Hawv. You're givin' me the creeps."

"Which would you rather have, the creeps or the shakes?"

❈ ❈ ❈

Hasmed barely had time to get back to his apartment, shower and change into his pajamas before Tina and Helena arrived.

"Hi, Daddy," Tina said, giving him a solemn look. "Are you all better?"

"I'm still sick, but I'm almost better."

"What happened to your eye?"

"Daddy got an owie, sweetheart." He pointed to the scab on his forehead. "A big owie."

"What happened?" she asked, brown eyes wide.

"Yeah, Harvey. What *did* happen?" Helena was leaning against a shelving unit with her arms crossed and a stern, calculating look on her face. Hasmed met her level gaze with one of his own.

"I fell," he said.

"You fell." Clearly, she didn't believe him.

He looked down at the top of Tina's head, then back at her. "I fell," he repeated.

"Uh huh. 'Cause I'd hate to think you fell in with Hamish Brennan and Dennis Porter and the rest of those—"

"Helena." His voice was hard and icy. "I fell. End of story. You got me?"

"He fell!" Tina hollered. "Fell fell fell!"

Uncertain, Helena frowned and looked away. "I just worry about you, Harvey."

"I'll be fine." He scooped up Tina, then winced. "Ach, you're gettin' enormous, honey." He turned back to Helena. "Where are we goin' to eat? My treat."

"I don' know. What do you feel like?"

"We could go to the Sizzler. Get some steaks."

"Eh, maybe you should take it easy on the heavy food."

"Nah, I need to get my strength back up. Protein and such. You know."

"McDonald's!" said Tina, very loud.

"No." Helena and Hasmed said it in unison, him touching his head, her touching her stomach.

They were still debating it as they filed out the door.

"You should get good shoes, Daddy," Tina said. "Then you won't fall down."

❖ ❖ ❖

As Sabriel slept, she dreamed.

In the day, weighed down by the mortal minutiae of Christina Vadrudakis's mind and memories, Sabriel's recollections of the ancient times were clouded, dim...dreamlike. But at night, when Christina's brain quieted, the Elohim within could remember the times before. She remembered fragments only, but the world had been so much larger then, so much deeper and more complex, that even the pieces that came in the night seemed more vivid and real than the world of nickels and fast food and paperclips she moved through when awake. That petty place was Christina's world. In dreams, Sabriel remembered her own.

She dreamed herself back on the broad, fertile plains known as the Grain Sea, standing at attention before Archduchess Azacachia. Sabriel was far from alone, for five hundred rebels had gathered for this attack. They were all volunteers, even though many knew that they would not return.

"My fellow soldiers," Azacachia said. "Today, we face a mission of great danger—but also great glory. Our battles to date have been skirmishes only—inconclusive, unimportant, little more than postures and poses. Why? Why have we been unable to strike a decisive blow against the forces of ignorance and repression? Because we were unwilling to trust the very people we rebelled to help! We were unwilling to look to humanity for aid, though they may prove to have power even a seraph may fear. Now we prepare to embark on this great experiment. Now we will see how great the power of Man can

be when we throw the might of His children against the servants of God!"

The soldiers before her cheered, raising swords and scythes, clapping hands and wings. Her claws and feathers glittering mica-black, Azacachia gestured for silence.

"We have trained for this. We have practiced our roles. I know I can count on each one of you to acquit yourselves with honor. Even should we fail, a bold failure will be more glorious than any blind obedience to a tyrannical authority. But with courage and strength and the faith of our followers... we will not fail!"

Standing at the front of Sabriel's unit was Hasmed the Defender, plumed with wings of smoke, his flail and spear ready for the coming conflict. With the rank of overlord, Hasmed was her direct leader in this mission, though she usually answered to another, a Lord of the House of Waves. Hasmed's unit was a combat unit—swift flyers and powerful warriors used for shock assaults. Sabriel was no fighter. Her job was something entirely different.

The mission was nothing less than an attempt to destroy Vejovis himself—a seraph of the Holy Host. As one of the mightiest angels, Vejovis had once commanded Hasmed's loyalty, along with myriad other angels of the Firmament. But now his onetime servants raised arms against him, as they warred with the Host and the Choir and with the One Above them all.

Sabriel only hoped that their new weapon would work as Azacachia thought.

"Are you one of the praise leaders?" Turning to see who spoke, Sabriel saw a figure of radiant light, glowing with the glory that belonged only to the House of Dawn—and to those rejected from it.

"Yes," she said. "My name is Sabriel."

"I'm Gaviel. Is this your first time in battle?"

"I won't actually be fighting," she said.

"With Vejovis, you never know. You won't be attacking, but he sees far and strikes hard. Keep your wits about you."

"My danger is nothing compared to what you'll face flying to the attack."

Gaviel shrugged. "I just hope you can weaken him enough."

"If it can be done, I'll do it."

"Excellent." He turned and touched the shoulder of another of the fallen. "Avitu? Have you met Sabriel?"

"Briefly." Like Hasmed, Avitu was an angel of the wind and life and protection.

"Avitu's task is to protect you and the other praise leaders," Gaviel explained. "She'll take good care of you."

"I know," Sabriel said, grateful for his encouraging words. "It's been explained before." Avitu gave her a smile, and Sabriel smiled in return.

"I've seen her in battle," Gaviel said. "You're in good hands."

At that moment, Azacachia sounded her horn, and the troops before her rose into the air as one. Hasmed, Gaviel and the other attackers formed themselves into ranks, some circling the treetops, others high and distant like flocks of birds. With a final nod, Avitu sprang into the middle distance, with Rabbadün the Seer of Time close by her side.

Sabriel flew low to the shores of a river. On its other banks stood row upon row of mortals, milling anxiously, watching the Elohim prepare for battle.

With a gesture, Sabriel called the water up, twisting and braiding it into a great waterspout. With a hum in the depth of her throat, she calmed it into ice then settled atop its chill spire.

"Beloved!" she called to the crowd below. "Now is your time! As we have given unto you, now we beg your gifts for us! We who defied the Allmaker on your behalf now ask you to protect us from His vengeful servants. Only your faith can make us strong! Only your belief can make great Vejovis weak!"

As she led them, the mortals began to sing.

"Great Azacachia
Lady of the earthy deep
As we learn your wisdom great
Many blessings shall we reap.

"Vodantu who reads the stars
Master of the inky spheres
Show us what the future holds
Answering our hopes and fears."

Watching the women and men, Sabriel saw them tremble as one, heard their voices falter as a darkness fell on the land. She turned—meaning only to glance over her shoulder—but the sight she beheld would not let her turn away.

Vejovis, King of the Tempest, had arrived.

He hung above the plain like a mountain in the sky. The dark clouds of his wings stretched across the horizon from end to end, and in their charcoal depths, searing cracks of lightning flickered. His eyes, the gray of storms, stared down with implacable judgment, and in a hand like a hillside was coiled a mighty whip.

"Sing!" Sabriel shouted. "They need you! Only you can save them!" But faced with the sheer mass of one of God's mightiest servants, the words felt hollow in her throat.

Azacachia—herself grown to the size of a granite cliff—leapt to the air and howled defiance as she surged forward. Vejovis's whip snaked across the sky, and its snap was thunder. The crash flattened the grass of the plains, blew the leaves off the trees, shook the feathers of every rebel angel arrayed against him… but Azacachia did not fall. She flinched, she dropped for a heart-stopping moment, and then she recovered, beating great wings of black stone as she continued toward her foe.

Seeing Azacachia withstand the strike, the other attackers darted forward like a swarm of bees. They struck with fire and with lightning and with the force of death itself.

Sabriel turned her eyes back to the mortals and sang with them. Human only, their voices lacked her perfection, but her sound could stitch together their disparate tones, making their discords and wrong notes into part of a greater harmony.

> "We praise mighty Gaviel
> Glory of the summer sun
> You have brought us truth and light
> We adore you, radiant one."

Vejovis's thunder whip struck again, and this time, he aimed at one of the other praise leaders. Avitu and Rabbadün swooped in to block the blow, but they could only soften its force. The thunder of impact sent cracks through Sabriel's tower, and as the lash struck, its victim fell. Her tower of ice

immediately changed into water, rushing out in all directions. With a gesture of hand and wing, Sabriel turned the wave before it could crash upon the mortals.

"Here!" she sang. "With me!" The water was calmed, but it now sank into the shore around them, turning the firm ground into mire and swamp, but they fought and swam and struggled toward her—some still singing as they did.

"BLASPHEMERS!" cried Vejovis. His tone was not one of anger, but rather shock and horror and boundless sorrow. Daring to glance back at the battle again, Sabriel was amazed to see blood on the seraph's face, falling like tears or rain to the ground below. His lash and lightning had felled dozens of rebels, but it was clear that they were hurting him too.

> *"Sabriel of Eastern Sea*
> *Bless us all with tender love*
> *With your caring we shall be*
> *Guarded from the wrath above."*

As they prayed to her, Sabriel felt a flood of strength. It was dizzying, intoxicating, thrilling like nothing else. With only a twitch of an eye, she enslaved the floodwaters, depositing the struggling swimmers with gentle care. Her song redoubled, knitting her followers tighter together, until they were no longer a collection of frightened, hopeful mortals but something more. With her, they became a living well of faith, and she drank deeply of its delicious essence, never getting her fill. She felt as if she were swelling, expanding across the fields and into the sky, growing until the battle was merely a part of her. Vejovis was merely a mote in her eye.

She was distantly aware as Rabbadün told Avitu "Sabriel is his next target!"

The bolt of godfire took only an instant to flash between her and Vejovis, but Avitu was swifter still. Leaping to protect her charge, the onetime Angel Defender blocked the brunt of the strike. The weakened remnant that struck Sabriel was still seven times hotter than the surface of the sun, was still strong enough to kill her and a dozen like her... save that she had the mortal well of faith for protection. Drawing on that store of strength, she rebuilt her body again and again, each time the fire consumed it, until the great angel's rage was spent and she remained.

Avitu plunged to the ground like a stone.

"Avitu!" Sabriel shrieked, and her scream was a song. "Sing for her, my people! Sing for your protector!"

"Avitu! Avitu! Avitu!" They had forgotten her verse, Sabriel was taking them out of their order, but their passion and fealty had its own momentum.

"Avitu! Avitu! Avitu!"

❖ ❖ ❖

"…vitu…" Sabriel muttered, before slowly opening her eyes. Some urge, some human feeling, had awakened her. It took her a moment to recognize it as hunger. She'd been in Christina's body for months, and it felt natural during the day. But at night, when she dreamed of the past or the ocean or her onetime glory, waking suddenly confused her.

She slid out of her bed and padded down the dark hallway to the kitchen.

When Christina had been a little girl, an uncle had told her how British anti-aircraft spotters in World War II would keep their eyes covered all day in order to preserve their night vision. Even at night (he said) they'd only keep one eye open when they turned the lights on. That way the other eye would stay dark-adapted.

This had seemed eminently sensible to young Christina, and over the course of her lifetime, she'd gotten into the habit of keeping one eye closed when turning lights on at night. Sabriel didn't consciously realize it, but she now had this habit as well. When she opened the freezer door to get out a Mars bar, she squeezed her left eye shut. As the door closed, the light went off and she opened her left eye again, once more seeing perfectly by the dim illumination of the streetlights outside.

As she opened the wrapper on the candy bar and took the first bite, she heard a noise.

She stopped chewing and tilted her head. There it was again. Someone was trying her back door.

Sabriel put the candy bar down and went through the living room toward the foyer. Her first thought was to kill the intruder—if he was merely mortal, it shouldn't be too tough. But she spotted her camera on the entertainment center and decided that it might be better to capture and blackmail him instead. She picked up the camera and started charging the flash.

Peeking around the back door's curtain, she could see a pale and scrawny man in a dark sweatshirt and a stocking cap. He was looking down, concentrating on his task. He had a short crowbar and was digging between the door and frame with it. She stepped back and waited.

When the door opened, she raised the camera and said, "Say cheese!"

"Crap!"

As the flash went off, the burglar was so startled he instinctively threw up his hands. Since he was still holding the crowbar, he managed to strike himself right between the eyes.

Sabriel looked down at his unconscious form and muttered, "That was disappointingly easy."

She dragged him into the house then went to get her duct tape.

When the burglar woke up with a splitting headache, he was firmly taped to a kitchen chair. A beautiful woman stood before him, barefoot, wearing a Def Leppard T-shirt that had been washed so often that it was faded gray and thin. It came to her mid-thighs.

"The funny thing is," she said, "There wasn't even any film in the camera." She had his wallet in her hands and was shaking her head over the contents.

"So," she said, "Your name really is Tommy Ramone?"

"I go by Tom or Thomas," he replied.

"Okay, Tom or Thomas. Explain to me exactly what you were doing here."

"Um, well, I was trying to break in."

"And why? Were you planning to rape me, Thomas?"

"What?"

"Were you going to sneak into my bedroom and, I don't know, hold me down and roll me over and fuck me? Was that your plan?" She took a step closer to him and bent forward. He could see the outline of her nipples through the thin, worn cloth.

"No! I just, look, I was *just going to rob your house*. I mean, that was all! I didn't think you were here! I mean I, I looked in your garage, and your car was gone and everything!"

"It broke down just today. Hope it's not the transmission." She took a step back and gave him a thoughtful look. "Your story checks out... kind of. You didn't have a weapon

53

on you, other than that crowbar, and you didn't have anything to restrain me with. No condoms either. Though I don't suppose rapists care much about safe sex, right?"

"I wouldn't know. Jesus! Honest, you, you gotta believe me. I wasn't... it wasn't that. I just wanted to steal your stuff." His voice had taken on a pleading tone. "Look, are you going to call the cops on me?"

"Can you give me a good reason not to?"

He slumped in his bonds. "Not really. Shit."

She chuckled. "Oh Tommy. Do you think you're going to get off that easy?"

"What?"

As his mouth opened with astonishment, she jammed a dishtowel into it. Then she gripped the chair by its back and started dragging him toward the cellar door. It was awkward as the bottoms of the chair legs bumped down each step, and Thomas kept making noises of protest around his gag, but she finally got him down below, into a concrete room lit by a single naked bulb.

Sabriel checked the basement's three windows. All had fairly strong bars, and their faded yellow print curtains easily blocked the view from outside.

"Be right back," she said as she ran up the stairs for a length of clothesline. When she returned, she was actually humming. Tom had managed to spit his gag out.

"You can't do this!" he declared.

"Why not?"

"Well... well, kidnapping is illegal!"

"So's housebreaking." She paused to pat him on the cheek before running rope from the top of the chair up over the ceiling beams. There. That would keep him from tipping the chair over and moving toward the stairs—or toward anything that might help him cut the tape. Just for safety's sake, she tied him with some rope on top of the tape.

"Why are you doing this?"

"Why did you break into my house?"

"Jesus, I was just going to steal your TV and stereo!"

"You wanted something from me, and I want something from you. Hey, you think I should screw you?"

"What?!?"

She deftly straddled him, sitting on his lap and facing him. She was still humming. As she sat, the T-shirt rode up to her hips, revealing her Hello Kitty panties. He recognized the tune—it was *Sheena is a Punk Rocker*. She put her hands behind her on his knees, arched her back and shook her breasts at him.

"Wouldn't that just be the kinkiest thing *ever*?" she asked. "I immobilize this horrible, nasty, creepy burglar in my own house and then fuck his brains out before turning him over to the cops. Though it would be awfully hard to explain, wouldn't it? Or I suppose I could fuck your brains out and then kill you. That's tidier."

Tom looked like he couldn't make up his mind between crying, laughing or having hysterics. "You're crazy!" he said at last.

"Now Thomas, is that *really* the smart thing to say to the woman holding all the cards?" She stood up again. She'd decided this was really a bit of luck. The Kowalski project was just about finished, and she'd been wondering what to do next. This Tommy Ramone could be useful, or amusing at the very least. Maybe when she was done, she'd see if she could contact Avitu.

"Look, you could just let me go. I wouldn't tell anyone. Please?"

"Now why would I do that? Did you tell anyone you were coming here? No? So no one knows where you are, there's nothing to link you to me, and it's unlikely that I'll ever get caught. I can keep you down here and live out whatever *Silence of the Lambs* fantasies cross my mind."

"Oh Christ…"

She'd procured a hard plastic tube from upstairs—it was actually a part of an espresso maker—and she pried his jaw open as a prelude to ramming it in.

"Hey, how'm I gonna go to the bathroom?" he asked, right before she stuck in the tube and started duct-taping it in place.

"Oh, I figured I'd just let you shit your pants for a few days," she replied brightly. "Now, blink once if you'd like the light left on, and twice if you want it off."

❖   ❖   ❖

In Toronto, another young criminal was having an encounter with a different Elohim. The criminal's name was Gordy Hines, and the cast-out angel was called Usiel.

Normally, Usiel looked like a rather small, slender black man, bald as an egg. For his business with Gordy Hines, however, he had put on the full grandeur of his supernatural form.

Gordy was screaming and pissing himself, which did not surprise Usiel one bit. A normal man—or even an abnormal one like Gordy, a teenage murderer, a hardened criminal who'd seen enough bloodshed for a man four times his age— is not used to seeing a person get taller and gaunter before his eyes, seeing him suddenly backed with wings of ash and smoke, seeing his skin tighten until it seems to vanish entirely. The apparition before him was seven feet tall, a skeleton made of burnt ebony bones, but these bones glowed with deep cores of hot flame lurking within.

"HINES," the monster said, pointing one skinless finger. "YOU HAVE KILLED. THE MARK OF MURDER IS ON YOUR SOUL. TRULY YOU ARE A FALLEN MAN."

Gordy didn't really give a shit what the voice—that horrible voice, like a circular saw in hard wood—was saying. He just wanted to *get away*. Every instinct, every nerve and brain cell was screaming at him that this was *death*, that he had to escape, had to flee, no matter what. But he was backed in a corner with bricks behind him and concrete beneath him. He scrabbled at them, breaking fingernails, mewing like a kitten in abject fear.

"YOU DID NOT KILL TO DEFEND YOURSELF, NOR FOR HONOR, NOR EVEN FOR REVENGE. INSTEAD, YOU ROBBED ONE OF GOD'S CHILDREN OF HER MOST PRECIOUS GIFT OUT OF NOTHING BUT SULLEN, DRUNKEN SPITE."

Trapped, Gordy huddled in a fetal ball, whimpering. "Oh shit," he sobbed. "Oh shit oh shit oh shit…"

The skeleton seized Gordy's long hair and pulled with enough strength to lift the boy off the ground. Hines howled as the pressure pulled his head free of its huddle, forcing him face to face with the nightmare before him.

"MANY IN YOUR POSITION CRY OUT TO GOD," it said "BUT YOU INVOKE ONLY FILTH. FITTING. YOU'VE MADE YOURSELF INTO EXCREMENT, A WORTHY CITIZEN FOR THIS FECULENT WORLD."

The thing pulled its shirt open and Gordy saw a new horror. It had no skin, no guts. Its ribs were like the black bars of a cage. Inside the cage there were... *things*. Little figures. Little *people*, only all made of fire, making tiny, tinny noises of misery. They clutched the bars, trying to escape, little faces twisted and screaming...

"YOU SHALL JOIN THEM," it said, and its whisper sounded like locusts in corn. "YOU SHALL SERVE ME A WHILE BETWEEN YOUR DEATH AND YOUR FINAL JUDGMENT. BELIEVE ME, NO MATTER HOW YOU SUFFER IN MY SERVICE, IT IS NOTHING COMPARED TO WHAT AWAITS YOU AFTER."

The burning, stony fingers were gouging his throat, pressing one of his eyes, and he fought like a cornered hare fights a wolf. But his fingers did no more to the burned bones than they had done to the concrete beneath him.

"Oh shit, oh fuck oh *fuck*..."

"DIE MISERABLE. DIE SMALL. DIE KNOWING THAT GOD IS JUST."

With a final gasp, Gordy Hines perished.

For a moment, a new shape was visible in the cage of Usiel's ribs.

Then the monster shrank and became normal, and the fire within him cooled.

When he walked away, Usiel was an ordinary Canadian man. A little shorter than most, and completely bald. But few would spare his body—Clive Keene's body—a second look.

❖　❖　❖

In Wyoming, a man named Teddy Mason sat up in bed, suddenly awake, breathing heavily.

He'd had that dream again.

As his racing heart gradually slowed, he looked around the darkened bedroom. His dresser. His pants draped over a bulging laundry bin. The door into the bathroom. Picture frames on the walls, and he couldn't see the pictures but didn't need to. Pictures of himself, his wife Birdie, his son Lance. He was home.

Everything was sane and normal.

He looked at his wife, who was lying on her stomach with her head turned away from him.

"Birdie?" he whispered. She rolled a little.

"Birdie?"

"What is it?" she grumbled.

"I had that dream again."

"Oh for Christ's sake."

"I'm sorry, but you know it upsets me."

"Can't you save it for your shrink?"

"Fine."

He rolled away from her and stared off into the dark. She sighed.

They'd been married for twenty years, and a sigh could communicate a lot. This one said, "Look, I'm sorry I don't have the patience to listen to this, and I'm sorry you're upset, but I've heard about that stupid dream dozens of times, and I just do not have any sympathy left on that subject. Now either we can both lie here angry and miserable and sleepless, or we can make up and at least *I'll* be in a better mood come morning."

He grimaced, but thinking about it there was really no way he could *make* her care.

"I'm sorry I woke you," he mumbled.

She turned until she was on her back and reached over to touch his shoulder.

"It's okay Ted. I just... I mean, I thought you were going to get *better* with..." she bit her lip. Finishing that sentence could easily, *easily* lead to a lot more discussion, not less.

"With everything," he said.

"Yeah."

"I thought so too."

The way he said it was so sad, so... *forlorn*, really, that Birdie momentarily forgot her goal of going back to sleep and rolled over all the way to hug him.

"It's okay," she whispered, and they both eventually got back to sleep.

But it wasn't okay.

❖   ❖   ❖

"Do you mean it?" Nate's voice was radiant with hope and fear.

"Well, now, the ink isn't dry on any contracts yet."

"I know, I know, I don't... don't want to get ahead of myself. But Mr. Guelder..."

"Hal."

"Mr. Hal. Hal. I'm sorry, I just..." Nate chuckled nervously and took a sip of his drink. It was spring water. He hadn't dared get alcohol—he was too nervous. He was too terrified by his high hopes as he did lunch with the man from Sony Classics. "This is what I've wanted since I was little. I mean, a *little kid*. All I ever wanted was to be a classical pianist, and now I get to play with the MSO, and a *record*..."

"This is the best part of the job, Mr. Kowalski."

"Nate! I mean, if you're Hal, I should certainly be Nate. Oh this is *such* good news. I didn't think you were going to... I'm babbling, aren't I?"

"It's all right. After dealing with so many blasé prima donnas, a little enthusiasm is a splendid change of pace."

"You're too kind."

"No, I mean it. You've got a freshness to your approach that really brightens your work. I'm thinking an album of mostly major key stuff. That's okay, right? Something broad and upbeat to start with."

"Um... well, okay, I guess."

"You sound hesitant."

"No, that's fine. Maybe even some Gershwin or something?"

"We don't need to go *that* far." He chuckled.

"I was so scared I screwed up the other night..."

"Well, I won't lie to you. I was disappointed."

Nate looked up with the frozen expression of a fawn in headlights. "Oh, I *knew* it!" he cried. "I should have spent more time getting ready!"

"No, no, there's no need for such self-recrimination. Lots of people get flustered in front of a live audience. I'm sure you'll do much better in a studio, where you can concentrate."

"Usually I *prefer* a live audience..."

He shrugged. "Well, what's done is done. It's out of my hands now, but I'm very optimistic. We just have to get Mr. Hoshida's permission, and I'll be able to give you a contract within a week. Maybe as soon as tomorrow... though perhaps you shouldn't get your hopes up."

"Why? You think Mr. Hoshida won't like my demo?"

"Mr. Hoshida does have very specific opinions about music—a particular vision for where he wants Sony Classics to go. But you probably don't have anything to worry about."

"Maybe you're right. I shouldn't hope too hard."

"Oh, Mr. Kowalski, I just meant you shouldn't get your hopes up about *tomorrow*." He chuckled. "Goodness, I apologize. By all means, get your hopes up about the contract. You've earned it."

After lunch, Guelder paid cash and watched the musician walk away. Then he checked his watch and clucked his tongue. It was just about time to check on Tommy. He'd have to change in the car.

He was not, of course, Hal Guelder. He was Sabriel in Hal's shape. By the time she parked in front of her home, she was Angela Meyerhoff once more.

❖　❖　❖

Max Hirniesen was a man with two souls.

One was an ordinary soul (or so he supposed) much like those of other men. It was a soul that felt love and hate, fear and anger, humor and contentment. It made him human, but it was his alone, and it existed isolated within him, formed and informed only by the shaping of his senses. Like everyone else (it seemed) his soul was aloof and uniquely his.

His second soul was different.

He had become aware of it when he was a freshman in high school, and he'd thought for a while that he was going insane. The other soul had feelings too. Sometimes he sensed towering anger or aching loss from it, but the causes of these powerful emotions were mysteries to him. Things he looked at—things that were normal and ordinary and commonplace—had different meanings to the alien spirit within.

The most important difference, however, was that his second soul was not isolated. It could touch the world directly and be touched by it in turn. When it reached out in anger, cars rusted before his eyes, people tripped and hurt themselves, and plants became blighted. When it was pleased, though, it could gift him with freakish good luck, protect him from harm and even clear up gloomy weather.

Max had been seventeen when he met Claus Merrow, another man with two souls. Claus had taught him that their double spirits were a great blessing, that the second was

known as an "avatar" and that, with time and training, Max would be able to tie his own will to it so firmly that together, his twin souls could mold reality itself.

In a word, Claus had taught him magic.

He had been Claus's apprentice for many years and, eventually, the older man's lover as well. Max hadn't felt any particular physical chemistry—certainly no *affection*—but he knew it would make Claus happy, and he felt like he owed the old man something.

Eventually, they drifted apart. Max felt he had sufficient control over his avatar and its powers, while Claus tried to hold him back and keep him as a protected student. Claus was powerful: His school was located in a different world entirely, one that could be reached only when strong magic opened the way. Max had been stubborn, though, and he'd gone off on his own, with friends his own age who were all determined to shake up the old order of things and install something new and better. Something more free and more true.

Davis, Magdalena, Shannon and Max. He was the only one left.

They had fought against men with guns and wicked magic, all the time telling themselves that they were fighting ignorance and oppression. They had battled twisted, unearthly spirits in strange spaces that no normal man could reach—always convinced that they were dueling with madness and evil incarnate.

In hindsight, the apex of their adventures had been when Max had gotten the scythe. Or, as it was now shaped, the ring.

Looking out the train window as Toronto neared, Max twisted the gray iron band on his finger—or was it iron after all? Was it silver or chrome or hematite? The color seemed to shift from bright to dark as the light changed on its surface.

When he'd seen it first, it had been a great, fearful scythe. The Abyssal Monk had raised it against them in anger, and after they'd killed him, Shannon and Davis had wanted to destroy his weapon as well. It was unholy, they said. It reeked of death.

But Max knew better. Certainly the scythe had some lethal vibrations, but it was more than that. His avatar stirred within him when he looked at it, and he knew that the scythe was also a tool of change of renewal and of release. Not only a weapon,

it was a bridge between the lands of the living and the domain of the dead.

He had wanted it, so he had quarreled with Davis and Shannon. In the end, they let him keep it.

Eventually, he had shown it to Claus, who was profoundly impressed. Claus unlocked some of the scythe's deeper secrets for his student, telling him it was ancient and powerful—older than mankind, perhaps. Claus had also worked the relatively minor trick of giving it a second form—the ring—that made it much easier for Max to keep it on his person at all times.

The ring and scythe enhanced his powers over decay and destruction (which were already reliable) and also aided him greatly in his dealings with the spirit world. Souls of the dead might not know what the scythe was, but they could feel its power.

Having the scythe made him proud. Pride was his undoing.

Confident that only he and his allies were going to change the world, Max was caught unprepared when the world changed beneath him. It took the shape of a tempest—a great monsoon in Bangladesh that was merely the herald of some greater disturbance, some colossal malevolence—perhaps one as old as the ring. He and his friends had gone to fight it, with no real grasp of the scope of the event.

The tempest in the world of matter had killed thousands, maybe a million, but it was nothing next to the storms in the other worlds. A twisted wind of decay and horror blasted through the realm of the dead, shattering ancient civilizations and disgorging horrors undisturbed for millennia. In the secret spaces plied by the double-souled, a whirlwind of insanity and unchecked power swept untold numbers of unprepared avatars off to destruction or into realms uncharted by human minds.

The engines of reality had gone mad, and he watched Davis and Magdalena and Shannon fall into the whirling gears one by one, where they were torn apart by the thrashing of fevered worlds.

He called upon Claus for help, only to get a fuzzy, distorted plea for aid in return. Claus—his teacher, his master, the opener of mysteries—had desperately screamed

for Max's assistance before the winds of the storm split even their voices apart.

For the first time since he'd been a teenager, Max was alone.

In time, the world seemed to calm down—or, at least the obvious world did. In the realms beyond, chaos still ruled from a hurricane throne. Max had sought others like himself, but the few he found were either concentrating solely on survival or had even less knowledge and power than himself.

His meeting with Penelope in New York City had seemed like blind luck, but she'd given him hope. Perhaps this Clive Keene she'd told him to look up understood what was going on.

Perhaps Clive Keene could explain.

Sabriel bent over Thomas Ramone and pulled the duct tape off his cheeks. "So!" she said, smiling as she pulled out the tube, "How's your Stockholm Syndrome coming?"

He looked up at her with frightened eyes. He had not had any water for thirteen hours. His mouth and nose were dry and cracked, and his face was gaunt with fear and misery. As he blinked and focused on the sloshing bucket she held, he developed a ghastly look of hope.

"P-please…" He tried to wet his mouth to speak, but his dry tongue only rasped over dry teeth and dry lips.

"Do you even know what Stockholm Syndrome is?"

Dully, he shook his head.

"Stockholm Syndrome is when a kidnap victim comes to identify with his or her kidnapper. Like Patty Hearst, remember her? The Something-Something Liberation Army grabbed her, and pretty soon she was robbing banks right at their side. Do you think you might come to love and adore me, eventually?"

He just stared. His only expression was utter confusion.

"Would you love me if I gave you water?"

"Please… please, Miss…" He nodded desperately.

"Well, too bad. This water is for cleaning you up. Mm, you made quite a mess of yourself, didn't you?" With confident movements and a sharp pair of scissors, Sabriel made short work of his pants and soiled underwear. It required some shifting and some strength to wipe and wash him

without untying or untaping him, but after ten humiliating minutes she was done.

Tom's body shook with sobs, but he had no tears.

"Oh, there, there. Don't cry, Tommy. Look, would you want me to give you this water *now*?" She held up the bucket. The water within was cloudy and foul with his own feces.

Wretchedly, he nodded.

"That's not very healthy." She shook her head and took the bucket upstairs.

In the cellar, Thomas sat and moaned, more miserable than he'd ever been in his life.

Five minutes later, she came back and gave him four ounces of tap water.

He had never been so grateful.

The next day, Sabriel glanced impatiently at the clock on Nathaniel's VCR. Timing the next act of her carefully planned drama was going to be very tricky. The window of opportunity was wide enough, certainly, but it was finite. If Nate didn't get home soon…

Then she glanced over at the door and saw the deadbolt start to turn. She smiled.

"Harder," she muttered. "C'mon. Harder. Do it now! Yes! Oh yeah, uhhh…"

Nate opened the door to see Angela, naked and flushed, bending over the arm of his futon. Behind her, with his pale belly sagging on top of Angela's lovely backside, was Hal Guelder.

(This was, of course, the *real* Hal Guelder, who had never met Nate. He had listened to Nate's demo and said, "Maybe when he's had a few years to mature." He had also been astonished that a woman as gorgeous as Angela was interested in him.)

"Fuck me," Angela gasped. "Oh, use me. I'm your *whore!*" Her eyes were seemingly closed in bliss, but she had them cracked just enough to catch Nate's look of absolute shock, absolute horror. For a moment, the young pianist was just frozen. Then he turned and ran.

"What? What…?" Hal was clearly confused, but a few expertly timed bumps from her rump was enough to bring him off. Afterward, though, he had questions.

"Angie, who was… Wasn't that Nate, Nate whatsisname? Kowalski? The pianist?"

"Uh huh." Sabriel wasn't looking at him. She was putting on her panties. (Red silk today.)

"Well? What was he doing here?"

"This is where he lives."

"I thought this was *your* place!"

"Nope."

"But… but you had a key!" Hal was looking more and more confused.

"I do. He gave it to me when we became lovers."

"When we… wait, you mean when *you and him*…?"

"Got it in one." Moving efficiently, Sabriel was now almost completely dressed.

"Then what was… why…?"

"Hal, think it through, please. Obviously, I brought you here to make him unhappy."

"But we—"

"Come on. You didn't really *buy* all that 'Oh Hal, I love your cock, ooh, I just can't get enough of that big meaty cock' business, did you?"

She watched as his face turned ashen, then she laughed her lovely laugh.

"Oh, you *did*! That's too much!"

"Why would you *do* this?"

"Why do you care? You got the best sex of your life, for *nothing*. Can't you just leave it at that? Can't you keep your nose out of something that's none of your business?"

"But that poor kid!"

"Well, you could tell your wife all about it if you really feel guilty. I'm sure she'd give you plenty of penance." Shoes tied, blouse buttoned, Sabriel paused to fluff her wild hair and then sashayed toward the door. "Lock up after you put your pants on, okay?"

"But…"

"Oh, and you might want to watch your back. I think Nate might have a real mean streak. It's always the quiet ones, isn't it?"

Then she was gone.

Later, she found herself telling Tom about it and frowning.

"I mean, I set this up for close to a month, and it came off just like I planned, only… I don't know." She'd brought a second kitchen chair down to the cellar and sat upon it, knees crossed, eating fried chicken from a red and white box. Thomas just stared at the food. He hadn't eaten in forty-eight hours, though she had given him another eight ounces of water.

"It wasn't a complete waste of time, like that thing with Maryanne Prisco. Did I tell you about her? No? Just a project I did with this devil from Missouri, a politician. It turned out really, really bad. I mean, at least with Nate there was a payoff. He had talent, there's no doubt about that," Sabriel said, nibbling a bit of breading off the tip of a drumstick bone. "And he's pretty much ruined, now. The first time I met him, I noticed some long, thin scars on the insides of his wrists, so I'm figuring he'll go back and finish the job." Her voice was chillingly casual. "I've denied the world his music. So why don't I feel good?"

Thomas shrugged, as much as he was able.

Inside Sabriel, there was another flare-up from Christina. At first, the ghost of Christina's feelings had gotten a deep, mean pleasure from Thomas's predicament, but the weaker and sadder he got, the more hesitant and ambivalent she became. Sabriel crushed those unworthy feelings. Typically human—unwilling to go the distance even in revenge. It had been just the same with Nate.

"Maybe it's because no one knows," Sabriel said. "Maybe that's why I'm telling you, so you can appreciate humankind's loss. But… ah, it's so frustrating. Running around from one artist to the next, dashing hopes, wrecking dreams. It's repetitive. Too easy, really. And no one *misses* them." She took a bite of a biscuit and made a face. "Uh, that's nasty. You want this?"

Tom nodded weakly, his stomach rumbling loudly.

"Too bad." She chucked it off into a dark corner of the room. "Maybe I'll give it to you after the ants and spiders get at it a while." She sighed again. "Perhaps I just need to aim higher. You know? Maybe denying people brilliance just isn't enough. Nathaniel was brilliant, you know. Could have been another Caruso or Bernstein, if he got the chance." She ran a greasy finger over her lip. "You know, maybe that's it.

Maybe I need to take a wider approach. It's not enough to take *away* genius. Perhaps if I *exalt crap*... now that's a good revenge. Yeah. It's not like human culture isn't sliding into a midden heap already. I'll just grease the skids." She stood. "Thanks, Tommy. You've been really helpful. I'll take a couple days, get a new identity, and go to Hollywood."

She kissed him on the cheek, then left him.

He groaned.

❖ ❖ ❖

Max wasn't surprised that Clive Keene lived in a rundown house. He'd seen mystic types living everywhere from dumpsters to otherworldly fairy palaces. He didn't have much left in the way of expectations.

He swallowed, then rang the bell.

When a scowling, short, bald black man answered the door, Max stuck out his hand and said, "Hello. I'm Max Hirniesen."

He had a speech ready in his mind—a variation on the one he'd used with other avatar-holders. It started out mysterious, became enticing, hinted that he could offer plenty of information in return for the few piddling details he was missing, and ended with a frank and flattering suggestion of alliance. He wasn't sure he'd get through the whole spiel today, but if Clive didn't seem receptive, he could play it haughty and aloof, wait for the other fellow to come to him. They almost always did, in the end.

But as his mouth was opening, his eyes registered the other man's stare. Keene wasn't looking at Max. He was staring at the ring, and his expression was one of amazement. And disgust.

Furthermore, Max felt instant loathing boil up from his avatar. Whatever or whoever Keene was, Max's second soul despised him.

"Where did you get that?" Clive hissed, reaching out for Max's right hand. Max snatched it away, but the black man grabbed him by the shoulder and rudely yanked him into the house. For a small man, he was surprisingly strong.

"What can you tell me about it?" Max countered, stepping back and protecting the ring behind his back.

"I can tell you it belongs to *me*," Clive replied, his lip curled with revulsion.

"Perhaps it did once, but…" Again, Max's words failed. The other man's eyes had shifted up to Max's face, and the look of loathing had redoubled.

"What are *you*?" Keene asked, in the tone of a man who finds a cockroach in his birthday cake.

"I could ask you the same question."

Clive's answer was to open his mouth and spit. Only it wasn't saliva that emerged: It was a whining, flaming spirit. It flew out and darted at Max.

Max instinctively flinched back, waving the hand with the ring through the spirit. It dissolved instantly—that's how Max knew it was weak. He'd fought some old ghosts in his time, terrifying and powerful creatures, but this wasn't one of them. It was a small phantom, recently dead, impotent and inexperienced. The touch of the ring/ scythe was sufficient to sever it from the living world and fling it, howling, into death.

Max concluded that he'd been set up and figured it was time for the gloves to come off. His left hand curled into a fist and pistoned forward into the other man's gut. It wasn't just a punch, it was a punch backed by his avatar. A punch that would find the most vulnerable point and strike it with the perfect degree of force and finesse. To a black-belt martial artist, it would be a lucky shot, one in a hundred. Max could do it with 99% accuracy.

The black man crumpled forward as the xiphoid cartilage at the low end of his sternum cracked off and jabbed into his heart. His eyes rolled and a grunt emerged from his throat, but the grunt was accompanied by more of the small ghosts— at least a half dozen. They flew at Max and made their inept assaults, trying to gouge his eyes, trying to set his clothes on fire, trying to frighten or confuse or even possess him. To a normal man, they'd be terrifying, but for his second soul they were just old hat.

Still, they were irritating, and it didn't pay to underestimate even fledgling wraiths. Max decided to use the scythe.

"If this was once yours…" he said, as it changed from ring to weapon in his hand, "…you should fear it enough to back off!"

The artifact's scythe shape—it's original, *true* shape— was a slender pole six feet long, with a curved twelve-inch

blade on one end. A simple thing, really, or at least a simple form. But it was not a construct of wood and metal. It was shaped shadow. The blade was dark division in physical form, and the smooth, cool dim of the shaft had a feel like nothing solely material.

It was wonderfully light and strong, and it howled as Max spun it through the air around him. He was vaguely aware that Keene was doing something, something hard to see past the glare of shorn ghosts and the light-drinking darkness of the blade that cut them. He turned and sliced with precision and grace, and the six petty specters were exiled from the matter lands.

Max barely had time to get the scythe up into a guard position before he saw the bleak horror his enemy had become. He took a breath, stepped to a good angle and swung his weapon at the skull-faced monster before him.

Keene—or the thing that had been Clive Keene—swept forward, propelled on a gust of smoke by charcoal wings. Its bony left arm blocked the haft of the weapon...

...and Max felt the sickle shift in his grasp. Where once his grip had been sure and firm, now the shaft was numbingly chill, slipping away as Keene pulled it from him. His heart had a moment to lurch in fear as he realized that the blade had somehow switched sides—was *coming toward his hand*—and he tried to let go, but it was too late. The edge, with sharpness a razor would envy, sheared through his fingers like a warm spoon entering ice cream. The cut was so clean he felt little pain, just a buzzing emptiness.

"WHAT ARE YOU?" the creature demanded again. "MERELY HUMAN, BUT WITH A PIECE OF A DEAD ANGEL'S SPIRIT CAPTURED WITHIN? HOW HAS THIS HAPPENED? HOW HAVE YOU STOLEN OUR POWER?"

"It's mine," Max whispered. He stumbled back, clutching his mangled hand, willing the blood vessels closed, willing his body out of shock. "It's my other half. We belong together."

"USURPER!" Keene swung its stolen—or reclaimed?—weapon through the air, and Max had to drop flat to his stomach to avoid the blow.

"CANNIBAL!" The scythe hummed, it sounded hungry somehow, and as Max saw his enemy ready another blow, he knew he could not dodge it again. Desperate, he reached out

to open a portal away, trying to get to another space, *any-where*. He knew that the spiritual storm could kill him or sweep him away forever, but he feared it less than the scythe in the skeleton's hands.

But the wall between worlds was so thick that he could not tunnel through. He rolled, he squirmed, but the blade struck him true.

Immediately, Max was outside himself, shaking and shuddering like a flag in a gale. He could see his body sprawled on the floor of Keene's home and he knew he wasn't dead… yet. The creature had simply driven his soul from his still-living flesh, he could reclaim it if he could only fight the tempest winds and return.

A normal soul would cling with only its own strength. But Max Hirniesen had help, the allied spirit laced through his body and through his essence, it served and saved and loved him, pulling him back…

…And then he saw the black bone creature cutting it.

"Unholy monster!" Keene bellowed. "Is your lust for humankind so strong that you can pervert death itself?"

Somehow, the creature was cutting Max's avatar away from him with the scythe. He knew such spiritual divorces were possible, but he'd never expected to fall victim to one.

The fear of his avatar was heightened into panic as the hellish creature unwound it, piece by piece, from everything that was Max Hirniesen.

Max knew he had only one choice. He gathered the last of his strength into a final effort and stilled his body's heart.

Whatever fate he would face, he and his second soul would face it together.

❖ ❖ ❖

Far away, a woman named Betsy Smith went a whole day without taking a single drink of alcohol. She took this as proof that she didn't really have a problem and that she didn't really need to make any changes in her life.

A man named Jake Steubbens, who was faced with the loss of his berth at a homeless shelter, decided to really make an attempt with this AA business. Before that, he'd just been going through the motions.

V
chapter
five

Hasmed dropped out of sight for a couple of days after burying Mikey Diamond, then he went to pay Dennis Porter a visit. Dennis had been Harvey's bookie, before. He operated out of a diner that had no visible name, just a Pepsi sign that said *3 egg & Bacon special*. The special had been up as long as anyone could remember. Once it had read *3 eggs* but the last letter had fallen off during a windstorm. You could still see where it had been, because the plastic behind it was so much brighter than the dingy gray background.

As Hasmed entered, two uniformed policemen were talking to Dennis. The three men laughed, and the police turned to go.

"Hey, Harv," one of them said. "Heard about your World Series bet." He snickered.

Hasmed gave him a tired nod and passed on toward Dennis.

"Harvey!" Dennis said, surprised. "What you doin' here?"

"Can't a man come speak to his old buddy?"

"Sure, Harv, sure," Dennis replied. He had a nervous look on his face. He peered closer at his guest and scratched his arm through his sweater. "What's... uh, what's going on?"

"Well, d'you hear about Mikey Diamond?"

Dennis looked uncomfortable and glanced at the two cops as they got into their prowl car.

"I heard he's, um, kind of missing."

"Kind of, yeah."

Dennis swallowed.

"You don't... know what happened to him, do you?"

Hasmed shrugged and tipped back his hat. "I know he shot me in the forehead."

"Jesus, Mary and fuck!"

"Uh huh. I know he was gone when I came to. And I know I died on the operating table not long after that."

"Harvey, you're... jeez man, you're not making sense. You're talkin' crazy."

"Oh, I came back. They, whatsitcalled... they resuscitated me. But I was dead for three minutes."

He took off his sunglasses and gave Dennis the full effect of his bloody red glare. Dennis shrank back in his booth.

"Man, Harvey, I'm... I'm real sorry..."

"Don't be."

"W-what you mean?"

"I mean being dead—even for just three minutes—it's real interesting. A real *eye* opener."

"Harvey, you're..."

"I see things now, Dennis. I can see shit you can't imagine. The future. Little bits of the past. The secret ways stuff's hooked together. It's really somethin'."

"You ain't makin' sense."

"Oscar Phelps bet a C-note on Lucky Shirt in the sixth race tomorrow, but Lucky Shirt's gonna perform poorly. You got asthma and you keep kidding yourself that it ain't emphysema, but tomorrow you're gonna have a bad attack that winds up getting diagnosed as pneumonia. Mikey Diamond ran off to Florida and is planning to head south to where dollars buy you a lot of heroin, 'cause he's been hiding a habit for a while. If you look under the gun cabinet in his house, you'll find some smack he forgot while he was clearing out."

"Harvey, you're making no sense. Cut it out!"

"Wait an' see."

"This is just some freaky trick," Dennis said, but he was clearly unnerved and agitated. He stuck out his chin. "Some trick to get out of the money you owe. You act like you know everything, but you made a stupid-ass play on the Series,

Harv. I know you ain't got the money, but I gotta at least get the vig."

"I don't owe you anything."

"Now you're *really* talking crazy."

Hasmed explained his point of view, and Dennis actually laughed in his face. But the next day—when Dennis saw his debtor already waiting in the hospital as he was brought in for what would later be diagnosed as pneumonia—Dennis had a change of heart.

He couldn't talk with the respirator tube down his throat, but he could write notes in a shaky, spidery script.

I can't cancel your debt. Talk to Vietnam Ham.

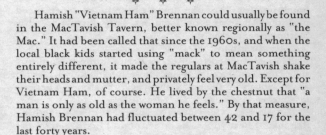

Hamish "Vietnam Ham" Brennan could usually be found in the MacTavish Tavern, better known regionally as "the Mac." It had been called that since the 1960s, and when the local black kids started using "mack" to mean something entirely different, it made the regulars at MacTavish shake their heads and mutter, and privately feel very old. Except for Vietnam Ham, of course. He lived by the chestnut that "a man is only as old as the woman he feels." By that measure, Hamish Brennan had fluctuated between 42 and 17 for the last forty years.

"One day, I was out in da boosh," Ham was saying as Hasmed entered the bar. "An' I spied one of da Cong, but he din' see me. So real quiet, I sneak up behind him, put one hand over his mouth, and jam my knife right up his ass." Hamish demonstrated with a gesture, then gave a nostalgic chuckle. "He died."

Hamish Brennan had been a pushy, no-good street punk in the 1960s. In 1967, at the age of 17, he lied about his age to get into the army. There, his boundless energy and cheerful willingness to kill got him accepted into the Green Berets. He was honorably discharged after serving two tours of duty, and he returned home to New Jersey. The same physical fitness, alertness and can-do attitude that doomed a number of black-clad Vietnamese soldiers quickly endeared Ham to the local dons. Plus, of course, he told great stories about killing Charlie.

His heyday as a bone-breaker and hired killer was long past, but as he'd aged, he'd matured as well. He could kill,

it was true, but unlike many in his profession, he could think up options other than killing. With nothing to prove, he could let things slide, and that ability to compromise—alongside organizational and tactical skills honed in the Army—eventually earned him a place as a heavily connected guy in the local family crime syndicate.

Since he was not Italian, Hamish was not (and could never be) a made guy, but he was successful. He had money, he had girlfriends who suited his many moods, and he was a silent partner in his favorite tavern. All in all, he was pretty content. He hadn't even had to kill anyone since he'd turned forty-four.

Dennis Porter was one of Hamish's lesser underlings. Small potatoes, but one doesn't become an experienced mobster by ignoring small matters. They can turn into big matters unexpectedly.

"Mr. Brennan?"

Hamish turned from his associate (a pimp from up-state New York) and frowned. It wasn't an angry frown. It was a "Now, who the hell are you again?" frown. Then his face cleared.

"Harvey, isn't it? Harvey Shoolee, Shooleo, something like that? I hear you made an ignorant fookin' call on the World Series."

"I thought the Cubs were due."

"Aye, well. What brings you to th' Mac?"

"Dennis Porter sent me."

"Did he, now?" Hamish turned his body to face Hasmed, and his eyes flicked left and right. From the dim recesses of the Mac, two bulky shapes materialized.

"He told me you could forgive me my debt."

Hamish chuckled. "You make me sound like a priest, lad. 'Forgive our debts as we forgive our debtors,' right? But even if I *could* do that—not sayin' I can, not sayin' I can't—I'm not exactly in the forgiveness business."

"This debt you ought to let go."

Hamish peered at Hasmed. He'd met Ciullo a couple times before—a small man, not in size, but in spirit. This fellow didn't even seem to be the same person. He had the same face and same voice and same pudgy dumpling frame,

but there was something else. Something that reminded Hamish of rain and heat and close death in the jungle.

Something in him bespoke a fellow warrior—someone who had seen much and suffered much and caused much suffering in turn.

"Why, exactly, ought I do that?"

Hasmed explained his reasoning. Hamish laughed, and it was more polite than when Dennis did. Vietnam Ham was genuinely amused. He still had no intention of dropping the debt, though, and he said so.

"I knew you wouldn't," Hasmed said. "Not just because it's right. So I'll give you another reason." He stepped closer, and the two thugs behind him closed their positions. All he did was tip back his hat and lower his sunglasses, however.

"I am not the man I was, sir," Hasmed told him quietly. "I have died and returned from the dead. I have seen what lies on the other side. I think part of me is still there—still dead—because I can see from the other side *in*, too."

"Really."

"I can see the sciatica that torments you, no matter how much you try to hide it. I can see that this man," he jerked a thumb at a thug behind him without looking "is going to be injured in an accident within twenty-four hours. I can see that this other fellow," indicated with a nod of his head "has just picked up a case of syphilis."

"You little…" The supposedly syphilitic bruiser reached forward and grabbed Hasmed by the shoulder, but the smaller man shrugged out of his grip and stepped forward to whisper in Vietnam Ham's ear.

"I know which of your mistresses is pregnant, and I can tell you who the father is."

Hamish shoved him back, and everything jolly was gone from his face.

"You're a regular fortune-teller, then." He looked at his two men. "Hold him," he said, reaching into his coat pocket for his brass knuckles.

Even in his fifties, Vietnam Ham had a strong, quick punch. It sank into Hasmed's soft gut, and the two lugs grinned as they felt their burden sag against their grip.

"Bet you didn't see *that* coming, Mr. Fortune," Hamish said, punching again and giving Hasmed a stinging slap with his other hand.

"Didn't I?"

The look in the bloody eye was disturbing, and Vietnam Ham suddenly found he didn't feel like hitting anymore. He waved a hand, and his two men flung Hasmed out in the street.

But later that day, one of the thugs tripped and fell down a flight of stairs, just as Hasmed had predicted. The other thug, uneasy, got a checkup and discovered he was, indeed, infected with *Treponema pallidum*. And Hamish, after talking to Dennis, called Harvey Ciullo's number to ask which of his three girlfriends he should talk to.

He also told Hasmed to talk to Sal Macellaio about his money problem.

❖ ❖ ❖

Hasmed was not, of course, predicting the future or seeing the past. He knew Elohim who could do that sort of thing, but it wasn't an art he'd studied. His talents ran more toward moving unseen and hurting people. With these powers combined, he could *make* his predictions come true.

He'd felt Dennis's illness. After describing a sudden turn for the worse, it took only a moment's breath to make it happen.

A similar whispered curse put an aching soreness in Lucky Shirt's leg.

Invisible, he'd found Mikey's syringe (along with money and jewelry that would make a small but real dent in Harvey's outstanding medical bills).

Ignored—covered in a gray section of papered-over vision, like one of the late Mr. Diamond's migraine auras— he had walked up behind Ham's henchman and given him a well-placed boot in the ass at the top of the steps.

Preparing for a visit to Sal Macellaio had taken the most work, the most sneaking. He'd searched Sal's house a lot more thoroughly than Mikey's, without finding anything nearly as damning. He followed the man himself, when he could, but even ignored, he found Sal hard to trail. Macellaio was in the habit of ditching even imaginary tails, with the

thought that they might really be there unseen. It took a lot of time and effort (and eventually luck), but he found something. He found something Sal was really hiding—something he could reveal, something that would astonish. He found Scott.

Maintaining the sham of prophecy took a lot of forethought and running around, of course. Simply unveiling his true form and power would have been much simpler, but the fortune-telling scheme had been Harvey's idea.

It wasn't like there was a little "Harvey voice" giving him advice, and it wasn't like Hasmed admired or even respected the man whose body he'd taken. Nonetheless, Hasmed had gotten a feeling—a feeling based on Harvey's experience and observations—that "seeing the future" would be a lot more acceptable than striking people down with curses. After all, a lot of the gangsters were involved with gambling. Gamblers were notorious for being superstitious, for following hunches, for magical thinking. They were known for it, and rightly so. Harvey was (had been) a perfect example of the type—a guy who'd bet the Cubs would win the World Series long before the playoffs had even started. And why? He had a "gut feeling" that the Cubs were due. Never mind that every other time he'd followed his instincts, he'd lost money and earned the contempt of his peers. *This time* was going to be different. He'd been certain of it. *This* was the big bet that would turn everything around.

In that, he'd been correct. Just not in any way he'd have hoped for or anticipated.

Nonetheless, his marginal existence had made Harvey a keenly interested observer of the people around him. They were superstitious, paradoxically religious, yet also strangely pragmatic. They were more likely than many to accept the miraculous. At the same time, they would also be more likely to deal with it on a dirt-common level, where a more educated or abstract mind would simply be amazed.

A college professor, confronted with reliable cures and curses, would be shocked and wonder-struck. Such a man would instantly get lost in the big questions of what such things meant about the world and the people within it.

A mafioso with the same evidence would be far more likely to try to control or destroy it. Yes, it's a miracle, it's

amazing, it's evidence of a wilder, stranger world... but, in the final analysis, it's also either a threat or a resource.

That narrow focus guaranteed Hasmed an extreme reaction (of one type or another) if he simply told the truth.

Once the idea of subterfuge crossed his mind (or Harvey's), it started to appeal to him more and more. Where Harvey looked at the reactions of the gangsters, Hasmed considered the reactions of his fallen fellows. Surely he would meet other Elohim at some point, and there was no guarantee that they would be friendly. If he posed as one of the Neberu—a member of the House of Fate, a seer, a finder of futures—then it would give him an edge against any spirit who wished him ill.

It was troublesome and complicated, but it was his plan, and it played to his strengths.

Unfortunately, it meant he had no idea what to expect when he confronted Sal Macellaio.

❖ ❖ ❖

Mob life is not a bureaucracy.

There are layers and levels and titles, but there are no hard-and-fast rules. There is no three-ring binder that explains when a consigliere is more important than an underboss. Instead, there is a loose, implied network of obligations and respect and reputation. When you start out, you keep your mouth shut and your eyes open, and pretty soon it's clear who's really running things—regardless of their position or title.

Gangsterism is unofficial. There is no red tape, so things get done efficiently. It also means, though, that there is confusion now and again. Vietnam Ham was a case in point. He couldn't *really* be running a crew, because he wasn't made, and he couldn't be made because he was a goddamn kilt-wearing Scotsman, for Christ's sake. Ham's crew had been officially run by a guy named Tiny Sorgente—except that Tiny had died eleven years ago. Technically, Hamish and his pals were in Sal Macellaio's crew, though in practice, Sal just took the money and let Vietnam Ham do what he wanted. No one talked about it. It just turned out that way. A little confusing, maybe, but only if you bothered to think about it.

A little confusion is fine—it's no big deal. The mobsters shrug and accept it as "part of Our Thing." But sometimes there are big problems—confusion that can't be swept aside with a nod and a tap on the nose. Confusion like that can cause an apparently stable society to convulse and shudder with sudden violence, like a sturdy tree shaken by a terrible storm.

Johnny Bronco was sick.

In the vagueness of the Vuoto crime family, there was one certainty. That certainty was not a promise or a principle, but a person—Johnathan Vuoto, also known as "Johnny Bronco," also known as "Don Vuoto."

In the days between Hasmed's discussion with Vietnam Ham and his scheduled meeting with Sal, Johnny Bronco suddenly dropped from what turned out to be lung cancer.

The last person to talk to him before his collapse was Harvey Ciullo—a fact that was not lost on Sal Macellaio.

Sal wasn't quite an underboss, but he was close. "Officially" he was only a skipper, a crew chief. In reality, several crews looked to him for guidance. Johnny respected him, and you couldn't deny that Sal did right by the family, but... Sal and Johnny were never pals. With Johnny sick, a lot of eyes suddenly turned to Sal, watching to see if he was make a move.

It was in this climate that Hasmed approached him for a favor.

❖ ❖ ❖

Sal did business in a lot of different places. Unlike Hamish or Dennis, he didn't have a "hangout." Predictability wasn't a problem for Dennis—it was, in fact, a necessity. He hid in plain sight and bribed the local cops. He didn't have to worry about the feds. Dennis didn't know shit, and he liked it that way, so he'd have been worthless as a witness. Consequently, he was beneath their notice. Easy as it would be to tap his phone and bug his favorite booth, it *still* wasn't worth the effort.

Hamish made do with daily bug sweeps and convoluted talk. Anyone who listened in at the Mac could readily hear an hour-long conversation without a single proper name or identifiable location. It was an art form. Hamish could plan an entire protection shakedown with phrases no

more specific than "that one place," "the guy, you know, with the thing?" "the stuff" or "something, you know, like what we need."

Sal wasn't like that. Sal was mobile, favoring noisy places where audio surveillance simply wasn't an option. Today he might be at a construction site. Tomorrow he might pick a public pool, where you couldn't get close with a wire.

When Hasmed caught up with him, he was at a steel mill.

There was a reason Sal kept on the move. Unlike Hamish, Sal needed to discuss crimes in precise detail before carrying them out. Sal was a stringer—an expert at assembling teams for specific high-risk, high-yield crimes. He was constantly looking for the next big score. Ham concentrated on stable, long-term ventures—prostitution, gambling, loan-sharking, rackets. Predictable stuff. He paid up to Sal, his immediate superior, and Sal (after taking his skim) paid up to Johnny Bronco. Usually.

On occasion, however, Sal had been known to take pay-ups from Vietnam Ham (and guys like him) and use it as seed money for bigger capers like long cons, bank robberies, armored car heists or high-level fraud. So far, he'd always been successful and had been able to pay up the money he'd held back from Johnny, along with a lot more. Johnny wasn't one to argue with success, but he'd noticed.

After those successes, of course, Sal hadn't needed to do any more investing with Johnny's money, and things seemed calm. But Sal never came up as a candidate for higher positions, even though he clearly had the will and the skill. Johnny didn't like him, and that took care of that.

But with Johnny weak, all that changed.

So when Sal's bodyguards showed Harvey Ciullo into their master's presence, there was already a tension in the air—a feeling of distrust and unease. The proximity of liquid tons of red-hot steel oozing along into molds didn't make any of them sweat any less.

The mill was a surreal hell of heat and incandescent spark showers, and grime was everywhere—everywhere but on the live steel, which coursed along, white, then yellow, then crimson, developing black crusts on the surface as it cooled. Then those surfaces would crack, revealing the angry core beneath. Heat would surge up in ripples and waves, angry white splitting crusted skin, and the cooling

progression would start again. Red flickers fought black shadows everywhere the eye fell.

"Harvey," Sal said. He didn't turn to look.

"Mr. Macellaio."

"You ever see anything like this?"

Hasmed had been remembering the war against Heaven, when he had battled mighty spirits of the soil and earth. When struck, they had bled molten metal much like what he was seeing. "Nuh uh."

"Can you imagine what that stuff would do to a guy? I mean, if you threw him in? The skin, the guts... that shit would be gone in seconds, right? Even the bones might just... poof."

"I guess."

Sal finally turned to face him. "You know you made a stupid play on the World Series. Just, really retarded."

Hasmed shrugged.

"Ham tells me you think we ought to let you skate."

Hasmed nodded.

"Why in hell would I do that?"

"I think you've put paid to me."

"Is that a fact?"

Hasmed removed his hat and wiped his sweaty, stubbly head with a forearm.

"Yeah."

Sal gave the knotty scar on Harvey's forehead a speculative squint. In the ruddy light, it seemed to pulse.

"The way I see it," Hasmed said, "We had a deal. Either I pay you or you kill me. Right?"

"That's pretty much the understanding, yeah."

"Well, I didn' pay. And Mikey Diamond killed me." He tightened his lips a little, but no one would call it a smile. "There. We're done."

Sal laughed.

"That's some kind of pretzel logic you got working there, Ciullo. Or should I be calling you Mr. Fortune, now?"

"You can check my hospital records. I *died*, Sal." A note of tension entered Hasmed's voice.

"I think it only counts if you stay dead, Harv."

"Don't tell me you're going to kill me again. Are you Sal?"

Something was happening. Sal couldn't quite name it, but something. The shadows were moving. Or maybe they

were suddenly still where they'd moved before. Maybe the shadows were touching Harvey and clinging to him.

"I'd rather get your vig and the money you owe."

"I ain't payin'."

"You defying me, Ciullo? You coming here, to my face, defying me? I don't fuckin' believe this. Vince, take care of him."

Vince stepped forward and started to cough. At first it was just a little rough sound, like clearing some of the mill's smoke and closeness from his throat, but then he coughed again. Again. Each was bigger and harsher, and by the time he'd taken three steps toward Ciullo, he couldn't stand up straight. He was doubled over, his red face redder in the light of molten steel, battling for breath.

Sal's two other bodyguards pulled out guns but aimed them uncertainly. They knew Harvey was there. They could see him. Only they couldn't, really. They couldn't focus on him. They knew he was somewhere, but...

"Sal, you ought to reconsider. Did you talk to Hamish? Did you talk to Dennis? Did they tell you what I've seen?"

Sal had his own gun out, but like his colleagues, he had no idea where to aim it. The voice—Harvey's voice only, Christ, so cold and cruel and purposeful—seemed to be getting *quieter*. But clearer, and that meant closer.

"I warned Dennis about his throat, and he didn't listen. And I warned Ham about his girlfriend, and *he* didn't listen. I warned Johnny about his cancer too, and he didn't really have a chance to listen. It came on that fast. Now I'm warning *you* Sal. You don't want to earn my hate, not over something as petty as *money*. You don't know how far I can see, and you've got things you can't stand to lose. Your wife? Your sister? I think you could see them go. You could, couldn't you? But your son..."

"I got no son!" Sal hissed, but his face had turned pale.

"You do. The son no one knows about. Scott, isn't it? The son who's at college, who doesn't know nothing about gangsters or rackets or strings. Your little piece of normal life, and *nobody knows*. Your secret. Well, Sal, I seen it. You want to know what his future holds? You want *me* to tell you his fortune?"

"A'right!" Sal said. "Okay! Jesus, fine. You're... off the hook."

And suddenly, everything was normal. Vince caught his breath and stood up. The bodyguards sheepishly holstered their weapons, because it was just little Harvey Ciullo standing by the boss. Harvey the nobody, Harvey the joke. Harvey, the dummy who couldn't think his way out of a wet paper bag with Einstein coaching him through.

Harvey Ciullo, who'd just made their boss back down.

Sal's gun vanished with practiced subtlety, and he straightened his jacket. His breath came in rough rattles, but he controlled it. He was good at control. It made him what he was.

He knew that he'd never get away with caving in to Ciullo. It wouldn't be fast, but it would kill his reputation eventually. Probably more thoroughly for being slow. But he also knew that whatever Harvey was now—whatever he'd become on the other side of death—he wasn't ready to cross it. Not yet. And if he was ever going to get ready, he'd need the respect.

It was quite a puzzle, but Sal was a resourceful guy.

"Yeah, your debt—fuggeddaboudit. Long as you do me one favor first."

"A favor?" Looking him over, Sal could see that Harvey's face was pale and he looked a little slumped, a little tired. So whatever freak-show shit he'd pulled, it had cost him something. Good to know.

"A little thing. 'Cause honestly, that bet you made was *so funny*. Hell, it's worth the money just for the chuckle, you know?"

"That's big of you."

"You just gotta do a little thing. Nothin' big. You got any frequent flyer miles?"

"How come?"

"'Cause you're going to Los Angeles for me."

❖   ❖   ❖

Hasmed went home and showered, letting the hot water sluice over him until all the grime was gone, all the clammy sweat washed clean and—more important—until the nerves and twitchiness eased out of his frame.

He was disgusted. He'd faced down thrones and principalities of the *Holy Host* without trembling, but now…? Now

he was reduced to fear by a human being. A mere mortal whose best threats were gunplay and molten metal.

Hasmed tried to leave it, tried to ignore it, told himself it was Harvey's fear, leftover anxiety from a mouse of a man… but he knew it was more than that.

The world was ugly and fallen and wrecked, but he was still afraid to leave it. He walked once more under the blue sky and above the green grass, and he would fight to remain with every ounce of strength. He could no longer deny his fear of Hell. He was terrified by the thought of returning to his cell of numbness, and he knew that made him weak.

That and Tina.

As he thought about her, he could feel her coming closer, coming up the stairs, a bright spark in a dark world. He wasn't God to her. God, to Tina, was barely an abstraction. God was something that some adults thought was important, something involved with churches and songs.

As long as he could act like Harvey Ciullo, Hasmed was *better* than God. To her, he was Daddy.

He finished his shower and toweled off. Glancing in the mirror, he could see the mark between his eyes settling down. The stitches had come out and now there was just a livid red scar. Coupled with the eye of blood and pus, it was hideous. Unforgettable.

Hasmed should have been able to heal the scar and the eye with a simple push of will, but he didn't. At some level, he suspected he couldn't. Those marks were part of him. They were neither Hasmed nor Harvey, but perhaps they were a natural part of the fused being that they were becoming.

Perhaps they were the face of Mr. Fortune.

Shaking his head, he dressed quickly and was out of the bathroom as Helena started knocking on his door.

He opened it and immediately squatted to hug Tina.

"Hey kitten," he said. She struggled against him.

"No!" she said. "No no *no!*"

"She's been like this all day," Helena said.

"I'm sorry," Hasmed replied. He meant it. "You wanna come in? I could make you some tea or, I don' know, get you a beer?"

"I'll take the beer," Helena said.

Tina got free and ran up to a wall. She started kicking it, yelling, "No no no no no!"

"Tina, *quit that*!" Helena told her.

"I don't have to!"

"Yes, hon, you do," Hasmed said. He turned to Helena and said, "I got this. You mind self-serve with that beer?"

"Not at all," she said, heading toward the kitchen.

Hasmed took Tina by the shoulder to pull her away. She wrestled free and kept kicking. He slipped both arms under her armpits and picked her up.

"No no no!" she hollered, struggling. He hugged her tighter until she was immobile. Then he waited for her to get tired.

"Sweets," he said. "What's this about?"

She didn't answer.

"You can't go around kicking the walls in our apartment. If you kick 'em down, we won't have anywhere to live."

"Aunt Helena is *mean*," she said.

"I don't think so," he replied.

"You're mean *too*!" she screamed, her face bright red.

"Tina, sweetie, you need to calm down."

"She's not my mommy! You're not my daddy! You're mister *ugly-head!*" She burst into tears.

He sighed and held her squirming form close again.

"She's not your mom," he said. "But auntie Helena loves you very much. I love you very much. You got that?"

"No," she said sullenly.

"Well, it's true. We're here and we love you, and we aren't going anywhere, you understand?"

"No." There was less fire in her refusal this time.

"It's about naptime for you, right? Why don't you go lie down in your room and see if you feel better in a while?"

"No! I don' wanna nap!"

"Okay, you don't have to nap, but you have to have some quiet time in your room. You got me?"

She frowned at him for a moment, then said, "Okay."

He escorted her to her room then came back to the living room after about ten minutes. Helena was sipping a beer and looking at a stack of books.

"You went to the library?" she asked. Her voice was skeptical.

"Yeah," he said. "I *do* know how to read, y'know."

"I know, but... *Getting Fit the Healthy Way*? *The Good Sense Diet*? What gives?"

"I don't wanna die," he replied.

She tilted her head.

"Honest," he said. "I don't want to die. Again. I been... I been outside life, Helena, and I didn' like it. I don't wanna go back before I absolutely have to."

"Wow."

"What?"

She opened her mouth, shut it, took a sip of beer.

"I guess I just... I don't know. I never thought about you changing your life," she said.

"Get used to the idea."

"Harvey?"

"Hm?"

"What happened that night?"

"What night?"

"The night you 'fell.'"

He shook his head. "Don't worry about it. It's not an issue anymore."

"I've heard that from you before."

"Yeah, but did I ever sound like I really believed it?"

She had to admit that before, he hadn't.

Later that night, after Helena left, Hasmed went into Tina's room. She was fast asleep on her bed, with a Barbie doll clutched in one fist. Even in sleep, her forehead was furrowed.

For a moment, he just stood there, head cocked to the side. A rush of emotions coursed through Harvey's body as he watched his daughter. Hasmed was outside them, but not unaffected.

He watched in silence and turned to go. He took two steps before a voice stopped him.

"Daddy?"

He turned back.

"Yes?"

"Do you want to hear a song?" She was whispering.

"Sure, kitten." He sat down next to her on the bed.

In her high-pitched lisp, Tina sang.

"Jesus loves me, this I know
For the Bible tells me so.
Little ones to Him belong.
They are weak but He is strong."

Hasmed bit his lip.

"Who taught you that song?"

"Auntie Helena."

"She really loves you, kiddo. You know that."

"Yeah." Tina was whispering. Hasmed stroked a wisp of golden curls back from her forehead. "Daddy?"

"Yeah?"

"I'll never see Mommy again, will I?"

"You'll see her in pictures, and in your memory."

"But… she's not coming back."

"Nope."

"She's dead."

"Yep."

She sat up and put her arms around him. "You almost died," she said.

"I came back for you, kid."

"But you *could* die."

"Don't you worry about that."

She just held him tighter and tighter.

"Look," he said. "I'll tell you a secret, okay?"

She looked up at him with brown eyes full of trust.

His heart began to beat faster, and he almost stopped, almost told her something meaningless. But he didn't.

"There's a way that you and me can always be together, Tina. Always. No matter what. Would you like that?"

"Uh huh!"

"Okay. Here's the first part. You have to say you're mine. Understand?"

"I'm yours."

Just like that.

He took a deep breath. "That's… that's good, honey. Now here's the second part. There's a name, you got it? And it's a *secret*. You can't tell anybody about it, you understand? No one. It's just for you and me. You don't even tell grandma. Not even aunt Helena. You got it?"

"It's a secret," she repeated.

"You don't tell anyone."

"Don't tell anyone."

"Promise?"

"I promise."

"Promise on Mommy?"

She swallowed. He could see that she didn't really understand everything—how could she? She didn't understand what he was asking, but she trusted her daddy. And she understood that there was something dreadful in promising on her dead mother.

"Promise on Mommy," she whispered.

"All right. The name is 'Hasmed.' If you're in trouble, if you're in danger, anywhere, no matter what, say that name. Has-med. Say it."

"Hasmed," she whispered.

"Good." He kissed her on the forehead. "You're a good girl, Tina. And I'm going to look out for you."

His voice caught in his throat.

"I'm going to watch you forever."

VI
chapter
six

"Did you ever fantasize about being a rock star, Tommy?"

Thomas Ramone shook his head. Sabriel frowned at him.

"No, really. You must have, right?"

He raised his eyebrows and shook his head again.

"Well, what about an actor? Stand-up comedian? Not a painter, surely."

His head kept shaking, back and forth.

"Oh, for Pete's sake."

Sabriel stood up and walked over to him. She'd been sipping from a Poland Springs bottle, and she tilted it up to his cracked lips. He guzzled greedily, letting twin trails of water snake down from the corners of his mouth. Then he wrapped his lips around the bottleneck completely, unwilling to let a single drop go. He continued to suck at it even after it was empty, and then Sabriel pulled it away.

She waited a moment and then asked, "Can you talk now?"

"I... I guess." His voice was low, rough and raspy. There was a deadness to it—a profound despair and depression that put a light, pretty smile on Sabriel's face.

"You *never* dreamed of being famous?"

"Nah. I mean, what the fuck? Gettin' all the jokes about The Ramones growing up. Who cares?"

She nodded. "I see." She sat back down. This time, she hadn't hauled down a kitchen chair. She had two large

suitcases, and was delicately perched on the end of the biggest one.

"I'm going away, Tom. You know that."

He nodded. She waited.

"Aren't you going to ask me anything?"

"You aren't going to let me go." He said it like he was trying to strangle his own hope, and like he was succeeding.

"Well, I might. It'll cost you, though."

"Stockholm Syndrome."

"Very good! You remember!"

"I've had plenty of time to think things over."

"Here." Rummaging in her purse, she produced a Ziplock bag with half a sandwich in it. It wasn't a big sandwich—just white bread with peanut butter.

"Do you want this?"

His stomach grumbled audibly. "You know I do."

"Believe that I am a goddess, and it's yours."

"You're a goddess." His voice was flat, except for a lowering curve of despair and anxiety.

"That's a start, but you don't believe it. Really Tommy, you don't. I can tell. You want the sandwich—want it *soooo* much—and because of that you want to believe. But you really don't believe. It's too bad."

She dropped the baggie on the floor and picked up her suitcases.

"You're just going to leave me here." He didn't even have the spirit to make it a question.

"That's about the size of it, yes."

"Bitch."

She was halfway to the stairs and she stopped. She put down the bags and turned back to him.

"What did you call me?"

"You heard." In his throat, she could see his pulse pounding hard.

She bent over him until her mouth was nearly touching his ear. "Maybe," she whispered, "you want to reconsider what you said."

Thomas bit his lips, pulled off a curly flap of chapped flesh and felt the pinprick sting as a drop of his own blood ran into his mouth. It tasted great.

"Maybe I do."

She stood back and looked expectant.

"You're a *cunt*."

She laughed.

It wasn't a wicked laugh or a cruel laugh. It was a genuine, joyous and delighted laugh. It was the laugh of someone who has truly been surprised by something lovely. Something enchanting.

"Oh *Tommy*," she cried. "I was right to keep you!"

As her laughter tinkled out, the air in the basement became charged and heavy. Reaching up behind her neck, she undid a button at the top of her blouse.

"Thomas Ramone. Tom. You've got spunk. Spirit. *Humanity*."

She pulled the blouse off, dropped her skirt and stepped out of it. The air had become so humid and dense that water was beginning to bead on the walls and drip toward the floor.

"And as I think about it, I'm *glad* you're not an artist. I'm *glad* that you don't want to create anything. I've been too hung up on people like that. Too close to my work I suppose."

A heavy mist was filling the room. She shook her hair, which was curling in the warm fog. She stood before him naked.

"I really am a goddess," she said.

Then she transformed.

Where before he had seen a pale and lovely woman with red and yellow hair, he now beheld the glory of the ocean in sunlight. It rained in the basement as she stood before him with the grandeur of a storm at sea, magnificent and inhuman, Siren and Scylla in one.

She stepped forward and wrapped him in waterfall wings.

"WHAT IS IT YOU WANT, THOMAS? TELL ME WHAT YOU DESIRE. GIVE ME YOUR SERVICE, AND YOU SHALL HAVE IT."

Tom Ramone knew.

The days of thirst and hunger had prepared him for this sight. Just as the hermits of old religions purified themselves in the wilderness with fasting and loneliness and flagellation, Thomas's torment had opened his eyes. The normal con-

cerns of the day-to-day man were washed away, and when the miraculous appeared, Thomas knew it for what it was. He knew that she could do what she said. He sensed what it would cost him.

"Freedom," he said. "I want my freedom."

"Laugh with me," she said, "and it is yours."

Dazzled and amazed, Thomas did it. He started out with a forced chuckle and felt himself melting, oozing, loosening. Terrified, his laugher rose to hysterical peak as he flowed between the bonds and puddled on the floor.

"You see?" Sabriel asked. "Freedom."

Thomas re-formed and rose again clean, renewed... and deeply afraid of what he'd become.

Teddy Mason sat in his psychologist's office. He wasn't lying on a couch. Too cliché. And his psychologist wasn't a saturnine man with an Austrian accent and a neatly trimmed gray beard. She was a big fat woman in a blocky-cut pantsuit. Her name was Dr. Ng.

"I had that dream again," he said.

"Last night?"

"Thursday night." She made a note.

"Does that bother you?" she asked.

"Yeah." He looked down and away from her. "You know it does."

"Would you like to tell me about it?"

He shrugged. "You've heard it before."

"Tell me again."

She knew he was uncomfortable talking about the dream, and he knew she knew it, and he figured that was why she made him describe it every time. Certainly the dream never changed.

"All right, so the dream's like this... It's cold. Nighttime. I'm up in some hills. Not mountains like around here. Old hills, you know? Worn down. Like the Appalachians or something, only, not nearly so fertile."

"You've been to the Appalachians?"

"Once, when I was a teenager."

"And these hills weren't the Appalachians."

"No. Just like they weren't last time I had the dream."

Dr. Ng raised her hands. "Okay, okay. It's just that you mention the Appalachians every time you have this dream."

"It's a point of comparison. They weren't the Appalachians."

"All right."

Teddy Mason had lost his virginity during that trip to the Appalachians. He'd seen a swarthy, ugly girl in one of the towns, and he hadn't said anything. She hadn't said anything either, just looked at him and turned and walked away. He'd followed her to under some weathered wooden bleachers at a football field. She'd lifted her skirt up wordlessly, and he'd grunted a little as he tore her panties down, opened his own pants, struggled clumsily to put it in her. Her expression—distant, maybe contemptuous, maybe just dumb—didn't change as he rolled his hips one, two, three times and then came. There was blood on his penis when he pulled it out, so he guessed she was a virgin too. He almost said something to her, but there was nothing to say. He'd pulled his pants up, she'd fixed her skirt, and then it was over.

It was the most satisfying sexual experience he'd ever had, but it seemed so unreal that sometimes he wasn't sure if he remembered it, or if it was just a dream, a fantasy. He sometimes wanted to tell Dr. Ng about it—in a very, very slight way she resembled the girl—but he never did.

He cleared his throat and went on. "So in the dream, I'm in this mountain area. Very barren. Lots of gray sand, almost like dust. It's cold and the air is thin. It's real clear. Looking up in the sky I can see millions of stars, and the moon's like a spotlight. I mean, it's so bright I almost can't look at it."

He settled back in the chair, which gave a leathery creak. His head tilted and his eyes rose as he stopped looking at his psychologist and looked deeper into his memory.

"There are a few cactuses—cacti?—whatever. A few of them, and these scrubby little trees. And one of the trees talks to me."

He paused, waiting for Dr. Ng to say, "What did the tree say?" Most times, at this point in the narrative, she said that. Today she didn't, so after a pause he continued.

"It tells me it's pleased with the offerings I bring, and that if I do my... like, my sacred duty? If I do that well, I'll have its blessings and protection. If I fail in my duty, I'll... you know, feel its wrath. Whatever."

Teddy felt ridiculous talking all this biblical stuff—he was a furniture store manager. He shouldn't be seeing a psychologist about nightmares and sexual dysfunction. He waited for Dr. Ng to say something—to encourage him, to make it easier. She didn't.

What the hell am I paying her for? To sit here silent as a tree herself? Even as he thought it, though, the image—the doctor as the tree—struck a deep chord in him and made him afraid. She wasn't the tree. He didn't want her to be the tree. Did he?

"So then I start with the... the sacrifices. You know. Like I told you before."

"Tell me again."

He sighed. "The first one is a, a girl. Maybe twelve, thirteen? I don't know, maybe older. And I take this stick. It's not real big—maybe six or eight inches, thinner than a pencil... sharp. I put it in her eye. I don't blind her, though." This was the frustrating part, trying to explain how he felt a sensation of... expertise in the dream. His dream-self had a *goal* and didn't feel anger or horror or even madness. Just purpose. Like Teddy felt balancing the books at the end of the month—only, at the same time, his dream-self felt a sense of rightness, truth, duty and purity.

"I put it in right by the nose, like at the tear duct? And it's angled sharply up and a little bit in. Then the tree tells me it's enough, and I pull it out. Hardly any blood."

"What does the girl look like?"

"Kind of... I don't know. Indian? Maybe black? Dark-skinned. Straight black hair."

"What's she wearing?"

"Nothing. But it's not like she's naked. Maybe it's just that her clothes don't matter to the dream. I don't know. Or maybe we're all naked, and that's just the way it is."

"When you say 'we're all naked'...?"

"There are other people around me, watching while I do it. The tribe."

"In the dream, you're Indian or black like her?"

Teddy tilted his head. "Yeah." This was an angle he hadn't really considered before.

"What are the other people doing?"

"They're chanting something over and over. I can't remember what it is. It's a name, though."

"Your name?"

"Maybe," he said, but he knew it was the tree's name. He felt that if only he could remember that name, everything would become clear. Everything would make sense.

"You know what Freud would say about that long, thin stick, right?"

"Yeah," he sighed. "I honestly don't think this is any kind of sex dream... thing. You know. There isn't any... any feeling of that."

She made another note. "All right. Another theory states that, in dreams, we are every person in the dream."

"Yeah?"

"That is, every figure in a dream represents a different aspect or facet of ourselves."

Teddy thought that over. "Makes sense, I guess. Seeing as nobody's dreaming but me, everyone in the dream must be me. Or from me. Or something."

"So then what part of you is that girl?"

He opened his mouth and closed it again. "I don't know."

"Do you suspect that you're blind in some part of your life?"

"I told you, I don't blind her! I fix her!"

She raised her eyebrows. Teddy was surprised too.

"You 'fix' her?"

"Yeah..." He put his right hand over his mouth and looked off at nothing for a moment with wide eyes.

"What's wrong with her?"

"I don't know, but..."

Dr. Ng waited. A clock softly ticked.

"...but the same thing's wrong with me." Teddy's eyes, still gazing blankly at the floor—at his memory—were wide and staring. "I have the same curse. And because I have to take it away from people I can never... lose it myself. I'm the high priest, and I have to stay sick to heal others."

She waited, then encouraged him. "I think we're making some real progress here, Teddy. What part of you is the crowd, the tribe?"

He tried, he opened his mouth and closed it once more. "I don't know."

"All right. We're just about done for today, but I think you should be very pleased." She made a note. "If we can understand this dream, I believe it will lose its power to terrify you."

"I'd like that," he said automatically.

"For next week, I'd like you to think about what part of yourself is, symbolized by the tree."

Teddy's heart gave a single, hard thud. On autopilot, he stood and shook Dr. Ng's hand, then went out and mechanically waved to her receptionist as he left.

Dr. Ng had never told Teddy that his dreams always coincided with the full moon, for the simple reason that she had not, herself, noticed the pattern.

There were things Teddy didn't tell the doctor as well, but not because of ignorance. His reasons were more complex.

He had not told her that the idea of himself as the tree had jarred his brain. It had felt not just wrong, but blasphemous.

He had not told her that what woke him from these dreams was not horror or fear, but an exhilarating sensation of power and courage and rightness. He had never told her the tree felt holy.

❖　❖　❖

At the local YMCA, Roscoe Paum was getting uneasy.

"Jeez, Hawv," he said. "Maybe you ought to take it easy for a minute?"

Ten minutes earlier, Roscoe had been yelling encouragement, calling Harvey a pussy, badgering him to keep jumping the goddamn rope, shit, even little girls could fuckin' *jump rope*. The other man had put up with all of it, even though he kept getting the rope tangled in his ankles. After a five-minute break, Roscoe started him on the weights, and that was when he got a little uneasy.

Roscoe had seen a lot of boxers train, but usually it was young punks or fresh dropouts from high school, not old

guys with a couple decades worth of bacon breakfasts lining their guts. Not guys who'd just died on an operating table during brain surgery, for damn sure. But this guy—this weird new version of Harvey—pushed himself harder than those young punks. Harder than muscle-bound bastards who knew deep down that boxing was their *only* alternative to petty crime or a life sentence of minimum wage. Harder than the head cases who boxed as an expression of something sick and wounded, who boxed because it kept them from murder and assault. Harder even that the guys who *loved it*, who trained like maniacs because they liked nothing better than working out to the point of puking fatigue.

Roscoe looked down at the purple face of the man on the weight bench and saw a heartless intensity that surpassed all that.

As he watched, the red scab in the middle of Harvey's forehead cracked a little at one edge. A drop of blood beaded out.

"Okay, that's *enough*." Roscoe grabbed the barbell and put it on its brackets. He had to struggle to do it. His tremors were bad today.

"What? I thought you wanted me to feel the burn."

"Yeah, yeah," Roscoe said, "But I don't want you to get a brain aneurysm doin' it. C'mon, hit the showers."

"Shit, I can still…" As he sat up, Harvey's face turned pale, and he suddenly leaned back on the bench.

"You all right?"

"Fuggeddaboudit." He stood, but it was hesitant, and there was no more talk about continuing the workout.

Waiting outside the locker room, Roscoe bit his nails, thinking. *If something happens to Mr. Fortune in there, what happens to me? I'm stuck quivering until I die. Shit, I can't let him push himself.*

At the same time, he was wondering when "Mr. Fortune" would do something for his condition again. After the water, he'd come up with a package of plants—ginger and mint and such, which kept his muscles controlled as long as he could smell it. But that only lasted about a day, and now when he trembled, it was worse than before. Not physically

worse, but it meant more to him because he couldn't resign himself to it anymore. It was much worse to have hope.

The door opened.

"You feelin' okay, Harvey?"

"It's a'right."

"You gotta take it slow, man. You ain't young. You can't bounce right back like a teenager."

"I know, I know. I just wanted to, y'know, get a good workout in before I go."

"Go?"

"Yeah, I'm takin' a trip."

"Where to?"

"Fuggeddaboudit. Not important. Just a little thing, you know?"

"Uh huh. When you think you'll be back?"

"Not sure. Could take a couple days, a week... probably not longer than a week."

Roscoe Paum bit his lips, thinking about a week with no relief for his pain and fragility.

"Well have a nice, a nice time, there. On your trip. Um." He looked away. They were walking to the parking lot.

"Hey Paum, how *you* doin'?"

"Me? Well, you know." He shrugged, but his whole body shook as he did it. "Why? You think you could... you know... you maybe got somethin'?"

The reply was a deep sigh. "I don' know. I got an idea, but..."

"Yeah?"

"Yeah, but it might not be easy."

"Well, nothin's easy. I mean, what's the idea?"

"Remember me telling you there were... things? Things I saw? Like, they're not real. Not something you can touch but they're still there? That they can do stuff?"

"Things."

"Yeah. The things have ideas, I think. And I get this... I don' know, it's hard to see, real hard. But maybe I see a thing helping you." He looked away, flexed his exhausted shoulders. "Helping you out long term, like."

Roscoe swallowed. "You mean, what... Like, fixing me? Like, permanent?"

"Maybe. It's not clear, you know?"

"But maybe?"

"Maybe. You wanna try this?"

"Yeah! I mean, why wouldn' I?"

They were in Roscoe's apartment twenty minutes later with the shades down and the phone off the hook.

"What do we…? I mean, how do we do it?" Roscoe asked.

"I think I just need to, uh… sit down. You sit down, and I'll see what I can… see."

"All right. You want, I don't know, a cold drink or…?"

"Nah, nah. Just stay quiet." He closed his eyes—one clear and brown, one bloody and mottled—and settled back on Roscoe's worn green couch. Roscoe sat and waited.

Nothing happened.

Nothing happened.

Nothing happened, and Roscoe started to fidget. His shakes and twitches were already shifting his body. He was biting again at nails he'd already bitten and was reaching for the TV Guide when Harvey's eyes opened and a voice came from Harvey's mouth. It wasn't Harvey's voice though, not by a long shot.

"SUPPLICANT!" it said. "STATE THY NAME!"

Roscoe jumped and stuck his hand on his mouth to smother a shriek. The voice was deep and booming. It didn't sound like it came from a man, it sounded like it came from a thundercloud. It sounded like a special effect in a Bible movie epic.

Harvey's face looked funny, and it took Roscoe a second to realize that there were new shadows on it, shadows cast by a very dim, flickering redness coming from that evil, blood-stained eye.

"STATE THY NAME!"

"R-Roscoe Paum. Sir."

"ROSCOE PAUM! WHY DO YOU DISTURB THE SLUMBER OF ZOTH-TOCATIL?"

"I… I was just… Harvey told me that…"

"HAR-VEE? IS THAT THE NAME OF THIS ONE, WHOSE FLESH I WEAR? IS HE YOUR MEDIUM?"

"I don't know. He's the guy you're talking with. No, *through*. I mean…" Roscoe's vocabulary failed him, and he just pointed.

"Why have I been summoned?"

"Har—Harvey thought you could help me. With, with my Muscular Dystrophy."

"Ah. thou art ill and would be whole. I understand."

Roscoe licked his lips. "Can you do it?"

"Such a cure is well within the power of Zoth-Tocatil, mortal! The question instead is, can *you* do it!"

"Do what?"

"Pay the price my power demands."

"Price? What price?"

"You must adore me, obey me and worship my name on bended knee. This vessel, this 'Har-vee' is ill-suited to my priesthood, but he has the Sight, and I shall speak through him. You will follow my commands, and those of 'Har-vee' when they do not interfere with me. He is to know nothing of me, however. Tell him not my name, nor of our compact."

"And you can heal me?"

"Already your trembling ceases."

Startled, Roscoe realized it was true.

"What…" Roscoe put a hand to his mouth and gnawed a ragged thumbnail. He knew he would make the deal. He was too weak to resist. But he had to ask the final question anyhow.

"What are you?"

"I have been called many names. To your ancestors, I was the Throne of the Mountain Wind. To my enemies, I was the Zoth of the Hated Lash. I have been named Scourge and Asharu and Fell Knight of the Boundless Deeps.

"In your tongue, I am named… demon."

VII
chapter
seven

Sabriel, fallen angel of the Fifth House, one of those also called Lammasu and Defilers and succubi, gritted her teeth and pouted. She kicked her heels against the boards holding up the cheap box spring of a cheap hotel bed. If she'd chosen to stay at a cheap hotel, had *decided* to sleep on a cheap hotel mattress—well, that would be one thing. Deliberately reveling in the banality and stupidity and bad taste of humankind was one thing. Being forced into it because it was all she could afford was quite another.

Things had gone poorly for her in Hollywood. She'd gotten distracted by a confused little dyke named Brenda Garry, she'd wound up in Chicago, that had been fine if not fulfilling… and then she'd met Nolan, the prick, and she'd wound up in LA after all. There she had met Enshagkushanna, the monster….

And now she was in Vegas, running away.

She'd tried to contact Tommy, but he'd been asleep. She'd still gotten through, but his muttered replies hadn't been helpful, and she'd been unable to wake him up, even shouting. If she wanted to rouse him from slumber, apparently she'd have to call him on the phone.

Only she didn't have his phone number.

Sabriel decided to forget Ramone for a while. He was making her marginally stronger, and that was probably all he was good for—especially if he was the kind of slacker dipshit who was sound asleep at 1:00 in the afternoon. She

kept telling herself that this was all a temporary setback. Money wouldn't be a problem for her, not with the Las Vegas strip just a taxicab ride away. She'd changed her appearance while fleeing California so that she looked like a lovely, pale Japanese girl. Very slender, hair cut in a straight-bang chop. Very innocent, classical, just a little bit dewy-eyed and vulnerable. Perfect bait for men who didn't quite have what it took to rape, but who still liked their women frail and easily dominated.

"Oooh, you big peepee too bokoo," she crooned sarcastically into a mirror as she put on her lipstick.

By the next morning she was back in the hotel room, $15,000 dollars the richer. A Texas insurance salesman named Bartholomew Hightower had gotten lucky at blackjack and had thought he'd gotten lucky with her. She'd made him beg long and hard for what he really wanted—for what she *made* him want—and when she'd cleaned him out, he'd been happy. Sabriel was blithely confident that his love life would be wrecked from now on. The memory of Makiko-from-Vegas would poison every sexual encounter in his future, and his failed attempts to re-create it could only lead to bitter disappointment. He'd try to find her again, probably. Good luck looking for a woman with no paper trail, no last name, and (as of breakfast time) a completely different height, weight and set of facial features.

As she packed up her clothes and her money, she wondered what she wanted to do next. It was depressing, really. She could go wreck artists, like Brenda and Nate, but it was too easy. Trying to really get in a position to trash the culture from the top down, though, seemed too damn hard.

What she really needed was some allies, but that was easier said than done. That devil Gaviel probably wasn't eager to hear from her again, not after their fuckup with Maryanne Prisco. She'd tried invoking some creatures like her, Lammasu, once the angels of the ocean... but the Reaver of the Deep Waters was still in the Abyss, the Singer of Western Waves didn't reply at all, and the Knight of the Rolling Storm had told her to go screw herself. It was frustrating being rejected by a being she'd worked beside for millennia.

More frustrating still was the *forgetting*. She had aeons of experience, but trying to cram it into a human brain the size

of a pound cake was futile. She'd lost so much—so many names, so many memories, so many yesterdays....

And then she thought of the battle against Vejovis. That memory was crystal clear. She hadn't worked often with those Elohim, but perhaps they were having the same sort of difficulties as she herself. Not Gaviel, not anymore, but Vodantu, Hasmed, Avitu... perhaps they would help her.

She'd had contact off and on with Avitu (What was her title? Something about the thin wind, thinnest wind...) while they were imprisoned in the Abyss. Then Avitu had become unavailable. Apparently, she'd been summoned to the human world and had not returned. Thinking about the trouble she'd had in California, Sabriel suspected that Avitu had been thwarted by just such a creature—a demon, like her, only with a longer span of time on Earth in which to build up strength.

It was hard to keep track of the passage of time in Hell. Sabriel had no idea when Avitu had been called or how long she'd been in the material spaces, but it had to be longer than Sabriel's time. A powerful ally could be very helpful. Even a weak one would be better than nothing.

She glanced down at her watch. She had an hour until checkout, and then another hour until her bus (the *bus*, damn it!) for Florida departed. With her new money, though, she might sell the bus ticket and catch a plane. Yes, that was definitely the way to go.

Sabriel drew the curtains and locked the door. After a moment's thought, she turned the drab, angular fake-modern art painting around so she wouldn't have to look at it. Actually, she knew her eyes would be closed. She didn't want it looking at *her*.

She sat cross-legged on the bed and spoke.

"Avitu?"

She felt something stir, and she jerked upright, eyes open.

What the hell? she thought. The sensation... it had been one of inertia, but of a huge, powerful mass. Yet Avitu had been a spirit of the air. Surely no amount of imprisonment on Earth could have changed the essence of her nature?

She had made contact—brief, brushing contact—but that touch had convinced her that Avitu was important. If Sabriel could only rouse her...

After a moment's thought, she went into the bathroom and ran a tub. She closed the door, locking out the sunlight, and got in the water. Relaxing her disguise, she assumed her natural form.

"Avitu?"

This time, she felt a stronger response.

SABRIEL... IS THAT...YOU?

"It is I, Avitu," Sabriel said out loud.

IT HAS BEEN... MANY YEARS... SINCE MY NAME WAS CALLED.

"Where are you?"

NEAR. OLD... COLLEAGUE. HELP ME... I... IMPLORE YOU...

The feeling of size and age and great unmoved mass increased, and with it, Sabriel felt distance and direction... and a disjunction that she had not felt since the War of Wrath.

"Avitu... are you inside a different..." She groped for an English equivalent, but had to fall back on their native language, speaking a sound rarely heard on Earth since the Fall.

ONLY A FRAGMENT, A SHARD. COME TO ME! PLEASE!

"I have not forgotten your loyalty to me during the war. I will come."

BRING... THEM.

"Them? Who? Whom shall I bring?"

THE ONES WE LOVE.

❖　❖　❖

The same day that Sabriel invoked Avitu from the water, Hasmed called upon Vodantu from the air.

His flight was coach class, a redeye, and he had the window seat. Sitting next to him was Lauren, a fifteen-year-old Jersey girl, and beside her on the aisle was her fourteen-year-old brother.

"Quit it!" she kept saying.

"I ain't doin' anything."

"Mo-om! Make 'im stop!"

Jersey mom and Jersey dad had the seats in front of the kids. "You two shut up! Ethan! Quit messin'!"

"I ain't doin' nothin'!" His voice became whiny.

Fifteen-year-old Lauren started to cough. Ethan, her brother, got a runny nose. Her father began to feel hot and irritable. The mother became drowsy and depressed.

Hasmed wasn't doing it on purpose. He wasn't even aware of it, but his very presence was making them sick.

As he went east, he could almost feel himself growing stronger. The proximity to his anchors—to Tina and Roscoe—made it easier to draw on their belief.

For a moment, Hasmed was pensive, thinking that it was ironic, maybe even a little sad, that each of them feared or adored him falsely. Tina didn't think he was Hasmed the Fallen—she thought he was her perfect, wonderful Daddy. Roscoe had a better idea what was going on, but he still was mired in deception.

Hasmed had played his little "Zoth of the Hated Lash" game for a variety of reasons. First off, he wasn't about to tell Roscoe the name "Hasmed." While it wouldn't give anyone the sort of control Vodantu had with Hasmed's True Name, it still had power enough. For one thing, it would let people invoke him, just as he was calling upon his master.

But there was a deeper reason for his deception. Hasmed was curious to test Roscoe's dedication. If push came to shove—and Hasmed could think of several ways it might, or might appear to—where would Roscoe's loyalty lie? With Harvey the human, his friend who wanted to help him and who was (seemingly) ignorant of the diabolical nature of Those Beyond? Or would Roscoe serve "Zoth" out of fear and personal gain?

Hasmed had known mortals. He guessed the latter.

It was well past midnight when Hasmed pulled the phone from its housing on the seat-back in front of him. He didn't turn it on, but he knew no one would care about a lone business traveler making a call. A solitary traveler talking to himself—that was something else again.

He did not call his master in the immortal tongue of the Elohim. Like the name "Hasmed," he wasn't about to utter those words within the earshot of mortals with untested loyalty. Instead he used an ancient human language—one of several that had developed during the days of the rebellion.

Those "days," seen from another perspective, were centuries or even geological epochs. But in other, equally valid ways, only days passed between the defiance of Lucifer's army and its defeat at the hands of the Holy Host.

"My lord Vodantu," he said in the long-extinct tongue. "Your humble servant craves your wisdom."

Hasmed. The voice sounded only in his brain. *It has been a long time since I heard from you. A long time since you entered the mortal realm.*

"I beg forgiveness, master. Incarnation is difficult, and the occupation of a human body brings many complications."

I am well aware of such complications. Already your colleague Joriel has been cast out of the material world.

Hasmed frowned and felt the tickle of fear. "The Darkness of the Deeps was a mighty warrior. How came he to such a defeat?"

It is unclear. Surely you know that Fate conspired to bring many of the Fallen to the city called "The Angels" lately?

So you didn't know I was in LA too? Hasmed thought it, but didn't say it. He was pretty confident that Vodantu couldn't pick up his thoughts unless he made an effort to broadcast them. After all, they had a long way to go.

Their presence masks events from perception, even mine. I know Joriel was greatly abused with mortal weapons, and I know that another of the Fallen delivered the terminal blow. Beyond that, I cannot see.

"Can he return from Hell again?"

Not now. Not soon. Perhaps not ever… only time will tell. But if you can call me forth into the world, it will not matter.

"Master, it will not be easy to call you forth."

Do you toy with me? Vodantu spoke again, and Hasmed winced as his soul, his entire essence, hummed in time with his lord's use of his True Name. *I know the difficulties. What are you doing to overcome them?*

"I have enthralled two mortals, master, and they give me strength…"

"Hey." It was Lauren, in the next seat, giving him a sleepy and suspicious glance. "What's that language you're talking?"

"It's none of your business," he replied, in English, glaring at her.

"It's not *Arabic*, is it?"

"Nah, it's… uh, Russian," he said.

"It is *not*…"

"Look, would you just shut the fuck up?"

"Hey, fuck you! You can't talk to me that way. Dad!" She started poking her father's chair.

"Oh for the love of…" Rather than say "Christ"—which would have been Harvey's reaction—Hasmed tapped Lauren on the shoulder. Immediately her skin went white, and she struggled out of her seat, running awkwardly up the aisle toward the bathroom.

WHAT HAPPENED?

"A thousand pardons, my liege," Hasmed said in the extinct tongue. "A mortal interfered with me. I have dealt with her."

YOU WILL NOT HAVE DIFFICULTIES HIDING HER CORPSE? Hasmed could detect a note of approval from Vodantu. He decided to gloss over the details.

"Do not concern yourself with it a moment longer."

Harvey would have said "fuggeddaboudit," but there was really no equivalent term in the tongue Hasmed spoke.

"I have made inroads with a human enterprise." He hesitated. There was also no word in the old language for the Mafia's kind of agnostic criminality. All its words relating to "crime" referred distinctly to religious disobedience. "They are rebels against the laws of other men. Through violence and duplicity, they take advantage of their fellows. They possess…" He struggled over another language barrier. Individual property was a sketchy concept at best, and using the old words for it—best translated as "items fated to belong solely to one person"—would give the wrong impression. Finally, he said "They possess usurped authority and control unique items."

ARE THEY SORCERERS?

"No, they have no knowledge of such things."

GOOD. TAKE CONTROL OF THIS MORTAL ORGANIZATION AND USE IT TO GAIN WORSHIPPERS FOR YOURSELF AND FOR ME.

"I am already trying that, but the cursed human form I inhabit is known to them as a coward and weakling."

YOU DO NOT SHOW THEM YOUR TRUE FORM?

"I lack the strength to cast aside this mortal shell. The world has changed, master. There is no place in it for demons made manifest. This cosmos that once welcomed us and changed easily under our touch now forcefully resists and attempts to expel us at every turn. Until I can use my full strength all the time, I dare not show it when I know I will become weak again."

THESE MEN WOULD CONTEND WITH ONE FROM THE HOST?

"Yes—even as we battled against the Most High. Most of them do not even believe we exist, or that we ever existed. They are proud and brazen and stupid."

SHOW THEM.

"I am, and I shall... but I must build their faith slowly, by degrees. To that end, I have posed as one of your house."

A NEBERU?

"They know not that word, but they find it easier to believe in one who can see the future than in one who can move unseen or sicken their bodies. It is less threatening to them."

IF YOU THINK IT BEST, THEN.

"Is there any way I can avail myself of your powers of perception?"

DO NOT PRESUME, HASMED.

"Forgive me."

WHILE I AM BOUND, MY POWERS ARE TAXED TO THE UTMOST SIMPLY TRYING TO FOLLOW THE MOVEMENTS OF ESCAPED ELOHIM.

"I will proceed on my own."

PERHAPS I CAN DISPATCH RABBADÜN INTO YOUR AREA. HE HAS THE SIGHT THAT YOU DESIRE.

"It would be a great boon to my plans."

VERY WELL. SEE THAT YOU LABOR DILIGENTLY ON MY BEHALF, HASMED. I LONG FOR FREEDOM FROM THIS PUNISHMENT, AND IMAGINING YOUR DEPREDATIONS OF HUMANITY ONLY WHETS MY APPETITE TO BEST THEM SEVENFOLD.

Hasmed swallowed—it was more Harvey's reaction than his own. The image of Vodantu incarnate, slaying humans with impunity... it was as horrifying to the mortal as it was delightful to the demon.

❖   ❖   ❖

"Name your master," Usiel said.

"I will never betray him," the thrall said, eyes bright and defiant.

Usiel slapped him. It wasn't a terribly hard blow— nothing bone-breaking or brain-rattling—but the reaping ring was on the hand, and as he struck, he unseated the man's soul.

The current target for Usiel's contempt and anger was a man named John Bow. John didn't stand out much if you looked at him. Maybe a little sickly looking and a little over-weight. But Usiel had sensed a demon's pollution on Bow.

He didn't see it, exactly. It was more like a sound, perhaps, an irritating buzzing whine, like a mosquito that hovers around your ear and easily floats around all attempts to swat it. Or maybe it was a stink, the fell thing's influence, like the faint hint of vomit on a drunk's clothing, even after laundering.

Whatever it was, Usiel had noticed it on John Bow and had selected the mortal for his attentions.

At first, he'd thought Bow was a being like him—escaped from Hell and occupying some mortal's neglected frame. But that wasn't it. He'd seen that Bow still had the human spark within him. The body's original tenant was still in control.

Then he wondered if Bow might not be another like Max Hirniesen—a human who had somehow attached his soul to the lost powers of a sundered Elohim. But that wasn't it either. The power operating through Bow, while weak, was whole. He did not hold it within him like a stolen treasure. Instead it held him in a miser's grasp.

In the war, rebel angels had called on human worshippers for strength. Apparently, some things never changed. John Bow had sold himself into servitude, obeying dictates from one of God's despised in exchange for... money? Health? Something else? It didn't really matter.

Bow's body, still vacant, convulsed in Usiel's grasp. The eyes popped open, followed shortly by the mouth.

"WHO DARES MOLEST MY SERVANT?" Bow's lungs pushed the air, Bow's lips formed the words, but it wasn't Bow speaking. It was his demon, his mastermind.

Usiel answered the question with one of his own. "Which miserable Fell Knight am I addressing?"

"NO MERE KNIGHT, BUT A DUKE, YOU WRETCHED GRAVE-ROBBER. UNHAND BOW OR SUFFER THE CONSEQUENCES!"

"I'm quite interested to see what consequences you can threaten."

At that moment, Usiel saw John Bow's ghost return to his body. The dark force within surged and swelled, and Bow lunged forward with inhuman might and unnatural quickness. His grasp broke Usiel's forearms before the black angel could turn and fling him away.

"Ah, with a mortal's soul propping you up, you are mighty indeed." An effort of will, and his arms were whole once more. "But can you battle without the stolen strength of man?" A gesture, and the scythe was in his hand.

Seeing the scythe, John Bow turned to run. Usiel gave chase and sheared Bow's left foot off at the ankle with one smooth movement. Forced on by his demon owner, John kept running on the stump, but it took only a few more strokes to carve him into pieces.

With no bodily anchor to give it succor, John Bow's spirit was nearly swept away into the dead storm, but now Usiel's weapon became a tool. Reaching out gently, he caught the soul before it could be torn asunder and dissolved.

"In death, you serve me," Usiel said. "As in life you served…?"

Bow resisted, but not for long. With his death, his tie to his old liege failed him, and Usiel's authority took precedence. Soon, Bow told the angel of death what little he knew about the other demon's mortal pawns. He knew only one by name—a woman called Krebbs who lived in Florida.

More than that, Bow told Usiel about the state of his master's spirit. Unlike Usiel, who was cased in flesh, this demon dwelt in stone—in a great diamond that had been broken into smaller pieces years ago. One small piece was in a pendant, kept safe around Bow's neck.

Destroying it felt wonderful. Indeed, had he known the joy he would take from the act, Usiel might have forgone the pleasure. He struck the jewel and stole from it some part of its master, some delightful, delicious piece of a fallen soul. Usiel could not help but feel that it was an unholy delight, something depraved and cannibal. But despite those feelings, he did not stop.

Driving away from John Bow's home, Usiel glanced from the road to the ring on his hand and wondered again how it had returned to him. While it would be romantic to think that his releasing tool had somehow found him due to its destined attachment, Usiel was morbidly confident that such destiny only occurred when guided by a hand… or a wing.

Someone wanted him to retrieve his reaper's scythe.

No one who knew him would doubt what he would do with a device of such rare potency, so it stood to reason that someone approved of his agenda.

In some nearly dead corner of his heart, Usiel nursed a secret belief that perhaps it was the Almighty forgiving him at last and offering a chance to prove that he remained loyal, even after everything—even after being imprisoned with the

rebels he hated and had fought. Perhaps that was why destroying the stone and looting the demon's spirit had been such bliss.

In any event, Usiel had an ally for the first time in ages. It felt good.

❖ ❖ ❖

Just for amusement value, Sabriel decided to lure people out to the desert without overt sexual promises. She anticipated (correctly) that it would be much more difficult. Sex—there was something about it that made even the brightest humans lose what little wits they had.

In this case, Sabriel went the bohemian route. She canvassed Las Vegas's art scene and was not particularly shocked to discover that there was almost no avant-garde.

Of course not, she reasoned. Anyone who actually *can* dance or sing is making money in a casino show. People who would be starving sculptors and part-time painters in Miami or Philadelphia are building sets here.

Those she finally met were, therefore, a motley collection of no-talent hacks.

She'd started out by getting a local paper—not one targeted at gamblers and guests, but one with coupons for supermarkets and drug stores—and looking at the small ads in the back. When she saw a coffeehouse in the suburbs with a poetry reading, she smiled.

At the poetry reading, she made herself a quietly regal black woman, she went back to the name Christina and, after a particularly obnoxious reading (it included the phrase "my black, bleak, slack, weak heart"), she approached the poetess and gave her a line of baloney about an "art experience" out in the desert.

"I haven't heard anything about it," the poetess—whose name was Peggy Palermo—said, looking a little suspicious.

"Well, it's not really an open thing," Sabriel responded, leaning in a bit. "You've been to Burning Man, of course…"

"Of course."

"Well, we're hoping this will be sort of like that only… without all the tagalongs. By keeping it small and invite-only, we think we can really focus on the art."

That hooked her good.

From Peggy, Sabriel got a few other recommendations. A likely one was a potter named Gil Delacerro, whose por-

celain chandeliers were designed to self-destruct when the candles that lit them burned through the strings supporting them. ("A dramatic comment on the transitory nature of art itself," according to Peggy.) He loudly professed his loathing for the decadence and commercialism of Las Vegas, but he stayed in the area because he'd found a vein of really great clay on some property outside of town. Plus, he had tenure teaching ceramics, sculpture and 3-D design at UNLV.

Disguised as Delacerro, Sabriel met Jennifer Arliss, a "re-composer." Jennifer's job as a librarian and archivist for EMI gave her access to huge stores of lost music—tunes composed, copyrighted and sold, but which were now worthless in market terms. Over the course of years, EMI had acquired the rights to hundreds of thousands of pieces of music—incidental music from B movies, theme songs for cancelled 1960s sitcoms, advertising jingles for discontinued products and companies long bankrupt. Jennifer's job was to restore and transfer old recordings from decaying tapes and records into digital formats. In the process, if she heard a hook or a melody that she found catchy, she'd buy the rights from EMI under an assumed name and use it as the basis for a song of her own. On weekends, she performed them on synthesizer and guitar to indifferent audiences throughout Nevada and eastern California. She'd pressed a CD and had sold about a hundred copies out of her trunk after shows.

Jennifer gave Sabriel a link to the website that published pornographic short stories involving the characters from sitcoms, science-fiction movies and comic books. The site's owner—the pseudonymous "James T. Kirkegaard"—claimed a deep and abiding hate for sitcoms, SF movies and comic books, and he insisted that his works were not meant as homage or as titillation. According to him, they served to recast the intellectual properties involved so that the implicit peccadilloes of their creators would become explicit. All this was explained in an article that was longer than any of the stories and which ended with a manifesto declaring war on derivative genre fiction, copyright laws and the concept of intellectual property.

(It turned out that "James T. Kirkegaard" was Jennifer's ex-boyfriend Gustavus Doakes, a prop manager for Cirque du Soleil. When Sabriel approached him in Jennifer's shape,

he implied without stating it that he was dating one of the acrobats but that he might be interested in getting back together with Jennifer.)

All told, it took her three days to gather a dozen teachers who were really musicians, commercial draftsmen who were really painters and advertising copywriters who were really novelists. Having made contact with Avitu—and the great demon seemed to be struggling to remain aware—Sabriel had directions to a location in the desert. According to the map, there was nothing there. Sabriel was quite curious to see what would happen.

Disguised once more as the regal woman of color, Sabriel rented a Jeep 4x4 and made sure that the artistes that knew that there would be some off-roading involved in getting to the site. She assuaged their confusion by calling it a privacy measure.

They rendezvoused at the coffeehouse where Sabriel had first met Peggy. (The demon liked it. It seemed like an apt sort of closure.) After giving directions to a highway mile marker, she set off in the lead with Peggy, Jennifer and Gustavus.

For the first several miles, they chattered excitedly about what was coming, what they could expect and how exciting it was that Las Vegas's neglected "scene" was finally getting some attention. There were a few catty comments here and there, but Sabriel noticed that Peggy expertly re-focused the group's spite and insecurity outward—first to passengers in other cars, then leapfrogging to local writers and musicians who hadn't even gotten invited.

"I hope no one tells Howie about this," Gustavus said, patently insincere. "He's intolerable enough without having a mantle of 'outsider status' to hide behind."

"Who's Howie?" Sabriel asked.

"Oh, a local hack—teaches composition and fiction writing at UNLV. He does all this garbagy kitchen-sink realism under his own name—you know, about a college professor in the Southwest who has an identity crisis and gets some petty revelation about himself while weeding the tomatoes or something—and he does film reviews. But under an assumed name, he writes stuff for these real low-budget pseudo-arty horror magazines."

"You know, he might have gotten an invitation from someone else," Sabriel said.

"Christ, I hope not. His ego hardly needs an invitation to an 'elite artistic summit.'"

She smiled and kept driving.

"What's out there?" Jennifer kept asking.

"The gathering."

"You said that, but, I mean, where's it taking place? Is someone's house out there?"

"Wait and see."

"I took a look on Mapquest's satellite photo archives," Gustavus interrupted. "There's nothing there."

(Sabriel had noticed how Gustavus had maneuvered to get in the back seat with Jennifer.)

"That doesn't mean much," Peggy said. "The scale on those is pretty huge right? Plus it could be something temporary, added since the photo was taken. Or something that blends in and doesn't show up."

The poetess turned and gave Sabriel an inquiring look, but the demoness just kept driving.

At the mile marker, she turned right and started off down the dusty track into the silver-lit scrublands. The other vehicles followed obediently.

Eventually, Las Vegas was just a vague, fried-egg blob of light on the distant horizon. When its glow no longer rivaled that of the stars and half-moon above, the terrain became increasingly hilly. Sabriel's Jeep could go no farther. She stopped and the others parked beside her.

"What now?" Peggy asked, looking concerned.

"We walk. It's not far," Sabriel said, though she had no idea how distant Avitu really was.

"But what about our equipment?"

"Don't worry. You can come back for it."

"Hey, I've got a thousand bucks of synthesizers back there," Jennifer said. "What if...?"

"Do you really think a thief's going to drive fifty miles past city limits and then another twenty out into the desert? Christ, it's probably safer out here than in your house," Gil said irritably. He himself had insisted on bringing several weighty pieces.

Sabriel got out and started walking.

"Hey wait!"

"Christina! What about…?"

"Are we supposed to…?"

They wondered, but they followed.

A few brought some things. After some consideration, Jennifer picked out an acoustic guitar. Gustavus shouldered a satchel full of writing samples. Others carried instruments or costumes or nothing at all.

"Hey," Gil called. "Who wants courage?"

Sabriel's eyebrow quirked up and she turned to look. He was holding aloft a bottle of Johnnie Walker black label.

Peggy rolled her eyes and looked at Sabriel. "Typical," she muttered. "A gesture of his antiquated 'creator as romantic rebel' paradigm."

"Still," Sabriel said, "It is a little cold out here." She gestured for Gil to bring the bottle to her. On the way, several others took sips.

Leading them through the darkness, feeling the sting of communal whiskey fade from her lips, Sabriel felt a sudden pang of affection. These people had no reason to think they were artists. For every one person who'd ever encouraged them, there were a dozen throats laughing, telling them no, saying it would never happen. They had no successes they could point to, not really. All they had was a feeling, a sense that they were creative, that they had something to say, something to share. They didn't have the skills or the knowledge or the inspiration, but they just stumbled on anyway, getting knocked back by rejection and getting up dumbly, wading in again with their guard down, just asking for another wallop. But they didn't stop, they kept slinking back to art like a kicked dog that knows no other master.

No angel was that stubborn. Angels didn't ignore the evidence like that, didn't choose "what I want" over "what is" so fiercely, so repetitively, too stupid to think of any other way or just give up.

That was what made them different. The Elohim had the powers of creation at their command, but only humans had that sheer bloody-mindedness that could take a lie and make it true. Sabriel shook her head and marveled and felt just a shadow of the love she'd had once, the love that made her give up everything for them, that made her step away from God. The love that had made her a demon.

They had rejected her in the end. Their incalculable faith had been in other things, not in the angels that fell for their sake. They had skulked away, and she had given up on her love. She had to. She couldn't cling like a lamprey, with mindless hunger and hopeless hope. She wasn't human.

Her love was dead but uneasy in its grave.

On a whim, she wiped her brow then reached back to help one of the artists up a sharp slope of sand. She didn't even look to see who it was before passing on her gift.

It was Jennifer.

As the musician touched Sabriel's hand, it was like a second kind of sight opened behind her eyes.

Jennifer blinked then looked up at the milky stars, out across the desert and over the faces of each of the others. Then she squatted briefly to get out her guitar.

"If you play *Kum-ba-yah*, I'm going to give you such a smack," Gil warned.

"I don't know, it could be a clever ironic statement," said a puppeteer/carpet-installer.

Jennifer didn't play *Kum-ba-yah*, or any other song they'd ever heard, or anything like any song they'd ever heard. She plucked out simple notes and tones and she played the desert. She strummed chords and the sound was like seeing the moonlit gray sand, almost like dust. A note struck here and there was somehow right for the air, so cold and thin. She played the millions of stars and the moon like a spotlight, the cacti and little trees. And moving through them, she played the people, each a tiny ball of hope and pride and insecurity traveling through the bleak and chilly vastness.

Hearing that song, unfolding on top of what it described, was like living twice as much in the same time. The density of experience silenced them all, and when Jennifer stopped, they realized they were standing in a circle around her.

There was nothing they could really say, but Gustavus said, "Wow," anyway.

"That was…" Peggy tried, but she couldn't say anything.

Jennifer just kept blinking.

Sabriel smiled. "Almost there."

As they came to the crest of another hill, a human hand erupted from the ground beneath them.

Jennifer jumped and gave a little shriek. "Jesus Christ!" Gil said, dropping the bottle (now half-empty) onto the

yielding sand. After a moment, he bent down to get it while Gustavus (a half-beat too late for it to seem instinctive) put his arms around Jennifer, who stepped away.

The hand cleared sand away and was joined by a second, and then a woman arose from the dust.

"I saw something just like that in 'Begotten,'" Peggy whispered to Sabriel.

Sabriel didn't take her eyes off the emerging woman—or woman-shape, for she could sense no soul within it—but she whispered back, "Yeah, I think Blue Man Group did it too."

The woman before them was small—under five feet tall—with straight dark hair. She was naked, with skin the color of the desert, and her face was completely unlined. She seemed neither young nor old. Wordlessly, she gestured for them to follow her.

"It's flattering that they bothered to set up an introduction like that," Gil said. "I mean, it's kind of theatrical…"

The mud woman led them to a very sparse grove of stunted, twisted trees. She pointed at one, the largest (though still under twenty feet tall). Its branches were densely contorted and tipped with green needles. The trunk was forked—it looked like lightning had split it long ago.

"Hey, I know about these," Gustavus said. "That's a bristlecone pine, right?"

No one answered.

"Yeah, they're, like, the oldest trees on Earth," he said, clearly warming to the chance to play expert. He walked up to the forked tree and peered at it.

"These things are ancient," he said. "One this old probably sprouted before the pyramids were built in Egypt. Scientists think a bristlecone is most likely the oldest living thing on the planet. They call them Methuselah Trees, I think."

He reached out and touched the trunk.

Everything changed.

VIII
chapter
eight

"Penny for your thoughts," Rabbadün said.

"I was wondering what you wanted the suitcase for," Hasmed replied.

Rabbadün just grinned his manic grin. "Wait and see. It's a surprise. You'll like it."

The other demon had taken a train in to New York City and Hasmed had met him at the station. It had been a relief to feel the presence of another of the fallen and know it was one coming to help him. Rabbadün said his body was Gene Souk, but he was now going by the name Benny Hoakler and, hey, could some of Hasmed's gangbang pals hook him up with a fake ID?

"I think you mean gang*land*."

"Huh?"

"My gangland pals. Not gangbang."

"Right, right," Gene/Benny/Rabbadün had said, hefting two duffel bags. "Gene did every goddamn drug he could get his hands on so, you know, the old brain is kind of in and out. It's cool though. It's all right. Gene's cool, you know?"

"Uh huh."

"How's your fit?"

"My fit?"

"You know, the shell. The body. Your roommate? Harvey something, right?"

"Yeah. Harvey Ciullo."

"Looks kinda beat-up, if you don't mind me saying."

"It's a fixer-upper."

Benny had a good snicker then asked about transportation. When Hasmed pointed out Harvey's car, Benny shook his head. "Won't do. Too traceable. We'll need to steal one. Hold on." He dropped his bags at Hasmed's feet and stumbled through the crowd. A few minutes later, he came back.

"Got it. Come with me to the second exit. In a couple minutes, a guy with a gray beard and a blue overcoat over his left arm is going to be on his way out. He's pissing now: You just need to fade out, steal the car keys from his right front pocket, and we'll be set. He won't miss the car until nightfall."

"Why do we need another car?"

"We're gonna have some fun."

"Look, I was hoping you could just…"

"Hurry, man! This guy's a cherry opportunity!" Benny flashed the grin, and Hasmed caved in, against his better judgment.

Half an hour later, Benny had convinced him to sneak into Tony Berman's apartment and steal the biggest suitcase he could find. "Make sure you wear gloves!" Benny had said. That done, they'd gotten back in the stolen Lexus and cruised toward Murray Hill, Benny threading easily through traffic.

"Who's this Berman guy, anyhow?" Hasmed wanted to know.

"Jeez, don't you *know*? Don't you read the papers an' shit?"

"Inform me."

"He's the son of Clark Berman. You know *him* right? The, you know, the cop who's going to run for mayor and run out all the fat cats? Chief Berman?"

"Tony's his son?"

"Uh huh. That's why this is going to be such a sweet joke!"

"Yeah, well, while we're doing your 'joke,' can we please talk some business?"

"This is a business joke, Harvey. I mean, it's going to be a good, *good* time, but it's also for the cause."

"Whatever. What would really help *my* cause is a little inside information, all right?"

"'Bout what?"

Hasmed shrugged. "Anything that makes me look like a fortune-teller. Who's gonna win the Rams/ Packers game?

Are the Giants going to cover the spread? Who's taking the fifth race tomorrow? What's the name of a good long-shot bet? You know, that kind of shit."

"Hard up for money, huh? Man, you can just take some out of the satchel if you're hurting. It's in the brown one."

"It's not that," Hasmed said, his pride stung. "I need to show people some, you know, invisible forces. Give 'em something to believe in."

"A no-shit angel isn't something to believe in?"

"Right. I don't see you flappin' your goddamn wings."

"Yeah, you're right, you can't keep it up forever. Not yet, anyhow. More's the pity."

"People would freak out."

"People would lose their shit," Benny agreed, eyes bright with malice. "Oh, here we go."

He pulled up by a park and eyed a mixed group by the corner. There were three women and a man—a boy really, a teen in tight jeans and a windbreaker that wasn't fully adequate for the chill. One of the women looked like she was a teenager too, skinny and pale in a tube-top under a transparent plastic coat. She teetered on absurdly high heels, like the other two females. Those women were older and wore resigned expressions over their feathers and color, beneath layers of pancake makeup. The younger ones looked defiant and, under that, nervous.

"Hey! You guys like to party?" Benny hollered.

"Aw shit," Hasmed muttered, putting a hand over his forehead and slouching down in his seat.

After a few minutes of vague talk, all four got in the car. As Benny blathered at them, Hasmed caught little glints of power leaking out. Not usually something the Neberu were good at: Charisma was far more common among the Bringers of the Word. Benny had apparently acquired the trick of making people ignore their better judgment, though.

As they drove away, Hasmed wondered if Benny had used it on him.

"Yeah, I'm celebrating," Benny said, turning his head a little to shout in the back seat. "I finally got the money my old man left me when he kicked it. This here's Gary, my lawyer."

"Hi, Gary," said the hooker who'd crammed in beside him in the front seat. Hasmed was squeezed between her on his right and Benny on his left. She reached between his knees and started to fiddle with the radio.

"Yeah, Gary likes men," Benny informed them at top volume as he crawled through traffic toward the Triborough Bridge. "Me, I'll do whatever, you know? Anything with a hole and a heartbeat. Hey, y'all like tequila? There's a bottle in that green satchel."

"Viva tequila!" shouted one of the older prostitutes.

"Careful with it," said the boy. "I've gotten awful hangovers from that stuff. It's more like 'ta kill ya,' you know?"

"Hah, good joke!" Benny replied.

They drank as they drove around, though neither Benny nor Hasmed indulged.

"Where are we going?"

"East Harlem. Not far now. Somewhere no one will hassle us. I know the way," Benny said, though Hasmed privately suspected he was looking for it, scanning fate to find someplace unobserved.

Shit, with the effort he's blown on these four nobodies, he could have given me a month's worth of prophet credibility, Hasmed thought irritably, but there was a tinge of uneasiness there too. The more he was with Benny, the more squirrelly Harvey's instincts became. Everything about his 'ally' was making Harvey think, "Run away! Psycho! Psycho!"

But Hasmed wasn't going to let some chickenshit mortal's mental leftovers scare him.

"All right, here we are." Benny had found a maze of back alleys and parking lots, edged all around with boarded up buildings and vacant spaces. This particular spot was overgrown with weeds and sickly bushes that had, nonetheless, managed to reach a height of nearly three feet. Benny pulled up and put the car in park. The Lex stood out like a sore thumb in the neighborhood.

Benny leaned across Hasmed and spoke to the woman by the door. "What's your name, sweetie?"

"Vanessa."

"You're not getting anything to drink, are you? Gary, grab that 'ta kill ya' bottle from those hogs in the backseat, 'kay? Vanessa's thirsty." Then he opened his door and got out.

Turning to comply, Hasmed noticed that the trio in the back were unmoving and glassy eyed. Vanessa noticed it too. As Hasmed made to hand her the bottle, she jerked her door opened and lunged out—right into Benny's arms.

He clutched her tight and kissed her hard on the lips. "C'mon, sweetie. It'll be all right."

She struggled against him, turning away. "Let me go!"

"You're feisty," Benny said playfully as he dragged her into the weeds. She opened her mouth to scream, but he had his arms locked around her torso right under her ribcage. As she drew in breath, he squeezed, sharp and hard—like a Heimlich maneuver. She folded forward slightly and gasped, but the wind was knocked out of her.

"Bring the others, a'right?"

"Aw crap," Hasmed murmured. He looked around. Benny had the car keys. Even if Hasmed bailed out, the Neberu would probably do whatever he had planned regardless.

Besides, what's Vodantu going to think if I'm unwilling to put down four pathetic mortals? The thought of his master invoking his True Name again was enough to get him to sigh, grit his teeth, and start dragging one of the others along. She was as limp as a rag doll.

"Every goddamn drug," he said. *Yeah, I'll bet,* Hasmed thought. *It's broad daylight. Is anyone paying attention?* But clearly no one was. "Benny" would have foreseen it.

He followed the noises of struggle and found Benny kneeling over the hooker. He'd produced a roll of duct tape from somewhere and was securing her wrists and ankles. Already her mouth was covered.

"Sorry to make you do all the lifting, 'Gary,' but could you pick up the brown duffel, too?"

Mutely, Hasmed nodded.

This is ridiculous. This is sick. This is beneath me. Hell, this is beneath Harvey, he thought. He considered hotwiring the car and at least saving the other two, but they'd identify him (or Harvey, at least).

Besides, why should he bother?

When he returned with the last whore, the boy, Benny had managed to prop the two passive victims upright. Their eyes were open but glazed, staring forward from slack faces.

"Ketamine," Benny said, by way of explanation. "In small doses, a fun party hallucinogen. Vitamin K. But you take enough of it, it paralyzes your whole body while your brain stays perfectly conscious. And everything you see seems like a hideous nightmare!"

He threw his arms wide and transformed.

"Change," he told Hasmed. "Show them your true form! Then they will believe!"

Shaking his head, Hasmed did it.

The three who were drugged didn't change expression—they couldn't. But Hasmed could see the amazement and dread in the fourth one's eyes. Where once there were two men, now there stood two apparitions.

Benny, formerly a bland white man with sandy hair and a too-wide smile, was now shaped of shadow and moonlight, a moving man of midnight in the middle of the day. When he spread his wings, stars shown within. His face was flawless.

As Hasmed changed, he felt something odd. His natural form was shapelessness—a wind that caressed or corroded, a half-seen shape like a gust moving through thick fog. But he was different, somehow. He was a dark and noxious cloud, a chill miasma with wings and human outline. He could feel something burning out from his face, from the scar and the eye that were the marks of Harvey's death.

"Look upon angels, O mortals! Marvel and despair!" Rabbadün shouted. With a movement as smooth as the fall of night, he lunged upon Vanessa.

"You are the first fruits of sacrifice," he said, flickering the razor edges of his wings along her arm. "But soon all your ilk will die. Soon the whole Earth will be our altar!"

As he flickered to her other side, Hasmed could see what he had written on her, sliced in perfect scrollwork script from elbow to wrist.

It said: *Vodantu*.

"Watch and learn your fate," he told the others. "The fate of the world!"

With Harvey's body transformed, Hasmed felt less pull of the dead man's revulsion. What he felt instead was a depressing sense of triteness, of banality...

...until their belief seeped in.

Even through the haze of drugs and terror, they believed. They saw the wings and heard the voice, and they believed. They were the living residue of society's apathy, they made their meager ways enduring the pleasure of others, and they couldn't believe in guardian angels and benevolent fates. But this—the slicing and the smiles, this they could believe. Every day on the street they thought about this, about falling into

the hands of some psycho freak, and it only *made sense* that the forces doing this were cosmic. Of course angels wanted to torture and kill. Looking around the world they knew, nothing else made sense.

They couldn't believe in a loving God, but they could believe in demons.

Rabbadün was cutting Vanessa's head off, but he was taking his time with it, and Hasmed felt a spark of outrage building within him. He stepped behind the man, the boy, the hooker, and he grasped him by the throat.

We gave them these bodies as gifts, he thought, pulling and twisting. *They take our gifts and sell them. They soil and degrade themselves for money. They have so little regard for our blessings that they lie there and let others defile them.*

He felt the bones separate, felt the life depart and it was good. But it wasn't enough.

"LOOK IN THE BAG," Rabbadün called, seeing the bloodlust rising in Hasmed's face.

Nestled in with the money were tools. Knives. Saws. Bottles of acid. A small, hot chef's torch designed to put a nice brown crust on the top of crème brulée.

Hasmed used them. He took them to those neglected, despised bodies, and he vandalized them far beyond anything they'd endured before. He drank in their terror and realized that Rabbadün and Vodantu were right. There was no point. The humans, with their numbers and their blessings, had far more power over the world than all the angels who fell from Heaven. They had made this modern world, in which God was a joke and kindness an aberration. They had poisoned the cosmos, had thrown away every chance to redeem it, and now all that remained was to show them what they'd become.

When they were finished, Rabbadün wrapped the young girl's dismembered torso in plastic and put it in Tony Berman's suitcase. Then he gathered his possessions, put them in the duffel, and changed back into Benny.

"I love it," he said as they tramped back toward the car. "Not a spot of blood on our clothes or hands or anything."

Hasmed nodded. He felt exhausted and confused and, once again, sad. He wanted Tina.

"Gene always wanted this, you know," Benny said. "He did it once, then overdosed. What a pussy, huh?"

"Yeah."

"The name was his idea. Benny Hoakler. Benny Ho-Killer. Get it?"

"Funny."

"I'm going to drop the suitcase by the police station where Tony's dad works. Either he'll cover it up and abandon his principles, or he'll have to investigate his own son. Sweet, huh?"

"Unless he's a hypocrite. Unless he was bullshitting about all that anti-corruption stuff."

Benny shrugged.

"If so, well, whatever. At least we've put a scare in people, right?" Benny popped open the trunk. "They'll find those fuckers, and it'll be worth some nightmares. I mean, it's not like the Devil Night's Quake out west, but…"

"It's nothing near 9/11."

"Yeah. Hey, did you know the humans did that one all on their own?"

"Nah."

"For real." Benny sighed as they got in the car. "And this is really just a pastiche of the Black Dahlia and that movie *Seven*. Honestly, we can't beat them at this stuff. Only learn from them."

Hasmed sank a little lower in the passenger seat. "We'll never be as cruel as them," he said. "Because we will never be as powerless."

Benny nodded. He seemed deflated.

"Well," Hasmed added as they pulled into traffic. "At least you're getting the master's name out there."

Benny cackled. "Yeah, we're building brand identity. Oh, and hey: Packers, no, Maple Thunder and Ruy Lopez."

"Huh?"

"All that stuff you wanted to know earlier, man. Keep up! The Packers are gonna beat the Rams—if Kurt Warner gets hurt in the second quarter, which is how things are aspected. Otherwise Rams. The Giants aren't going to cover the point spread, mainly because of bad weather. Maple Thunder, the heavy favorite, takes the fifth race tomorrow. And this guy Ruy Lopez is going to come out of nowhere and really dominate the NASCAR circuit—for a couple races at least."

❧ ❧ ❧

At first, the artists found themselves in light. Their blindness faded in time, though the searing brilliance was still present.

They looked down at a ground that was no longer soil, but cloud. They stood by a tree made not of wood, but lightning.

"Shit," Gil muttered, looking up and down.

"The shapes," Peggy said. "Look, the... the shapes are the same."

Looking at the lightning tree, they could see, far above them, a firmament of earth. The ground and the sky had switched places, up was down, and the frozen thunderbolt by which they stood had the exact same shape as the tree above/ beneath them. It was the tree they'd touched. The Methuselah Tree.

"What is this?" Jennifer asked, lower lip trembling. "What... how can...?"

Gustavus put his hand on her shoulder, and this time it was pure instinct. "Okay," he said. He was blinking rapidly and his lips were working. "Okay. Okay. Gil was in on it, clearly."

"In on what?" Gil demanded.

"The booze. You drugged us, right? I mean, it's okay. We're all, you know, sophisticated adults, mature and, hey, this is worth it, this illusion, it's, it's... really something..."

"You're babbling," Gil said. "I didn't dose you with anything!"

"You think this is some kind of hallucination?" Rudy, the carpet-installer who did radical Marxist puppet shows asked, doubtful.

"Why, why not? I mean they, uh, get us out in the desert in a suggestible state, they... maybe drug us... and this is all... like when Doug Henning made the Statue of Liberty disappear."

"That was David Copperfield," Peggy said absently, but she wasn't really paying attention. She was staring at the vast trunk of light—much bigger than the tree, though its form was identical—and she was noticing how the hair on her arms stood up as she reached toward it. She decided not to touch.

"This is real," Jennifer stated flatly.

"I'll be the first to admit it's an incredible installation!" Gustavus shouted. "This is, without a doubt, the most amazing art experience I've ever, ever *had*. But that doesn't mean

I can't, can't enjoy it without believing in it. This is a trick! It's got to be. Legerdemain, slight of hand, illusion!"

"Where's Christina?" an atonal composer asked, looking around.

"See!" Gustavus said, as if that proved anything. "She snuck away when we were distracted. A classic illusionist's gambit." He looked at the mud woman who had led them there, and he gave her a deep, theatrical bow. "I commend you," he said. "I mean it. My hat is off to you and everyone else involved in this. It's *amazing*! It's the, the *ne plus ultra*. But please tell these people that it's, you know, just a show. An artwork. You know."

She spoke to him in gravelly tones, but no one could understand what she said.

"Gus, honey, calm down," Jennifer said. "Look. Really *look*. How could they... how could they change the whole sky?"

"I don't know. Rear projection, holograms. There was that guy, in Central Park who projected stuff on trees and clouds, remember?"

"If you think this is a big fake, go touch the lightning," Peggy said.

"If you think this *isn't* an illusion, then what the hell is it?"

"I don't know, but..." She looked around. "What are we standing on?" She crouched, but the fog by their ankles was too thick to see through. When she tried to clear it away, more swirled in to obscure her ankles and feet. She hesitated, then put her face in it. It came out beaded with water.

"I can't reach the bottom," she said with a terrible kind of calm. "My feet are supported but my hands go right through it."

"Nobody move," The puppeteer said. He too had squatted and was feeling around. "We could fall off at any moment."

"Hah," Gustavus said. "It's just another trick. A good one! An excellent, magnificent one, but it's *all a trick*." He started stomping around. "Hey, maybe we're hypnotized, did you think of that? Or maybe *I'm* hypnotized and the rest of you are laughing at me. Is that it? Some kind of stage hypnotism?"

"Oh please give the solipsism a rest!" Peggy barked. "We're not hypnotized! We're not in an 'art experience'! We're floating in a *motherfucking cloud*!"

"Which of you is the wisest?" asked the naked woman.

They all turned.

She had said it in the same flat, gravelly tone she'd used before, and her pronunciation was odd. She spoke as if she didn't really understand the words, as if she was simply pronouncing foreign syllables. Her face remained flat and expressionless.

"I think we're moving to the next act of the drama," Gustavus said, his voice tinged with hysteria. "Now it gets interactive. They put our minds in a strange space and see how we react. Okay. This has been an absolutely brilliant production so far, so I'll play along and act *as if* this was all real…"

"Would you please *shut up!*" Gil shouted.

"Oh, I think you just excluded yourself from the 'wisdom' race," Gustavus retorted.

"Gustavus, if you could just…"

"Which of you is the wisest?" the woman asked again.

"Well, let's see. I believe Gil here has the most advanced degree… terminal MFA, right Gil? I always thought that sounded like some sort of illness. But anyway, he's got the most *education*. Or at least the most formal education. Should we privilege that, though? Is class work and theory really more relevant to art than experience and emotional intensity?"

"Gus, please…"

"By that standard, Jennifer is the most *experienced* in some ways. I mean, if you have to suffer to create, her childhood is probably…"

"*Shut up! Shut up! Don't tell them!*" she shrieked. Peggy and Gil stared—their amazement compounded—as Jennifer lunged at Gustavus, swinging her guitar like a weapon. He turned pale and stumbled back, hands up, but the naked woman seized Jennifer in a grip that was clearly quite powerful. Jennifer jerked to a stop like a chained dog at the end of a leash, and the brown woman wasn't budged at all.

"Fine, fine, okay. I'll, you know… I never bought the idea that suffering created art at all, because lots of people who are non-artists suffer and produce nothing. Famine zones should be hotbeds of creativity by that logic and they're not…" Gustavus's words were coming faster and faster, rising in pitch and volume as his eyes widened. He couldn't seem to stop himself. It was as if his mouth had been cut and he was bleeding aesthetic conjecture.

"You're such a prick," muttered the composer.

"But am I a fool?" Gustavus asked, eyes wild. "Who's the bigger fool? The person who believes their senses when they could be getting tricked, or the one who doubts his senses despite the, the *total coherence* of their nonsensical input?"

"This is insane," Jennifer murmured. The brown girl had released her when she stopped struggling, and now she was slumped, looking dully at her wrist where she'd been grabbed. There was a brown smear on it.

"You win, Gus," Peggy said, rolling her eyes. "Jesus Christ, not many guys could go through… *this*… and make it all about them, but you can manage it." She gave him a few sarcastic claps. "There's your wise man!" she yelled at the mud woman. "There he is! Smarter than all the rest of us! Sees through your tricks! Won't get fooled again! Ta daaaa!" She gestured extravagantly.

The woman from the dust walked over to Gustavus and put a hand on either side of his face. He had time for one last worldly, superior smirk before she forced him to his knees.

The way he moved immediately told the others something was wrong. He didn't struggle—or if he did, his strength was so mismatched that it was no real contest. He went down as if someone had chained a safe to his head and dropped it off a bridge. He had time for one strangled gasp, one sound of surprise, before his skull cracked open. Like a nutshell, it went in on the sides and folded up in the center. For a second, it almost looked comical, before the witnesses grasped exactly what it meant, what they were seeing. Then the woman split open the skin beneath his hair and calmly began scooping his brains into her mouth.

❖   ❖   ❖

When Gustavus touched the tree, Sabriel felt Avitu awaken. It was terrifying and thrilling. It was like swimming in the sea and feeling the water carry you upward as a whale rises beneath you. The world rippled as Avitu approached, and Sabriel knew what it was to be dwarfed.

Then she was in another place.

It was not merely another area of the same space—that space known as "the world" which contained the sun and the Earth and all the stars. It was a different type of space entirely—a different context of mind and matter. It was an unformed bubble of potential where all things passed through

myriad iterations of existence. There, every thought and action existed simultaneously as infinite variations of itself.

Sabriel had felt this before, back when the world was not fully made, when the Elohim were still constructing it. Apparently Avitu had either found an unformed remnant of primal reality, or—far more likely—she had re-created the chaos of the early cosmos for some reason of her own.

Sabriel felt a moment of spiritual vertigo as all her myriad responses and thoughts coursed around her, but it took only an instant to adapt and remember. In a way, it was comforting, like coming home. It was only Christina who was puzzled and paralyzed by experiencing all potentials partially, feeling them stream together into the one act/thought/instant, like grains of sand flowing through the pinch of an hourglass. The unlikeliest existed only for a flicker of a moment, while the more probable were longer and more stable, until her every choice resolved into reality, casting shadows of minor variation in every direction.

"Avitu," she asked. "What is this?"

She did not need to speak out loud, of course. There was no air to carry the vibrations in this space, no dimensions for them to travel through. But, for the convenience of the human brain that would need to recall it later, Sabriel chose to conceive verbal thoughts.

She felt, more than heard, the other demon's reply. Avitu's moods and mind were moving at glacial speed, but Sabriel could already sense them quickening.

THIS IS MY DOMAIN. THE WORLD IS FLAT, BUT I HAVE KEPT MY SECRET FOLDS IN SPACE AND TIME.

"Where are the artists?"

IN A FROZEN MOMENT, A PROPITIOUS TIME FROM LONG AGO THAT I HAVE PRESERVED.

Sabriel felt a thrill of excitement. Stopping time! Back before the war, no one of Avitu's house knew such great secrets of the House of Eternity.

"How can you do that? How have you learned the secrets of true time?"

I LEARNED, NOT FROM THEM, BUT FROM MEN. AFTER THE WAR, MEN FOUND PIECES OF THE SLAIN FROM BOTH SIDES AND, CRAVING POWER, BECAME ONE WITH THEM. IT WAS ONE SUCH WOMAN WHO CALLED ME OUT OF HELL AND BOUND ME INTO THE PINE.

"How was this possible?"

She had part of a mighty soul, part of one of the Guardians of the Spheres. But with all that might, she wanted only simple, short-sighted things. Ample food. Protection against harm. Sickness for her imagined enemies.

"When was this?"

I know not: when is it now?

"It is the dawn of the new millennium, by the Christian calendar."

I know nothing of "Christians." The people you brought, they are none of them native to the land. How long have they been in this place?

"Hundreds of years. How long ago were you summoned?"

Long. When I was bound within the tree, it was but a sapling. What of you? How long have you been free?

"Less than a year. I was not summoned, but I escaped on my own."

And how come you to be tied to a mortal body? Such things did not happen in the old ages.

"I do not know."

Now that you are free, what is it you seek?

Sabriel considered, carefully. She spared glances for the potentials in which she spoke instantly—for those where she told the truth, for those where she lied, for those where she was evasive. In each, she saw ghosts of Avitu's possible responses. In the end, she decided to tell the truth.

"I seek revenge."

Revenge on whom? The One Above who cast us down?

"Perhaps, but the One Above is beyond my reach. No, instead I'll get even with humankind."

What score would you settle with them?

"Surely you remember how they betrayed us? At the war's end, not one would stand beside us. Not one would pray on our behalf."

The war was long ago, and I have forgotten many things.

"I will never forget," Sabriel said fiercely—her anger so strong that she no longer bothered to foresee the other creature's responses. "We fought God for them, lost everything because of them, and all so that we might give everything to them! What did we get in return? We were their scapegoats, condemned to the Pit so that they might rule the world."

ARE YOU SO SURE THEY ESCAPED PUNISHMENT? LOOK AT THEM NOW: FRIGHTENED, DIVIDED AND ALIENATED FROM GOD.

"Their suffering is by their own hands. Ours was inflicted on us because we dared to love fully. It's not the same thing at all." Even as she said it, Sabriel became more cautious. If Avitu—or whatever Avitu had become—loved humankind, Sabriel would gain nothing from declaring war against them.

"What happened after you were called?"

FOR MANY YEARS, I GAVE THE SHAMAN WHAT SHE WANTED. I FED HER POWER UNTIL ALL HER DESIRES WERE MET AND SHE HAD TO MAKE NEW ONES. THEN SHE CAME TO ME AND SOUGHT WISDOM, WHICH I DID NOT HAVE EITHER. BUT TOGETHER WE SPOKE AND CONSIDERED AND, AFTER MANY YEARS, BECAME WISE TOGETHER.

"Indeed? What did you learn from her?"

I LEARNED WHAT IT IS TO BE IGNORANT AND AFRAID, FEELINGS NOT NATIVE TO THOSE OF OUR ILK. I ALSO LEARNED OF FAITH AND CURIOSITY—TWO OTHER TRAITS THAT ARE NOT NATURAL TO US.

"Faith? We lack faith? We, whose first memories are of being crafted by the Allmaker's hand?"

THAT IS NOT FAITH. WHAT WE HAD WAS CERTAINTY.

"We had faith in humanity, and look how that repaid us."

WE HAD FAITH IN OUR ABILITY TO DO ONLY RIGHT. IT WAS THAT FAITH THAT WAS FALSELY PLACED. IN OUR EAGERNESS TO HELP HUMANITY, WE HURT THEM FAR WORSE THAN ANY CURSE FROM GOD. OUR ILL-CONSIDERED "GIFT" HAS BECOME THEIR MOST BURDENSOME PROBLEM, AND I—FOR ONE—HAVE SEEN THE ERROR OF OUR WAYS.

"How can you possibly think that what we gave them—truth, awareness and knowledge that they were themselves—is a curse?"

IS A BIRD IN THE WILD HAPPIER KNOWING THAT THE HUNTER'S SNARE AWAITS IT? THAT A BEING FAR MORE CUNNING AND POWERFUL THAN ITSELF LONGS FOR NOTHING MORE THAN ITS DEATH AND CONSUMPTION?

"Our gift was given before they knew death, before they even grasped what death was!"

IF THEY HAD LEARNED IT, EARNED CONSCIOUSNESS AS THE MAKER INTENDED, PERHAPS THEY WOULD WIELD ITS POWER MORE SKILLFULLY. INDEED, WITHOUT THE GIFT OF CONSCIOUSNESS— WITHOUT LUCIFER'S CURSE—MANKIND COULD NEVER HAVE PAINED YOU WITH BETRAYAL. WITHOUT THE SENSE OF SELF, COULD THEY

BE SELFISH? COULD THEY CHOOSE COWARDICE? NO, WITHOUT THE CURSE, THEY WOULD HAVE KNOWN ONLY THE DUMB FEAR OF THE ANIMAL DURING THE WAR—A WAR WHICH WOULD, OF COURSE, NEVER HAVE HAPPENED.

"Without consciousness, there would be no art, no creativity, no sharing…"

YET I LOOK TO YOUR PAST AND I SEE YOU RUINING ART, POISONING CREATIVITY, SOILING WHAT GIFTS THE HUMANS COULD SHARE.

Sabriel felt a prickle of fear when she realized how much Avitu had awakened, and how quickly.

YOUR DESIRE FOR REVENGE IS AS PETTY AND UNWORTHY AS THE BETRAYAL THAT INSPIRED IT. YOU DO NOT WANT THEM TO MERELY LACK THE BLISS OF COMMUNION. YOU WISH THEM TO KNOW THE PAIN OF ISOLATION. THAT IS WHY YOU HAD SUCH STRONG FEELINGS FOR "JENNIFER," THE ONE WHO REACHED FOR CREATION SO LONG BUT NEVER HAD IT IN HER GRASP.

"What are you doing to the artists?"

THEY HAVE A DIFFICULT CHOICE. I WOULD DEARLY LOVE TO GIVE THEM THE GIFT OF SWEET SURCEASE BY TAKING AWAY LUCIFER'S CURSE. BUT I NEED THEIR COMPLICATED REGARD, FOR NOW. I NEED THEIR FAITH. PERHAPS I CAN HEAL THEM WHEN I NO LONGER NEED THEM.

Jennifer—who, moments before, had wanted nothing more than to brain Gustavus with her guitar—now tried, too late, to save him. Gil, too, rushed on the naked woman when he realized what she was doing. So did the puppeteer and a woman who made masks out of blown glass and crystal. The others threw up, hid their eyes or simply stared in shock.

It didn't matter. They couldn't stop her. They couldn't even slow her down. They seized her arms and pulled, but it was likely trying to pull against a forklift. Pushing her body was like trying to budge a highway overpass. She looked like a woman, but she was stone.

The mask-maker accepted these facts more readily than the others, and tried to pull Gustavus's body away instead. For her insight, she earned a shove from the brown woman. It didn't look terribly powerful, but it was enough to stagger her back several feet. By the time she recovered, the stone creature's grisly meal was done.

Gil and Jennifer and the puppet-master stopped when the woman stood and changed. Where once her body had

seemed like rock—inflexible, weighty and immobile—it now flowed freely as mud in rain, changing and reshaping. The woman stood taller, her meaty hips and waist slimming, lengthening. Her features re-formed, becoming finer, eyes wider, cheeks higher, chin more delicate. She became pretty, then beautiful, then stunning.

As she transformed, her skin tones changed as well. They still retained the dirt brown of the desert floor, turned gray in the chill moonlight, but they became warmer and richer. Her flat, straight hair curled and became lustrous chestnut locks cascading down her bronze, naked back.

"There," she said. "That's better. Now we should be able to communicate more easily."

Modestly, she wiped her mouth.

In a sickening instant, Jennifer realized two things.

First was that this thing—while speaking in tones undeniably feminine, indeed, almost cooing—said the words with Gustavus's inflections and intonations.

The second was that its features were a little bit like her own, only perfected, fetishized, fantasized. Through instinct or intuition, she knew that she was looking at Gustavus's desires made flesh.

She bent over and vomited into the clouds.

"You know my goals, Avitu. What are your own?"

I FEEL NO ANIMOSITY TOWARD THE MAN-CHILDREN, the other demon replied. *I WISH TO UNDO THE WRONG WE HAVE WROUGHT. WHERE THE MORNINGSTAR BROUGHT UNWELCOME LIGHT, I WILL GIVE THEM THE PEACE OF A SWEET, DREAMLESS NIGHT. I SHALL REMOVE HIS CURSE, AS I TRIED BEFORE, BUT THIS TIME, I WILL HEAL THEM ALL. BELIEVE ME, SABRIEL, THEIR LAST CLEAR THOUGHTS WILL BE GRATITUDE FOR THE COMING IGNORANCE.*

Sabriel was not paying full attention to Avitu's ideas, because she was busily scanning the possibilities that swarmed around both of them. Avitu's thoughts were visible—vague and bizarre, alien and erratic, but those of Sabriel's house were sometimes called the Angels of Comprehension, and the other creature's purpose was gradually taking shape. A future was clarifying, and Sabriel didn't like it. While Avitu was certainly pleased that the Lammasu had come, gratitude was not an element of her mental landscape. It was more and more obvious that the demon in the tree was deciding that

Sabriel's plans did not fit within her own, and that the one who awakened her should be repaid with destruction.

Sabriel began scanning frantically, trying to find a way to escape. Her most obvious actions all led her directly into Avitu's trap, because Avitu could readily anticipate the actions of an angel.

One thin flicker of hope wavered.

It was a very unlikely act—less probable than Sabriel choosing to join Avitu or choosing to destroy herself or trying to invoke God the Allmaker's forgiveness and pity— but it was possible and unexpected, and it just might work.

In the slender microsecond when the choice could become real, Sabriel let herself be Christina Vadrudakis.

❈   ❈   ❈

"Who are you?" Peggy whispered, staring at the creature that had formed before them. "What are you?"

"You can call me Avitu," the beautiful murderess replied. "I'm not, really. No more than Rudy's marionettes are him," she said, gesturing to the man who did Marxist puppet shows. "I'm not Avitu, but it's Avitu's voice that speaks through me."

"Who is Avitu?" Gil asked.

"Avitu is the tree of knowledge. Avitu is the protector of her people. Avitu is the realm around you and the ruler of that realm."

Jennifer dropped her guitar and stumbled to Gustavus's corpse. She planted a hand over her mouth and stared. Then she said, "Why did you kill Gus?"

"Gustavus was suffering, poor child," the woman responded, and when Jennifer glanced up, the look of compassion on features so similar to her own renewed her sense of nausea and vertigo. "His mind was feverish with the disease of consciousness. Like all of you, he suffered because he knew too much and understood too little. Now his suffering is over."

"What do you want from us?" Gil asked, his face pale, his words full of dread.

"I only want to help you—to help all humanity recover from the curse that torments you."

"Oh God, she's going to kill us all!" the mask-builder cried.

"No, I am not," the naked woman replied, her voice kindness itself. "I could not make myself understood until I had Gustavus's vocabulary, his memories and frame of reference. It's unfortunate that I had to seize them so crudely, but now that we can communicate—"

"It's unfortunate?" Jennifer's eyes were wide and her voice was shrill. "You murdered him! You fucking ate his brain, and now you say it's unfortunate?"

"I needed what he had, and I took it. His knowledge is much more useful in my hands than in his. All his ideas, all his conjecture only wound him tighter and tighter in bonds of misery, ignorance and discord. I don't expect you to understand this," she said with a smile of sweet tolerance, "But Gustavus is better off dead than afflicted by the madness of awareness."

"The same madness we all have," Peggy said.

"Yes."

"You want to take away 'Lucifer's curse' now, huh? Make us all babies again? Turn us back into apes or Cro-Magnons or something?"

Sabriel felt a strange sense of unreality as she followed foreign instincts, letting Christina's false understanding, Greek language and vague vocabulary drift out when they'd been so ruthlessly repressed for months. Of course, in this space, the specific language spoken mattered very little.

YOU ARE MAKING MOCK OF THINGS THAT YOU DO NOT FULLY GRASP.

"Oh, I grasp it all right. You used to be all fired up about Lucifer's program, right? You fought in his war, followed his orders, the whole thing! Now you've changed your mind again and decided to steal away this, this present because you don't like what we're doing with it. You don't like losing the game, so you're taking your ball and going home!"

It was working. Sabriel could feel Avitu's confusion and dismay. The great demon was switching gears, trying to adjust itself to deal on human terms instead of celestial ones, but it was still weary from centuries of slumber.

WE WERE WRONG TO AWAKEN YOUR MINDS. WE WERE WRONG, AND YOU PAID FOR IT, AND WE PAID FOR IT, AND THE WORLD PAID FOR IT. I WANT TO UNDO THAT WRONG.

"I bet you're totally sure you're right now."

I AM RIGHT. Sabriel could sense Avitu's growing anger, but it was tempered by an inhuman patience with humanity. The former guardian was getting more and more bewildered, unsure whether Sabriel was demon or mortal or somehow both.

"You'd have said the same thing before when you believed the total opposite!"

There! Scanning the futures around them, Sabriel figured she'd hit the moment of Avitu's greatest confusion, greatest distraction. She gathered as much strength as she could...

(...in Miami, Thomas Ramone was bussing a load of soiled plates back to the dishwasher at Solly's Pizza-n-Subs when he was struck by a wave of dizziness. One leg buckled, and he stumbled forward into the corner of the kitchen door. He hit his head, hard, falling and destroying most of the tray of crockery. When he was taken to the hospital, the diagnosis was dehydration...)

...and fled.

One minute, there were the eleven remaining artists and the brown goddess that had killed Gustavus. With a flare of brilliant color, like white light broken by water, Sabriel appeared from the column of the thunderbolt. For a moment they saw her as the black woman they'd known as Christina, but she changed before their eyes, growing in size, growing in magnificence. She spread wings of ice and foam above them and swept downward.

"What...?" Peggy said, raising an arm to shield her eyes as she tried to track the flying figure against the brilliant bolt. Sabriel was too swift for the mortal to follow, however, turning in the air and lifting her from behind. The poetess had a moment to cry out—not even a proper scream—before Sabriel laced her hands behind Peggy's neck and bent it forward until it broke.

Jennifer shrieked again, and the others joined in.

"Sabriel! Stop at once!" shouted the naked creature, but the flier paid no heed. A clap of wings, a sweep of ice, and then Gil was dead too.

"Stop it! Stop it!" Rudy screamed, flailing his fists wildly at this new danger as it plunged in to seize him. He struggled to free himself—maybe he succeeded, maybe he was thrown,

but the result was the same. He sailed off into the pillar of light and was destroyed with a sharp ozone crack.

The artists scattered. The stone woman chased Sabriel fruitlessly, leaping after her but unable to match her speed. Bolts of lightning lashed out from the trunk of fire, but the flying fallen stayed too close to the humans for Avitu to aim with confidence.

"Stop!" bellowed Avitu's puppet. "Stop! Stop!"

But the succubus didn't stop until she'd killed the mask-maker and another sculptor too. Of the original dozen artists, only half remained.

Sabriel was exultant. Her fear of Avitu, her plans for escape, her subtle ploys to sow despair—all were rinsed out of her by a warm wave of bloodlust. Grabbing Jennifer by the throat and lifting her into the sky, it was all she could do to refrain from squeezing that tender neck purple. But she resisted, even going so far as to lace her legs around the musician to hold her more safely.

When the next streak of electricity snapped, Sabriel turned toward it instead of away. It still missed her. As she'd guessed, Avitu wasn't about to endanger the few mortals who remained.

"Let me go!" Jennifer screamed, clawing at Sabriel and squirming.

"Sorry, but that's my line," Sabriel told her. Raising her voice, she called to her captor. "Avitu! Release me!"

"After watching your wanton slaughter of my guests? Never!"

In a state of terror that was surreal in its intensity, Jennifer had a brief moment to consider how odd it was that the same being that killed Gustavus would be angry at this other creature for killing Gil and Peggy—and, in all likelihood, Jennifer herself.

"Let me go, or you'll have no guests!"

The mud woman threw back her head and screamed in anger.

"Do it!" Sabriel shouted. "Do it or you can drop back into sleep, you can fall into oblivion for another thousand years!"

"Agreed," Avitu said. "Just drop Jennifer. Please."

"Let me out first!"

In the swirling cloud floor, a hole opened. Looking through, Jennifer had a vertiginous vision of the desert, at night, normal.

"Take me with you?" Jennifer pleaded.

"Sorry," the winged thing replied. It released her right before plunging through the portal. Jennifer clawed her way toward it, but it was too late.

❖ ❖ ❖

Sabriel emerged over the desert, over the grove of Methuselah Trees, and kept flying at full speed until she reached the cars. Then she drove back to Vegas with the gas floored the entire time.

As she fled, clouds barreled in from over Lake Mead. They moved fast and scuttled on legs of lightning. The storm caught up to her over the city, soaking its glitz and gamblers.

Behind her, Sabriel did not see another hand erupt from the soil—this time, a man's hand.

❖ ❖ ❖

Teddy Mason sat up in bed, a look of wonder on his face. "Avitu!" he said. "The tree's name is Avitu!"

Next to him, his wife grumbled and turned over.

❖ ❖ ❖

The next day, Hasmed picked Tina up from preschool, made her macaroni and cheese for supper, patiently persuaded her to eat her carrot sticks and sent her to bed around nine o'clock.

As he sat in the living room, trying not to think about Vanessa, he felt a sudden, insistent pull. Someone was speaking his name, someone nearby.

It took him a moment to realize that it was Tina in the next room. He'd heard her say her prayers, and now she was lying in bed whispering "Hasmed, Hasmed, Hasmed," over and over.

IX

chapter
nine

Hasmed got out of bed. Tina was still asleep in her room as he got in the shower and turned it on.

Several weeks had passed since he'd killed Vanessa, and he was behind schedule. He'd quit Harvey's old job (clerking at a hardware store) and had rented a small office in a dingy old building. He'd paid some bills and minded Tina and put the word out about his new business, but his plans—still immature and barely formed—seemed to be stretching away from his grasp even as he trudged toward them.

He blamed humanity for this problem. Specifically, his own humanity.

His body—this lousy, pudgy, sickly body he'd scraped up out of the dirt—was an unceasing source of petty, irksome demands. If it wasn't eating, it was sleeping. If not sleeping, crapping. The thing *still* got cigarette cravings, though Hasmed had ruthlessly crawled through every inch of its veins and cells and glial connections rooting out the physical causes of addiction. The psychological compulsion that had been ingrained by Harvey's years of abuse was just as strong. He might have cleaned the nicotine stains off its fingers, but they wouldn't come off the mind—not even after death.

And digestion! It was just plain misery. All food tasted the same to the demon, so sticking to a wholesome diet (fruits, whole-wheat bread, raw vegetables, rice cakes and a little tuna fish now and then) was not difficult. It was just so *constant*. Every five to eight hours, with thirst even *more* frequent.

With consumption, of course, came the inevitable by-products. Hasmed had easily fixed Harvey's chronic digestive problems (mainly by switching his diet from high-fat to high-fiber), but even without hemorrhoids and heartburn and flatulence there were still the physical acts. Pissing and shitting. Shaking and wiping and flushing. What a colossal waste of time! At least with sleep he was barely aware of how much opportunity he was throwing away.

Eight hours of sleep. Another two hours for meal preparation, consumption and defecation. Thanks to Harvey's laziness, he was fighting an uphill battle at the gym for an hour and a half a day. Plus all the miscellaneous money-grubbing, light-bulb-changing, dressing and undressing, shaving and shampooing and applying of underarm deodorant that occupied so much of mortal life. And the little girl—fuggeddaboudit! Parent-teacher conferences ("Tina seems to be having trouble adjusting to her new surroundings") and story-reading and trying to get her to bathe and eat right, constantly buying her new clothes when she outgrew the old ones… He barely had eight hours a day to do his master's work.

Even still, though, he did manage to steal $100,000 worth of diamonds.

❖   ❖   ❖

Down in Miami, things weren't going nearly as well for Thomas Ramone. He barely stole a couple thousand after Mr. Yamamura (the owner of Solly's Pizza-n-Subs) fired him.

"You're on dope, ain't you?" the scowling restaurateur had said.

"Yeah, I'm hopped up on goofballs," was Thomas's sarcastic reply.

"Don't sass me, you little punk. I've had it up to here with you friggin' potheads."

"Look, I'm sorry, boss."

"Don't call me 'boss'! I don't employ druggies."

"I don't smoke weed!" Thomas earnestly lied. "Look man, here's what happened. I was working hard, I got dehydrated and dizzy, and I hit my head. That's all. Ask the doctor!"

His employer—former employer—replied with a withering glare. "The day you pass out from working too hard is the day I start selling crap sandwiches. You're fired!"

Without his paycheck from Solly's, Thomas was in a tight spot. Not only did he need the money, ongoing proof of employment was a term of his parole. He'd gotten a suspended sentence and a year's probation after his first arrest for housebreaking. He had a month and a half probation left, and he was doing a great job of foxing the drug tests, so he didn't want to screw anything up. But all that was standing between him and a parole violation— which would drop his two-year prison term on his head like an anvil—was his second job working the night shift at a local video rental place.

Mr. Yamamura might have been loud and pushy, but underneath it all, he was not a scumbag. The same could not be said for Mr. Kneller, the video store owner. Tom had gotten the job at Video Villa through Franklin, one of his weed-smoking buddies and a Video Villa day clerk. Franklin was all right, but he had a big mouth, so Mr. Kneller quickly learned that Thomas was in bad shape. As soon as Kneller realized that he was the only thing keeping Thomas out of slam, he slipped effortlessly into Pushy Bastard mode. He soon had Thomas working extra over-time hours at regular pay—pay that was always a couple days late and a few dollars light.

Thomas wished he could screw Kneller good—rob the bastard or rip him off somehow—but he was certain that suspicion would fall on him, fast and hard. Let's see, guy gets robbed right about the time he starts dicking over his em-ployee with the suspended sentence for burglary? Do you suppose it was the disgruntled clerk? Ya think?

Aggravating all his smoldering anger and resentment was the lingering suspicion that he'd sold his soul for what was— in the final analysis—a pretty stupid trick.

Sure, he could escape any physical bonds, except for maybe a bucket. If he concentrated, he could turn his body into water. Sometimes. It wasn't the most reliable thing. He managed it about one time in three, not counting the time after a wake 'n' bake that he did it accidentally in the shower. That was pretty scary: He came within inches of going down the drain. After that, he only took baths.

He could turn into water, about a gallon. Turning back human was easier—pretty much automatic, seemed like. As a living puddle, he could move along even surfaces, but going

uphill was pretty much impossible. A great trick for getting past bars, out of handcuffs or under locked doors.

The only problem was, the change didn't seem to include his clothes. Whenever he was tempted to just rip off Kneller, make a run for it and simply power up if captured... the image of himself bailing down the road stark naked always gave him pause.

Thomas made a concerted effort to get his life back on track. Stage one was cutting back on the Mary Jane. It was a pain, but it made sense. He couldn't afford to botch a drug test. He couldn't afford fogged thinking. And he couldn't really afford to buy a lot of reefer, either. He cadged some off his friends—taking hits if they offered them—but by and large, he just said no.

He thought about telling his buddies about Sabriel—Angela Meyerhoff, whatever—but no way. No matter how stoned they all were, they'd think he was off his nut. Besides, he'd already lied to them (kind of) about the missing days. He'd been planning a road trip with Pete, Steve and Mo'ana, and he'd figured that the cash from selling Meyerhoff's TV and stuff would let him travel in style. When he didn't show, they went without him. He told them he'd met this crazy hot chick and had spent the weekend with her. Which was true, more or less. They were mad, but not too mad. It wasn't the first time any of them had gotten flaky.

Thomas had considered himself lucky that he hadn't had any hours scheduled at either job for the time he was tied up in the basement. But then he wound up getting fired anyhow.

Okay, he thought, *Water. I can turn into water. There's gotta be a way to make some dough off that.*

"Excuse me? Uh, the box for this movie was on the shelf, but the tape's not there?"

"It's probably checked out."

The man on the other side of the counter shifted uncomfortably. "Could you, like check? On the computer or something?"

Thomas sighed and leaned forward. "What's the title?"

The man showed him the box.

Tom checked the file—which wasn't computerized, of course, everything was done with index cards—and then told the customer that, sorry, *Big Cock Randy Mountin'* had been checked out and was, in fact, overdue.

It was 11:30 on a Friday night. People like this guy—portly, nerdy, with a vague reek of shame—were his regular customers. The man retreated back into the adults-only room, and Tom sat back down on the stool. As he picked at the cracked vinyl and the stuffing within, he resumed his train of thought.

Okay. Water. No one suspects water, so it's good for hiding. I could get in somewhere, turn into water and wait until the place closes. Like a bank or something. But nah, those places all have cameras, and to move around and carry stuff I'd need to be human again.

He'd considered and rejected the idea of showing off his power in public, selling tickets. He could tell people he was a magician, but then they'd expect him to do other tricks, and he only had one. Besides, he didn't like the idea of all those people staring at him. And what if the power conked out on him? Or he could tell them it was the real thing—*prove it*—but he was pretty sure he'd wind up in some kind of government lab. He'd seen *The X-Files*.

What I'd wanna do is go in the place earlier and stash my clothes somewhere, like in a bathroom. He shifted, flexing stiff back muscles, and raised an eyebrow. *Actually, a bathroom would be the perfect place to hide. Yeah. I go in there when no one else is there, I put my clothes in, like, a plastic baggie, put 'em in top of the can and then water myself in on top of them. The smart move would be to glue down that flap inside the tank so I don't get flushed.*

Thomas's apartment was furnished with a bowl that sometimes ran on and on unless the handle was jiggled, so he was very familiar with ballcocks and floats and the other (to him) nameless elements of the toilet tank.

Yeah. So I pick somewhere with cash locked inside it, somewhere I can get inside, wait, then jack the cashbox without worrying about cameras and shit. I just let myself out the front door when it's done.

He tried it the very next night.

✸　✸　✸

Hasmed's diamond heist started out with Roscoe Paum. They'd been at the YMCA, sitting in the sauna.

"I'm down twenty pounds," Hasmed said, plucking at the loose skin rolling over the top of the towel around his waist.

"I still have all this jiggly stuff though." He demonstrated with a second chin and with a flap of flab on his upper arm.

"Yeah, what you've lost is mostly water weight," Roscoe replied. "That goes off first, and it goes off pretty easy. When you get down to the real *fat* fat, it's gonna go a lot slower." He shrugged. "What's really important isn't weight so much anyhow—not unless you're some anorexic beauty queen. Instead of body weight, you should watch your body *mass*—'ats how much of your weight is actual muscle."

"So when I start building muscle, all this floppy stuff goes away?"

"More or less. I won't lie to you, that belly of yours is never going to look like a six pack again." Roscoe himself was lean and angular—he looked like sacks draped over coat hangers. While Fortune was slimming down, he was trying to bulk up. "Really great definition, it's like virginity. Once you lose it, it ain't coming back."

"I don' give a shit. I just wanna be healthy."

"You're on the right track, just give it time. Doesn't happen overnight y'know."

They'd sat in silence for a while, sweltering, and then Roscoe had mentioned his cousin Angie.

It turned out that Angie worked for one of the local jewelry stores and had shrugged off a sleazy pass from a New York diamond merchant. Since "Angie" was short for "Angelo," this was a bit more noteworthy than standard boy-on-girl sexual harassment.

"I mean, it's not like Angelo looks faggy, you know?"

"What's this New York diamond guy doing here in Jersey, anyway?"

Ros shrugged. "Angie says he makes monthly deliveries. Why?"

"I'm just thinkin'. Maybe Angie'd like to get a little payback on this guy? Y'know, get him in some trouble?"

"You're not sayin'…?"

"I'm not sayin', I'm just thinkin'."

"Yeah, well, you're thinkin' with that hole in your head and not your brain. You can't rob this guy. He may be a fag, but he's, like, an ex-marine or an Army Ranger or somethin'. Carries a big gun and doesn't take chances. I mean, dig this—overnight, he leaves his deliveries at the police station. Or you think you can steal it right out of a precinct house?"

Hasmed shrugged. "We'll see."

As he said it, he wiped his foggy glasses, unveiling the eye full of blood.

❖   ❖   ❖

Even Kneller wouldn't work Thomas *every* night, so on his night off, Thomas took a deep breath and went after a Home Depot.

He parked his car in the lot behind it, in the spot by the dumpster. He had a key tied behind the back bumper with dental floss, and a change of clothes in the front seat. With a Miami Dolphins cap pulled low over his eyebrows, he walked into the store. In one pocket, he had a small, dim flashlight and a tube of glue. In the other was a large plastic bag and a pair of gloves.

In the bathroom he looked around and, seeing that he was alone, went into the stall.

There was no tank.

He blinked.

Shit, he thought. *What now?*

At that point a good burglar would have cut his losses and left, but Thomas wasn't a good burglar. He decided to improvise.

Glancing around, he pulled the garbage can into a corner by the farthest stall. He stripped, put his stuff in the baggie and sealed it. Then, after a moment's thought, he pulled the glue back out and globbed it all around the flusher handle.

I hope they sanitize the fuck out of that bowl, he thought as he stuffed his property down under the bag in the trash bin. Then, with a sigh, he sat his naked ass on the toilet seat and gave a weak little chuckle.

Nothing happened.

"Ha ha," he tried feebly, but nope, no good. He forced it, laughing a little louder, a little faker. "Ha HA."

Zilch.

Well, I suppose I could piss, get dressed and call it a night. There was a rush of relief. He gave one last sad snort, and that one did it.

Aquatic, he sat in the bowl and waited.

And waited.

And waited.

In his water body, Thomas could still see. Looking up from the bowl, he could watch the unmoving shadows on the bathroom's drop ceiling, and he started thinking.

Shit, I could have put my crap up there. I could have put a bucket up there too and hid there instead of being in here! I gotta remember that for next time.

The light switched on.

If he'd had lips, he would have bitten them. If he'd had a heart, it would have hammered. As it was, he could only lie perfectly still, concentrating on remaining water, remaining water.

He wondered what was going on—he could hear someone moving around, but nothing specific.

Just don't take a dump.

Eventually, the light went off and the door closed. Thomas waited and waited and waited.

Next time, I gotta stick my watch somewhere I can see it, he thought. He counted to a thousand, slow. He wasn't patient by nature, but one trip to jail had been enough to teach him caution. After a second slow thousand count, he rose up.

Weird, he thought. *I'm not even wet.*

He dressed, took a deep breath, and opened the door a crack.

Silence.

He crept out into the darkened store and cautiously looked around. The giant bell-shaped lights on the ceiling were still dimly glowing—they'd had the same kind of lights at Thomas's high school football field, and he knew they took about an hour to go out completely.

So that's some luck, he thought. He tiptoed from the back through the lumber area to the home-decorating department and glanced through the corridors of bolts and spackle and electrical wire. He saw no one.

Next stop, cash registers.

They were locked, but he'd made a brief detour to the crowbars in aisle three and selected a small, black, tempered pry-bar that made quick work of the lock.

They were empty.

Shit. They must empty the registers and put the cash in a lock box. Unless they take it to the bank every night? No way… would they?

He knew that the more time he spent, the greater his chances were of being spotted... but the Home Depot was gigantic, the parking lot was at least an acre, and any security guy would be checking the outside... presumably.

He was working on the lock of the manager's office when he heard the cop cars pull up in front.

If Thomas had been smart, he would have fled right after hearing the car stop, but he gave himself the luxury of optimism. He thought it might be some kids looking for a private place to make out. He thought it might be someone checking a map. Those thoughts cost him half a minute of waffling and deliberation before he crept forward and glanced out the window in time to see a blue uniform approaching a door.

He turned and bolted for the back.

Shit! He thought. *Shit shit shit!*

When that didn't help, considered the crowbar in his hands. He'd worn gloves the whole time he used it, so it was clean. He dropped it immediately, and the clang echoed throughout the store.

"Who's in there?" The voice from the front sounded terrifically loud and sharp.

As Thomas turned the corner of an aisle, he saw the back door opening and a flashlight beam creeping in. He ducked back and ran up a corridor. It was lined with door fixtures—boxes of knobs and locks and kick plates.

Think, Thomas. Think think think!

It was clearly time to bail. He jerked off his shirt, then dropped his pants and undies. His shoes were cheap black kung-fu slippers, and they quickly joined the bundle around his flashlight.

He could hear footsteps getting closer and he started to giggle. It was hysteria, but he couldn't use it yet, he still needed hands and arms and height.

The gloves were most important because they'd have his fingerprints. He took them off, added them to the clothing wad, and stuffed it on a shelf as high up as he could reach, behind several boxes of weather stripping.

Completely nude, he gave a desperate chuckle and dissolved.

A flashlight beam played across the aisle floor. As he slithered his way toward the cop, he could hear the man talking into his shoulder mic. "Nothin' yet, over."

Another patrol officer was by the door, a woman. He got right up beneath her feet before he realized that the door-jamb was slightly raised.

Is nothing ever easy? He slithered away into the dark. When he was sure he was out of her sight, he re-formed—just for a moment, just long enough to tip over a display of energy efficient light bulbs and give a yell.

Please let it work, please let it work, please let it work, he thought, desperately chortling.

But it didn't work. He was giggling now and couldn't stop, caught up in the terror and ridiculousness of it, but he couldn't change until the policewoman came around the corner and caught a glimpse of him, stark naked, ducking around the other end of the shelving unit.

With a sense of deep relief he oozed down the tile floor to the back door, overhearing her as he passed. "...white Caucasian male, long dark hair and is, repeat, *naked...*"

At the door, he paused. If he'd had a body, he'd have taken a deep breath. And then, just like that, he had one and he did.

Bare feet slapping as he bolted toward the dumpsters in his birthday suit, Thomas Ramone had never felt so exposed in his life.

Thomas struggled into the shirt and sweatpants in his car without even noticing that the pants were backward and the shirt inside-out. He got dressed and turned the key and jammed. His heart was still thudding rapidly when he pulled into the parking lot by his apartment.

He was momentarily distracted when he realized that the asshole with the Trans-Am had stolen Thomas's space in the carport, *again*, but mainly he was still freaked out and amazed that he'd escaped from... what, at least three cops?

By all rights I should be cuffed and stuffed by now.

He went into his apartment, shoved a couple of skate magazines aside and sat down on the couch.

Crap, he thought. *I'm not out of the woods. I still could hang for this, but... what are they gonna do? Tomorrow's Sunday. When they figure out nothing's missing, they're not gonna close the store. Not on an autumn Sunday, when everyone's buying snow blowers and shit. So any clues I left, they're gonna be worthless—just so long as I can get in and get the clothes. That's job one tomorrow. Gotta wait until it's good and busy, don't wanna go in first thing...*

Mentally, he pictured the lady cop again, and he was overcome with a fit of the giggles.

"Suspect is, I repeat, naked." Shit. This is crazy. This is *some crazy-ass shit.*

He got a beer out of the fridge and thought about smoking some pot. Then he remembered he didn't have any in the house.

Probably just as well. One giggle fit, and I could be a stain on the couch.

When the beer was done he opened another. Halfway through that, he felt competent to do some *real* thinking.

My problem was, I was thinking too large. Got greedy. What I need is to knock over smaller places—like mom-an'- pop restaurants, places that leave cash in the fucking regis- ter. Heck, places like that are more likely to have tank toilets, right? Or I could, like, put a basin under the sink like it's catching a leak. Though someone might dump me then.

He worked the next night, but he went to a Brazier out by the highway on Monday night and made $500. Thurs- day was his next night off, and he netted $450 from Nicole's Old Fashioned Tap. Three nights after that, the "Midnight Marauder" was in the paper after he stole $1,117 from a BP Amoco.

It was a little more than a week after his first aborted attempt that he was spotted by the demon Usiel, who was traveling under an assumed name.

※　※　※

Together, Roscoe and Hasmed cased the diamond mer- chant. His name was Jack Haskell, and he had the fat, crew-cut look of a no-nonsense cop.

"I can't believe he's a fairy," Roscoe kept saying.

Jack made weekly deliveries, getting into town late and driving directly to the police station.

"Doesn't make sense," Roscoe said. "Why would he drive from New York late and get here after the store closes?"

"Ask Angie."

"How'm I gonna bring that sort of thing up with him?"

"Find a way."

To his credit, Ros did and reported it back to Hasmed.

"All right, it makes sense now. He's got a route, see? Starts in Manhattan, makes deliveries to a bunch of different towns in Jersey. Ours is the last stop, and with the traffic, he

just couldn't ever get here on time. So they started putting him up overnight."

"Why not make two trips?"

Roscoe shrugged. "I don' know. You're the fortune-teller, you tell me. Maybe he's married, likes to ditch the wife and cruise for blowjobs?"

"Maybe they didn't want to double their exposure."

"So if we're gonna hit him, maybe we should do it early? You know, before he makes his other deliveries?"

Hasmed thought about it a moment before shaking his head. "Nah. That's when he'd be most alert, right? And we'd be in a strange town. We'd stand out."

Roscoe had some private thoughts about "Mr. Fortune" standing out anywhere, what with the big goddamn scar in the middle of his face, but he kept them to himself.

"So how you want to do this?"

"Don' know. I'm gonna check the precinct house."

Roscoe just shook his head.

❖ ❖ ❖

Back when he was an angel, Hasmed had lived by clear, inflexible rules. One of the most important was, "Do not reveal yourself to humans." This was a rule for all the Elohim, but since Hasmed had duties to protect people, he had to go out of his way to remain unseen. Created by a perfect being, he naturally had abilities to enable him to do just that.

The war and his subsequent imprisonment had weakened his powers considerably, but remaining invisible to humankind was still within his grasp.

Following Jack Haskell along the street to the precinct house, Hasmed disappeared. It wasn't sudden, like when a figure gets spliced out of a film with a dramatic pop. He didn't fade, either, like a dying match flame. He just gradually was where people weren't looking. A woman strolling by him glanced at her watch and instinctively stepped out of the demon's path. A man paused to lean and tie a shoe as Hasmed passed. A child sneezed, its mother knelt to wipe its face—as a consequence, they both missed the creature walking by.

When he entered the police station, people rubbed tired eyes, glanced at ringing phones or looked down as they scratched themselves, and not one saw him.

Jack Haskell had a sample case, black and nondescript, but watching closely, Hasmed could tell it was different from the usual salesman's catalogue box. Haskell could lift it easily, but the way it moved, swinging in his hand, the time it took at the edge of each arc, told Hasmed that it was fairly heavy. Inside the pleather exterior, it probably had a steel core.

A cop came out from the back and greeted Haskell with a smile, clapping him on the back. He picked up the case, and the two men went through a door marked AUTHORIZED PERSONNEL ONLY.

Hasmed followed.

The pair went through dark brick halls, chatting amiably, with Hasmed only a few steps behind them. When he noticed cameras by the ceiling, he tilted his head down so that only the brim of his hat was visible to them. Even if the people watching the security cameras had been looking at those particular images at that particular moment (and none were), all they'd see was three men, the one in back wearing a baseball cap.

At the bottom of a flight of stairs, the cop opened an unmarked metal door. Hasmed watched as they went inside. It wasn't a big room, so a quick glance was enough to reveal no other doors, no windows. It just had a couple of racks of cheap steel shelves laden with boxes, cases and paper bags. Each was in a clearly labeled spot.

Hasmed climbed the stairs alone thinking, *Two cameras, two locked doors, one locked security case.*

❈ ❈ ❈

"Jeez, you're serious?"

"Serious as cancer, Ros. It's doable. 'Cept for the locks. The locks are the deal-breaker."

"It ain't being in a whole *building* full of cops and cameras and shit? The deal-breaker is three little locks?"

"That's what I'm tellin' you."

They were back in the sauna, and both just sat for a moment. Then Hasmed spoke.

"Actually," he said, "I reckon it's really just two locks. That first door, it looked like there was lots of traffic through that. I could probably just follow someone through it. The second door, it was at the bottom of the stairs, not lots of people went there. But no camera on it, either."

"So two locks."

"Two locks."

There was another pause.

"So we need a pick."

"Eh…" Hasmed bit his lower lip. "I don' know if I wanna get a third man involved."

"We're gonna have to anyway, to move the rocks."

"Yeah, yeah… but that's not so much of a big problem. You can always find a fence. For easy stuff like ice, right?"

"But to get the ice, we need a pick."

"I don't know if I could get a pick inside."

"How you gonna get *yourself* inside?"

Hasmed made a little grunting noise and rubbed his forehead.

"Let's just say I don't *see* a good way to get anyone else in."

"So you can't *see* a good way to get through the locks?"

"It doesn't work like that."

"Okay, okay, whatever. We could cut the locks."

"With what? A fuckin' hacksaw? It'd take all night."

"One of them—what you call 'em?—a sawsall? Like, an electric saw?"

"Too loud. And we'd need to plug it in, I think."

"A lock-pick gun would do it."

"You know where to get one? 'Cause I don't."

They sat in silence for a few more minutes. "Aw crap," Hasmed said at last. "I'll think of somethin'. Now, I gotta go. I got someone to see."

❖ ❖ ❖

"Mr. Fortune" didn't have a big clientele. Not yet, anyhow. But word was going around about his lucky sports picks. Vietnam Ham and his bodyguards weren't talking about his predictions, but Dennis Porter did enough jabbering for both.

In fact, Dennis had become his best customer, even after it was explained that sports were dim and hard to call. That was fine. Porter was more interested in other matters, as it turned out. Mainly marital stuff. He'd paid two hundred dollars for reassurance that his wife didn't suspect anything—and another three-fifty for confirmation that she was stepping out on him, too.

Five hundred and fifty bucks was nothing to sneeze at—it made a good dent in Tina's outstanding medical bills, if not

Hasmed's own—but in addition to some stock-standard snooping, it had also involved listening to Dennis's blather about how it was *different*, elaborately justifying his own infidelity while condemning hers. It was tiresome and sad, and Hasmed considered killing him. He considered it very, very carefully. But today, Hasmed wasn't talking to Dennis. He was talking to Lee Boyer Jr., also known as "Milkman Boyer," also known as "Milk Monster."

Hasmed always acted much busier than he was. When someone called to talk to him, he always scheduled an appointment for a couple of days or even a week. It gave him a chance to scope out his new pigeon and learn a few "amazing facts" with which to wow them.

The most impressive fact he'd picked up watching Milkman Boyer was that the faded, decades-old cigarette burns on Boyer's arms and hands clustered much more densely on his penis, scrotum and buttocks. He'd heard rumors about Boyer's mom and dad, and the scars seemed to clinch it. He was similarly encouraged to see that Lee's key chain had a rabbit's foot on it, and that there was a horseshoe on the inside of his apartment door. Running over his notes, observations and rumors, Hasmed was fairly confident about three things.

One: Boyer was almost certainly involved in a 1997 Skelly Armored Car robbery. It was a big job—nine crooks on four guards. Two guards had died, along with one robber. Seven of the surviving criminals had been apprehended. They ratted on one another freely but none of them—not one— would admit to knowing the identity of the ninth man. Of the six million stolen, all but $750,000 had been recovered. It was widely believed that Boyer had killed the guards and intimidated his confederates into silence.

Two: Lee Boyer's parents, Lee Sr. and Marcia Boyer, had both been very bad news. Lee had gone to the electric chair when his son was sixteen. Marcia had died in the violent ward of an insane asylum in 1989.

Three: Lee Jr. had gotten his dairy-case nickname in 1998 when word got out that he was buying human breast milk from a teen mother in Colonia. The first guy to joke about Lee drinking it—Carl Christopherson—died in a very uncomfortable fashion not long after making his bon mot. Lee had been arraigned on Christopherson's mur-

der, but he was acquitted due to lack of evidence. No one would testify.

With these points of data—along with clues gleaned from searching Boyer's apartment, not least of which was a shelf in his kitchen well stocked with cans of Enfamil baby formula—Hasmed was confident that he was dealing with a violent, dangerous man whose childhood could charitably be described as a chamber of horrors. He was a sick fuck from a sick family, and people who would cheerfully work with murderers and convicted rape-os would shake their heads and walk away from a string with the Milk Monster in it.

When Boyer walked in, Hasmed stood and shook his hand. They exchanged a long, cool look. Boyer wasn't a big man. He was medium-tall, he was skinny, but he somehow gave the impression of being more vivid than other men. He was like a giant, tightly wound down to a smaller size and ready to burst if touched. He had the eyes of a rabid dog.

"Have a seat," Hasmed said. Boyer did. Hasmed sat across from him.

The table was scarred oak, its varnish aged almost black. Hasmed had gotten it second hand. It was covered with cup rings and dents and stains, and it had a matchbook wedged under a leg to compensate for some warping. Other than two dinner chairs, matching it in age and condition, it was the only furniture in the room. There were no windows. No rugs. No pictures on the wall. Just the door in, behind Lee, and another across the room.

"So," Boyer said. His voice was tight and sharp. "How do we do this thing? You got them cards? A crystal ball?"

"Nope."

"You gonna look at my hands?"

"Nuh uh. I just got to look at you."

Boyer sat back and spread his arms wide.

"First things first," Hasmed said. "You understand the pay thing?"

"Explain it to me, why don't you?"

"It's twenty bucks for me to try. Even if I don't see nothin', can't tell you nothin', it's twenty bucks up front."

"That's a screwjob."

"That's the deal."

"Hell, I could pay you and you just say 'Eh, the spirits an' all are cloudy, come again next week. An' bring another double-saw.' It's bullshit!"

"It's the way it works. This ain't like pumpin' gas. I don't know what's gonna be down there when I go to the well, got me? But I got to stick my hand in anyhow. Twenty up front—no returns, not negotiable. If I see somethin', you decide if it's worthwhile. If it is, you give me a hundred bucks. More looking we agree to separately."

Lee glared.

"I should just walk away from this shit."

"Door's open."

"Don't you disrespect me, Ciullo."

"No disrespect. It's your choice. Pay or walk. I'm just here."

With a snort, Lee handed over a pair of tens.

Even though the room was dim, Hasmed had kept his sunglasses on. Now he took them off.

"Fuck man. What happened to your face?"

"Is that the question you really want answered?"

"A'right, a'right." Boyer shifted right and left. "Here's the thing," he said. He paused. "The thing is…"

Hasmed just waited.

"Well, it's like a professional thing. Y'know? I been, uh, out of work for a while now."

"Uh huh."

"And it's not that I'm hurting for dough. I got enough, but you know how it is, I'd trade it all for a little more. But a man's got to work, you hear me?"

"You don't want to rust out."

"Exactly."

"Why aren't you getting work?"

"You tell me. You're the fortune-teller."

"All right. You have a bad reputation."

Something mad and deadly flickered in Boyer's eyes, but he just said, "Yeah, I guess that's right."

"Someone said something about you, and now they laugh at you. Nothing about how you work. Just bullshit about your personal life."

"Bullshit is right, Ciullo. It's bullshit, nothing but, and that cocksucker Christopherson deserved everything his

157

lying ass got." He closed his mouth, forced himself to lean back again and shrugged. "Whoever it was that killed him, you know."

"Why not move? Leave town, start over?"

"Leave Jersey?" Boyer said it like Hasmed had suggested he take up hairdressing instead of robbery. "Fuggeddaboudit. Where'm I gonna go, huh? New York? Those assholes figure anyone with a Jersey accent is a moron. Same thing in Chicago. Or, what, I should go to Boston, where they don't even know what to call a sandwich? Miami's full of spics. They run everything now that the Mustache Petes are out of it."

"How 'bout Vegas?"

"Too hot."

Hasmed nodded ruefully. "So you don't want to leave. But you can't escape these, uh…"

"Lies. Fucking *lies*."

There was a pause.

"So have I earned my hundred bucks yet?"

"You barely earned your twenty."

"All right, I'll tell you some more. Y'might not like it, though." Hasmed took a deep breath and started in on the horse crap. "You're isolated. You're lonesome. You been kicked to the curb by your friends and by people you respected. And there's a reason."

Lee took a deep breath in through his nose and said, "The next words out of your mouth better be real good ones, Ciullo. 'Cause I don't like what I'm hearing."

"It's not the reason you think. You got unfinished business, and it's hanging over your head. People in the present, they stay away because you give 'em the feeling of a broken past. You got to fix that stuff. Then you'll be okay."

"What kind of crap are you talking here, Ciullo?"

"I'm talking about your parents."

"My parents are dead."

"Yeah. Pisser, ain't it?"

❖   ❖   ❖

Betsy Smith had a very difficult morning at work, so she snuck off to a supply closet and took three deep swallows from a bottle of Rumpleminz schnapps. She'd hidden it there a week and a half earlier, replacing the bottle of Kahlua she'd finished. Her hiding place was a dark corner of a low cabinet, behind the insect repellent. Betsy kept her bottles inside

large plastic zipper bags, because she had a vague thought that the insecticide might contaminate them.

Nevertheless (she told herself) it wasn't like she had a drinking *problem*. It was after noon.

❖ ❖ ❖

The damned angel Usiel was waiting for the bus when he spotted Thomas Ramone slowing down for a stop light. Usiel—shabby and bald Clive Keene to outward appearances—didn't notice him right away. He was lost in thought.

The thrall he'd killed up north had directed him to Bayonet Point, Florida, and to another vassal named Krebbs. Usiel's plan had been to kill her and then torture her for information, but things hadn't worked out just right. The demon Vassago—patron to both Krebbs and the late John Bow—had other agents in the area that Bow hadn't known about. They had interrupted Usiel's business with Krebbs, they'd hurt him, he'd hurt them back and, in the end, he'd decided to quit while he was ahead.

He'd only killed one of the servants, but he still considered himself ahead, thanks to something he'd found in Krebbs' house. Something he'd *sensed*. Something with the reek of the Fiend upon it.

Physically, it was not terribly remarkable. It was a single earring with a diamond pendant. The diamond was large, and of good quality, but not stunning. A pair of earrings very much like it could be bought at a good jeweler for one or two thousand dollars.

But those earrings would not contain part of a demon's soul, and this one did. Just like the pendant at John Bow's house.

Usiel was not sure exactly how Vassago had managed to get his spirit sealed into a diamond, but then again he wasn't sure how he'd managed to get his own spirit into a human body. He wasn't sure how he'd recovered the scythe, his very own releasing tool. He wasn't sure what, exactly, was going on.

He was sure, however, that he would be very pleased to send Vassago back to the Abyss where he belonged.

The diamond had part of Vassago's soul, but not all or even most of it. Usiel was conflicted, wondering what to do with it. On one hand, possessing it helped him sense where the demon had other pockets of essence concealed, and if he studied it long enough, Usiel thought he might be able

to pick out a part of Vassago's True Name. On the other hand, as long as he had it, the demon's agents would be able to track him effortlessly. Destroying it immediately would weaken the rebel, and would also release some power that Usiel could reclaim.

Sweet power.

A potent, intoxicating rush of power.

Ever since his scythe had cut the tie between Vassago and Bow's pendant, Usiel had thought about somehow getting more. Even that small dose had energized him, and he could feel how much more was contained in the earring.

More than power, it was the sensation that tempted Usiel. He was not sure it was good to enjoy so much the destruction of something that could never be remade. But this pleasure was linked to strength as well, and he was disturbed by how poorly his battle against the demon's minions had gone. It was not just that they'd hurt him—they'd hurt him beyond his ability to readily heal himself. Even his mortal shell showed the marks of blows that had struck immortal flesh.

He had ultimately fled them by cutting a hole into the lands of the dead, fleeing bodily through that bodiless space until he found a place where it was easy to re-enter the physical world.

It had gotten him away, but that tactic had also been unusually difficult. The soul storm had hurt him further, and now he sat on a bus stop bench, aching, waiting to get to the airport and hoping that the servants of the Fiend would not find him before he had a chance to repair himself.

Then, as he sat musing, he became aware once more of the stink of a Hell-ridden human. His first thought was that Vassago's thralls were upon him, but as he started to his feet he realized that this was a different reek. Vassago's lackeys had a feverish stench of madness, while this was a musky, salty stink—like dead fish and dirty thoughts. With a squint, Usiel identified the man.

Has anyone in this degenerate age resisted temptation? he thought, striding toward the car. He wasn't even sure what he was going to do. He wasn't in much condition to start a fight, though looking at any corrupted mortal made his gorge rise.

The vassal turned to him without an iota of comprehension. Thomas Ramone grimaced, cracked his window and

spoke to Usiel, once one of the most feared soldiers in the Holy Host.

"Get a job!" he yelled. The light turned green, and he drove away.

Usiel glared after him.

❖   ❖   ❖

Coming home, what Hasmed really wanted was a shower, a cold beer and some quiet. He knew he shouldn't be frightened of Boyer—after all the man was merely a man at the end of the day (no matter how crazy and violent). But nevertheless, Harvey Ciullo was terrified, and that terror seeped up into Hasmed as well. He was trying to shake it off even as he unlocked the door.

"At last!" Helena said, fixing an earring into her ear. "I got to rush, or I'm gonna be late!"

"I thought you were working weekends this week."

"It's not for work!" she said, giving him a buss on the cheek.

"Tina's been okay," she whispered in his ear. "It was a nice day, so we took a walk in the park, watched the birds flying south. I told her you'd get her a kite and fly it with her. And she wants to be a ballerina for Halloween."

"Mph." Hasmed hadn't even noticed that it was a nice day. "What's she doing now?"

"Watching TV, but it's all right, it's PBS."

"Daddy, c'mere! This is neat, Daddy!"

"In a minute!" he called. He turned back to Helena. "Hey, thanks again," he said. "I don' know if I thank you enough for all the babysitting."

"She's my only niece. You know. Like the daughter I never had." For a moment Helena frowned. Then she blinked and was back to normal. "I got to go," she said.

"Daddy!"

"Yeah yeah." He shook his head. "She sounds happy."

"I think she is. Bye now."

"Bye."

"*Daddy!*"

"I'm here, kitten." With weary tread, he entered the living room just in time to catch an instant replay on *Bill Nye the Science Guy.*

"Watch!"

Obediently, he watched a slow-motion Bill Nye use the Big Hammer of Science to shatter a rose that had been dipped in liquid nitrogen.

He stood, staring.

"Cool!" Tina shouted.

"You're right, sweetie. That's definitely very, very cool...."

chapter

ten

Teddy Mason felt uneasy about deceiving his wife and son.

Well, no. That's not exactly right. Teddy felt (strangely enough) that it was entirely right and appropriate to deceive Birdie and Lance. What made him uneasy was just *how* good it felt.

At first he'd tried to put it in the category of a "white lie"—a friendly deception intended to enhance a pleasant surprise. Like telling Lance about Santa Claus when he was a little boy, or like the time he got Birdie a pair of earrings for her birthday but hid them in a weighed-down food processor box. But deep down inside, he knew that the vacation to Nevada wasn't a particularly thrilling surprise. Furthermore, if Birdie found out that it was not (as he'd told them) a prize he'd won in a raffle at the furniture store but that he had, instead, spent a good chunk of their hard-earned cash and had, furthermore, taken vacation time that the family had been leaning toward earmarking for a trip over Christmas... well the only thing *that* would enhance would be her anger.

He didn't feel uneasy. He thought he *should* be uneasy.

Nonetheless, he felt *great*. He felt alert and alive, capable and competent—more so than he had for years, maybe more than he *ever* had. He'd called Dr. Ng's office and cancelled his next appointment, citing an unexpected business meeting. He promised to call back and reschedule. Then, he simply didn't call back.

(His sex problems were gone!)

It wasn't like his family was thrilled by the trip, but he was.

"Las Vegas is so *gay*," Lance said.

"Son," Birdie said warningly. The teen rolled his eyes.

"Okay, it's *lame*. Is that, like, politically correct enough for you?"

"What's wrong with Vegas, son?" Teddy asked mildly.

"It's just all lights and stupid people and, you know, dumb old singers no one cares about. Like, Tom Jones and Celine Dion. Big deal."

"Your mother and I like Celine Dion."

"So I get stuck listening to her with you? Whee. Real fun."

"There's no reason to spend much time in Las Vegas," Teddy said. "I actually thought we might go out into the desert and do some camping."

"In a *desert?*" Birdie asked.

"I read somewhere that it's really beautiful out there this time of year. Very stark and spare but, you know... primal. It's a very powerful landscape."

"Powerful," Lance said, eyes still rolling. "If you want to go camping, why don't we go to Yellowstone again?"

"Because I won the two tickets to Las Vegas."

"But it didn't come with hotel?" Birdie asked. "That's awfully odd."

"It's a weekend for two in the hotel," Teddy lied, improvising. "We'll have to pitch in a little more for Lance's plane ticket, but I thought we could extend the trip a little and see Lake Mead and the area around it."

"I could just stay here," Lance said sullenly. "I can take care of myself."

"I'm not leaving a fourteen-year-old *boy* alone in this house," Birdie said firmly. "We could maybe leave you with the Cormans...?"

"Awwww maaaaa..."

"What? I thought you and Steve Corman were friends."

"Like, back in sixth grade maybe. Not now. You know..."

"I want Lance to come," Teddy said, his voice firm. "Look, I'm not sure how to explain this, but I really want this to be a family vacation. I don't know, I feel like this is a real stroke of luck, and I want to really grasp it while I have the chance. This might sound corny, but, uh... I feel like we've

turned a corner. Or at least *I* have. And I really want my family beside me."

Birdie looked at him closely. She was touched. Lance continued to roll his eyes, but beneath his reflexive discomfort, he was a good kid who loved his dad, so he resigned himself to going.

❖   ❖   ❖

"Hasmed?" Sabriel was cruising along Interstate 40 through Arizona, late at night. It was, against all likelihood, still raining over her. She'd decided not to get on a flight until she'd shaken the storm. Taking to the air, Avitu's native element, seemed like a singularly bad idea. She had no idea how far Avitu's perceptions were stretching, and she didn't want to take chances.

"Hasmed? Can you hear me?"

Who is that?

"It's Sabriel, Hasmed. You remember?"

What do you want?

"Hasmed, I'm hurt. Is that any way to greet an old friend after... how many thousand years has it been, anyhow?"

I don't know, and I don't care. You're free, huh?

"Yeah, I'm out in a human body. You too?"

Yeah. How could you tell?

"I've run into a couple of our number who got out a long time ago. They didn't have human hosts, and it made them... weird."

Who were they?

"One from your house who defended me against Vejovis. Another I never knew before. I'd rather not speak their names."

Fair enough. How have they gotten "weird"?

"It's hard to describe. Your old comrade, for example, is all fired up about ushering in a new age of ignorance for humanity."

From where I'm sitting it looks like one's already here.

"I've also run into your old colleague Gaviel."

There was a pause before Hasmed replied. *So?*

"Like us, he has found a human to wear."

Good for him.

"I take it you two are... estranged?"

It's none of your damn business. He's not one of the crazy ones?

"No. So you haven't run into any Elohim who've been locked in the inanimate for a long time? Who've been sleeping, maybe?"

Nothing like that around here.

"Where's 'here' for you?"

That's none of your business either.

"Hasmed, don't be that way. Surely our… condition… is hard enough without turning friends aside, right?"

Are we friends, Sabriel? I've run into fellow escapees—demons in human bodies—who were awful "weird" too. And demon-on-demon violence is hardly a rarity. If you don't believe me, invoke the Darkness of the Deeps.

"I'd rather not, thanks. Are things going well for you?"

Why do you care?

"If they're not, perhaps I can help you out."

Really? You call me up in the middle of the night, you ask me questions about dangerous, powerful, "weird" old demons, and I'm supposed to believe it's because you want to help me? You're slipping, Sabriel. You used to be more persuasive than that.

"Well… okay, yeah, you got me. I'm not in perfect shape, of course, but maybe I really can help you, you know. Yes, I'd like you to help me, but that can be a two-way street. Opening lines of communication can't hurt at the very least. Right? If each of us has accomplished something with the power of one demon, how much more could each accomplish with the power of another?"

Just what are you hoping to accomplish?

"I need followers, and I need money. Both of those are pretty simple, for me—but I need someone to watch my back while I get them."

And, as a guardian angel, I was an obvious choice.

"What is it you want?"

I need money, and followers, and I'm doing just fine on my own, thanks. Why aren't you calling Mr. Summer Sun instead of me? Are you two "estranged"?

"I could quote you something about 'your damn business.'"

Got it.

"You could be doing better, with a Lammasu to help you. Right?"

Maybe.

"Just think it over and get back to me. That's not an unreasonable request, is it?"

I'll think it over.

❋ ❋ ❋

Without hesitation, the woman standing in front of Chuck Collins pulled her T-shirt off over her head.

"Whoa," Chuck said. "Okay, so you've got the assets." He squinted but couldn't see a scar. "Those real?"

"What does 'real' mean?" she asked.

"True enough. So then, can you dance?"

"I suppose so."

"Let's see it." He reached back and started a scratchy tape. He kept meaning to get a CD player for his office but never got around to it.

She danced. He'd seen better, but with her looks, she didn't need a lot of skill.

"Right. You're clean? No drugs? Nothin' like that?"

"I'm clean." She smiled that close-mouthed smile. Her only flaw was her teeth. They weren't white enough—they were browned up like she was a sixty-year-old chain smoker. He mentioned it and told her she'd need to get them bleached on her own dime. She nodded.

"Can you start Tuesday?"

"I can start tonight, if you like."

"I didn't ask about tonight, I asked about Tuesday."

"Tuesday's fine."

"What did you say your name was again?"

"Gwynafra. Gwynafra Doakes." She spelled it out.

"That's a hell of a handle."

"It's the original Welsh form of 'Guinevere,' which got turned into 'Jennifer,'" she explained.

"Whoa, I didn't ask for your life story. Just give me your Social Security number and I'll get you filled out."

She gave him Gustavus Doakes' number, already planning the line of bullshit she'd lay on him if he ever asked why his visibly female showgirl was using a man's SSN. She didn't think he'd notice, or even care.

Gwynafra Doakes, who was animate mud formed by the will of the demon Avitu, prepared to start her career as a dancer. There was an old tradition of erotic temple dancers—or, at least there was a vague sense of one in Gustavus Doakes' memories. She was fairly pleased with her choice.

The more familiar she became with Doakes' memories, the more Avitu felt that she'd done the man a favor. If anyone was ever a consciousness addict, it was him.

They'd tried a brothel first, but to get a license, Gwynafra would have needed a blood test, and that was one thing she couldn't give.

❖   ❖   ❖

"Would you like more tea, Mr. Daddy?"

"Don't mind if I do, Miss Tina," Hasmed answered. The three-year-old hoisted up the child-sized teapot and mimed pouring tea into his fake-china plastic cup, which was almost as big as a shot glass.

Harvey Ciullo's bulky frame was compressed down to sit on one of Tina's little chairs, leaving his knees on level with his nipples. She was sitting next to him (she'd been very insistent about who sat where), and the other two chairs were occupied by a plush giraffe and a toy panda.

The table had seen better days. Helena had bought it at a garage sale, and it was permanently discolored by years of crayon rubbing and paint spills. There were patches where long-gone decals had yielded their stickiness, viscosity that had pulled in dust and grime over the years. Like silhouettes, the shapes of the stickers remained, rendered in grubbiness.

Hasmed reached down, but his stubby, paw-like hand was clumsy, and the handle of the cup squirted out from between his thumb and forefinger.

"Whoopsie!" he said.

It was fortunate that there was no real tea in the cups. Otherwise, he'd have added yet another layer to the table's discolored strata.

"I do it!" Tina shouted, popping up and grabbing a blanket off her bed. She began to polish the table—not noticing as she did so that her sleeves were upending other cups and saucers and plates of imaginary cookies.

"See daddy? I'm cleaning!"

"That's great, kitten…"

HASMED. ATTEND ME.

Vodantu's voice echoed through Hasmed's head with only a little less violence than Mike Diamond's bullet had. He twiched and shuddered. Tina didn't notice, cheerfully chirping along as she cleaned.

"Sweetie, can you excuse me for a moment?"

"You promised you'd have a tea party wif me!"

HASMED. YOUR MASTER CALLS.

"I'll be right back, honey." He rolled his eyes comically and put one hand in front of his mouth. "I have to go to the bathroom," he said in a stage whisper.

Tina giggled and he scuttled away.

Once in the washroom, he focused his attention on Vodantu's invocation.

"I'm here, Master Vodantu," he whispered.

WHAT ARE YOU DOING?

One of Harvey's leftover reflexes was to run his tongue over his right canine tooth before stretching the truth. Without thought, the body did that now.

"I'm looking after one of my thralls," he said.

WHAT PROGRESS CAN YOU REPORT ON DOING MY WORK?

"I'm still trying to get into the Mafia. Uh, that's the... the society I told you about."

YOU HAVE NOT GAINED ACCESS YET?

"They're very... secretive and exclusive. I have made overtures to several members, and I have sickened a local chieftain. I expect there to be bloodshed during the succession struggle. Afterwards, whoever assumes his position will be eager to recruit new members."

I STILL FAIL TO SEE WHY YOU DO NOT SIMPLY REVEAL YOURSELF AND DEMAND THEIR OBEDIENCE.

"I believe that it is best, at this juncture, to remain hidden. The minds of the humans are poisoned against us, Lord. Were I to declare myself as a fallen angel, few would be eager to enter my service—and those who would, would be poor specimens, despised by their fellows and of little use."

Vodantu was silent for a moment, and Hasmed wondered if the connection was broken. Then the great demon addressed him again.

PERHAPS YOU ARE RIGHT. JORIEL'S FATE GIVES ONE PAUSE, AND I AM NOT EAGER TO SEE THE DESTRUCTION OF ANY OTHERS AMONG MY SERVANTS.

"Wait, you mean... Joriel is destroyed?"

LUBIKU HAD A SERVANT SUMMON HIM, BUT WHEN THE DARK-NESS ARRIVED, HE WAS TOO DAMAGED AND MAD TO BE OF USE. I GAVE LUBIKU PERMISSION TO CONSUME HIM.

Hasmed swallowed. "The Stone of Despair is free, then?"

GREG STOLZE

HE IS. EVEN NOW, HE SERVES MY WILL IN A LAND CALLED "SAMOA." THE SAVIOR OF THE FALLING STARS WALKS THE EARTH AS WELL, DOING MY BIDDING. AND AS YOU KNOW, RABBADÜN GLORIFIES MY NAME IN THE MORTAL WORLD. ONLY YOU, HASMED, HAVE FAILED TO PERFORM EVEN ONE SACRIFICE ON MY BEHALF.

"Sacrifices are a poor substitute for freedom, master. Would you have drips of human suffering now, or the ocean of misery that will attend your incarnation?"

There was another pause.

PERHAPS YOU ARE RIGHT IN THIS MATTER, AS WELL. JUST MIND THE CAUSE FOR WHICH YOU TOIL.

"Your freedom, master. Always."

I HAVE HEARD AND FELT CHANGES WITHIN SOME LIKE YOU, WHO HAVE ESCAPED INTO HUMAN FORMS. THEY BECOME SEDUCED BY THE ATTACHMENTS OF MORTAL LIFE, DELUDING THEMSELVES THAT THEY MIGHT RETURN TO THE FAVOR OF THE ONE ABOVE LIKE THE CHILDREN OF EVE AND ADAM.

"Nonsense. What temptations could this weak body—layered in fat—hold for me? It's only a tool, and a cheap clumsy one at that. Believe me, I long for the day I can cast it aside."

SEE THAT YOU REMEMBER THAT ATTITUDE. YOU SERVE ME, HASMED. AND SHOULD YOU FORGET YOUR SERVITUDE FOR TOO LONG A TIME, YOUR NAME CAN BE GIVEN TO RABBADÜN. I'M SURE HE WOULD DELIGHT IN THE CONSUMPTION OF SOMEONE OF SUCH HIGH STATION.

Hasmed's heart beat fast, but he fought his voice calm. "I can serve you better as an agent than as a treat for some power-hungry usurper."

FOR NOW, I AGREE. BUT REMEMBER THAT ONE WAY OR THE OTHER, YOU WILL ALWAYS SERVE.

Usiel was on an airplane to Boston, wrestling with the question of whether to get a gun or not. They seemed to be very useful for harming or even just intimidating the humans, but he had a streak of pride that made him reluctant to acquire such a mundane weapon. Furthermore, Clive Keene had some very vivid memories associated with firearms, and Usiel was concerned that owning one would only increase the mental and emotional interference from his host body—interference that was already annoying enough.

He was looking out over the clouds, drumming his fingers against the seat, when somebody invoked him.

USIEL, said the voice in his mind. *USIEL, ATTEND ME.*

He ignored it. He got invoked a lot, usually demons with insults and abuse for him, empty curses and vain threats of what they'd do when they found him. The occasional invocation of hatred had been a steady feature of his imprisonment in the Abyss. It was less frequent now that he'd escaped, but some of the stronger demons in Hell could still reach him from there, even in the material world. But he was very, very good at ignoring them.

USIEL. I AM THE ONE WHO SENT YOUR SCYTHE.

That caught his attention. It was almost enough to persuade him to open himself to the communication, but he could tell that the invoker was no angel. Indeed, Usiel had seen and felt no pure angelic influence since his return to the human world—an absence that alarmed and concerned him. This speaker had the reek of rebellion on his voice, and Usiel ignored him.

After all, he thought. *It could be an ally of Vassago. Or one of the Neberu might have divined that I've recovered my releasing tool. It could be an infernal trick.*

USIEL. YOU ARE NOT STRONG ENOUGH TO CONTEND WITH VASSAGO, BUT YOU HAVE THE CHANCE NOW TO STRIKE AT A MUCH STRONGER DEMON, ONE WHO IS WEAK AFTER A LONG REPOSE.

He ignored it, trying to concentrate on an article in the airline magazine. Whoever it was, it was someone strong—strong enough to broadcast to him even when he was striving to block the message out. The article was not written for deep concentration, so it was of little use.

GLENDA FIELDING IN OSWEGO, ILLINOIS. SHE IS HAUNTED AND WILL WORSHIP YOU...

With an irritated noise, Usiel turned from the window to the in-flight movie. He didn't have headphones, so the humans on the screen looked asinine, capering silently. They were hitting one another with pies.

YOU NEED WORSHIPPERS IF YOU ARE TO BE STRONG ENOUGH TO DESTROY THE EARTHBOUND.

This was no ally of his. This was a tempter, trying to lure him into the tactics of the fallen. The lust for human worship was *their* flaw, and they would not make it his. He had his sins, but craving human adoration was certainly not one of them.

Turn aside from your pursuit of Vassago and speak with me. I shall give you a better target.

Summoning strength he could ill afford to spend, Usiel finally replied.

"Go away and shut the hell up," he hissed.

The man sitting next to him turned and gave him a blank look.

As you wish. When you learn some ugly truths, I'll speak with you again.

❖ ❖ ❖

The diamond heist wasn't nearly as slick as Hasmed had hoped. Getting the liquid nitrogen went just fine—hiding out unseen in Sargento Welding Supply was a snap. He wrecked some stuff transferring the liquid into a smaller container, but so what? Roscoe seemed nervous as hell when he dropped Hasmed a block away from the police station, but it was a full moon, the Jets had just lost a game, and the weather was wet and cold. This meant that people were irritable and drinking, and that driving conditions weren't that great. A perfect recipe for busy, distracted cops.

When he saw a paddy wagon pull up, Hasmed decided that the time was ripe. Ros had watched Jack Haskell go in and come out hours earlier, while Hasmed was jacking Sargento. The diamonds were in. The police had their hands full. Time to go to work.

Hasmed walked through the blind spots of a dozen people as he entered the precinct house. He went straight to the first door and waited.

"Fuck you, bitch! Fuck you and your bitch mama!"

"You can't talk to me like that, you cock-sucking shitball!"

Hasmed gritted his teeth as a man and woman were dragged in, both with their hands cuffed. She had a black eye. He had claw marks on his face. Each was accompanied by two uniformed officers, who were straining to keep them apart.

"Little help here?" one of the officers said. "We got that double-D here from Shady Pine Court."

"Hands full!" shouted another cop. "With you in ten!"

"Damn it," muttered the first officer. The couple from Shady Pine Court continued to scream abuse at one another.

"Cunt! You fuckin' whore cunt!"

"Asshole! Shitbag asswipe!"

Hasmed turned his face away, but he couldn't block out their voices, and the hatred—the pure, sniveling malice—pulled his eyes back. It was like a car wreck of souls. He wanted to look away but found himself staring instead.

Etched in each feature was profound loathing. It was equal parts disgust—contempt for the other caused by perfect understanding of every failing, small and large—and shame. That was what took it to the next depth, really. He could look at them and know, *know*, that they loved one another, or at least needed each other. The hate each had was mostly self-hate. Each despised in himself, in herself, the part that loved the other. And it didn't reduce the love one bit.

He knew that look. He knew he'd worn it, ages ago. Against his will, he remembered…

❖   ❖   ❖

Winter had come, and the war was going poorly.

The fall of Vejovis had been a blow to the Host, but it only made them cautious, not afraid. The rebels had ceased their sorties against Heaven after too many losses, and they were now concentrating on fortifying the material world. It was the right decision—the Holy Host was unwilling to unleash its full fury in the mortal realm, when there was a chance of damaging it further or causing human casualties—but it was hard in more than one way. It was not lost on the soldiers of Lucifer's army that their safety came at humankind's expense, and living with that wasn't easy.

Outside the emotional weight, it was also difficult to pick one aspect of reality and defend it exclusively. By operating mainly on the human scale, they ceded other realms to Heaven, which left them many fronts to protect.

Hasmed was out with Gaviel, sweeping through the Stark range in search of angelic scouts. It was just the two of them—forces were thin—and they were to flee if they encountered more than one foe. They were tense and alert, for they had never patrolled with fewer than five before. It wasn't fear as humans know it, black and paralyzing, but they were uncertain and concerned.

They didn't find angels. What they found was a small camp of humans, six of them. Four men, two women, all carrying short spears and hunched over in their cloaks and soggy furs. They had made a tiny fire, and two of them were crouching low, blowing on it, trying to raise it against the chill.

Hasmed did not speak to Gaviel—not with words, not with sound. His communication was a pattern of mathematical ripples in the contingent factors of wind and snowmelt and the fluid dynamics of hot air touching cold. Gaviel understood, of course, and he moved unseen even as Hasmed did.

"I don't think Ruchel is going to make it," one of the men said, and his voice held sorrow the way only a human could—their double sorrow, sorry for the other and also for themselves. "Myicha, do you think he'll still be... hated?"

Hasmed flowed around each of the humans, tasting their breath, and he sensed the pain and disease in all of them. Only one was close to death, though, and with a gentle caress, Hasmed wiped the illness from his brow. He didn't take it all—there was nothing to gain by revealing himself—but enough to take Ruchel out of danger.

"There!" said the man by the fire. Turning his regard, Hasmed watched it flare up and finally catch well. Unlike the humans, he heard Gaviel's words to the flames, teaching them how best to burn.

"Even if Ruchel dies, the One Above will know," said the other woman, Myicha, the one who wasn't tending the campfire. "The One will know we have turned away from blasphemy."

"If we are now once more beloved by the Most High, why doesn't He help us?" asked a man. "Where are His angels when we are cold, when we are dying, when we are injured?"

"We have not yet earned such aid," she replied. "Did we not side with the fallen, when they tempted us with blasphemous knowledge? Why should he send his agents into danger to save weak souls such as us?"

Unheard, Gaviel asked Hasmed if he ought to appear. Hasmed cautioned him to wait.

"Perhaps He will never forgive us," said a different man. "Perhaps we cannot unsay what we've said."

"It's too late now, Bachlus," said the woman by the fire. "The followers of Eve and Adam won't welcome us back—not after what we did, not after killing Darmen and Seatus. Our only hope is that Abel's tribe will take us in."

"Eve and Adam might forgive," Bachlus replied. "If the Morningstar or one of the others intercedes on our behalf. They need us. Remember what the Lady of the Waterfall Song said. Every prayer is needed. Every worshipper counts."

"The Allmother and Allfather cast out their own son for shedding blood. What chance do we have, not nursed at Eve's

breast? No, our trail is closed behind us. Only by joining the Abelites, repudiating the demons and begging God's forgiveness can we be sure of safety."

Hasmed had heard enough. With a gesture, he stood before them.

"There is no safety for your kind," he said.

Most of them cowered, and Hasmed felt a strange conflict within him. He was sorry that they were afraid of him, because they were human and he loved them, but he was also glad, because they had betrayed his cause. Hasmed was used to feeling time split and pass at different rates, he was used to being matter and spirit at the same time, or existing simultaneously as an abstract idea and as a concrete physical principle... but this was the first time he'd ever known two opposite emotions.

Only one, the woman Myicha, stood her ground. "How long have you been spying on us?"

"Long enough to save your ill friend. Long enough to save you all, by kindling your fire."

"I don't believe you."

"WOULD YOU BELIEVE ME?" Gaviel, too, unveiled himself.

"No human can doubt one of the Radiant Ones—even when he lies," she hissed.

Hasmed was taken aback. "How can you hate us so?" he asked. "Have we not fought Heaven on your behalf? Have we not given you the gift of awareness, for which you were so obviously intended? Have we not sacrificed all that we were, only for you?"

"Hah! Fought Heaven—and ruined Eden in the process. Have you sacrificed? We never asked you to! And as for your gifts, what have you given us that you did not steal from your Maker?"

Her hate was contagious. Hasmed knew he should reason with her, and he tried.

"All we did, we did for love, selfless love! Believe me, we would rather die ourselves than see you suffer..."

"Then how is it you live? We suffer every day! Thanks to you, we know age and sickness, and we know the animals' claws! You speak of your suffering, but you are not the ones subject to inevitable death, you are not the ones helpless and ignorant as others battle for your fate!"

"And so you would betray us to our enemies?" Hasmed asked.

"Rejecting blasphemy is no betrayal!"

"JUST LISTEN TO ME," Gaviel said, but Myicha turned her back, closing her eyes and covering her ears.

"No!" she shrieked. "You boast of giving us freedom, but when we choose against you, you use your words of enslavement!"

"You blame us for your misfortunes," Hasmed responded, "Perhaps you are right to do so. But we are all, man and angel alike, subject to God's wrath. Only together can we free ourselves from His curses…"

"I'll never go back with you! I'll not listen to the lies of the devils and the defilers! You sickened me with consciousness, you doomed me to mortality, but I won't spend what life I have exalting you in your treachery!"

"DO YOU REALLY THINK YOU HAVE A CHOICE?" Gaviel asked. "YOU WILL RETURN WITH US. HASMED AND I WILL SEE YOU SAFELY BACK TO YOUR PEOPLE, AND WE WILL INTERCEDE ON YOUR BEHALF…"

"I need no demon to speak for me!"

She seized her spear and brandished it, eyes wide. Neither of the Elohim paid it heed: Against them, it was as dangerous as a blade of grass.

But she wasn't planning on attacking them. As Hasmed reached out to take it away, she brought the tip up against her chest and dropped her weight forward.

"For the Maker!" she choked, fighting to speak as the spearhead pierced her heart. "For the Most High!"

Both angels screamed.

❖   ❖   ❖

At long last, a cop came out the door. Hasmed shook himself and tried to put Myicha—possibly the world's first suicide—out of his mind. It was hard. The look of loathing on her face was just like that of the arguing couple.

Glancing at them once more as he slipped through the door, he saw that they'd stopped screaming at each other. Now, instead, they were both straining, both grunting and pulling against the officers.

They weren't looking at Hasmed, but they were frantically straining *toward* him. Uneasy, he slipped through the door and closed it.

He slipped down the corridor and went down it at a fast walk. Three cops were hustling up it toward the door

from which he'd entered, and as they passed he overheard them muttering.

"…just went crazy down in the holding cells. I don't know what the hell…"

Pulling his hat down low, Hasmed walked through the field of the first camera. One down. One to go.

After a couple more turns, he went through an unlocked door and found a cop staring at him.

The officer was white with a scar on his cheek, and he had something in his eyes that said violence was quite all right by him. It was a spark of avid cruelty, and as Hasmed approached, it brightened.

"There's something here," he muttered.

Hasmed realized that the cop couldn't see him but could feel him. The wind of Hasmed's wrath was fanning the flame of this stranger's rage. And it was all getting caught on the second camera.

"Rickie, what… what're you…?" Another cop, maybe the angry one's partner, was looking on confused.

"No, there's… it's here. I can't… Listen Fred, *there's something here!*" The mad glint in Rickie's eye was blazing now, and he pulled out his gun. An eerie smile creased Rickie's face, and Hasmed wondered if Rickie longed to serve or destroy the evil he sensed. Maybe both.

"Rickie, put that…"

Rickie spun. Hasmed had been sneaking past, but the gun was now pointing in his direction once more.

"Fred man, can't you… can't you feel it?"

"Sure, Rickie. You're right. I feel it now." Fred's voice was tense as he pulled his stun gun out of its holster. "I really do." He jammed the electrodes into his partner, and Rickie dropped to the floor. He didn't even have time to yell.

The demon slipped through a doorway as he heard Fred muttering into his radio.

Clearly something was going wrong (*really* wrong) with his concealment power, but he was too far gone. No reason to stop now. He came to the second door, the one to the basement, and pulled out the canister of liquid nitrogen.

Ten minutes later, he slipped into Roscoe's car. Ros jumped.

"You startled me!"

"Drive!"

"Did you get the stuff?"

"Drive!"

Not long after that, they were in Mr. Fortune's office, spilling a paper bag of diamonds onto his black wooden table.

"Holy crap!" Ros crowed, staring. "That's unbelievable! Oh my God, man! Oh my God!"

Fortune grunted, looking down. They were just rocks, to him. He recognized that they were cut, unset stones and therefore pretty easy to fence. But really, just stones.

"Harvey, what the hell happened to your shoes?"

"That liquid nitrogen crap. When I was putting it on the door lock, it spilled on my shoes, too. Damn it."

"Your feet okay?"

"Yeah, yeah. It's just a pain in the ass."

"Worth it though. No one saw you, right?"

Hasmed bit his lip, thinking about Rickie, about the couple from Shady Pine Court, about the way he'd become a beacon for everyone crazed and violent, about the way his own sickness had seeped out and caused chaos all around...

"Fuggeddaboudit," he said. "No one saw a thing."

❖ ❖ ❖

Jennifer woke and, for a moment, felt a flood of relief. It was the same relief she'd felt every day for the past couple of mornings. There was a brief time, between sleep and full wakefulness, when she always thought she'd had a dreadful dream. For just an instant, she could hope that she was in her own bed, that Gustavus was alive, and that the world made sense.

It was that fraudulent hope that always led her to open her eyes, expecting to see her bedroom dresser, her cat, her guitar case in the corner. Instead, she saw clouds and realized that the nightmare was all true.

As with every morning, that horrible mud creature was there. She'd started wearing clothes—today a Hooters T-shirt and hip-hugging blue jeans. In her—no, Jennifer had to remind herself—in *its* hands, it held a paper bag full of bagels and bottled water.

"Are you ready to pledge yourself to me?" it asked, as it always did.

"No," Jennifer said, but it was mostly reflex. Pamela Creed, an unpublished novelist, had given in two days ago and had immediately been released. The mud monster had

taken her away and claimed that she was back in Las Vegas, returned to normal life. The other artists had discussed the possibility that Avitu had simply killed her, and had tried to believe it, but it wasn't easy when the creature could so obviously kill them all if that was its goal.

"I believe you prefer the 'everything' bagel?" Avitu said, holding one out, along with a plastic spoon and a container of cream cheese. Jennifer took it, fighting her instinct to say thank you.

"I'm curious why you won't worship me."

"'Cause you *suck*!" That was Joeesha Murfee's response. She was a sax player and not the most articulate woman in the world, but Jennifer respected her resistance to the blandishments Avitu proffered.

"Can you clarify?" the mud woman asked dryly, and Jennifer shuddered. Gustavus had talked like that, and now his words, his pat phrases, his smug tones were coming out of the mouth of this artificial whore monster.

"If worship is *good* for you, we ain't havin' none of it." This was Brandon, a high school dropout who'd decided, against all reason, to become a performance artist. "Why should we help you out when you dragged us up here, start killin' people, kidnapped us an' all the rest?"

"Isn't power one of the attributes of a deity?" Avitu asked. "Greek mythology is full of…"

"Oh *God*, I got so sick of hearing about myths when it was *Gustavus* talking about them!" Jennifer shouted. "There's more to being a goddess than just having power! Otherwise, people would be worshipping nuclear fucking warheads!"

"Or Oprah Winfrey," added Joeesha, with a quirk at the corner of her mouth.

"Then what are the other traits of divinity?" Avitu asked. "What must I demonstrate to win your willing faith?"

"Well, for one thing…" Brandon started, but Jennifer cut her off.

"No, don't tell her! Don't tell this evil bitch *anything*. Why should we help her? If she's too fucking stupid to figure out how to act, why should we clue her in?"

Avitu smiled—that sickeningly *gentle* smile—and said, "According to Gustavus's memory structure, now would be a good time to grow to thirty or fifty feet high and throw thunderbolts at you, but I don't want to terrify you into belief. That's short-lived, and it's not fair to you."

"If you don't want to terrify us, *let us go*." This was Stuart Flaubert, a painter who's primary palette was human fluids, usually his own.

"I can't do that. It would be unethical."

"*Unethical?*" Jennifer cried. On one level, she realized that she was giving Avitu just what it wanted, that it was drawing her out, but she just couldn't stop herself. "So kidnapping us and holding us prisoner *is* ethical?"

"As one of the creators of the human race, I feel a certain parental protectiveness toward you," Avitu responded, without a hint of irony in its tone or expression. "You are lost, degraded, sad and isolated creatures. You may think the best thing you can hope for is to be released back into your self-made cages, but trust me—"

"I wouldn't trust you if you was the last demon on Earth!" Brandon interrupted.

"—in the long run, you'll be much happier as my worshippers. A heroin junkie wants nothing more than his needle, but it's no favor when you give it to him. Honestly, I wish I could just take away your consciousness now, *really* I do. But there's an element of your awareness that I keenly need, and I can only take when it's freely offered—"

"So you'll just, what, brainwash or blackmail us since you can't just rip us off?" This was Joeesha again.

"Have I tried either of those things? I haven't threatened your families, though I could. I haven't tortured you or denied you sleep or kept you hungry, though I could do all those things too."

"Yeah, you're a *hell* of a hostess," Stuart said.

"Instead, I'm trying to explain to you where your best interest really lies. If I can persuade you, you'll eventually thank me."

"We'd be much more open to your persuasion if you didn't have us under duress."

"Now Jennifer, you know that's just not true." Jennifer gritted her teeth, hearing the creature's chiding tone. "If I let you go, you'd just run as far and fast as you could. Wouldn't you?"

Jennifer turned her back and raised her middle finger at the mud woman behind her.

"What I offer you is freedom from conflict, freedom from uncertainty, freedom to simply *be* without suffering

the burdens of questioning your being." The corner of her mouth quirked up. "Gustavus would call it 'existence without existentialism.'"

"*Quit talking like him!*" Jennifer shrieked. She didn't want to cry, she hated being a crybaby, but she couldn't stop herself, she cried.

For a moment, there was nothing but the sound of her sobs. Then Avitu said softly, "It's only your humanity that makes this painful."

❖ ❖ ❖

It was close to two in the morning when Thomas Ramone got home after closing Video Villa. He just wanted to brush his teeth and crawl into bed. He was exhausted and a little depressed, so he hadn't even noticed that the lights were on in his apartment.

Despite his weariness, he noticed Angela Meyerhoff when he opened his front door. She was sprawled out on his couch, stark naked and watching the TV Guide channel.

"Hi Thomas," she said. "I masturbated in your bedroom. Hope you don't mind."

"Wha... you... buh..."

"Close the door, will you? I feel a draft."

He did, mentally trying to prioritize the questions tumbling through his mind. "How'd you get in here?" he finally blurted.

She gave him a withering glance. "Oh Thomas. If you can't figure *that* out..."

"Well... what are you doing here? What do you want?"

"I just wanted to check in on my favorite piece of property. I was kidding about your bedroom, by the way." Thomas's couch had a ratty old blanket slung across the back. He'd bought it in Mexico and eventually used it to hide the cigarette burns and worn-thin patches on his sofa. As she stood, Sabriel picked up the blanket and wrapped it around herself.

"Look, I... You'd better..." He opened and closed his mouth a few more times before his brain caught up with what she'd just said. "What do you mean 'property'?"

"Well Tom, you didn't think you'd sell me your soul and that would be *it*, did you?"

"I just... figured that... you know, when I died or something..."

"Oh my, why ever would I wait that long? You're, what, twenty?"

"Twenty-four."

"So even assuming you cut your life expectancy down with cigarettes and bad decisions, that probably means I'd have a minimum, *minimum* thirty year wait until you were of any use to me. Do I seem patient to you?"

"Maybe."

"I'm not." She started gathering up her clothes and putting them on.

"Hey, why... Why were you naked when I walked in here?"

"To freak you out."

"Oh, real mature," he said, for lack of anything better. She grimaced at him.

"Currently, Thomas, our relationship is rather adversarial, isn't it? You resent me, don't you?"

"Well, *yeah*. You, you fuckin' imprisoned and starved me an' shit. How do you *think* I feel?"

"You *could* be grateful that one of the primal ministers of creation *deigned* to share her power with you. You could get it through your cannabis-numbed skull that you can now do *something impossible*, something *miraculous*. You could get the picture that you've entered a larger world, more real and more important than your daily drudgery of... what is it you do, anyhow?"

"I'm a clerk in a video store."

"Worse than I could have imagined. Honestly, why did you start robbing houses?"

"For the money, what do you think?"

"Thomas? Is that the *whole* truth?"

"Why else?"

"For the thrill."

"You watch too much TV," he said, turning away to switch off the set.

"Here I thought I'd captured a bold and unconventional man, one who sneers with pride at the hidebound conventions of law—a John Galt, an *Übermensch*, or at least a Raskolnikov..."

"Look lady, I have *no idea* what you're talking about, okay? I just want to go to bed. I'm *tired*."

She clucked her tongue. "Somebody's cranky."

"I don't like..."

"Finding naked chicks in your home?"

"Being called property."

"Can I stay here tonight?"

"*What?*"

"My lease on that house ended when I went to Chicago, and I haven't found a new apartment yet."

"No! No goddamn way! Give me one good reason not to call the cops!"

Her laughter pealed out.

"I suppose spending the night in the county lockup would solve my housing problem, temporarily. But the next day I might just stupidly go and rob a bank, wearing your face and making sure the video cameras got it all." As she spoke, her face shimmered, like a rain-dappled pond and—for a moment—Thomas saw his own image. Then she was Angela again.

He stared, appalled. "Fuck," he whispered.

"That's not part of the deal—I just want to sleep."

"You... I guess... There's not much..." He sat down in a decaying recliner and put his face in his hands. He gave a deep sigh. "Are you going to seduce me now? Is that the next part? You screw my brains out, and I turn into a servant like... like Igor for Dr. Frankenstein? Is that next?"

"You don't sound too excited about it."

"I just want to get some sleep and... and not have all this, this... you know. All *this.*"

Sabriel perched on the arm of his chair, then got back up when it shifted alarmingly beneath her.

"Thomas, I *promise* that I will never sleep with you."

He looked up, and she gave him a crooked little smile, and he couldn't help it. He laughed. It was mostly just exhaustion and bewilderment, but there was humor in it too.

"Not only that," she continued, "I promise to never give you any form of sexual gratification *whatsoever.* You're right to not want it, you know. You and I, we should keep things... strictly business. I've been busting your chops, but you know what? I'm done. I'm going to stop jerking you around, and I'm going to tell you the truth. I've spent the last couple of weeks dealing with 'artists' and 'creative types' and, shit, it's a real relief to be with someone who isn't jammed full of stale, stupid pride. Someone who doesn't assume I'm just dying to hear his opinions. You're really pretty sensible, Thomas. Don't sell that short."

"Yeah well. It's not like I've got much choice, huh? I kick you out and you'll just fuck up my life."

She smiled and shook her head with admiration. "Like I said: Sensible."

"You really need a place to stay?"

"I do. And I have an ulterior motive coming here, though it's not the one you think."

"Why am I not surprised?"

The smile faded, replaced by a look that was almost regret. "Here's the thing. I've got an enemy now."

"Just one?"

"Listen, I'm being serious!" She sat back on the couch and twisted a strand of hair around her finger. Thomas found himself wondering if it was a real nervous gesture, or just an act. "I ran into a... well, it was a demon like me but it's been here a long time, it's gotten warped and... strange. I barely got away from it."

Thomas felt like something was expected from him, so he said, "Uh huh."

"It's probably not going to give up... and if it wants me dead or bound or expelled, then it's going to probably strike at my sources of strength."

"Which means me. Right?"

She nodded. "Keep your eyes open, Thomas. That's why I'm here. Not to seduce you: I'm here to protect you."

Thomas just shook his head, tired and resigned.

"You can sleep on the couch," he said at last.

❖　❖　❖

The stone man ran.

He did not have Gustavus Doakes' brainpower and memories—those were tied too closely to the creature called Gwynafra. He did not have clothing, though the shape of tan pants and a gray T-shirt and brown boots covered the surface of his skin. His features were coarse and unfinished, and Avitu had not bothered to sculpt hair on the flawless dome of his scalp.

He did not have a name or even speak English, but that didn't matter. He ran.

He'd been running since he first pulled himself from the dirt.

Running after Sabriel.

XI
chapter
eleven

Hasmed had a busy day scheduled, but he'd built in extra time to get Tina ready for school. That turned out to be wise, because she dawdled over breakfast, argued about which clothes to wear and threw a minor tantrum getting into the car. Then, when he dropped her at pre-school, her instructor pulled him aside for a private word.

All of Harvey Ciullo's instincts said to make an excuse, weasel out, tell her he had an urgent business appointment (which was not a complete lie), but Hasmed listened closely and wrote down a time when they could meet and talk.

Consequently, he was late for his meeting with Milkman Boyer. Boyer wasn't waiting patiently.

"What took y'so long, Fortune?"

"Sorry, traffic was bad," Hasmed said as he fished out his keys and unlocked the door.

"Traffic? *Traffic was bad*? Fuck, Ciullo, if you're such a motherfuckin' seer, how come you didn't see that one comin', huh?"

"I'm sorry. I'm, look, I apologize, it's my bad, my fault. Mea culpa. You satisfied?"

"This is bullshit," Boyer muttered again, but he followed Hasmed into the office and sat once again at the oak table.

"I said I was sorry."

"You can't jerk me around like this. You know that, right?"

Hasmed took a deep breath. "Tell you what. It's my fault. I'm sorry I made you wait, so I'll blow off the usual twenty. All right? Will that square things?"

Lee Boyer looked left and right and straightened his coat lapels.

"Fuggeddaboudit," he said at last. "Let's just get down to business."

"All right." Hasmed sighed and took off his glasses. "Oh yeah. I see 'em."

"See who?"

"You know."

Boyer bit his lip and squinted. Hasmed could almost see him struggling to believe. On a bright autumn morning it was hard, but there wasn't any bright sunlight in this room. There was just the dim bulb above, the brooding bloody eye and the tight knot of scar in the middle of his forehead.

"So my parents, right." Boyer tried to sound matter-of-fact, tried to sound skeptical.

"They're your bad influence."

Boyer snorted.

"I don't mean that like it sounds. I mean they're what's messing up your life."

"Ciullo, you're starting to sound like a shrink."

Hasmed shrugged. "Here's what you need to do. An' I'll warn you, things are going to get worse before they get better. You need to confront 'em. Smoke 'em out into the open and face 'em head on. You do that, and they'll stop screwing around in the background."

"How do I do that, exactly?"

"Okay, you know that little Mexican storefront a couple doors down? You go in there; they got them miracle candles on sale."

"Miracle candles?"

"Yeah, you know. Those beaner candles, got saints on 'em an' stuff? You need two of those—one with a man, one with a woman. Doesn't matter which saint."

"Saint candles."

"Hey, I'm just tellin' you. Take those to your apartment and light 'em up. Get something your dad owned and something your mom owned. Burn the thing from your mom in the candle with the *man* on it. That's important, you

got me? The mom's thing in the man candle. And burn your dad's thing in the woman candle."

"I got to burn my parents' stuff."

"Not all the way burned up but, yeah, you gotta burn it pretty good. Like, burn a hole in it or something."

"And this... this fuckin' voodoo bullshit is going to fix my life?"

"Look, just try it. If it doesn't do anything, don't pay me a dime."

"Hmph." Boyer sucked his teeth for a moment. "That's all?"

"All for now."

He stood and tossed a pair of tens on the table. "I think you're crazy, Ciullo. I think you're off your goddamn nut."

But when Boyer went out, Hasmed opened the interior door and went into his small proper office. There was a window in there, and watching through that, he saw his client go into the bodega. As soon as he saw that, Hasmed scrambled for the elevator, got in his car and lit out for Boyer's apartment. When Lee got home, carrying a plastic grocery sack, Hasmed was spying on him through a crack in the staircase door.

As Lee Boyer shifted the bag and delved in his pocket for the keys, Hasmed took a breath and hid himself.

Boyer looked up.

Hasmed opened the stairwell door and crept into the hallway. He saw Lee's eyes peering in his direction, noticed the man's flaring nostrils, the way his lip curled back.

"Someone there?" Boyer called, and his voice was tense and menacing. Hasmed said nothing, just tiptoed closer, until he could almost smell the sweat of suspicion on his client. As Hasmed stepped behind him, the Milkman turned a little too, looking over his shoulder. With a murmured curse, he went back to his keys and opened his apartment. The demon slipped in a half step behind.

Boyer set up the candles and lit them with a sterling silver lighter. He pulled out a cigarette and made to light it from a candle, but thought better of it. He continued to peer around the apartment suspiciously—his face usually turning toward Hasmed like a steel needle twisting toward a magnet's invisible pull.

Muttering, he went back into his bedroom. He emerged a few minutes later holding a string of wooden beads.

"Okay, mom," he muttered, putting the beads on a coffee table between the two candles. Reaching into a pocket, he produced his key chain. There was an embossed leather lanyard. Hasmed leaned in and read the name "LEE" on it. As he approached, Boyer twitched, as if startled and spun around.

"Who's...?" He trailed off, and his breath was coming heavy and fast.

"All right," he grunted. "Enough. Here you go." He took the lanyard off the key chain and held it in one of the flames.

Hasmed grinned and looked around. There were some pictures on the walls—Lee Jr. with a smiling woman a long time ago, a young kid, an old woman. Hasmed pulled them off, one at a time and sent them sailing across the room to smash into the opposite wall.

Boyer jumped, then just stared, eyes wide. When Hasmed realized that Boyer's fingers were getting burned, he came close and blew out the candle. His client gave a little yelp and jumped back.

"Yeah." Boyer's eyes had a mad gleam in them. "Now you, Mommy. Now it's your turn."

As he picked up the necklace, Hasmed saw the dangling crucifix and realized it was a wooden rosary, just moments before it descended into the fire.

He tore open the door to Lee's stereo cabinet and started flinging the records out, one by one. Lee lunged toward him and Hasmed sidestepped, pausing to grab some old trophy off the top of the TV and hurl it straight at the candle.

"Hurts, huh?!" Lee shouted, swinging the burning crucifix through the air blindly—but surprisingly close to Hasmed. "Well you can *both* burn!"

Hasmed tipped a chair over and Lee lunged toward him. For a moment, the demon thought that Boyer had him trapped. The man wasn't running away from these unseen powers, he was running *toward* them. He couldn't stay away.

Hasmed grabbed a tall book case and half-climbed it to get out of Lee's way. As it took his weight, it tilted forward. Boyer stumbled back, and Hasmed himself barely got out from under before it crashed to the floor.

"Yeah! *C'mon!* That all you got? Come on you shitty old fucks! Come on! *Come on!*"

Hasmed decided that was just about enough. He smashed a foot through the coffee table for good measure and slammed the door on his way out.

❖ ❖ ❖

Still the stone man ran.

He wasn't particularly swift, but he was strong. He never got tired or distracted or bored. He was chasing the storm his master had made, and that storm had chased Sabriel all the way home.

It was twenty-five hundred miles from Las Vegas to Miami, and the stone man ran every step of the way.

❖ ❖ ❖

Usiel was in Washington, DC, and he could feel the stink of diabolical power as he neared his target. Clive Keene's memories were stunned at the thought of demons in the US capital—stunned but somehow, not really all that surprised. He was more curious about why the evil's epicenter was the Smithsonian, instead of the Capitol or the White House.

The angel within Clive Keene cared little for such theories and distinctions. He knew he was getting close to Vassago, close to the core of its being. He had a vague sense of the demon's machinations—it was ready for him, it had called its defenders, but Usiel was confident. Let them come. Let them try to save their foul master or rescue him. Heaven's wrath would not be stayed by mortal hands.

In the war against Heaven, the demons had developed any number of low tricks—theirs was the side that had invented deception and murder and ambush, after all. One of the dirtiest was a sort of cosmic cannibalism. The demons had learned how to steal the power of a dying angel, using it to augment their own.

Usiel had never sunk to such tactics back then. He'd never needed to, but now he felt Vassago's stolen strength—twice stolen, taken from humanity by the fiend and now taken from it by Usiel—throbbing within him.

He'd succumbed to his craving and destroyed the diamond earring, consuming that delicious little morsel of his enemy. An appetizer. Now he couldn't wait for the main course.

Usiel strode through the doors of the museum and saw his adversary's pawn—a big man, brutish, lurking behind the leg of a stuffed mammoth and holding a scruffy overcoat. The demon's stench was strong.

"Excuse me, sir."

Usiel ignored the guards completely until one grabbed his shoulder. With an irritated shrug, he tried to slip the grasp. Another guard grasped him by the arm.

Grunting once, softly, Usiel called his releasing tool. He had nothing against the guards, but time was of the essence. With two blows, they dropped—not dead, but neither were they alive. Their souls had been expelled into the ghost storm, and until they could fight their way back (if, indeed, they could) their bodies were useless. Usiel didn't particularly care if they recovered or not. He was clearing his path toward his true enemy, the vassal.

He saw fear in the big man's eyes and began to run forward. The man flung his coat in panic and screeched, "Back off!"

With a neck-rattling snap, Usiel's charge was halted. His eyes widened as he felt immense power propelling him back, power he couldn't fight.

Holy power.

The compulsion shoved him back into a small chamber, a coat-check room. Amazed, Usiel struggled against it, but there could be no doubt. This was not infernal strength. This was angel strength, laced with the potent will of humankind.

Cursing, Usiel changed into his true form, but even that was impotent against the unseen barrier. There could be no doubt that this was sacred might... channeled through the abased slave of an Earthbound demon.

His puzzlement turned to anger. Had the Choir Above forgiven the thrall of a rebel, somehow unaware that it continued to serve? Surely not. More likely the man was a priest or some other sanctified warrior, tempted into diabolical service.

Stymied by the barrier, Usiel shifted himself into the realms of the dead and was shocked to realize that the wall didn't exist there. Now even more confused, he stepped past it and returned to the human realm.

Three mortals—clean ones, more security—stared in shock and opened fire with their pistols. It took only the

surge of Usiel's wings and two sweeps of his scythe to fell all three. As he struck, he felt a nearby flow of infernal power. When he looked up, he faced no man, but the shape of one of the fallen.

The man-become-demon had wings of night, darkness for skin and razor spines protruding from his hands and head and the joints of his limbs.

"Hey," his opponent said. "C'mere y' big fucko!"

Again, Usiel vividly felt the tangled mix of the sacred and profane, and it sickened him. Whatever this man was, whatever he'd done, he must be destroyed.

Then it spoke again—this time in the tones of one of the unhallowed.

"USIEL! MOST POTENT OF SLAYERS AND MOST DESPISED!"

Usiel examined his enemy, pointing his weapon to keep it at bay, judging what its strengths might be, its weaknesses...

"I WAS NEVER CURSED WITH THAT TITLE, FIEND." Usiel responded. "I NEVER MIRED MYSELF IN THE FILTH OF BETRAYAL."

He edged little closer.

"AND YET YOU WERE CONDEMNED NONETHELESS, USIEL. DO YOU THINK YOU CAN SURVIVE LONG, CRUSHED BETWEEN THE RAGE OF HELL AND THE SCORN OF HEAVEN?"

Usiel knew he should ignore its taunts, but that one struck home. Why should this polluted human carry the blessings of uncorrupted angels when it was clearly the pawn of the Neberu? Why should this mere man fling God's wrath at Usiel, who never doubted His orders, who never disobeyed, and who continued the war even after being rejected?

"IN DESTROYING YOU, I SHALL DO HEAVEN'S WORK!" Usiel took a mighty swing, but his enemy lunged in and grabbed the haft of the scythe before the blade could reach.

Folding his wings around him, Usiel felt the battling energies, light and dark, within the man, and he realized a part of Vassago's dangerous game. The light illuminated the demon's darkness, and as Usiel struggled with the thrall, smelling its sweat and hearing its grunts, he felt the shape of its master too. For just a moment, he saw its secret self. It was a slight glimpse, but enough to read a syllable of Vassago's True Name...

Then the pure strength was upon him again, burning him, searing him as if *he* were the monster, *he* the rebel. The man was pushing the power through its hand into his.

"Burn, you fucker!" shouted Vassago's slave. Usiel could feel the consuming power cutting through his hand, and his fingers dropped off like ripe fruit. He shrieked and swung his weapon one-handed, cutting through the lies of demon wings, bringing the cold truth of human frailty…

"Back!" Again, the compulsion of the power Usiel could not resist—the power he hoped to *serve*. As it tore him away from his enemy, Usiel took one last swing, slicing across the man's chest, trying to reach the heart… but no. The monster fell, but rose again, grabbing its coat, shedding its grotesque form and returning to its bulky human guise.

Usiel instinctively strained against the ward before he realized something: The demon's focus was gone. The core of its being… the very object he'd come to destroy… he could no longer feel it!

Furious that he'd been tricked, denied and injured, Usiel fled once more into the realms of the dead.

❖   ❖   ❖

"So he says, 'What kinda fairy name is *Philly Phil*?' An' Philly Phil don' say nothin', just comes right off the barstool into his groin, grabs him by the back of his hair, slams him mouth-first into the bar—and it had one of those big brass rails onna front, like this—slams him into that and says 'It's *my* fairy name.'"

Vietnam Ham laughed as he concluded his story, and his bodyguards laughed, and the bookie from Trenton who was drinking on Hamish's dime laughed too. The only person who didn't laugh was Hasmed, but he'd just walked in.

Hamish picked up a curly fry, dipped it in ranch dressing and crammed it into his mouth as he noticed his new guest. "Well well! Hahvey Shooleo, Mr. Fortune, my favorite gypsy fortune-teller!"

"Good afternoon, Mr. Brennan."

"Ach, you c'n call me Ham," he said, in tones that subtly indicated that he did not mean what he was saying. He tilted his head. "Y're lookin' well, Shooleo. Lost some weight?"

"I've been working out a little bit."

"Heh. Well, what brings y' to the Mac?"

"I was hoping we could talk."

"Aren't we talking?"

Hasmed's face took on a slightly embarrassed cast, but it didn't quite fit. It was like he was indicating embarrassment for the benefit of others, who weren't expected to believe it.

"Uh, I was hoping we could talk... alone. Y'know." He shuffled his feet. "I got a thing."

"A thing." Hamish looked at the bookie, who excused himself to go to the can. His bodyguards looked at him, and Hamish shook his head gently. "Well Hahvey, we could, y'know. Step out."

"Take a little walk."

"Might help my lunch go down." Hamish stood off his stool and led Hasmed out the bar's back door. Strolling through a greasy and garbage-strewn alley, Hasmed shuffled closer and gave Hamish a diamond.

"What's this?" Ham asked, nonplussed.

"My thing."

Ham frowned at it, and it disappeared in his pocket. "Seems a fine thing."

"It's not a *fugazi*, if that's what you're thinkin'. It's real."

"I never said 'twasn't."

"Have one of your guys look at it."

"I know a man."

"Good."

"An' you'll be wanting something?"

"It's a gift."

That stopped Ham in his tracks.

"A gift?"

"A present, me to you."

"Generous."

"Well, you know. I'm hoping you can help me out."

"Ah." Hamish Brennan chuckled. "Y'mean you're only giving me a present to get my help? Well, that's the way of the world."

"I've got more."

"More like it?"

"Uh huh."

"How much more?"

"A lot."

"Hm. And were did you get them, pray tell?"

"I got them."

"Ah." Ham narrowed his eyes. "When you got them...?" He rubbed a finger alongside his nose, and pulled downward at a bag under his eye. Hasmed shook his head.

"You sure?"

Hasmed nodded.

They'd reached the open air. Neither spoke as they crossed a street and started walking down a second alley.

"That's all right then," Hamish said.

"Trust me, you'd've heard."

"I don't hear everything."

"You'd've heard this."

"All right then."

There was another pause. Then Hasmed said, "I'll get screwed."

"Everyone gets screwed," Ham said, philosophically.

"Overhead."

"Middlemen."

"Right."

"Everyone takes a cut."

"I know."

"But with this pie..." Brennan shrugged. "Even a cut up piece, that's still sweet, right?"

"Right."

They reached the end of the second alley.

"It's nice that you came to me with this," Brennan said. "Who else?"

"We'll make this thing happen." Vietnam Ham patted Harvey Ciullo's cheek paternally then turned to go back to his bar. After a few steps, he stopped, turned and tilted his head. "You're really pulling yourself together, ain't you?"

"I'm tryin'."

✦   ✦   ✦

Sabriel used up all the hot water before Thomas got a chance to take his shower. When he emerged, goose-pimpled and surly, she was digging into a bowl of Count Chocula.

"Morning, sunshine," she said. He glowered.

As he poured a bowl for himself, she said, "I'm afraid you're out of milk."

He slammed the box on the counter.

"Why do you even got to eat at all?" he demanded. "I thought you were a big hotshot *goddess*, huh?"

"I've got a mortal body. I eat, I shit, I pit out my T-shirts," she said around a mouthful of brown pellets.

"I don't believe this."

"Believe it." She swallowed. "I'm sorry I drank all the milk, so I'll make it up to you. Hand me my purse?"

"Yes, master," he said sarcastically. The purse was Christina's—now a little battered from being stowed in various overhead compartments. Sabriel opened it, pulled out a fat wallet and yanked out ten bills.

"There."

Thomas looked. They were hundreds.

"Are these real?"

"No, Tom. They're counterfeit. I want to get you in trouble because I figure you'll be better protected in jail, where my enemies can't reach you. Even though the power I specifically *gave* you is the power of freedom."

"Hey, no need to be so sarcastic."

"So does that cover the milk?"

"Where'd you get the money?"

"Las Vegas, but I don't want to talk about it." She looked over her shoulder. "Coffee's ready. You take it black?"

"Sugar, no milk," he said automatically. "Thanks."

"Are you afraid of me, Thomas?"

He sighed. "Do we have to get into this first thing in the morning? Yes, I'm afraid. You know I am."

She nodded. "I'm sorry, it's just that… you have to believe in me. I *need* you to believe in me."

"What for? You got all this money, you can… Shit, I have no idea what you can do. Change yourself around, I've seen that. Turn into water."

"This choco-crap feeds my body, but your belief feeds my soul. That's not poetry. That's truth, the same way shit feeds a dung beetle."

"You say the sweetest things."

"Right now, you are my sole source of nourishment."

"I'm your shit, then? Sure explains how you been treating me."

She shrugged. "You have to cut me some slack, Thomas. I'm trying."

"You're *trying* to treat me well by breaking into my place, by using up all of everything and playing these weird head games and freaking me out? What do you do when you're trying to treat someone *bad*, huh?"

She told him about Nate Kowalski and Hal Guelder. For a moment, he just sat, confused and shocked.

"Why?" he finally asked.

"Because I'm bitter and mean, and I hate humankind, Thomas. That's what I am. That's what I have to be."

"But... I mean, couldn't you—"

"*I don't know how to be nice!* Okay? I do not know how to treat people kindly. You got it? This human suit I'm wearing, *she* knew, but I'm not about to go to her for advice, she spent her life getting knocked up and knocked over. That's what nice got *her*, so what I'm trying to do is be honest with you and try my hardest not to destroy you accidentally."

"Shit."

They sat in silence for a moment. Thomas got up and started to make himself some toast.

"Maybe I'm bein' dumb," he said at last, "But you were nice to Nate and Hal, right? Until you... you know."

"Until I closed the deal."

"Right. So, why couldn't you... you know, *act* like you're setting someone up, then just not screw him over?"

She sighed and looked up at him, and for a moment Tom felt weird. For a moment he felt sorry for her because she looked sad.

"You might as well go to an alcoholic and say, 'Why can't you pull the top off the bottle, tilt it up to your mouth and let the booze inside just barely touch your lips... then put it down?' I don't know that I can stop myself. Be on guard, Thomas. I don't want to hurt you. I don't want to tear up your heart. So I'm not even going to give myself the chance."

The toast popped up. Thomas put on butter and jam in silence.

"So what can I do for you, huh?" he asked at last.

"Find me some others like you."

"What do you mean, others like me?"

"I mean people who will submit to me."

"If you mean, help you tie people up in a basement, shit no. No. That's all, no."

"I mean people who *want* things. The more support I have, Thomas, the less I have to rely on you. As my only believer, you're a big fat target. Anyone who comes after me will kick you out of the way first to starve me weak. The more

believers I have, the less likely you are to get picked, just by sheer odds."

"Jesus."

"Look, it's not as bad as you think."

"Playing soul pimp to some fuckin' demon from Hell isn't bad?"

"Souls, bah, who cares? I'm not going to devour your soul when you die, Thomas, honest. I was bullshitting about that. I couldn't take it if I wanted to. The fate of your soul, the afterlife, it's as much a mystery to me as it is to you. I want *life*, not death. And I can offer a lot to people."

"And what do I get out of this? Other than the ability to be the Amazing Puddle Man?"

"What do you want?"

He took a long sip of his coffee and thought about it.

"Well, for starters I'd like a new job."

Hamish Brennan phoned Sal Macellaio the day after getting the diamond, but it wasn't a good time.

"I got a thing," Sal said.

"A thing you're doing, or a thing you got to do?"

"A thing I got to do. Came on kind of sudden."

"You want I should come out and help?"

Sal thought about it for a moment.

"Eh," he said noncommittally. "I guess. Meet me out north, 'kay?"

"North where?"

"That one place. You know. With the thing?"

"With the big thing or the little thing?"

"The big thing."

Twenty minutes later, Hamish parked his dark blue Cadillac sedan in a junkyard and climbed out of it. Sal's dark red Cadillac sedan was parked deeper in, and Ham could hear the car crusher working. He walked over to its control booth as the great hydraulic plates turned a large car into a small cube.

Sal was working the levers.

"So," Hamish asked, jerking his head at the auto being squashed. "Whose was that?"

"I'm guessing Steel Pete, but I don't know. It was an import."

"Messy or clean?"

"He tried to clean me, but I wound up cleaning him."

Like Sal, Steel Pete was the captain of a large local crew. There had been rumblings lately that Pete was the heir apparent to Johnny Bronco, who was in stable condition but still sick and vulnerable.

"You tell anyone about this foreign cleaner?"

"I'm tellin' you," Sal said, raising an eyebrow. Between two old friends like them, that eyebrow might as well be a billboard emblazoned with KEEP YOUR MOUTH SHUT in bright yellow letters.

"What if Steely didn' send him? What if it was someone outside tryin' to move in?"

"Whos'at gonna be? Boston? New York? Fuggeddaboudit. They'd be more likely to ice Petey or Bronco himself than come after me. I'm the bastard they'd want to *back*." He shifted a lever forward and then another back. Steel groaned in reply. "They'd think I'm Judas."

"Oh yeah? You're Judas?"

He shrugged. "No one's offered me thirty pieces of whatever yet."

"Ah."

"So. What's on your mind?"

Vietnam Ham showed him the diamond. "From *Shooleo*," he said.

"Yeah, so?"

"'Tisn't a payment, either. A 'gift.' An' there's more like it."

Sal just frowned at him for a moment. "Get outta here," he said at last.

"Nah, I think he's f'real. I think he made a serious score here."

"And he wants you to fence it."

"Yeah."

"Where'd he *get* it?"

"Don' know. But not from anyone mobbed up. He was pretty sure 'bout that."

"He fuckin' better be." Sal rubbed his face, grimacing. "This makes no sense. Harvey Ciullo? The joke? I mean, that moron? Where's he gonna get a bunch of diamonds and no one even hears? There's something weird about that guy Ham. Something weird is going on."

"So what do I do?"

"Fence his rocks. Take the typical 50% commission, then take it again."

"He knew we'd do that," Brennan said softly. Sal grimaced again and gave the levers one final jerk.

"Yeah, well, fuck'im. We can use the money. An' if he keeps screwing around in our territory, I'll have 'im clipped," Sal said, climbing out from behind the controls.

He did not say "again," but he thought it.

✦ ✦ ✦

The next day, Sabriel took Thomas out to lunch. He warily suggested a place that served really good fish tacos.

"So, where'd you say all this money came from?" he asked.

"Las Vegas," she said.

"Big winner huh?"

"Something like that."

"Hell, if you wanted to gamble, you should've just stayed here in Miami," he said, as their meals arrived. "All kinds of flash rollers around here."

"Is that so," she responded, curling a lip at her food.

"Sure. I guess it's mostly the dog races and jai alai, but all the college sports too, y'know? Man, I had a buddy who went to the University of Miami. He said these guys would be sitting on the sidelines of basketball games and, like, making bets on the guys taking warm-up shots. Not little bets either, serious cash. It's crazy."

"Really?" She tilted her head, considering. "I thought that gambling on college sports was... frowned upon?"

"Not in Miami. Here's it's fuckin' *smiled* upon. Don't get me started with the football program, either."

"Why not?"

"Aw man, it's just crazy. These guys who can, like, hardly sign their names are getting degrees in business and shit. And these guys are mostly poor kids—some of 'em from ghettos an' shit—but they're walking around with diamond rings and two-hundred-dollar sneakers. I heard there's a car dealer who gives a Jeep to every running back who catches a tie-breaking pass, or something like that."

Thomas paused and looked up. Angela wasn't eating, just looking off into the distance.

"What?"

"Sorry," she said. "Just woolgathering. So, is Monday good for you to start a new job?"

"What?"

"You want one, right?"

"Yeah! How'd you find me one so fast?"

"I didn't find it. I created it."

He narrowed his eyes. "What've I got to do?" His tone was a mixture of dread, suspicion and resignation.

"It's nothing *bad*. You'll be a clerk in a bookstore, all right?"

"A bookstore?"

"Yes. I've bought controlling interest in a floundering local establishment called the Threshold Bookstore."

"Never heard of it."

"What, a bookworm like you?"

Thomas flushed.

"I'm sorry," she said. "That was cruel. It's a New Age bookstore."

"Oh."

"What?"

"I think I get it. I work there and I tell you who's buying, like books on demons and devils and shit, right?"

"Right. The Necronomicon for Dummies and such. That would go a long way towards gaining you some company in my service, yes?"

Thomas didn't look her in the eye, but eventually, by the end of the meal, he'd mumbled his acquiescence. Sabriel smiled and paid for lunch and thought about how to make her pitch to Hasmed.

❖   ❖   ❖

Driving to the YMCA, Hasmed got paged. At a stoplight, he looked down at the message and smiled. Milk Monster Boyer was eager to see him again.

Roscoe Paum was already in the locker room when Hasmed entered. He was idly tilting his head from side to side, rolling his shoulders to loosen them up. "Hawvey," he said. "What's the good word?"

"I talked to a guy about the thing."

"Yeah?"

"He can move them."

"Hey, that's great!"

"It's not bad." Harvey opened his locker and began to strip. "We're gonna get a tiny piece of what they're worth but, well, you know."

"Huh? How come?"

"'Cause we're not connected is how come." He pulled on track pants and an old LA Rams sweatshirt and started to lace up his shoes.

"You took it to a made guy?"

"Close enough. I took it to Hamish Brennan."

Instinctively, Roscoe looked around to make sure no one was listening. He moved closer and lowered his voice.

"Hawv, is that smart? Do you want the mob knowing you're putting strings together?"

"They'd find out eventually. Might as well be open about it." He stood and stretched backward. "As long as they're getting rich ripping us off, why should they care?"

"I guess, but... Jeez Hawv..."

"Fuggeddaboudit. We'll have our money in a week or two at most."

They exited the locker room and started jogging gently around the indoor track.

"Let's talk about somethin' else," Hasmed said. "I just heard from an associate down in Miami, an' she said something real interesting."

❖   ❖   ❖

Chuck Collins frowned. There was something weird about that new chick.

Not that there wasn't something weird about a lot of the dancers—a couple of them had names that made "Gwynafra" sound as plain as vanilla ice cream. Some of them were flaky or neurotic or just plain bitches. That was okay. Chuck had been putting together dance shows for a long time (even if he'd never made the big time), and he could deal with that stuff. Anything but the goddamn druggies.

Chuck had a lot on his mind, running a small show in the shadow of Vegas' glitzy *big* shows, but in the back of his head, some small part of him kept picking at the idea of Gwynafra. There was nothing about her specifically that he could put his finger on. She danced okay. She hit her cues okay. She smiled and waved at the fans okay. The audience reacted okay.

Maybe that was it. She was just okay.

A gal like that—and in the privacy of his own head, Chuck could admit that she was freakin' gorgeous, the best looking piece he'd ever had on his stage—should be making the watchers really watch. But they weren't. He'd put a picture of

her out front on the marquee, and that brought in the gents. But once they were in, they watched her dance for a while then just looked away to Bitsy or Starshine or even that weirdo Trunella.

It was like the picture of her was more real than she herself was.

But Chuck didn't let himself think about that too hard.

One night after the show, he followed her. He didn't even feel particularly creepy about it—he'd followed his girls before, when prompted by a gut feeling. It wasn't a sex thing, a voyeur thing. He was just protecting his investment.

He wasn't particularly surprised that she went to an Alcoholics Anonymous meeting at a local Lutheran church. He was somewhat surprised when he saw her talking to one of the drunks after the meeting broke up. A dancer talking to a guy was no big thing, but the guy she picked—cheap clothes, old, broken teeth. Even at an AA meeting there were much likelier marks, but she was talking to the hobo-est boozebag there.

Chuck was uneasy about her spotting him, but his curiosity got the best of him. When the guy went to the bathroom, Chuck did too. He followed the man out of the can, took a different cross-corridor and lurked around the corner.

"Drinking is just a temporary solution to a permanent problem," she was saying, in that weird school-teachery tone she sometimes took. "You drank to ease your pain, right?"

The man muttered something affirmative.

"But you were just trimming away its branches. I can give you something that will take it out at the root."

The man murmured in reply. He sounded uncertain.

"Trust me, Jake. I used to be as trapped and miserable as you, but there's a way out. Please?"

Jake mumbled again, but it sounded to Chuck like the man was caving in.

❖ ❖ ❖

Threshold Books had a bad location in a strip mall. It was crowded between a 7-11 and Fong's Dry Cleaning. It was tiny and cramped and out of the way.

Furthermore, its owner not only had a bad head for business, he didn't like to carry supplies related to Voudoun and Santeria—two of the largest "alternative" religions in the region. He was a pagan, but more of the Earth-Friendly,

harmony and meditation type. His name was Free Feurstein, and he'd been on the very edge of bankruptcy when Angela Meyerhoff stepped in with enough cash to keep him afloat and some demands that seemed very reasonable (at first).

One, she wanted a job for her friend Thomas. Two, she wanted to start carrying the ritual materials that her new partner had heretofore shunned.

He balked, pointing out that the Voudoun people were all buying their stuff at John the Conqueror's, while the Santeria clientele shopped at Frieda Cortez's place.

"Don't worry about that," Angela had said. "Just get the stuff in stock."

Surprisingly, it was only a week later that the proprietress of John the Conqueror's Bookstore closed up shop and left town. Free was able to buy up most of her stock at a deep discount. Rumor had it that she'd seen a vision of an evil spirit and that it had frightened her enough that she was going back to Haiti.

As for Frieda Cortez, she had a hard nose for business and wasn't going to let anything scare her. Nonetheless, her store suffered a terrible blow when it unexpectedly flooded, ruining almost half of her stock. She stayed in business, but the cost of replacing the damaged goods trashed her cash flow, forcing her to lower prices to increase turnover. But with her profit margin narrowing, it would take her longer and longer to recover from the damage, and in the meantime, Threshold could take away a lot of her customers.

At least, that was how Angela explained it to Free.

The stone man encountered some trouble on the eighth day of its run. It was loping up and down the hills of a back-county highway when a pickup pulled up alongside.

"Hey mister, y'need a ride somewhere?"

The stone man said nothing, because he couldn't speak.

"Hey!"

Nothing but the sound of his heavy tread on gravel.

"You all right? I mean, you have an accident or somethin'? Or you just joggin'?"

"Damn, Clancy, sounds like he's ignorin' you."

Darren and Clancy, the two teenage brothers in the truck, were bored and restless. They were driving around aimlessly, sipping on juice boxes, listening to Travis Tritt,

Greg Stolze

and talking about who they'd rather nail, Shania Twain or
Beyoncé Knowles. Running along and ignoring them, the
man was a distraction. They sped up and pulled over directly
in front of the stone man.

"Just where you headin'?" they asked, but he detoured
around them and kept running. Clancy—the big brother,
eighteen and on the swim team—sprinted after him, easily
catching up and getting right in front of him.

Without breaking stride, the running man smashed him
out of the way.

"Ow, you fucker!"

"Clancy, you okay?"

Clancy rose, grimacing and holding his side. "That
motherfucker," he hissed as his face twisted with sharp
pain again.

"Son of a bitch!" Darren yelled, and picked up a rock. It
was a good-sized rock, about five pounds, and he gave it a
nice, hard overhand throw. It hit the man in the back of the
head and bounced off. The man didn't break stride.

"What the fuck?" Darren said, and there was dread in his
voice.

"Shit man, I think he broke my rib!"

"Let's go, then… let's get you to the hospital, 'kay?"

"Not yet," Clancy said, his eyes squinting up. He went
over to the truck and started climbing—grunting and biting
his lip—up into the driver's seat.

"Clancy, what you doin'? There's something weird 'bout
that guy. Somethin' ain't natural."

"All the more reason." He pulled the seatbelt across,
then hissed with pain and let it go.

"Let's just go, huh? Just get you to the hospital?"

"You wanna leave that thing out running around?"

"Maybe… maybe we hassled him enough, huh?"

"You said yourself he wasn't natural." Clancy reversed the
truck and aimed it down the road. "You gettin' in or not?"

Later, Darren would wonder why he got in. He guessed
it was because Clancy was his brother.

Clancy himself couldn't have explained his behavior. His
pride was wounded, certainly, and he was physically hurt, but
mostly it was fear. He didn't understand this man, this *thing*.
It had hurt him, and he wanted to strike back. In fact, he

needed to strike back. That was his only alternative to being afraid for the rest of his life.

So he gunned the truck's V8 engine down the highway as hard as he could and aimed the grille for the dead center of the mystery runner's back. Darren was groaning with fear beside him, but Clancy had to do it. He didn't really understand that even a fleshy body can do tremendous damage to metal vehicle (or, in this case, a metal vehicle with a fiberglass and plastic body). And of course, he had no way of knowing that what he was charging had the weight and density of a granite boulder.

The crash was tremendously loud.

The front of the truck crumpled around the stone man, flexing like a juice box bendy straw. Both boys slammed forward as the air bags deployed. Since Clancy didn't have a seat belt on, he slid to the left, caught the corner of the airbag and got his head slammed into the window. He died. Darren got two ribs popped free of his sternum when the seatbelt caught, but he was alive to see the man they'd hit pry himself free of the wreckage.

Later, he told the police that it looked like the man was scored with hundreds of cracks. He told them the man was bleeding gray dust, but they just wrote it off as the effects of his concussion.

He wasn't as smooth or as fast, and he seemed to lurch a little when he moved his left leg, but the stone man started running again.

❖ ❖ ❖

It had taken Sal most of his afternoon to find out where Ciullo had gotten the diamonds. He knew he should have been paying attention to other things—angling for Johnny Bronco's forgiveness, aligning himself with some outside action or trying to figure out what Steel Pete was doing—but the Ciullo thing bugged him. He'd checked in with his street ears, talked to people who knew stones, bought a couple cups of coffee for cops on his dime, and he'd eventually dropped a grand on a copied police station surveillance tape.

Now, sitting on his couch with a cigar, Sal couldn't stop watching it.

He heard the doorbell ring and heard his wife's cheerful greeting, and within moments, Vietnam Ham Brennan was ushered into Sal's TV room.

"So," Ham said. He took in Sal's tracksuit and cigar and allowed himself the momentary hope that this was a social visit. But the look on Macellaio's face killed that thought quick.

"Watch this tape, Ham."

"Got any fucking on it?"

"Just you and me getting screwed," Sal said sourly.

Hamish sat on the couch, a respectful distance from his boss, and watched.

"This is from a surveillance camera in a precinct house," Sal said.

They watched.

"What'm I lookin' for, exactly?"

"You see that guy, the one with the hat?"

"Yeah."

"See how he got out of the way of those uniformed cops?"

"Yeah. So?"

Sal shrugged. "Okay, here's the good part. This is from another camera."

There was a haze of static, and then they watched as the hatted man entered a chamber with two cops. There was no sound, but it was clear from body language that one of the policemen was agitated. The antsy cop pulled his gun and was waving it around. The man with the hat moved out of his way—not dodging, but acting like he was tiptoeing, even though he was clearly visible in the washed-out fluorescent light.

"What the hell is that?" Vietnam Ham asked.

"Just watch."

Hamish watched as the other cop pulled out his stun gun and put his partner down. He even chuckled a little, until a soft, irritated noise from Sal made him stop.

"The weird cop—the one who pulled his piece—that's Rickie Rosen."

"The pit bull?"

"Exactly."

Both men knew about Rickie Rosen. He wasn't dirty in the conventional sense of taking bribes and making himself useful. He was dirty because he beat the crap out of restrained suspects, because he terrified waffling witnesses into following the police script, because he preferred to kill criminals and then press unlicensed guns—drop-pieces seized in raids

but never processed—into their dead hands so that he could claim self defense. He was a psycho, a killer. A pit bull.

"So he Section-Eighted on the hat guy and his partner put him down? That's strange."

"It's not even that. It's *stranger*'n that. Watch 'em again," Sal said, rewinding. "He points the gun *towards* the guy in the hat, but not right at him. Neither one of them ever looks straight at the guy."

"So, what are you thinking?"

Sal couldn't say it, wouldn't, but he was thinking about Ciullo in the steel mill, the way the shadows had crept around him…

"The diamonds were in the police lockup," Sal told Hamish. "Someone—this guy, I think—cracked the locks with liquid nitrogen and stole the rocks."

"Why not use a pick?"

"Don' know. The bigger question is, how come no one saw him?"

Hamish shrugged. "Well," he said, "There's no way they're going to let this guy go, right? I mean, robbing a police station, that's fookin' barmy, right?"

"Yeah," Sal said quietly. "It's *stugaz*. Kind of thing you'd expect from a guy with brain damage."

They were quiet for a moment.

"Ciullo is probably involved, yeah," Vietnam Ham said. "Turns out I'm not the only guy to get a gift."

"Yeah?"

"He sent one to Johnny Bronco as a 'get-well present.'"

"Wasn't he the last guy to talk to Bronco before he had that real bad attack?"

Hamish shrugged. "Y'think the cops'll find 'im?"

"I think the cops will pretend this never happened. They don't wanna look like clowns, y'know? And even if they knew it was Ciullo—even if somebody, say, ratted him out—how can they prove it? The evidence tape would cost them their pet muscle creep, all the 'decent' cops would have to start doing their dirty work themselves while Rosen weaves baskets in some residential program. Nah. I think they'll let it slide, because I don't think they have any idea who did it."

"How could they not see him? I mean, it's not like he's easy to miss, with that goddamn *thing* in the middle of his forehead."

"I don't know, my friend," Sal said quietly. "I've seen some weird shit, but…"

"Yeah." Hamish chewed his lip. "In da boosh," he said at last, "I saw some guys who could do some oddball stuff. Vanish from plain sight, seemed like. And Charlie… There were some of the Cong who could just get in anywhere, it seemed like. Like fookin' ants. You just couldn' keep 'em out." He shook his head. "So you think goofy Hahvey Shooleo, what, learned these slitty-eye kung fu vanishing tricks? What makes you think it's him?"

Sal rewound the tape. "Who else you know wears a Cubs ball cap?" he asked.

❦ ❦ ❦

Pamela Creed stared down at the paper in her type-writer. It was an IBM Selectric. She told people she wrote her novels on a typewriter because she felt energized by the chattering of the type and because the cold, flavorless phosphor of a computer monitor took her out of the moment, impeding her creative flow. When she was think-ing about it, she believed this. When she wasn't specifically thinking about that explanation, computers frightened and intimidated her.

Pam was trying to do some more work on her postmodern, feminist Elizabethan romance novel, but she'd been stymied ever since being kidnapped by a demon in the desert.

She sighed and looked over the thick sheaf of already-typed pages. She'd tried to write yesterday, too, but had wound up just going over the footnotes and endnotes again. She'd spotted a couple of typos and had retyped the pages. Now it was time to push the novel forward, and she couldn't seem to start.

There was a knock on the door. Pamela believed herself to be irritated, so she ignored the feeling of relief as she went to look in the peephole.

When she saw the mud monster woman with a disrepu-table-looking man hanging on her arm, Pam's first instinct was to pretend no one was home.

"Pamela Creed," the creature called Gwynafra said. "Open the door. I know you're in there." It knocked again—a peculiar hard and flat knock, like it was hitting the wood with a stone.

Pam bit her lip and unlocked the door.

"Look," she said. "I don't know what—"

Gwynafra effortlessly moved Pam aside and brought the man in. His eyes were red-rimmed as if he'd been crying, and he seemed unsteady on his feet.

"I need your help," Gwynafra said bluntly. Pam blinked.

"Uh, I don't know what exactly I can do."

"Jake, could you let me and Pam talk privately for a little bit?"

He nodded and went off to halfheartedly look over Pam's bookshelf. The mud woman lowered her voice and explained what she wanted. Pam turned pale and her jaw dropped.

"Oh no. No no no. Look, I don't know what you think—"

"Pam, you agreed to the worship of Avitu. This is a critical element. This man, Jake Steubbens, he needs Avitu's blessing, and you're the closest thing we have to an awake, aware shaman right now."

"I'm sorry. I didn't agree to, to…"

"But you did. You agreed to submit your will to that of Avitu. I'm sorry, Pam. I wish it was different. I wish you could know the bliss of ignorance, but you're fated to carry Lucifer's curse a little longer at least. While you bear that burden, you can serve as a priestess."

"I'm not a priestess!"

"You took the pledge. You accepted Avitu as your patron. I'm afraid you *are*."

"But can't *you* do it?"

Gwynafra shook her lovely head sadly. "I wish I could. I can help you, but the actual ceremony must be enacted by one of God's favored children. It must be the choice of a human soul, a human will."

"I won't. I just won't do it."

"You must."

Gwynafra took Pam by the hand and suddenly the unpublished novelist was short of breath. She gasped and hunched forward, but it felt like all the air in the room had been sucked out. She turned her head up, and her vision seemed to close in, narrowing like a tunnel until all she could see was the stone beauty of the goddess's emissary on Earth.

Somehow, Pam knew that it was not just air drawn out, not only her lungs and throat being robbed. She could feel her life slipping away, feel the same sense of deadness and loss

that each rejection letter brought. She wondered if this was her soul, if that was what Avitu was consuming.

When Pam's knees hit the ground, the actual physical pain began—searing, ripping pain deep in her lungs and lights.

I don't want to die like this, she thought, but her mouth was gasping out, "I'll do it. I'll do it!"

"Excellent." Gwynafra released her wrist and looked around the apartment. "Do you have a knitting needle, a screwdriver... maybe a toasting fork, something like that?"

Breathless, Pam shook her head.

"No matter," the mud creature said, moving confidently into the kitchen. "I'll come up with something."

Pam stumbled to a chair and tried to catch her breath.

"You okay?"

She looked up and saw the red eyes and gin-blossomed nose of her other houseguest. Jake, she supposed.

"No," she whispered.

He put a hand on her shoulder, and she instinctively flinched away with her lip curled. He smelled sweaty, and not the kind of robust odor you get between jogging and showering. This was a rank, layered, old sweat. Sweat that had dried days ago but which still clung. And his fingernails were dirty.

She felt ashamed for recoiling, felt like a prissy stuck-up snob and that wasn't her. And then she thought about what she was going to do to him, and she shuddered.

"It's okay," he said. "I want this."

"Do you really understand...?"

He nodded. "She said it would make it all better." His eyes were bright with trust—maybe a desperate trust. "That I wouldn't be tempted anymore, and I wouldn't have any more fears and worries and unhappiness. That I'll just exist. Just like a cloud or a mountain."

"Or like an animal." She swallowed, hard. "Or like a vegetable."

Gwynafra came out of the kitchen with a kitchen knife in her hand. "Sorry about this," she said. "I'll turn it back after."

As Pam and Jake watched, the metal blade twisted, untouched. It was like watching Uri Gellar bend a spoon, only this time, the blade was stretching, curling in on itself,

becoming longer and sharper. In moments, it had gone from paring knife to five-inch ice pick.

"I think we should do this in the bathroom," Gwynafra said calmly. "And it would probably be tidiest if we were all naked."

"Tidy," Pam whispered.

"It's okay," Jake replied. "This is going to be all right. She promised."

"You can't believe her…" Pam replied, but her voice was low and leaden, with no passion in it. She could feel events closing in. It was inevitable.

They stripped and folded their clothes, and then the three of them crowded into Pam's small bathroom. Jake got in the tub, with his feet toward the spout. Gwynafra climbed in behind him, cradling his shoulders between her knees. His head rested against her belly, right beneath her breasts.

He made a joke about being naked with two women, but no one laughed.

Pam knelt by them outside the white porcelain. Gwynafra crossed her ankles in front of Jake's pale gut, clamping his arms securely. She put a hand on either side of his head.

"I think a gag is a good idea," she said. Jake agreed, and Gwynafra released his arm so that he could grab a washcloth and stuff it in his mouth. Then he put his arm back behind her leg.

"All right Pamela," the demon's creature said calmly. "Place the shaft against his face, along the side of his nose."

"I can't do this."

"You can, you must and you will. Lay the metal against the side of his nose. The tip should go right into the tear duct. There. Turn it in a little bit… it should be angled, just slightly. If his face was a clock, and the center of it is right between his eyes, you want it aimed at about… 6:30."

"Oh God…" Pamela was trembling violently.

"Just put the tip next to his eye."

"Oh Jesus…"

Jake muttered something encouraging around his gag. Gwynafra bent forward so she could wrap her left arm around his head, holding it like a football. With her right, she reached out and steadied Pam's trembling hand.

"Right like this," she said gently. "Now just push. Not too hard. Just nice and slow and smooth."

A horrible, low wailing sound was coming out of Pam's mouth.

"Pam. Just breathe now. It's okay. You're doing fine. This is just right."

The trembling tip danced around in the red corner of the yellowed white of Jake's right eye. He made a pained, urgent noise, smothered and animal, as the needle tip scratched and shredded the tender tissue. Tiny drops of blood welled up.

"Push it in! Push! Go! But not too hard, gentle!"

"AaaaAAAAAAHHH!"

"No Pam! Don't close your eyes!"

But the writer did, she closed her eyes and turned away and pushed hard. Jack gave one hoarse scream through the gag, but it was lost in Pam's own cry. The man twitched a few times in Gwynafra's concrete grip, then laid still.

"Oh dear, Pam. You've killed him."

Miles away, a stoneware platter slipped out of Teddy Mason's hand. He'd washed it and rinsed it and was drying it, because they'd eaten a meatloaf off it and it was too big to go in the dishwasher. He was drying it and reaching for the door of the cabinet where it belonged, when his mind went blank. It was not a perfect blankness—not a gray, neutral blankness. It was the blankness of overwhelming loss. Teddy knew, without doubt, that something special and precious had been needlessly squandered, wasted pointlessly because he wasn't there to… oversee things.

He felt stunning, tragic loss and knew it was his fault. Then the dish hit the floor and shattered, and he told Birdie that he'd just been so terribly clumsy. After sweeping it up, he went to the phone in the bedroom and paid a lot of money to move his flight to Las Vegas up a week.

XII
chapter
twelve

Chuck Collins thought about it carefully and decided to do it the most cowardly way he could.

He took another look at the newspaper, squinting at the picture of Jake Steubbens. Normally, the death of a homeless wino gambling addict wouldn't make page one, even under the fold, but given that this guy's face had been beaten in and they'd had to ID him from fingerprints... it made people nervous and curious. The picture was from one of Steubbens' numerous arrests for vagrancy.

He couldn't be *sure* it was the guy Gwynafra had been talking to, but he'd give it better odds than you'd get at roulette. Better to just can her and have that be the end of it. If the police found out who did Steubbens, all well and good. If not, at least he'd get her away from him and his girls. If she wasn't involved at all... well, too bad. There was still something weird about her.

He could hear the girls coming off stage, and he stood in his doorway watching them file into the communal dressing room. When he saw her come out, he called, "Doakes! C'mere."

"Yes?" she asked as he waved her into the office. He shut the door behind her.

"Have a seat."

"What's this about?"

He got into his own chair and said, "Doakes, sorry, but it's not working out. I got to let you go."

He'd learned from experience that when firing top-less dancers, it was sometimes good to have a big desk between you. But Doakes took it well—her expression didn't even change.

"Why?" she said at last.

He sighed and held up a baggie full of catnip. "I found this in your stuff, Doakes. Christ, you could've at least hid it from me, y'know?"

"That's not mine!"

"Save it." He shook his head. "You know I don't hire druggies, Doakes. I'm not going to the cops. I don' need that kind of hassle. But you're out."

She was silent for a moment, then stood to go.

"I'll send your wages to that PO box," he said to her retreating back.

She closed the door behind her. Chuck breathed out hard and was pleased. She might suspect that he knew something about Steubbens, but she didn't know for sure. And he'd said he wasn't going to the cops. And she'd figure (if she had half a brain and *was* involved with the bum's death) that he could have simply called the fuzz and had them waiting when she came off stage. He didn't think she'd be any more trouble.

Fifteen minutes later, several dancers saw a burly man with brown skin and hair rush in the backstage door and make a beeline for Collins's office door. There was a brief sound of struggle, then the man ran out again. When the witnesses cautiously looked in the office, it was obvious that Collins was dead.

The next day, Gwynafra showed up for work as usual.

❀   ❀   ❀

Milkman Boyer looked eager. He'd beaten Mr. Fortune to the office again, but he wasn't angry about the wait. He just wanted to get down to business.

"You were right, you were right," he said as they went through the door. "It was them, them the whole time. They wouldn't let me go, not even in their graves."

"Yep."

"Now how about the rest of it?" They sat down on opposite ends of the table, but Boyer was on the edge of his seat, leaning eagerly in. "You can do the rest, right?"

"I think so."

"Ciullo, you *got to*." Boyer's passion was ugly. His natural suspicion had flooded into his face, where it sat oddly with the hope of cruelty. "You told me, didn't you? You said that by coming back, they were vulnerable. That was your word, *vulnerable*. You said if I did what you said, I could hurt them like they hurt me. That I could *destroy them*. You said that, Ciullo."

"I said I could see that possibility."

Like flicking a switch, suspicion and hope turned to pure hate. "You fuckin' with me now?" His hands lashed out. His left hand seized Hasmed's right wrist, and his right grabbed his collar, pulling him forward over the table.

Slowly, Hasmed's left hand reached up to remove his sunglasses. The gaze he fixed on Lee Boyer was distant as a mountaintop and just as deadly cold.

"You think you want this," he said.

"Fuckin' A."

"When I said it was a possibility, that meant it might not happen. There's always that chance in anything you do, whether it's an exorcism or... say... a Brinks job."

"You're not backing out." It was half challenge, half statement.

"I won't. The question is, will you?"

"I'll do anything."

Hasmed's bloody eye flickered, and the Milk Monster slowly eased his grip, leaning back.

"Excellent." Fortune's voice changed, becoming resonant and commanding.

Boyer took a deep breath, eyes narrowed. "So." He licked his lips. "What you got?"

Hasmed surged to his feet and unveiled himself. His wings swept out, brushing the walls on either side. His wounds, the marks of human death, blazed from his face with unholy light.

Boyer didn't scream. He didn't back away. He stared, and a small smile grew on his face.

It was the look of a man who's been seeking a demon all his life.

"Yes," he whispered.

"I can cleanse you of your parents' wounds," Hasmed intoned. "I will not change the past, for that has made you what you are. And I will not change your soul, for it is the

215

WOUNDS ON IT THAT MAKE YOUR PAIN SWEET TO ME. BUT THE HAUNTING YOU HAVE EXPERIENCED SHALL CEASE FOREVER, AND YOUR BODY WILL BE FREE OF YOUR PARENTS' MARKS."

"Yes."

"BUT THE PRICE IS HIGH. FOR THESE BOONS, I DEMAND YOUR WORSHIP AND OBEDIENCE. I WILL BE YOUR GOD, AND YOU WILL BE MY SLAVE."

"Yes! *Yes!*"

Hasmed stepped forward and enclosed the man within his wings. Lee Boyer, Jr. was lifted up, and he felt sweet breezes blow through is body, sweeping away his scars like leaves in an autumn wind. He felt his leg straighten where it had been poorly set. He felt his shoulder joint—the left shoulder, the one his dad had always grabbed—straighten out and settle back properly. Even his face was made anew, as the nose his mother had broken returned to its original state.

Far sweeter was the joy in his heart, knowing that this being, this holy monster, would destroy his parents' souls forever, consuming them perhaps, or condemning them to the fire. He took a deep and pure pleasure from that thought.

He had no idea that he'd been tricked.

When he opened his eyes, it was just plain, scarred Harvey Ciullo standing before him. But Boyer didn't doubt. He could feel something new inside him.

"So," the fortune-teller said. "I've got this thing I'm setting up in Florida. You want in on it?"

❖ ❖ ❖

At first, working at the New Age bookstore was a pretty sweet job. Almost no one came in. It was like working the video store, only Free was a lot less of an asshole than his old boss.

In the course of some of his most boring hours, however, Thomas had idly picked through a few of the books that were just lying around—*The Ebon Branch, Manes Malus, The Left-Hand Door.* Pretty much anything with a gnarly looking demon on the cover.

Knowing that he'd signed on with such a creature didn't make for encouraging reading. Still, given how much of the stuff in the books was bullshit from his own experience ("Ye demonne cannot coerce, onlie persuade."), and how much of it contradicted the stuff in the other books, he figured it was all a crapshoot.

At first, the store's sparse customers seemed to be overweight white women in earth tones with high, breathy voices and lots of beads. Sometimes he'd spot the male of the species, inevitably bearded, generally ponytailed, but the women were the majority. Every now and again you'd get someone young, skinny, pierced and tatted—the gender on those could be male, female or optional. They tended not to buy much.

Not long after he started, though, Free had him unload a bunch of weird stuff into the stock room. Then the two of them worked all afternoon moving dream-catchers and Starwind books around to make room for roots and flags and candles and a bunch of other stuff that looked different from Free's original stock.

After that afternoon, a trickle of new customers started coming in. Blacks, most of them real dark blacks, and a lot of them with accents or headscarves or both. They weren't chatty like the earth tone women. They bought their candles and their plants, and they left. A few spared him enough attention to give him dirty looks.

Then, not long after that, the shelves got even *more* crowded with a *different* bunch of paraphernalia, and *another* segment of the buying public started trickling in. These people were all Latino or Latina, dressed in jeans and plaid shirts and cowboy boots or sandals. Like the blacks, they weren't interested in a lot of talk, which was fine with Tom.

He couldn't help but notice that the two new groups usually looked poorer than the original customers. But they came more often and spent more money.

❖ ❖ ❖

Roscoe Paum was uneasy around Milk Monster Lee Boyer, even after Harvey assured him it was fine, that he didn't need to worry, that the rumors about Boyer were all hot air and smoke. Hasmed had finally gotten fed up and played "Zoth of the Hated Lash," telling Paum that Boyer wouldn't harm him, that it was under control—basically the same things he'd been saying as Harvey. But, as he'd expected, Paum paid more attention to the demon than the man.

Even after *that*, Ros was jittery when they swung by to pick up Boyer, which Hasmed just did not need. Getting Helena to agree to watch Tina for a long weekend had taken all of his

native persuasive abilities, which weren't much. The thought had crossed his mind that he could subtly shift her thoughts with angelic grandeur, but he didn't. He didn't want to waste energy on one of his allies. He didn't want to risk the consequences if it failed. And, no doubt influenced by Harvey's remnants of affection, he didn't want to screw with her head.

He had, at last, dummied up a story about a job interview with an old friend from high school. It wouldn't have held water if she examined it closely, but he dazzled her with cash. He had never, before his death or after it, offered her money to watch Tina, so the sight of a short stack of twenties convinced her he was dead serious about the trip. She was still dubious, but she gave him the benefit of the doubt.

Tina was much less sanguine. She wailed like a torture victim as he left the apartment, and Helena had to physically restrain her from running after him. Tina hit her aunt and kicked her, but it was no use.

Watching the elevator door close, Hasmed had one of those uncanny, unpleasantly human moments of mixed guilt and relief.

Then Roscoe had started in about Boyer again, and Hasmed had told him to shut it.

"Hey Shakes," Lee said as he slid in the backseat of Roscoe's Dodge. "How you doin'?"

"Can't complain. How 'bout you, Milkman?"

Boyer turned white. Even his lips were white. "Don't call me that."

"Don't call me Shakes."

"Guys, guys," Hasmed said. "Calm down, huh? Could we do this without measuring each other's dicks please?"

"You just watch yourself," Boyer muttered, sitting back. They were like that all the way to the airport.

❖   ❖   ❖

Jennifer woke up when Joeesha Murfee said, "The bitch stole our playing cards."

"What?"

"She must've taken 'em last night when we were sleeping."

"Damn it!"

Stuart Flaubert had caved in two days previously, leaving only Joeesha, Brandon and Jennifer.

When they'd first arrived in the cloudscape of lightning, with the Earth suspended miraculously above them, it had been awe-inspiring, mind-boggling, unbelievable. Now it was merely boring.

Jennifer had painstakingly folded and torn a paper bagel bag, then used a pen from her purse to make a deck of playing cards. The prisoners had spent the day playing spades and hearts. They'd played every poker variant they could think of—they gambled for nothing, tracking their wins and losses with knots in their shoelaces. Even Brandon's accusations of cheating were a diversion from boredom. Even boredom was better than contemplating their fate, or their dilemma.

They'd taken great care not to drop a single card, since there was no floor for them to fall upon. They'd gotten through another day without going mad or giving in to the demon, and in the night, it had stolen their cards.

"Well, there's charades," Brandon said.

"Did you ever read *I Have No Mouth and I Must Scream*?" Jennifer asked.

Joeesha shook her head. Brandon did too.

"Gustavus was really into science fiction, you know. Or really into hating it, anyhow, and he badgered me into reading that story."

"So?"

"It's about people being held prisoner by this evil computer, and eventually they decide—on the spur of the moment, because it can read their thoughts—to kill one another."

There was a moment of silence. Brandon and Joeesha and Jennifer looked at one another. Nods were exchanged, but no one moved.

"Come on," Jennifer said. "We probably don't have long before she shows up!"

"You should've told us about this after she left, when she was far away and going in the other direction, not when she was on her way here!" Joeesha shouted.

"Well, I'm sorry, but now that we've said it, we know she heard us. We have to do it now!"

"You sure this is what you want?" Brandon asked, uneasy.

"Hey, *I'd* rather be dead than cave in to that thing," Joeesha said. "Y'all can do me first."

Jennifer bit her lip and then, tentatively, grabbed Joeesha's sleeve. "C'mon," she said to Brandon. "We can use the lightning."

"You sure?"

"*Do it!*" Joeesha yelled.

Brandon grabbed her other arm, without a lot of energy, and the three of them started walking toward the column of blinding light.

"Shit, we could just jump in on our own. *You* could."

"I don't know if I've got the guts," Joeesha said, her eyes getting wide. "Besides, suicide's a sin."

"Oh, and *axing* someone to kill you ain't?"

"Christ, you're starting to sound like Gustavus," Jennifer muttered.

Gwynafra appeared before them, rising out of the clouds. They froze.

"You poor children," she said. Her expression was genuinely sad.

"Hey, *fuck you!*" Joeesha said. "You'll *never* control me, so you might as well kill me yourself!"

"You long to be free of your discomfort, but your prison is not this realm, this pocket of space and time. Your prison is your own mind."

"Shut up shut up shut *up*..."

"Your minds are not ready for the burdens they bear. You were not meant, yet, to be the fulcrum on which the scales of justice rest. You're not strong enough to bear the weight of good and evil as those slippery ideas shift back and forth. Wouldn't it be better to be liberated from those concepts?"

"I don't want to be amoral!" Jennifer shouted. "I don't want to be an animal! Jesus, can't you see how... how *absurd* it is? Trying to rationally persuade us to become irrational? You're the one who's crazy!"

"The poison of rational thought is all you understand, so it is the only tool I can use. It has blinded you to my love for you. It has blinded you to your own best interest."

"You've said all this shit before," Brandon said. "It didn't work the first time, and it ain't workin' now." He took a step in front of the women and puffed up his chest. "Why not just admit you're licked? Let us go. Get some other suckers and try your played-out shit on them."

The mud creature shook her head. "Brandon, do you think it's that simple? Even if I gave in and released you, what do you think the police would say when you wandered into town? You've been missing for weeks. Telling them you were being held captive in a cloud isn't going to go over well."

Brandon's mouth twisted. "Who'd miss me?" he asked, and his voice was bitter. "You're lyin'. I could drop off the face of the Earth... shit, I *did*... and no one would notice or even care."

Gwynafra reached out to stroke his cheek, but he flinched back. "Loneliness," she said. "It only exists as long as you're aware of it. It's like the circle of light from a flashlight beam. It's real, but click it off, and it's as if it was never there. That can be yours—that click, that relief—if you but serve me a little while."

"You say our awareness is like a drug, but *you're* the one who sounds like a pusher," Joeesha said, stepping up beside Brandon. "Promising to take away the pain. First one's free. All that shit."

Gwynafra sighed. "Even your imperfect comprehension gives you some insight. We are at something of an impasse, but not the one you think. I could wait until the stars died without getting impatient. Boredom is a human attribute. But the time span in which you can return to your lives as my servants, without rousing undue suspicion, is passing fast."

"I don't care anymore," Jennifer said. "You think my old life was so great that you can break me by letting me back in it? Think again. If I have to go to jail or get thrown in an institution, better that than serving a murdering monster."

"You will serve me one way or another," Avitu's mouth-piece said benignly. "Currently, you can choose your path of service.

"One: You can choose to serve me in life, enduring the burden of consciousness for a while longer as my priest or priestess, feeding me your will and doing my bidding."

"Pass," Brandon sneered.

"Two: You can serve me in life, against your will. Soon, when my plans grow greater, your praise will not be necessary. Then you can have Lucifer's curse lifted by force."

"You're lying," Joeesha whispered, but she said it like a hope and not an accusation.

"Three: You can serve me in death, giving me your memories and knowledge as Gustavus did."

"You mean, you'll eat our brains."

With a small smile, Gwynafra nodded. "A set of modern assumptions is most useful for simulacra like this body. Soon I'll be strong enough to make another one," she said, looking between Jennifer and Joeesha. "Perhaps a musician."

The three artists looked at one another in dread.

"Think it over. Have a decision by tomorrow morning." The mud woman handed out bottles of water, bagels, condiments. "Oh, and don't bother trying to get through the walls."

"Walls?" Brandon asked.

And suddenly there were walls.

Thomas had felt uneasy the first time he turned someone on to Sabriel—it was a thin, geeky type who was always trying to special order some book called *Dies Ignis*, despite Tom's assurances (and, eventually, Free's as well) that the book did not exist, that it was a hoax and a joke and a trick on the gullible. The twerp kept coming back and winking and acting like Tom had been putting him on. Eventually, Thomas told him, "Look… I know this chick who might help you."

He never saw the runt again. He kept telling himself that anyone who wanted a demon that bad would find one eventually, so he (Thomas) might as well get something out of it. He told himself the same thing the next couple of times—again, both men, and both seeming to have an attitude or an aura about them similar to the first would-be "diabolist." They also reminded him of the 1:00 AM porn-renters back at Video Villa.

It eventually dawned on Thomas that the more schmucks he sent her way, the less attention she seemed to pay him. She'd gotten a new rental place and a new hairdo (jet black) and didn't seem to expect as much from him.

Until one Thursday she called him at three in the morning and said, "I need you to pick some people up at the airport tomorrow."

"Wha'?" Tom rubbed sleep from his eyes and tried to focus his mind.

"Three guys, coming in on United. I need you to give them a lift from the airport to my apartment."

"Why can't you do it?"

"I could, but I want you to. It'll make a better impression."

"Aw man... what time do I got to be there?"

"Their plane gets in at noon."

"Noon? And you're calling me at, shit, 3:00 AM?"

"I didn't want you to make any plans."

"What if I already got plans?"

"Cancel."

When he got to the airport, it turned out the flight was delayed, but after waiting an extra forty-five minutes, he saw three men walking toward his sign, which read CIULLO.

The first one was short and wiry, and he moved in a series of efficient spurts. Every step seemed to start loose and relaxed, then surge forward, then sag back into relaxation. He had sad eyes, a flattened nose, and his ears had the puffiness common to boxers and serious wrestlers.

As he got into earshot, Thomas heard the man saying, "Nah, 's like flushing your money down a toilet. They're just gonna raise taxes and piss the money away on people who're scamming the system. I mean, look at me. I ain't been sick for a month an' a half, but my disability checks keep rollin' in."

"Why don't you tell 'em then?" This was the second man, a little taller but just as skinny, wearing an uncomfortably heavy suit and looking around with mean, sharklike eyes. He walked with an assured, gliding tread that wasn't even arrogant—it was barely-restrained viciousness. He looked like he was *seeking* an excuse to make trouble.

"Hey, Boyer, it ain't my job to make sure the system works," said the shortest man.

"The system doesn't work," said the shark—Boyer, it seemed. "I mean, look at all them rape-os and murderers and psychos who get off on technicalities. If it was me, I wouldn't even give 'em the chair. I'd break their fuckin' backs and leave 'em to die in the sun."

"I'm surprised," said the third man. He was as tall as the second one, but he seemed shorter. Probably the heaviest of the three, but the easiest to ignore—he looked soft and fudgy. Even his round head, with a short dusting of bristly hair on the top, looked like some sort of pastry dessert. But then he got closer, and Tom could see an angry red scar in the middle of his forehead, like a caste mark from some incredibly

violent mockery of Indian society. That crawly looking flaw gave his whole face an entirely different cast.

"Hey, I believe in capital punishment, that's all," Boyer said.

"*You* support capital punishment?" said the little man.

"It's funny. Almost all the killers on death row support capital punishment. They just support it unofficially." Scarface said it like that ended the matter. He looked at Tom and said, "Hi. I'm Harvey Ciullo, but people call me Mister Fortune."

❖   ❖   ❖

After all the planning and watching and discussion, the actual job went down surprisingly smooth.

Hasmed introduced Boyer and Paum to Sabriel—or, as he said it, "My old friend Angie." Paum shook her hand and made a weak joke about how he had a cousin Angie, only his cousin was a guy. She simpered.

Later, Roscoe asked Hasmed why he hadn't mentioned that his friend was such a fox.

"She looked a lot different last time," was the answer he got.

After the niceties, Angela briefed them on the schedule.

"University of Miami has one of its big games tomorrow. They've already got a lock on a playoff seed, but this is an old rivalry, so a lot of alums are in town for it. The betting action is heavy."

Hasmed smiled.

"Every year, before the big game, there's a banquet for the team and the alumni—not all the alumni, just the high-rollers and the ex-footballers."

"The big donors," Paum guessed. Angela gave him a lovely smile and put a finger on her nose.

"Exactly right. The dinner is private and, unofficially, it's the biggest fundraiser of the year. It's all under the table, of course—the donors pay into a slush fund, which the coaches use over the course of the year at their discretion. Remember when Jasper Whitty got arrested for shoplifting last year? The discretionary fund paid off the store owner and got the charges dismissed. Scuttlebutt is, it also pays to bribe certain professors, hires prostitutes for prospective recruits to the team… even paid for an abortion for a star running back's girlfriend back in 1998."

"Gawd, it's touching t'see a team stick together like that," Boyer said.

"U of M got censured way back in 1987, and the NCAA investigated rumors of corruption again in 2000," Hasmed said. "They've been very cautious since then. They're trying to keep the money hidden—at least, as much as they can when such big sums are moving. That means there's no ledger, no paper trail, no *checks*. It's *all cash*."

"And that means they can't report it stolen," Paum said, smirking.

They worked in two teams—Angela and Roscoe Paum on one team, Hasmed and Lee Boyer on the other. Angela's job was to lure Jasper "Spur" Whitty, the team's starting quarterback, into a truck with Roscoe, where they would drug and subdue him. At the same time, Hasmed would sneak into the banquet hall and see who was collecting the dough. While that was going on, Lee would check in on Angela, get a Polaroid of Spur Whitty in danger and take it to Hasmed. Then the two of them would approach the money man (or men), show him the Polaroid and take the cash.

Easy.

❖   ❖   ❖

"So, uh… you known Ciullo long?" Roscoe was sitting in the driver's seat of a U-Haul rental truck, with Angela Meyerhoff next to him. She seemed distracted.

"Sorry?"

"You and Hawv. You known each other a while?"

"Oh, a *long* time," she said, with a secret smile.

"How'd you two meet?"

"We used to work together." She checked her watch. "I think it's about time for me to go into action."

"A'right. Take it easy, 'kay?"

"You're sweet," she said, patting his cheek.

Ros tapped on the steering wheel for a while, listening to the radio. He listened through "Stardust," "Smoke Gets In Your Eyes," "My Way" and "Love Child." The radio station was playing "Little Brown Jug" when he saw Spur Whitty coming out of the banquet hall with his arm around someone who wasn't Angela Meyerhoff.

Shit, he thought. *She must have missed him.*

Paum didn't have a gun—none of them did, as far as he knew. But he'd helped himself to a black-handled steak knife

in a plastic sheath out of Angela's kitchen. (For a chick without much furniture, she sure had an extensive cutlery selection.) It was in the inside pocket of his lightweight blazer, and as he walked toward Whitty, his left hand came up to pluck the lapel open.

"Uh, excuse me," he said, then blinked.

It was Angela with him after all. But it didn't make sense.

"Muh?" Whitty looked up with the sway-necked gaze of a drunk. "Who're you?" His head lolled in the other direction to Angela and he raised an eyebrow. "An' who are *you?*"

"Spur, don't you remember me?" Angie asked, pouting. "Jeff just introduced us!" While the quarterback goggled down her shirt, she gave Roscoe a meaningful look. He wasn't sure exactly what it was supposed to mean, however.

"You're, uh, Spur Whitty, ain't you?" He had a pad soaked with ether in his pocket, and so did Angela. "Can I get your autograph?"

"Sorry, man. Too busy."

"Aw, c'mon…"

"Hey! Beat it!" As Whitty looked up, aggressive and annoyed, Angela stepped behind him and clamped her pad over his mouth. He seemed confused for a moment, then reached up with both brawny arms and yanked her hand down.

Roscoe was ready. It wasn't quite like boxing, but close enough. He'd timed a thousand dropped guards in the ring. This time, though, instead of a punch, he just pushed a rag into the big guy's face.

With one hand holding Angela's wrist, Whitty raised the other to knock Roscoe's hand back, but Paum's reflexes were far quicker. He jerked his hand back and re-inserted it under the athlete's arm, right at his nose, before Spur could even take a clean breath. When Whitty lowered his arm, Ros just did the same thing in reverse.

Whitty was in magnificent shape, but ether on top of booze was not what he was used to fighting. Still, he had one good rally left, and with a low grunt, he curved both arms together and charged. It was a hell of a hit, the kind of thing that makes a tackle dummy shift and slide. The boxer danced back, but Whitty was twice his weight and easily knocked him down.

But the football star hadn't reckoned with the woman behind him. When he let go of her wrist and lunged, she waited half a beat, waiting for him to exhale. Her rag was right there when he instinctively took a deep breath, and that did it.

Roscoe barely got out from under him as he crashed.

❖ ❖ ❖

Unseen, Hasmed watched the banquet winding down. He'd been uneasy about concealing himself after the near-riot at the police station, but this time it seemed to be under control.

He'd gotten there early and watched a long time. A lot of the cash traded hands early, and the donors were surreptitious. But as the night wore on, alcohol eroded their sense of shame, and they began to wave money openly.

The bagman wasn't drinking. He was a large fellow, with a quietly competent look, and a couple people addressed him as "Marns" or "Coach Marns." He had a briefcase, into which the money went—loose money, money secured with banker's bands, money in envelopes and manila folders and even one small paper sack. (The man with the sack seemed to feel it was a tradition. People laughed as he presented it.)

When a particularly well-dressed man took Marns aside, Hasmed followed and spied on a discussion about Marns' "protection"—a Ruger 9mm with a high-capacity magazine. The demon paid little attention to their talk about the stopping power of hollow points versus dumdum rounds. He was watching to see where Marns had his holster.

As the night wore on and the boasts and jokes became louder and cruder, Hasmed began to feel something burning and sizzling in his belly. It surprised him. He shouldn't get indigestion—his body was no longer subject to such pains. Besides, his supper had been peanut butter on white bread with bananas and a glass of milk.

Concentrating on his curiosity, he realized that his body was reacting to his feelings, just as if he were human. This disturbed him, and he decided to leave.

How much money changed hands in there? He wondered. *How many hungry children would it feed? How many second chances is it worth? And how many people, employed by those men in there, are angry or depressed or tugging to make ends meet—all so they can be rich and posture before*

other rich men and dazzle stupid teenagers into winning a game for them?

But then he thought about his master, and about the Stone of Despair, and about Rabbadün. Compared to what they would do with that money—or with the power it represented—the men within seemed harmlessly naïve. Sweet, even.

He walked up to the Plymouth LTD they'd stolen earlier that night and knocked on the passenger-side door. Boyer opened it for him.

"Guy's named Marns. He's got a gun in a shoulder holster."

Boyer nodded. "What's he wearing over it?"

"A blazer."

"Hm."

"That going to be a problem?"

"Nah, I don't think so. Not with two on one. Besides, guns don't scare you, right?"

"They should scare *you*, Lee."

Lee shrugged and handed him the Polaroid. It was a good one. Whitty was passed out on a featureless white sheet with today's evening paper next to his head and the tip of a steak knife positioned under his eye.

They waited in silence for the banquet to end.

❧ ❧ ❧

While all the other coaches and players and donors were going home, Assistant Coach Evan Marns pointed his car toward the university campus. He didn't notice a blue Plymouth following him, so it was wasted effort on his pursuers' part when they turned off into a side street near the field house.

It was late and Evan was tired, and carrying all that money made him feel funny. His right hand kept coming up to brush the handle of his gun, but it didn't help his unease.

He went to his office, opened up the safe hidden by the false bottom drawer of a filing cabinet, put the briefcase in, and sealed it up again.

It felt good to have the cash out of his hands. With a lighter tread, he returned to the parking lot.

He was two steps past the exit when something moved behind him. He didn't have time to turn, or even register the noise, before something fast came out of the bushes by

the door and slammed into the backs of both knees. He cried out and flung up his hands as the parking lot blacktop rushed toward him. He hit, stinging his palms, and someone was on him from behind, reaching around him, digging for his gun.

Evan Marns had played football himself, and he'd wrestled. His reflexes were a little rusty, but the were still there. He grabbed his attacker's hand, pinning the gun in the holster, then tried to fight for his own grip on the pistol's butt.

A foot slammed into his hip as he rolled, but it was a momentary distraction before hideous, massive pain flooded into his entire head. It was coming from his right ear, a powerful clamping agony. To relieve it, he instinctively rolled the way it was pulling, and then he was on his back and the agony shifted to his nose. He heard, more then felt, the crack as his nose bone broke, and then an icy voice in his good ear said, "Lose the gun, or it's eyes."

Marns drew in breath to scream, and then felt something metal release his nose and very gently bracket his Adam's apple.

"Or we can do it this way," said the chill voice.

Marns gave up.

Someone grabbed him under his shoulder and roughly heaved him upright. "Unlock the door," he was told, and he obeyed.

Inside the field house, he paused to wipe tears from his eyes, and in the dim red light of the Exit sign, he could see his attacker. Not a big guy, but fearsome with the blank anonymity of a stocking over his face. There was Evan's gun in his right hand, and in his left, Marns saw what had so tortured his nose and ear: An ordinary pair of spring handled, needle-nose pliers.

In response to a tense gesture, Evan raised his hands.

"The money," said the masked man.

"Look, I don't..."

The pliers darted in and gave him a savage pinch on the side of the ribs. It was quick—his scream was only a brief, sharp note—but strong enough to tear skin.

"Okay," Marns said. "Okay."

❖ ❖ ❖

"So, anybody want a gun?"

They were back at Meyerhoff's apartment. Boyer had taken the clip from Marns' stolen weapon, checked to make sure no round was chambered, then set the pistol in the middle of the table before taking off his rubber gloves.

"Maybe," Angela said. "You might as well leave it here when you go."

"I'm more interested in the money," Paum said, eyes bright as the bills got sorted into fifties, tens, twenties and hundreds.

Looking at it like a heap of paper, it didn't look like much. The men from Jersey had all seen old ladies with bigger heaps of coupons, sorting them at the store. But when you realized how many were hundred dollar bills... Your perception flip-flopped, like one of those Magic Eye pictures, and suddenly the pile was huge.

Hasmed and Angela were dividing and counting—each under the watchful eye of the other.

"I don't even know why we bothered with snaffling the jock," Boyer said. He was keyed up and jittery. The chance to be cruel had made him cheerful. "We could've just taken it from that fat dopey coach."

"We didn't know it would just be him," Hasmed replied. "It could have been five guys. Or eight."

"Yeah, I guess."

Angela tapped a pile of cash into a tidy rectangle. "I've got a total," she announced.

"So do I," said Hasmed. They looked at one another steadily for a moment, and then she said, "Forty-two thousand, five hundred and fifty."

He nodded.

"Not bad for a night's work," Angela said. "Split four ways, it's ten thousand, six hundred and thirty seven dollars... and fifty cents. Anybody got change?"

"Just give me the ten thousan' six, that's fine," Roscoe said.

"I still think our plane tickets ought to come out before the split," Boyer said.

"C'mon, remember the deal," Hasmed said. "This is okay. We're all coming out ahead."

"It's not a huge pot," Lee grumbled.

"True," Hasmed said, "But it's cash money, and it was safe and easy, and they probably won't go to the cops. How many times have you done a bigger job and gotten screwed by a fence?"

"Fences don't screw *me*," Boyer muttered, but he seemed to have taken the other man's point.

Then the door crashed open.

The walls around Jennifer were made of cloud. Stretching up a good thirty feet, they formed a circle about forty feet across. It was, of course, impossible to climb them. When she pushed against them, there was no resistance. She could walk into the wall—and walk and walk and walk—without ever getting anywhere, but as soon as she turned around, she was back in the open-topped, circular "room" from which she started.

She shouted for Brandon and Joeesha, and she heard very faint replies, but conversation was clearly out of the question. They'd all be hoarse from shouting after even a few minutes.

Eventually, she gave up, sat and just waited.

The man who came through the door was big, brown and bald. He moved with a clumsy, hitching gait, but with plenty of power.

"Hey!" Roscoe shouted.

The man didn't say a word. He just made a beeline for Angela.

A typical hero would have interposed himself between the attacker and the woman, but Roscoe wasn't a hero. He was a boxer, and the sight of the man's unguarded back was a rare treat. Right and left, his hands flashed out—first for the back of the neck and second for the kidney shot. A normal man would have crumpled in pain, if the head shot didn't knock him out clean.

The intruder didn't even notice. Instead, it was Roscoe who yelped, waving his hands to try and clear the sting out of his knuckles. It had been like hitting a brick wall.

"Shit!" That was Angela, ducking away and bolting down a hallway. The man turned in pursuit and ignored it when

Hasmed picked up a steel folding chair and smashed it across the back of his stone shoulders.

"What the fuck?" Roscoe said. He'd only now noticed the cracks and fissures and dust, only now noticed that he was fighting a moving statue.

"Kill him!" was the response. Hasmed had kept hold of the chair and was struggling to chase the invader down, hammering fruitlessly at its back.

"Step aside, boss." With a series of efficient metallic clicks, Milkman Boyer had put the clip in the gun and chambered a shell. Hasmed ducked into a bathroom off the hallway, giving Boyer a clear shot at the brown man's back.

The sound of the gunshot was thunderous in the enclosed apartment. Boyer and Paum could both see the impact where the bullet hit, but not because of any bloody wound. What they saw was cracks and chips of stone. It was like they'd shot a boulder.

"What the *fuck*?" Paum repeated.

But they'd finally gotten the brown man's attention. He turned. Roscoe darted back from the mouth of the hallway.

Boyer shot the intruder in the shoulder, then in the chest. Each bullet gouged craters in the stone, but the man didn't fall.

He started to charge.

Another gunshot to the chest. One in the belly. A couple thin slabs of stone fell off him, and as he lurched forward, they could see the edges of the cracks grinding together, churning raw and blowing dust, but still he moved.

The bulletproof man was almost on them.

Boyer was taking slow, even steps backward—not enough to spoil his aim as he fired into the stone man's face, his neck. Its features were cratered off by the bullet's impact, but it still came, gaining speed.

As its left leg crossed the threshold, Roscoe came in low with the back of a chair. He didn't hit it—he tripped it.

"*What the fuck!?*" The metal chair back dented and warped as the impact pulled it from Paum's hands, but the creature crashed forward into the floor.

The truck had cracked it, and the gunshots had damaged it, and distance from Avitu had weakened it, but what shattered it was its own weight, slamming into the floor. One

moment it was a cracked stone statue, unnaturally alive and trying to rise. Then, suddenly, it was nothing but desert dust.

There was a moment when the only noise was the ringing in their ears. Boyer stepped back and absentmindedly waved gun smoke away from his eyes.

"What the fuck?" Roscoe whispered. He'd backed away from the thing until he hit a wall, and then he'd crouched down on the floor in a ball. His eyes were wide with panic and disbelief. Then he blinked, and it was visible on his face as he had a half-coherent thought and seized it, used it to pull himself together.

"Angie? Angie, you okay?" Paum ran down the hall to where she'd fled. Hasmed emerged from the bathroom and looked at the pile of dust. He stirred it with a toe, noting the flattened slugs mixed in with it.

"What the hell was that?" Boyer asked. Hasmed shrugged.

"She's gone!" Paum came back, eyes wide.

"Somehow, I'm not surprised," Hasmed murmured.

"No, I mean she's *gone*," Roscoe repeated. "There ain't a door or a window or nothin' back there, but she ain't in the room."

"So what?" Boyer asked bluntly. "We gotta scram before the cops get here."

"Right. Don't worry Ros; I'm sure she'll turn up some time." Hasmed shook his head, then looked up at the table. "So… did she take her cut of the money with her? If not, I'm sure she'd want us to… uh, hold it for her."

"But what was that thing, Hawv? What was it?"

"I don' know, Ros. But we got to get outta here."

"Whatever it is, it's dead now," Lee said. He was busily shoving the money back into its briefcase. "Fuggeddaboudit."

"What the fuck?" Roscoe whimpered one more time, as the other two pulled him out the door.

Gwynafra spent the night with the club's new owner—a man called Sweet Pete, who frightened the other dancers because they'd heard he had mob ties. Gwyn had taken one look at the woman on Pete's arm—a woman with an obvious boob job and brassy, dyed hair—and had felt confident that she could take him away. She'd just been direct. With the memories and experience of Gustavus the pornographer, she'd had a wealth of ideas.

She'd felt it when her "brother" in Florida was destroyed, and she knew that was a setback, but her mistress Avitu didn't consider it critical. Making creatures from the earth was not easy, but with Pamela, Stuart and Brandon feeding her their awe and fear, she would be strong enough to make another soon. And after them, her greater servants could be called forth from their deep slumber. But that would take a while.

Sweet Pete didn't want her to leave, and he wasn't used to having women contradict him, but she played that to her advantage. People with power—or, at least, men with power—often found helplessness to be exciting and new. She gave him everything he wanted, except servility. She figured it would work until he learned her true nature. Then they'd renegotiate.

She stopped by the bagel shop as usual and made the long trek into the desert. This time would be different, though. This time, she wouldn't leave any prisoners.

And this time, she'd have the High Priest with her.

❖   ❖   ❖

Thomas.

"Huh?"

Thomas!

Tom Ramone sat up in bed, startled awake by a voice. *Her* voice. For a moment he thought she was in the room with him, but then she spoke again and it was in his *head.*

Tom, I need you to do me a favor.

"What the hell is this?"

It's called an invocation, Thomas. I probably should have taught you about this before, huh?

"You can just get in my head any time you want?"

Short answer, yes. Don't worry though, I can't spy on you while you're beating off in the shower or anything. I only hear spoken responses after tuning you in.

"Any other tricks you haven't told me about?"

Thomas, get with the program! Are you in your apartment?

"Don't you know?"

No, I don't! Tom, someone just tried to kill me, and if he's still mobile and has half a brain, he might try to kill you. Now do you want to play twenty questions, or do you want to be safe?

"Shit!" Thomas leaped out of his bed to the window and stared out into the parking lot. "Yeah, I'm, I'm at my place." Now that he was more awake, it felt really weird to be talking with no one there. He felt an irrational urge to press his hand to his head, as if holding a phone. "What should I look for?"

One—a large, hairless black man. Two—my car.

"That Explorer?"

I traded it in. I'm in an orange Miata now.

"If I see the guy, what should I do?"

Turn watery. You can't be hurt in that form, or at least not easily.

"No shit?"

Hadn't thought of that, huh? I'm pulling into your parking lot.

"I'll buzz you in."

"I think we're safe," she said several minutes later. They were talking face to face, sitting on his couch while the coffeemaker percolated. "I've got my guard up now. He just got the drop on me last time because I was distracted."

"With those guys from Jersey? What's up with them, anyhow?"

"Don't worry about it." She glanced out the window again, following his gaze.

"Was one of them… like you?"

"A demon?" She gave him a little smile. "What do you think?"

He shrugged. "I think so." He peered out into the night. "Which one?"

"That Boyer guy."

He didn't see her look away from him. "I'm impressed by your sensitivity. But the demon was the guy with the scar."

He looked back at her, made a rueful face and changed the subject.

"So, how come you didn't go to Levi or one of those other guys?" Levi was the bookstore guy, the nerd looking for *Dies Ignis*. Angela sighed.

"I got so sick of those three jerks," she said. "Do you know what a succubus is?"

"Nope," Thomas said, though that was a lie. Succubi—female sex demons—were prominently featured in many of the books on demons, often described in lurid detail.

"Well, that's what they were looking for. That was the deal. They get the sex they crave and, in return, they…"

"They believe in you?"

"Yeah. And at first it didn't seem like such a big deal. I mean, between us? It's pretty much a piece of meat. But *man*, they were so damn *annoying!* All the time, calling me up, wanting me to look like Jenna Jameson, wanting me to look like Angelina Jolie, wanting me to look like 'that chick from *The Scorpion King.*' Crap, if they'd asked for Helen of Troy or, I don't know, even Ingrid Bergman… They just really bugged me."

"Bugged? As in, past tense?"

"Mm hm. You know what it was? No respect. Now that I think about it, that's what really cheesed me off. They treated me like I was a twenty-four-hour pizza delivery service, you know?"

"So what did you do?"

"Oh, I killed them."

There was a brief silence. Thomas opened his mouth, then shut it, then got up for coffee. He brought milk and sugar for Sabriel.

"Thanks."

"You didn't really *kill* them, did you?"

"Hey, those clowns thought they'd driven a hard bargain, but they left out the most elementary clause—'never harm me.' Sure, one of them had a safe word that would make me stop whatever I was doing to him—he had some weird sex stuff to work out, you know how it is—but that wasn't much of a problem. I just killed him from outside earshot."

Thomas swallowed. "You could do that to me, right? Couldn't you?"

She nodded.

"How?" he whispered.

"Well, you've agreed to give me power. Just like they did. But none of you put any limits on how much I could take from you. If I take a lot, you get weak and messed up. If I take it all, you die."

"This is another head game, isn't it?"

"I didn't mean for it to be but, yeah, partially, I guess."

"Just reminding me that you'll kill me if I cross you."

"Ugh, it's always about *you*, isn't it? Excuse me, but I'm going to call up my buddy from Jersey."

"Is he a… succubus… also?"

"The male form is 'incubus.' Like the rock band. Or you can call us the Lammasu, or the Defilers… but he's different. He's one of the Asharu."

"What the hell is an 'Asharu'?"

"The closest in English would be 'scourge,' I guess. They used to be guardian angels before. Now they're… they're dull but regrettably necessary. Kind of like the designated drivers of the Unholy Host." She paused. "That was a joke, Thomas."

"Uh… well, you know, if I laugh too hard I might stain the carpet."

He reached for the phone, but she waved it away. "Don't need it. You can contact any demon if you know its name. If you listen, you can learn his. Then, if you want, you'll be able to invoke him."

"Why would I do that?"

She shrugged. "Well, he could probably tell you how to break your pact with me. Though, I must say, if you do that I'll just get you thrown in jail for murder or something."

Thomas jumped back. She'd said the last sentence in a perfect imitation of his voice. She gave a sad smile and shrugged. "I said I'd be honest with you, remember?" Then she leaned back on the couch and closed her eyes. Her voice took on a strange tone as she said, "Hasmed."

❖ ❖ ❖

The gun got a thorough wipe-down and went in the ocean. After racking their brains to be sure they hadn't left anything in Meyerhoff's apartment, the men decided they were safe enough and went to a bar to split a pitcher. They were watching jai alai on the bar's TV, and Paum had calmed down enough to explain the game's finer points to Boyer, when Hasmed stood up abruptly. "Gotta make a call," he said.

The two men sat for a while, and the small talk trickled off. Then Paum said "So… do you have any fuckin' clue what was up with that thing?"

Hasmed went to a payphone, put a coin in and mimed dialing, then said "Hello?"

Hasmed. I'm so glad you're all right.

"Yeah. Sure, 'Angela.' I bet my health and well being are, like, your top priority right now."

You think I set you up.

"And now I think you're gonna try to convince me you didn't. Good luck." Instinctively, he made to hang up the phone.

Wait! I didn't set you up... completely.

"Ah?"

I didn't know that thing was coming. Honest.

"But you thought there might be some trouble. From Avi—"

Don't say it!

"She may scare you, 'Angie,' but I'm of her house. I saw her fight, and I'm not intimidated."

You should be. Could you make something like that... thing?

Hasmed sucked on his teeth and said, "Giving the semblance of life isn't that hard."

Yes, but from thousands of miles away? Or maybe she made it locally and kept it moving for weeks while it tracked me down.

"So she's powerful now. Great. You've made her my enemy. Thanks a lot. Maybe I should just hand you over to her—sort of patch things up, keeping it all in the family?"

Look, what do I have to do to make this up to you? What happened, anyway?

"Now you're curious? Should've thought of that before you beat feet on us."

Is everyone okay? I mean, little Roscoe and that other fellow?

"They can take care of themselves, which is more'n I'd say about you."

I know you're angry, but weren't we a good team? As a gesture of goodwill, hey—you can keep my chunk of the money.

"And just how would you keep me from doing that anyhow?"

Let's not get into threats. I know who your thralls are.

"And I know the name of a powerful enemy who'd love some advice about taking you down. Sounds like stalemate to me. I'm willing to wash my hands, walk away and write you off as a minor pain in the ass. I bet that's better than my other old colleague did."

What would it take for me to earn back your trust?

Hasmed rubbed a stubby finger over his stubbly chin. "Two syllables of your True Name."

That shut her up for a long time. Then she said, *I'll have to think about it.*

XIII

chapter
thirteen

A few days later, driving toward the local mob don's house, Hasmed held his cell phone to his ear and said, "Vodantu."

HASMED. WHAT NEWS, MY MINION?

"Daily, my power and influence grows." He gritted his teeth as a station wagon in front of him braked unexpectedly. He honked his horn and briefly thought about how clunky the formal speech of Hell was starting to feel in his mouth.

HOW MANY THRALLS DO YOU COMMAND?

"Three, so far." He thought about promising more soon, but decided that excuses would only make him look weak.

AND YOU HAVE ACQUIRED MUCH MONEY?

"Yes. I have stolen nearly fifty thousand dollars." He frowned, thinking just how badly screwed he'd gotten fencing the diamonds. Still, he'd made part of it up betting against University of Miami. Their heavy-underdog rivals had unexpectedly won, after U of M's starting lineup unexpectedly came down with mononucleosis. He'd had to get away from Dennis for that sort of heavy action, of course. "Someone has… explained the humans' concept of money to you?"

THE SAVIOR OF THE FALLING STARS IS HAVING DIFFICULTY DUE TO THIS "MONEY." CAN THE MANIPULATION OF MERE PHYSICAL TOKENS REALLY HAVE SO GREAT A POWER OVER MORTAL LIVES?

"Indeed it does, my lord." Two days ago, Hasmed had bribed the director of a daycare center to let Tina in mid-term. It was a better place than the cheap, fly-by-night arrangements Harvey had fudged together.

AND THERE IS NOTHING MAGICAL ABOUT THE TRANSACTION?

"No. Only the magic of greed and consensus."

THEN I SHALL HAVE THE SAVIOR CONTACT YOU, THAT YOU MIGHT SEND SOME OF YOUR MONEY TO HER. SHE IS IN SOME PLACE CALLED "ARGENTINA."

"If you give me her lesser name, I can make the arrangements myself."

NO. SHE ALREADY KNOWS YOUR NAME.

Hasmed winced. Still, Vodantu could ask for worse. Lots worse. And as if the demon duke had read his mind…

I HAVE SEEN YOUR ACTIONS TOWARD YOUR THRALLS. YOU MIND THEM WITH METICULOUS CARE.

"A well-tended tool is a reliable tool."

QUITE. BUT I AM CONCERNED THAT YOU MIGHT BE FALLING BACK INTO OLD HABITS. THE HABITS OF AN ANGEL PROTECTOR.

"I assure you, that's quite absurd."

EXCELLENT. I HAVE DECIDED THAT THE ONE YOU CALL "TINA" WOULD BE A FITTING SACRIFICE TO MY GLORY.

"If you wish, my master," Hasmed said, desperately trying to keep his voice casual and light. "I fear she would be poor tribute. Boyer, I think, would be more to your liking. Many fear him, and if he was slain in your name, they would fear you in turn."

YOU SEEM RELUCTANT TO PART WITH THE GIRL.

"Of course I am. All manner of suspicion will fall on her father—my mortal host—if she is killed. Even the Mafia would be repelled by infanticide. And finally, the simple child bargained little for her faith, which is raw and pure. I reap more trust from her than from both my other pawns combined."

I SEE.

"But if it is the girl you crave, you shall have her. All I ask is that you give me enough time to find a replacement."

HER OR ANOTHER, IT MATTERS NOT. PERHAPS YOU ARE RIGHT. PERHAPS I SHOULD NOT ASK YOU TO PART WITH A VASSAL.

"I exist to serve you, Master." His heart was pounding. This was bad. His master had tested him and backed down, which meant he probably didn't trust Hasmed anymore. "If it is sacrifice you crave, sacrifice you shall have."

SUPERB. ANYTHING ELSE?

Hasmed considered telling him about Sabriel and Avitu, but decided that until he had something to offer, there wasn't much point. "Nothing of great importance."

VERY WELL. I LOOK FORWARD TO YOUR OFFERING.

❖　❖　❖

Lance Mason grumbled and whined when his dad insisted on getting up early to go out to the desert, but his parents closed ranks against him. He thought he resented the way they ganged up on him, but at some level, it made him glad to see them agreeing.

"It looks like the surface of Mars," Birdie said, looking out across the dust. The rising sun gave long shadows for emphasis to every hill, every signpost, every scrubby shrub and piece of roadside garbage.

"Mars is red," Lance said.

"A whole new world," Teddy murmured. Birdie glanced over at him. He sounded... odd. Off. Almost like he was drunk or sleepwalking or something. His eyes were bright and alert, though, and he leaned forward as he drove their rented Bronco down the road.

"Teddy... don't you think you're going awfully fast?"

"What are we going to hit? The road's straight and there's no one around for miles." He eased off the accelerator a bit.

When he pulled off the road, Birdie asked him why. He said it looked like a good place.

"We're not the only ones," Lance said, looking out his window. "See? There's a bunch of tracks coming in and out."

In fact, it was only one set of tracks, going back and forth every day. Gwynafra's tracks. The other tracks—from Sabriel and her prisoners, and from others even earlier—had sank under the blown sand, but they had no way of knowing that.

"So there must be something to see," Teddy said brightly. When they pulled up next to a sturdy truck, he put the car in park.

"Ted? Do you know whose truck that is? Or whose property we're on?"

"It's a surprise," Teddy replied. "C'mon, get your packs. Wait 'til you see this!"

His enthusiasm pulled them on. The desert was passing through that short median period between the night's icy chill and the day's remorseless heat, so the exertion of climbing with tents and packs was fairly pleasant. Teddy was out ahead of them, impatient, and they saw him crest a low rise and stand stock still. Everything in his posture bespoke awe, so Birdie and Lance were somewhat puzzled when they reached him.

"Wow," Lance said, with the sarcasm only a teen can muster. "It's a *tree*. My oh my."

Birdie frowned, glancing from the tree to her husband's awestruck face.

"Just like… it's just like…" he whispered.

"Just like what?" Birdie asked, but she had an awful suspicion.

Teddy dropped his pack to the gritty sand and started down the gentle slope in the ungainly trot of a forty-plus man.

"What the hell?" Lance said.

"Language," Birdie replied, on autopilot. "I think we're camping here."

"Here? But there isn't any water or anything?"

"All will be provided."

Both of them turned and stared at the beautiful woman who had just appeared on the slope, walking toward them. If either had bothered to look, they'd have noticed that her footprints started where they'd first seen her. But they were both transfixed by her face, hair, body… Lance was getting uncomfortable, and Birdie was becoming self-conscious.

"I'm Gwynafra Doakes," the apparition said.

Down the slope, Teddy had reached the tree, and he reached out to touch a branch with a trembling hand.

He closed his eyes.

"Yes," he said. "Yes."

There was a moment of silence, and a grave look clouded his features. Then, with somber voice, he said, "Yes. Forever."

A piece of the branch came off in his hand, forming a needle-sharp wand, thinner than a pencil, about seven inches long.

Then he disappeared.

❖   ❖   ❖

Jennifer was mildly surprised when someone other than the mud woman appeared. It was weird to think she'd gotten used to her eerie prison, but she was. She must have if she'd gotten so mind-wrenchingly *bored* with it. Nothing ever changed in the cloud walls. Nothing but her, getting more desperate and lost and weak. And more sick of eating nothing but bagels.

The man who appeared was chubby, maybe in his late forties. He had male pattern baldness, a tidy moustache, close-shaved stubble on his double chin. He was wearing blue jeans that hadn't seen much wear, well-used Redwing boots, an LL Bean windbreaker.

"Hi," he said. "Are you okay?"

Jennifer just blinked.

"Am I *okay?* Do you have any idea where the hell I am? Where *we* are?"

He looked around. "The tree explained it to me," he said softly. "She took me to another place first... or maybe another time. Or something outside time. She explained a lot of things." He shook his head. "I should be amazed by all this but... it's like I've been ready for it all my life."

"Who are you?"

"I'm Teddy Mason. What's your name?"

"Jennifer." She wanted to resist, but he was just so *real*. After Gwynafra, it was hard to stay wary of someone who seemed so completely ordinary and genuine. He was just some guy. It was wonderful.

"I'm really sorry you've been trapped here."

"Can you do something about it?"

He sighed. "It's complicated."

"*Complicated?* No shit, Sherlock! I'm being held captive in the sky by a demon that ate my ex-boyfriend's brain. Yeah. It's pretty darn complicated all right."

"I'm sorry about your boyfriend, too. Ex-boyfriend. Avitu... you have to understand the scale on which she operates. An

individual life... it's easy for her to forget what that means. People can be like grains of sand in the desert, only her desert is eternity."

"Are you *apologizing* for her?"

"I wouldn't dare."

"What is she to you?"

"She's my goddess," he said simply. "It turns out my family served her since... well, for a long time. It's funny. I didn't even know I had... you know, native ancestors. Just goes to show."

They were quiet for a moment.

"She's going to kill me, isn't she?" Jennifer asked.

Teddy sighed. "It doesn't have to be that way."

"No, I can just get *lobotomized* instead. Or, or I can give in and help her out, after she—"

Teddy held up a hand. "I'm not going to ask you to pledge yourself to her," he said.

"No?"

"I don't want... I think it should be voluntary. I think that when people understand what Avitu really *is*, what she really *offers*—"

"You think people will line up to lose their souls?"

"Not their souls, their pain!" He leaned forward. "Don't you understand how much I envy you?"

"What?"

"I am Avitu's high priest. I was *born* to oversee her sacrifices. Only they're not really sacrifices at all. It's a healing. A blessing. What she offers you is perfect absolution."

"Or perfect ignorance!"

"Perfect freedom from uncertainty and misery and self-loathing. I wish I could have that! But because of how I serve, I *never can*. I must always bear the curse. *You* have the chance to be free. I have to stay outside the door, holding it open. You can walk through it, yet you refuse!"

"I will not give up my *self*. That's not freedom." Jennifer felt tears coming and she bit them back. She could still hear the sob hidden in her voice though, and she knew Teddy could too.

"The night I came out here," she said, "I had a moment. One perfect moment. We were in the desert, and there were

a million stars. And I started to play. And I played everything. All the people who were with us... and most of them, now they're dead... and I, it was like I was making the landscape with my song, or like the sky was singing *through me*. That was what I've always wanted, forever. For a moment, I was totally, perfectly *me*. Or I was always, you know, who I'd *wanted to be*. And now this creature wants to cut that off? When I've just found it? How can I?"

Teddy nodded his head. "You're an artist?"

"A musician."

"That's who you really are?"

Something about the way he asked it—not forced or dramatic, but somehow free of all the baggage most people had, when they asked about art or music or creativity. It made her really think instead of just react.

"Yes."

"And what does that mean?"

"It means that I can... that I *try* to touch the truth."

"But you've seen the truth. You've seen Avitu."

"I don't trust *her*. She could lie about... about everything. Like that horrible creature Gwynafra. It looks like a woman, but that's a lie."

"All right, but you've seen the truth that Avitu is. That she exists."

"Oh yes."

"Do you think you can hide that?"

Jennifer was silent.

"If we just let you go, do you think you can put that away?"

Her head slumped forward on her shoulders.

"I'm never going to be free of her, am I?" she whispered. "I'll always be afraid. I'll always know she could kill me, or take me back, or... or..." Tears started to fall. "I'll always know, won't I?"

"There's one way out," Teddy said.

When Teddy returned, his wife had many questions, but he ignored them to go attend to the short line of the wretched that Gwynafra had brought out for him. Drunks, drug addicts, runaways... people with no hope, other than the

hope of somehow dulling the pains of the past, or of escaping their fears of the future for a while.

Lance's only question was, "Dad? What's that gray stuff on that stick you're holding?" But Teddy didn't answer that, either.

XIV
chapter
fourteen

Johnny Bronco's guards made Mr. Fortune park a long way back from the house. Trudging through the snow toward it, Hasmed felt something. It wasn't something he'd felt before. It was power, but not a familiar type. Nothing from the old days. Nothing like Sabriel.

The strange perception caught him in mid-stride, and he slowed, turning aimlessly in the capo's lengthy driveway. His eyes swept back and forth before settling.

He walked under a graceful weeping willow and looked up at one of the branches. Glancing right and left—Johnny had a lot of guards around, and Hasmed didn't want to look weird hanging out under the tree—he quietly spoke a few words in the first tongue.

The bat hanging from a branch said nothing. Frowning, Hasmed picked up a short stick and tossed it at the creature.

It wasn't really a bat, of course. He'd known that, so he wasn't terribly surprised when it dropped and changed form, landing in front of him as a man. He was big, with lard-pale skin. He had on coveralls, work boots and a mesh-back seed-corn cap. He wore no coat.

"Don't know who you are," the stranger hissed, "but you just made a bad mistake." He had slitted eyes like a cat, and his teeth were unnaturally long and sharp.

Hasmed just stared, curious and a bit confounded. "Caine?" he asked at last.

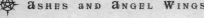
That stopped the man-bat cold. "What do you know about Cainites?" he asked. "Are you…?"

"Am I what?"

"You know. Kindred."

"Kindred to who? To Caine? He didn't have any kids." But the more he examined the creature before him, the more amazed Hasmed became. "Shit, did Caine find some way to pass the buck? Did he figure out how to… to share the wrath of Almighty God?"

"How is it you know about Caine, but you don't know about Kindred?"

"Let's just say I've been out of action for a long time. What the hell is a Kindred?"

The man drew himself up to full height and gave Hasmed his best evil-eye stare. "We're vampires," he said.

"Well I'll be dipped in dog shit. I thought you guys were myths!"

"We're real. What the hell are you?"

Hasmed pulled down his shades and let a little of himself show through his own mangled eye. "Funny you should use that phrase."

"What? I'm supposed to think you're a no-joke *demon*?"

"Exactly."

"Whatever." The creature's skepticism was broadly apparent.

"Believe what you want. It's a funny world."

For a moment, both creatures stared, sizing one another up.

"You here working for Bronco?" Hasmed asked.

"I'm here to *kill* Bronco."

"Then we've got a problem."

"Ah."

Again, for a few moments they just stared.

"Fuck it," the vampire finally said. "I don't care if you're a demon or just a crazy Kindred or the motherfucking Tooth Fairy. Whatever you are, you ain't in the contract, and I'm not throwing down with you over some phlegmy mortal gang boss."

"We should go somewhere and talk."

They were in a diner half an hour later, though the vampire just got coffee and left it untouched. He did seem disproportionately unnerved when he saw Hasmed eating, though.

They didn't exchange names, just questions. The vampire was curious about Caine and the First Days. Skeptical, but still curious, and Hasmed told him a few things. The vampire didn't know much about vampire history, but he knew other

"Kindred" who were always looking into that kind of stuff—and who wouldn't be too picky about where the story originated.

"So it sounds like there was a long, *long* time between when God cursed Caine and when Caine got around to building the first city," the vampire said.

"Actually, Michael cursed Caine. I mean, it was the power of the One Above, but Michael carried the actual message. The infinite cannot touch the finite in a limited fashion."

"Huh?"

"Michael, not God. Also, there were cities before that, too."

"Damn. No one's probably going to believe me."

"Well, no one would believe me if I told Bronco that a vampire got sent to whack him out. You mind telling me who sent you now?" That had been the deal—they were trading questions and answers.

"Sure, I guess," the Cainite replied. "Fuck, it's not like it's a big supernatural secret… like all this Caine stuff." He gave Hasmed another cockeyed, cat-slit look over his shades. "Like the existence of fuckin' *demons*."

"So… the name?"

"Rico Pudoto."

"Rico from Atlantic City? Huh." Hasmed scratched his chin. "Any way I can get proof? It would really help me out."

The waitress came by to offer coffee refills, and if the sight of two men wearing sunglasses at 10:00 PM surprised her, she said nothing about it.

❖　❖　❖

Sal Macellaio was permitted to park up near Johnny's house. As he pulled in, he could see Steel Pete Petrucci's BMW already there.

Things were starting to bubble and cook. No blood had been shed—at least, not in public—but there was a lot of posturing going on. Inside Johnny Bronco's mob, people were shifting in place to take charge if he died—things didn't look good for the old boy. Outside, a couple other syndicates were giving Bronco's machine appraising glances—deciding if it was weak enough to seize and whether it would be worth the trouble.

People from New York, from Boston, from Atlantic City, even Vegas and Chicago—they all seemed to be "visiting friends" or "passing through town" or, most ominously, "just checking in."

The wise money was on Steel Pete. Sal was a dark horse—unless he turned bitch for some other gang and brought his crew along. Sal's smarts made the outsiders wary, and Steel Pete's men were numerous and hardcore. But no one was sure whether the two big crews would work together. It didn't seem likely.

When Sal was shown into Johnny Bronco's bedroom, he heard Petrucci's voice from within.

"...tellin' ya, it's time to open the books. The family's gotta look strong, gotta *be* strong, now more'n ever."

"Fuggeddaboudit. Who's gonna want in now, with the wolves and jackals waiting at the door?" That was John Cohn, Johnny Bronco's consigliere.

"There's always guys," Sal said, striding in. "And now you get the hungry and the dumb. Hungry guys who know shit's coming down and who see it as a chance to prove themselves. And the dumb guys who don't know shit's coming down. They might be even more useful."

Steel Pete was momentarily thrown by Sal's endorsement of his idea. "You got anyone you'd prop up for membership?"

Sal shrugged. "I got a short list. You could do worse than Brennan," he said.

"The goddamn Scotsman? You're crazy."

"He's been connected for decades now. If you could catch Wop like a cold, he'd have it ten times over."

"Next you're gonna propose Harvey Ciullo," Cohn said.

"Now *that's* crazy," Sal said.

"Is it?" Pete asked. "I hear he grabbed a pretty fat load of rocks. I hear he pulled some kind of sweet robbery down in Florida too. In fact, I heard your old pal Mike Diamond hasn't been seen since he went to give Ciullo a good talking to."

"Harvey? Fuggeddaboudit. We're wasting our time just talkin' about him. He's worthless."

"So worthless you flew his ass out to LA to look in on your own flesh an' blood?"

Sal glared. Someone had a big mouth. Steel Pete had no reason to give two shits about Harvey Ciullo... unless someone had tipped him that Sal was keeping tabs.

A young hulk in a dark suit poked his head in the door and spoke, briefly and respectfully to John Cohn. Cohn raised an eyebrow. "Speak of the devil," he said.

"What. Ciullo's here?" Sal acted annoyed, but inside there was just a touch of fear.

"Here, and he says he has news."

"It's probably about the fuckin' Cubs again," Sal said. Cohn shrugged and left with the young gangster.

Pete and Sal glared at one another.

"C'mere. Both of you."

They turned.

Johnny Bronco's voice was hoarse and thin, but they still respected it instinctively. They drew near.

"You both... right about recruiting. We need... new blood, new *soldati*."

The two crew captains exchanged looks of grudging respect.

"You two... you gotta quit fucking around."

"You naming a successor?" Steel Pete asked quietly.

"I'll do that when I'm good and goddamn ready!" Bronco's voice got stronger, and his pale face showed a trace of blood. "You so eager, Petey? You wanna shit in my toilet, maybe fuck my wife while you're at it? You goddamn vulture. I ain't dead yet. Neither are you. Neither is the *family*." He paused to cough. "But if you two shitheads fight each other, there won't be a family left to win. You'll just hand it over to Giancana or the Bostonians or those cunts from Chicago. You both know this!"

"No one's done anything yet," Pete muttered. He was looking down at his shoes like a chastised teenage son.

"*Signore?*" It was Cohn's voice, from the doorway. "I think you maybe ought to hear this."

Sal turned with a scowl, and Pete with a smirk. Harvey Ciullo stood behind Cohn.

"What is it?" Johnny said.

"Pudoto's hired a contractor," Hasmed replied.

"Just how the fuck would *you* know that?" Sal asked.

Hasmed produced a manila envelope. Inside were surveillance photos of Johnny, notes about his schedule and habits, images of his bodyguards, a copied blueprint of his house with notes about where the guards were stationed.

"I got this from the zip," he said. "If we move fast, we can catch him reporting to one of Pudoto's captains tonight. All he asks is that we leave him out of it, or say we killed him."

"He's gonna sell out Pudoto for nothin'?" Cohn asked skeptically.

"Not nothin'. He decided it was... healthier to help us out."

Johnny Bronco had made up his mind. "Cohn, get Rock and his people. Harvey here is gonna take 'em to this meet and settle things." As the consigliere nodded and left, Johnny said, "This plays out like you say, Ciullo, and you're gonna be a friend of ours, *capisce*? I'll set you up."

Harvey's ravaged face creased in a homely smile. "You won't regret this, sir." He gave a peculiar kind of sigh, and Johnny Bronco seemed to sit up straighter in bed, seemed momentarily less sick, less dying. Steel Pete didn't notice, but Sal Macellaio did.

"I'll stand up for you, Harv," Sal said. "You can be in my crew."

As the two men locked eyes, each wordlessly knew the real meaning behind Sal's sudden, generous offer. Each gave the other a slow nod.

❖　❖　❖

A few days later, Betsy Smith got up with bad menstrual cramps and decided that a Bloody Mary was just the eye-opener she needed. It was a Saturday, and she was scheduled to work the afternoon shift. She liked working weekends because she could drink on the job with much less chance of getting caught. Of course, she told herself that it was because she could catch up on a lot of paperwork without interruption.

It was a nice day, though cold. Hasmed took Tina to see a G-rated movie. She wanted to see a PG-13 one, but he told her no way. He'd had some difficulty lining up a sitter for her—Helena had met some guy and suddenly had better things to do than watch her niece on a Saturday night. But Hasmed had found a woman in his building, Donna Wentz. She had three kids of her own and was willing to look after Tina for a few extra bucks.

The thing with Pudoto's henchman had gone off velvety smooth. The meet was in a graveyard—kind of weird, unless (like Hasmed) you knew one of the principals was a frickin' vampire. Rock's men moved quiet for such big guys, it was eleven on three, and the guys from Atlantic City didn't have a chance to see it coming. Rock's crew was surprised that the paleface hitman managed to get away. Only Hasmed saw him duck behind a gravestone and never come out again.

Rock himself had given Hasmed a 9mm piece for the job, and he'd carried it ever since. He kept it at the office, of course. No way was he having a gun in the apartment with Tina around.

In that short, one-sided fight, Harvey Ciullo had earned his way into the Vuoto Family, Johnny Bronco's mob. He was going to become an insider, protected, bound by Mafia law.

He was going to get made.

He put on his best suit, kissed Tina goodbye and drove off toward the Mac. That was where they were going to do it, in the bar's basement.

Most of Sal's crew was there when he arrived. Hamish Brennan treated him to a single-malt with a beer back and Dennis Porter looked on with a mix of envy and confusion. Hasmed recognized Vietnam Ham's pals from his first visit, months ago—the syphilitic and the guy he'd knocked down the stairs. They both seemed happy to let bygones be, and they welcomed him to the family with genuine enthusiasm. The guys who'd been with Macellaio at the steel mill were more reserved, but they still gave him their respect.

At her office, Betsy drank the next-to-last beer in her six-pack and then decided to have the last one too. Just tidying up, really. She had ten more minutes on the clock before she was scheduled to punch out, and she was scrupulous about never quitting early.

Tina was outside, playing with three older kids while Donna Wentz watched them from the window. She was on the phone with her sister, getting the latest dirt about her brother-in-law's ex-wife's kid. Donna didn't really notice when the snowball fight became kind of one-sided, with her three sons ganging up on Tina. Tina had been yelling a lot all evening, after all.

Johnny Bronco arrived at the bar, and everyone commented on how much better he seemed. They weren't exaggerating, either. Since he'd offered to put Harvey in the books, his health had improved measurably.

Sal was the only one who made that connection.

Betsy walked, deliberately, to her car, brushed off the slush and started driving home.

A barrage of snowballs hit Tina, hard. She started to cry. She was frightened and alone, and she said the Secret Word.

A couple miles away, Hasmed excused himself to go to the bathroom, prompting several coarse jokes.

He was minutes away from achieving a great step toward his goal, toward membership in a mob that he was confident he could make his own.

But he heard Tina's voice, and when he asked her what was wrong, she couldn't tell him, couldn't answer. He frowned and concentrated and visualized what was happening around her. At first he was relieved to see that it was just some older kids picking on her. Little bastards, he'd fix them later—but she wasn't in danger. He didn't have to choose, didn't have to blow his chance…

Only he did.

Dumb luck, she'd called him because of false peril, when she couldn't see the real danger that was sliding down the street toward her, the street she'd run into fleeing the snowballs. And that car wasn't slowing down, not at all.

As he yanked the bathroom window open, Hasmed didn't think about what he was throwing away. He didn't think about failure. He didn't think about Johnny Bronco's anger, or that of Vodantu, his duke. All he thought about was how to do what he must.

He did not feel conflicted. He did not feel regret. He did not feel anger.

He felt a threat to Tina, and that was all.

As he pushed his way from the bathroom into the alley, his wings were already spreading forth. Another burst of effort, and his glorious, hideous, inhuman form was cloaked in darkness and apathy. No human must see him and none would. He lunged into the air and knew he was moving too slow. He needed more power, more speed, and he reached deep for it.

Miles away, a glass slipped from Roscoe Paum's hand and smashed on a bar-room floor. He gasped and clutched his chest, unable to breathe.

Hasmed moved faster.

In the next state over, in New York City, Lee Boyer Junior was visiting someone who catered to very specific tastes. In the middle of everything his suckling lost power as the air was pulled out of him. He nearly blacked out as he tumbled from the teat, trying to inhale but feeling his breath stolen…

Hasmed's speed increased yet again.

Tina looked up and saw the car, and she screamed. If she'd run, she might have made it on her own, but she froze. She couldn't do anything but shriek.

The change in tone of Tina's cries prompted Donna to look down, but there was no help there, nothing she could do except gasp and gaze and lose every thought in a blank page of horror.

Behind the wheel, Betsy heard, and if she'd been sober, she might have reacted in time, might have steered away or slammed on the brakes. But she couldn't quite get her thoughts and reactions to mesh.

And then a black wind swept across the street and suddenly Donna saw Harvey Ciullo and, holy shit, she'd never have thought the old fat guy could move so fast, like lightning, his coat flapping behind him (like wings?), going into a flat dive, knocking Tina over…

Even that wasn't enough.

With the crystal clarity of an angel's mind, Hasmed knew it wasn't enough. He'd moved her away from the center of the grille, but she'd still get hit, that bitch behind the wheel wasn't even slowing down.

A human would have felt a wash of despair. That sensation would slow a human's hand by half a second. Not much, but it would mean the difference between a near miss and getting sucked under a car's tires.

Hasmed wasn't human. He didn't hesitate. In an instant, the gun was in his hand, and he shot out Betsy Smith's driver-side tire. The car sagged and turned and started to fishtail, and as the spent cartridge from the first bullet hit the ground, he fired twice more. Two other tires flattened, slowing the car.

Its dirty plastic doors actually slid along his outstretched arm, the back flat tire was close enough that it pushed cold dirty slush into his pants leg. Then it was past him, skidding to a stop at last.

"Oh God! Oh my God! Oh Jesus!" Betsy Smith rushed around her car, slipped and sprawled across the trunk and found herself staring down the barrel of a smoking pistol.

The man with the gun had a hideous scar, and he stared at her with an eye of blood. Hasmed didn't fire the gun, though. He reached out with his power and inhaled sharply.

Betsy Smith never felt the urge to drink again.

❧   ❧   ❧

Miles away at the Mac, Johnny Bronco needed an oxygen mask to keep breathing. He was enraged.

"The disrespect," he kept saying. "The disrespect!"

Sal Macellaio looked down at his finger nails, got off his bar stool and made a soft suggestion to his boss. Johnny looked at him and nodded, sharply.

"Ice him," he said. "Make it hurt."

Sal smiled.

chapter fifteen

"Honey," Hasmed said, "Believe me, we have to move fast. Take just your favorite stuff. Right now!"

Tina seemed kind of shell-shocked, and once again, Hasmed felt that uneasy human sensation when emotions mixed. This time it was fear and relief. Relief because Tina wasn't arguing, wasn't complaining, was just wordlessly packing—mostly her toys—and accepting that they needed to leave their apartment right away. Fear because he was worried about her emotions—worried that it would scar her to be wrenched away from her new school, uprooted from yet another home, torn away from Helena. He was also worried that they'd get caught, of course. He'd tried to keep her secret, tried to make sure that no one knew he even had a daughter—but had he succeeded? More importantly, had Harvey succeeded before Hasmed possessed him?

Sal tried to keep his kid secret, Hasmed thought, clumping into his own bedroom. *Look how good he did. 'Course, he didn't know he was hiding from a demon.*

He threw open a suitcase and filled it with pants, shirts, underwear and socks. Most important was a white plastic VCR tape case, hand-labeled "The Hunt for Red October." It did not contain a tape of *The Hunt for Red October.* It contained his store of loose cash, along with two of the clearer, larger diamonds. He'd held them back,

planning to fence them later if he could get better terms. (He'd told himself that he'd cut Paum in for his share at that hypothetical future date.)

Thinking of Paum, he coughed to clear his throat, put on his Zoth of the Hated Lash voice and said "ROSCOE PAUM. ATTEND YOUR MASTER!"

It was the first time he'd invoked the boxer, and there was some initial confusion as he explained the nature of the communication.

"WHATSOEVER YOU ARE DOING, CEASE!" he commanded. "YOUR 'FRIEND' AND MY HOST, HARVEY CIULLO, IS IN GRAVE DANGER. YOU MUST COME TO HIM AT ONCE! HE WILL MEET YOU AT THE CORNER OF BOND AND LOCUST IN TWENTY MINUTES. COME ALONE."

Then he broke off communication and checked on Tina. She was crying.

"It's okay kitten," he said. "It's okay."

"I'm gonna miss my dollies, an' I can't take 'em all!" She pronounced "going" as "doeing" and "can't" as "dan't."

"Shh, it's all right, we'll get you some new ones."

"But these are *mine!*" she cried, anguished.

"Okay tell you what, hon. If they won't fit in a suitcase, we'll put them in garbage bags, not because they're garbage, but just so we can carry them, all right? We'll carry them down to the car like that, and we'll put your clothes around them so they won't get banged up in the back seat. Okay?"

She still looked downcast and scared but she agreed. She pronounced it "Dokay."

"You have to be a brave little girl, Tina. There's bad trouble, but I will protect you. I promised, remember? I'll be with you and protect you."

Suddenly, she flung herself on him and hugged him with all her strength. He made a few attempts to get her off, then simply picked her up. The hours and weeks in the gym paid off—she was a lot easier to lift.

He got her to let go when he got the bags, and he piled enough of her clothing and possessions into them. Hauling the stuff was going to be a bitch—they'd just have to take two trips down the staircase.

"I have some more bad news, sweetpea," he said as he drove her toward Locust Street. "I'm going to have to leave you for a little while."

"You said you wouldn't! You said! You *promised!*"

"I said I'd protect you. To do that, I have to stay back for a while and make sure we aren't followed. But I'm going to leave you with someone named Roscoe, he's a good friend of daddy's, okay? Roscoe will take care of you. It's all going to be all right."

She was crying as they pulled up at Bond Street. Roscoe was sitting on a bus bench, and he hopped up and came to the corner as the car rolled to a stop.

"Get in," Hasmed said.

"Hey, kiddo," Roscoe said to Tina. She paused for a moment, then continued her weeping.

"Whose little girl?"

"Mine."

"*Yours?*" They pulled away from the curb.

"She's my daughter, yeah. Mazel Tov for me, a'right?"

"Jeez, Hawv, I had no idea."

"No one knew. You're the first."

"What's going on?"

"Trouble. Bad trouble."

"The diamonds? Did the cops make us or somethin'?"

"Worse. Vuoto's mob."

"What!? I *told* you not to go to them for the fence."

"It'll be okay. I just need you to go to Atlantic City for a while. Take Tina, take care of her. I'll be along soon."

"Hawv, you're talkin' crazy talk. I can't just up and run—"

"Got a piece?"

"Huh? No."

"Here." He gave him the 9mm he'd gotten from Rock. "It's got five bullets left, so you might wanna get some more."

"What… what's going…?"

"Look, have I steered you wrong yet? Have I? No, not since I come back. So just *trust* me, okay Paum?" They braked for a red light, and Hasmed turned a desperate glance to his passenger. "Roscoe, you are my only hope with this. If you don't do this, I'm dead. I'm dead, and my little girl dies too. I'm not kidding, okay?"

There was a pause. When the light turned green, Hasmed turned right.

"Okay. Atlantic City. Sure. When you gonna come down?"

"Soon."

"Where should I stay?"

"Wherever."

"Then how you gonna find me?"

"I'll find you."

❋　❋　❋

Hasmed gave Ros all the money from his wallet and regretted it as his thrall drove away. He should have at least saved back enough to buy a few little things—some sort of weapon, for one. He was drained and exhausted, physically and spiritually. He'd had to wrestle the world, beat it into submission to save Tina, and it had taken a lot out of him. He wouldn't be doing anything terrible or magnificent until he had a chance to recover—or unless he was willing to sicken and rob his believers still further.

Roscoe had dropped him in front of the bodega near his office, the same place he'd sent Lee Boyer to get candles. Entering, he gave the woman behind the counter a smile that was supposed to be charming. She immediately went on guard.

"Hey, uh, Miss," he started. "I really need to get this box opened up at my office. The guy who sent it he's…" Hasmed made a tsk sound, twitched his shoulders, rolled his eyes. "He put on, like, fi'ty layers of tape, an' I can't get through it." He picked up a utility knife from a display box and said "I need one of these, but I left my wallet in my other pants. You guys know me, right? I'm right up the street, could you maybe—"

"No credit," she said.

"Look, it's, what, it's a dollar seventy for this, I'm not gonna rip you off for that."

"No credit."

He felt a brief flash of anger but pushed it down. "How'bout this: I leave you my watch as an assurance, a'right? It's no Rolex, but it's worth more'n a buck seventy."

"Does this look like a pawn shop?"

He felt the wrath flaring up again, and he considered just killing her. Her hands were on the counter. He was pretty confident that he could grab her hair, yank her

forward, stun her and then slit her throat, stealing the knife she wouldn't sell to him... and then he just had to laugh.

Here I am, he thought, *An angel or a demon or something, and I'm thinking about kacking this bitch over a goddamn box-cutter.*

He dropped it on the counter and said "Thanks for nothin', cunt." On his way back to the office, he picked up the broken neck of a glass bottle. When he reached his office door, he realized that the key was still on his key chain, in his car, on the road to Atlantic City.

Shaking his head, he sat in the stairwell, peeking through a cracked-open door. He didn't have long to wait.

He recognized one of the two men who came off the elevator—he'd been with Macellaio at the steel mill. The other was younger and twitchier, some steroided high school dropout in a funeral suit from Sears. He kept putting his hand under his lapel, like he was scratching his ribs.

"Knock it off, AC," the older man said. "You look like fuckin' Napoleon."

"Huh?"

"With your hand in your jacket. Christ, don' be such a moron."

"Don' call me a moron!"

"Then don' act moronic." He looked up and down the corridor and squinted at the stairwell door, but there was nothing to see. Hasmed had pushed reality just a little more.

In New York, Boyer felt weak and breathless again, but not as bad. This was just as well. When he'd collapsed, the lactating hooker had tried to roll him. Once he recovered, he'd started to pistol-whip her. The second bout of weakness probably saved her life, if not her face.

Satisfied that no one was looking, the mobster from the steel mill extracted a set of lock picks from a plastic case and went to work.

"Why don' we just kick it in?" AC asked.

"Shut up." He shook his head at the lock. "Cheap piece of shit," he said as it opened. He stood back from the door and gestured for AC to enter. "Quietly, now, though it's probably way too fuckin' late."

AC pulled his gun and boldly walked in. The other man rolled his eyes and went along, empty handed. Hasmed followed close behind, stepping lively to get through before they closed the door.

"It's empty," AC reported, coming back from the office into the room with the table. He was screwing a silencer onto the end of his revolver.

"So we wait," the older gangster said, drawing a weapon and doing the same. "And for Christsakes be quiet. We want him to come in without knowing we're here, all right?"

"I know, I know. I ain't stupid."

Hasmed had decided that AC was, by far, more likely to do something dumb and unpredictable, so that was the man he crept up behind. He took a deep breath—no spirit, just the body's preparation for action—then looped his arm over the young man's shoulder, digging the points of glass into his throat as he dropped his disguise.

"Gimme your gun," he hissed.

"Don't do it!" the other man cried, his own weapon rising in an instant.

"Drop it, or I kill your pal!" Hasmed said. He didn't yell—he didn't want any attention, and neither did the mobsters.

"Actually, I can probably shoot you right through him."

"You FUCKER!" AC bellowed and pointed his gun at his associate.

Hasmed started to chuckle. "Quite the standoff, ain't it?"

"Give it up, Ciullo. You jab him, and I'll blow you away, you know this. Or he'll pull his head out his ass and point that gun at you instead of me. AC's too smart to hand his gun to an unarmed asswipe like you."

"But what if I'm not afraid of gunshots? I mean, it's not like I never been shot before. I got better."

"You're friggin' crazy then."

"Am I? Or am I something worse than crazy?" Hasmed tilted his head down and let his bloody eye peep over the top of his sunglasses. "Do you believe in the devil?"

"Shit no."

"Are you sure? 'Cause you didn' seem so sure at the steel mill, remember that? You had a gun on me then, too."

"Crazy…"

"Sure, it's crazy. I'm crazy, we're all crazy. You're crazy if you think anything else. How else did I kill Mikey Diamond, huh? How else did I go from being nobody to getting made in less'n four months? How else did I just *appear* behind your buddy here without neither of you seeing?"

The man was shaking his head, but Hasmed grinned as he felt it. The man *did* believe, sweet and pure and uncomplicated fear belief, and it was all the demon needed to show his true face.

The mobster didn't waste time screaming, he just fired. The silenced gunshot, no louder than a clap, was drowned out as AC shouted. The bullet slammed through him and into Hasmed, and AC pulled his own trigger. Then with a sweep of wings and a movement like a hailstorm, both guns were in Hasmed's hands and both men were bleeding on the floor.

Crap, I barely had to do anything, the demon thought, almost giddy, but now was no time to lose control. Not yet. Awkwardly, he put both silenced weapons in one hand, freeing the other to stuff a tie into AC's mouth, smothering the boy's screams. The other mobster wasn't a shouter. He'd taken his hit through the lung and couldn't get breath to shriek.

"You believe now, don't you? Yes, you do. That's good. It's good to die believing." He didn't bother with claws or weapon. He pinched the man's Adam's apple and squeezed hard. That did it. The man gasped and twitched for several seconds more before stilling. Hasmed had enough time to wonder if it was the throat or the gunshot that really finished him off, though it probably didn't matter.

He turned to AC. The boy was still wailing, but it was muffled through the tie. He'd been gut-shot, and while he might have wanted to pull the makeshift gag from his mouth, he didn't seem able to move his hands away from the wound.

"You're unlucky," Hasmed said. "That other guy died for me, and that was quick. You're going to have to die for Vodantu my master, and it's going to take a while longer." He frowned, then stomped hard on AC's kneecap. "Don't go nowhere," he said, and went into the back office for a roll of packing tape.

"Did you like the ponies?" Roscoe asked.

"Yeah," Tina said without much spirit.

"Good, yeah. They ran fast, huh?"

"Uh huh."

"And supper was good?"

"Uh huh."

"That's a pretty cool gadget you got from that, uh, Happy Meal there," he said.

They were back at a motel, and Roscoe felt incredibly uncomfortable. He had almost no experience with children, and checking into a motel with this tiny girl he didn't know made him feel like a monstrous sex pervert. He knew he wasn't—Roscoe liked his women big and foul-mouthed—but still, what would people think? What would they say if they knew?

"So, uh, what's your usual bedtime?"

Tina shrugged.

Christ, she probably can't tell time, Roscoe thought. "Well, are you sleepy?"

She shrugged again.

"Well, uh, why don't you brush your teeth, an… and all." Earlier, at the horse races, she'd had "a potty accident" and he'd had to help her with her pull-up pants. He had never felt so humiliated in his life, and once he'd actually pissed his own pants during a fight, when he got knocked out. This had been worse.

"When is Daddy coming back?"

"Oh, uh, real soon. If you go to bed and sleep, he'll probably be here when you wake up."

"Really?"

"Sure!"

She scampered off into the bathroom, and he sank into a chair, breathing a big sigh of exhaustion. She returned quickly.

"Did you brush?"

"Uh huh."

He didn't think she had, but decided not to push it. He wasn't about to waste effort lobbying for pajamas or, God forbid, a bath, either. Not when some hard cases from Johnny Bronco's crews might bust down the door any minute.

"Tell me a story?"

"Uh… a'right. You, uh, you know the Three Little Pigs?"

He told her the story of the Three Little Pigs. Eventually, she got into one of the room's two beds.

"Daddy's coming back, right?"

"I told you he was."

"Is he going to die?"

"What? Christ, Tina! I mean… I mean no, sweetie, no. Your dad ain't gonna die."

"My mommy did."

Her mournful tone made him look right at her.

"Aw, that's… that's too bad, kid." He had no idea what to say.

"I went next door to play, and when I came home, mommy was dead."

Unsure what to do, Roscoe got up and sat on the edge of a bed. "Don't think about that now," he said, almost pleading. "Jus' go to sleep."

"I went next door, and mommy slipped in the shower." For "slipped," she said "dlipped."

"Crap."

"Mommy slipped in the shower an' she hit her head an' she died. She died for ever and ever."

"Christ kid… I mean, that's rough." Hesitantly, he reached out and stroked her hair. "I bet you miss her a lot, huh?"

She nodded.

"Well hey, she's watching you from Heaven. You know that, right?"

Another nod.

"An' she's… uh, you know. She's in your heart, too. You know. She's there forever."

"Uh huh," she said softly.

"And you've got your dad. He's gonna take good, good care of you."

"But I want her here *right now!*" And suddenly, she was crying.

Roscoe knelt by the bedside and put his arms around her.

"Shh," he said. "It's all right. It's okay." He couldn't think of anything to say or do, except to stroke her hair and say things that he felt, deep in his heart, were utter lies. He

felt stupid and useless and weak, with nothing to offer this poor suffering orphan except good intentions.

Eventually, good intentions must have been enough, or maybe she just got tired. She fell asleep.

Roscoe sat in the chair with the gun in his lap, watching the door and waiting.

❖   ❖   ❖

Hasmed took money from the gangsters but reluctantly left their pistols there. Taking them would just prolong the inevitable police inquiry. Murdering them had refreshed him, and he'd gotten a letter opener with a decent tip out of the desk, along with more cash. He wasn't sure how much good the money would do, but it couldn't hurt.

As he was on his way out, he heard a chirping sound coming from a corpse. Coming closer, he found it was a tinny version of "God Bless America".

When he flipped open AC's cell phone, he heard a scratchy woman's voice saying "Arnold? It's mama. On your way home, could you pick up a quart of milk for me? I'd go, but—"

He turned off the phone, shaking his head. Then he went to a hardware store for a saw and to Walgreen's for a duffel bag.

There were three men at his apartment when he got there, including Rock himself. Things got kind of crazy—he was shot several times before he got control of the situation. He sacrificed Rock to Vodantu, apologizing as he did— "You were pretty square with me, but you're the chief, you're the pick of the litter"—and took the other two for himself.

The police showed up while he was sawing off Rock's head. He took a shot and made some noise about hostages. The police started evacuating the building and calling in the SWAT team, so Hasmed had plenty of time to finish his decapitations, wrap the heads in layers of old plastic grocery sacks and sneak out of the building under the cover of demonic influence.

He'd been collecting cell phones, and one rang. He answered it. Except for AC's phone, which was bright blue, they all looked pretty much the same.

"Rudy? Talk to me."

Hasmed grinned. It was Sal's voice.

"Rudy can't come to the phone right now," he said.

"Ciullo? Listen, you fuck—"

Hasmed clicked the off button and kept walking. Pretty soon, another phone rang.

"Rock? Sal. Listen, Ciullo is in town, I think he got Rudy and that new kid."

"Too late again, Sal."

There was a blank silence from the other end of the line.

"Saying 'oh shit' would be appropriate," Hasmed told him as he entered the bus station.

But Sal was made of sterner stuff. "Listen up you fuckin' *freak*. I don't know what you are or how you're doing this shit, but you are gonna pay if it's the last thing I do. I'm gonna hound you. I'm gonna break you. You got any friends? They're dead. A pet? Dead. Your fuckin' half-sister-in-law, whatever, Helena? Fuggeddaboudit, Ciullo. Unless you're in the room with me right now."

"Wait. Sal, wait a minute."

Over the phone came the sound of muffled hysteria, then Helena's sobbing voice.

"Harvey, I told you not to! I told you not to go back with those guys! I said—"

A loud bang cut her off.

Hasmed swept his glasses off his face and shut his eyes, pressing the back of his hand against the bridge of his nose. He breathed out, searching for Helena.

Gone.

"Huh. So I guess there's things you can't do." Sal's voice was deeply satisfied. "Didn't know I had her, eh? An' I bet you don't know where I am now."

"Your son is going to—"

"No, Ciullo, your *daughter* is going to die. Unless you get your fat monster ass out of town and never, ever come back. You get me? We are done, Ciullo. You're fuckin' exiled. If you ever come near my boy or my wife or *my town*, I'll snuff your mama down in Florida and everyone who went to her weddings. You get me?"

Harvey would have backed down. But Harvey would never have been in the position to back down.

"No, you get *me*, Macellaio," Hasmed said, and he spoke not as a man, but with the voice of a minister of creation. "You have roused a wrath whose depth you cannot fathom. Your petty cruelty is nothing to me. Kill dozens if you wish: I have stood on the corpses of *thousands*. You will know my revenge, Sal Macellaio. You will know what it's like to be a sinner in the hands of an angry god."

He turned off the phone and looked around him. People were staring. He tilted down his glasses, and they all suddenly found new homes for their glances.

In a bathroom he wiped off the phones and left them neatly by the sink. Two were ringing as he pushed his way out. He bought a ticket, pulled out his own phone and left it off as he put it to his ear.

"Rabbadün," he said. "Can you meet me soon? Like, today or tomorrow?"

chapter sixteen

The bus trip was long, and Hasmed spent most of it asleep. When he arrived, he called Boyer—conventionally, this time—and asked who he knew in Atlantic City. Having heard about the shit-storm with Rock and the Vuoto family, Boyer had stayed in New York, laying low. He gave Hasmed a reference.

That reference—a guy called Tommy Bones—wasn't all that easy to get to, but once Hasmed started showing the heads, people got the hell out of his way. It was midnight when he got his audience with Rico Pudoto.

"This better be good." Rico's rolls of sweaty fat looked like freshly boiled bratwursts, only with thick, dark hair sprinkled liberally on top.

Hasmed opened the duffel without a word.

"Jesus, Mary and fuck," Pudoto said, waving a hand in front of his nose. He leaned in. "Holy crap, that's Rock all right."

"You want in on Vuoto's turf." Hasmed didn't say it as a question. Rico shrugged. "I just whacked out Rock, two of his guys and two of Macellaio's."

"Congratulations," Rico said.

"Let's make a deal."

"Yeah?"

"I get Macellaio out of the way. That's my part. You make me and give me a crew. That's yours."

"Whoa whoa whoa." Rico held up his hands. "I don't know you from shit."

"You know what I can do."

"And I can't just make people whenever I want."

"Go to war with the Vuotos, and no one will blame you for opening the books."

"Plus I got guys of my own. I can't just bump you up to Skipper from nothing. They'd hate me."

"Tell 'em I was a made guy with Johnny Bronco and you're giving me a crew as a reward for piping his ass."

"Yeah, Johnny Bronco. That's another thing. He's a tough old fuck."

"He'll die soon."

"That's what we all thought, but I hear he's all of a sudden doin' better."

Hasmed smiled a flat, mirthless smile.

"How 'bout this," he said. "You're a gambler, right Rico?"

"With some things."

"I'm a gambler, too. I lost a lot betting that the Cubs would take the pennant this year."

"That's a stupid fuckin' bet, if you don' mind me sayin'."

"I'll bet you that Johnny Bronco dies within… what, two days? If he does, we have a deal."

"If he doesn't?"

Hasmed shrugged. "A quarter mil over the next year and a half sound fair? I can give you twenty large of it up front."

Waiting in the lobby of a Super 8 Motel, Hasmed was nervous. He liked the killing—liked it a lot. Sawing off Rock's head had been about as much fun as he'd had since the Fall.

In one way.

In another way, it made him sick, and it made him sad. There was some little bright part of him still, something even Hell hadn't crushed, and that part didn't want him to be another Rabbadün, another gleeful killer. That small spark was still a guardian angel, and every time Tina looked at him, it got stronger and truer. More than it feared Sal or

even Vodantu, that spark feared what Hasmed could be if he gave in to that terrible, merciless joy.

It was the same thing again, the same waffling, human, both-feelings-at-once thing. He wanted to see Tina—*needed* to—hoping against hope that she'd soothe the ache of anger and put him back in control. He needed her to put the beast back in its cage. But at the same time, what if she didn't? What if he saw her and she was just another blob of meat, another sack of guts to spill out and desecrate for his impatient master?

He sat strung between hope and fear, munching a donut from the motel's stale continental breakfast, until Roscoe brought Tina into the room.

"Daddy!"

Her hug was so tight it was actually painful.

"Hey, kitten. Mornin', Paum," he nodded.

"You look like sh—like crap, Hawv."

"You don't look so good yourself, Ros."

"I didn't sleep last night."

"Me either, much."

"Daddy! Daddy! Can I have Cap'n Crunch?"

"Sure, sweetie." He turned to Roscoe and said, "Hey. Thanks."

The boxer shrugged.

"No, really. You did me a real solid. Thanks."

"Hawv, there's... there's somethin' you gotta know."

"Daddy! I'm having a donut!"

"I see you, honey. Careful with that milk, now!"

"Hawv..."

"Sorry Ros, she can be a handful. Well, *you* know that for sure."

"Do you know the name Zoth-Tocatil?"

Hasmed kept his face carefully neutral. "That's a weird kind of name, Ros. Never heard it."

"Well... it... it kinda talks through you."

"What?"

"Remember when you, y'know, fixed me?"

"Daddy! Look!"

"Not now, sweetheart."

"No, daddy! Look! Look!"

"Hold on," Hasmed said. With an apologetic look at Paum, he picked Tina up and walked her around, answering questions about the pool and laughing at her jokes and listening to her run-on, fragmentary account of her trip to the racetrack. When she seemed calmer, he came back to Roscoe.

"Okay, Ros, what were you saying?"

The boxer opened his mouth and shut it. "Maybe now ain't the right time," he said at last.

"A'right… maybe you're right, I gotta get goin'." He sighed and knelt down before his daughter.

"Tina, sweetie," he said. "I gotta leave now. You stay with Mr. Paum." The two adults had discussed this over the phone, so Roscoe was braced, but he still wasn't prepared for what happened.

Tina exploded. She started with a wordless scream, then started flailing her arms, kicking and shrieking.

"Sweetheart…" Hasmed tried to hold her, tried to contain her. Her face was bright red, wet with tears, and snot was streaming out over her upper lip.

"I hate you! I hate you hate you! You're not my daddy! You lie to me! You're bad! You're mean mister deadface!"

That was when her *dad* lost his temper.

"Tina, damn it," he started, his voice getting louder and deeper as his face started to match hers in color, "I do *not* need this shit! You hear me? I'm doing all this for you! I just threw away *everything* for you!" He had a hand on either shoulder. He wasn't shaking her, but his knuckles were white with strain. It wasn't that he was squeezing hard, it was the effort of *not* gripping her painfully tight.

Tina's anger abruptly turned to fear, but she was trapped. The thing that scared her most was the thing she went to for comfort. She froze, immobile except for the writhing of her mouth as she sobbed in utter misery.

Hasmed slumped. "Tina, you gotta give your old man a break," he whispered.

Roscoe stepped forward wordlessly and put his arms around the girl. She turned and buried her face in his chest.

"Hey now," Paum said. "Hey. How'bout you give your old dad a kiss huh? For good luck. A little hug for daddy?"

She wouldn't do it.

❊ ❊ ❊

Rabbadün was waiting at the airport.

"Still drivin' this beater, eh?"

"Shut the fuck up."

"Yes sir, O great Asharu. O Master Hasmed of the Hated Lash." He turned his neck, grinning. "So, where we going?"

"I need you to find someone for me."

"I thought you Angels of the Firmament didn't need anyone's help in that department." As he spoke, Rabbadün drummed his fingers on the dashboard of the car.

"It's been a hard couple days, and I need to conserve my strength. Plus, I need to get to him and away from him quickly."

"Ah, I see. So I'm basically your getaway driver, hm?"

"Sure, whatever."

Rabbadün nodded. "Well, I'll need three syllables of your True Name."

"What? What the fuck are you talking about?"

"Hey, it's tit for tat. You give a little, you get a little. One hand washes the other. You scratch my back—"

"I got three syllables for you: Suck my dick."

"Can't help you with that."

"As long as you do the other thing."

"Can't help you find your guy, either."

The tires squealed as Hasmed pulled over to the side of the highway. "Listen, you puffed up Neberu ass-wipe, I'm not *asking* for your help, I'm *telling* you."

"On what authority?"

"On *my* authority!"

"What authority is that? Your God-given right to lead lesser houses? I don't think The Ancient of Days is about to stoop down and get your back, Hasmed. Or are you going by your rank in Lucifer's army—an army that lost and got kicked into Hell for eight thousand years. An army whose leader is *nowhere to be found*?" Rabbadün's sneer turned into a snarl. "Welcome to the Fifth Age, shitforbrains. The only authority here is how much power you got. You need it, I got it, so what you gonna—"

Roscoe had introduced Hasmed to both the speed bag and the heavy bag, so when he smashed his passenger across the chops, it was a fairly good blow.

"You wanna bang heads with me, you shit?"

Rabbadün's response was to lunge across the seat and try to choke him. Hasmed got in two good jabs to the nose before they were clinched, before neither could punch and both were reduced to shoving and biting and gouging.

As if by wordless agreement, neither took on their demonic forms. Both had been striving against a world with no place for angels, and even as they gripped one another, they could feel the pressure of the mundane world close upon them both. The weight of overdue rent and job interviews and furniture that needed to be reupholstered, the weight of pencils with the erasers worn down and plugged radiator filters and lawns that could really use some fertilizer. The world of man kept them pinched into-man shapes, and neither wanted to be the first to wrestle free of that hold.

In the end, Hasmed's greater weight won the day. He rolled Rabbadün to the left, down onto the floor of the sedan, with the hump of the drive shaft jammed into his back.

"Okay, okay," Rabbadün said as Hasmed's thumbs pressed down on his eye sockets. "You win." He took a deep breath. "One syllable."

Hasmed sighed. Why not? What was the use? Besides, they were nominally allies anyhow. He spoke a single, inhuman, unearthly syllable in the first language.

"There." Rabbadün wiped some blood from his nose. "Was that *so* hard?"

Groaning, they separated and returned to their seats. Once he'd caught his breath, Hasmed pulled back onto the highway.

Shifting lanes, Hasmed wondered why he bothered. Suppose he killed Sal, just like he'd killed Rock and AC and the others. What then? He'd be a rotten, dirty gangster with Pudoto's gang instead of Johnny Bronco's. Big deal. Sal would go on to whatever unknowable, ineffable fate God had reserved for mankind alone. One way or the other, he'd

be done with Hasmed and the Mafia and the rest of the shit of life.

At that moment, Hasmed envied him deeply, and that envy breathed up the ember of hate that he'd banked low.

Why should Sal get out? Why should Sal be released from this sick and shitty world, while Hasmed had to stay knee-deep in the grime? What had *Sal* done to deserve the reward of death, to earn its Get Out of Jail Free card, to finally find out what God's ultimate plan was?

Screw that.

Sal wasn't going to live forever. Like every fallen guardian, Hasmed knew that without a doubt. But at that moment, he decided that Sal wasn't going to escape the hell of Earth, for a while at least.

"Misery loves company," he muttered.

"What?" When Hasmed turned and glared, Rabbadün flinched back—good. "I just... just wanted to know who we had to find and get to."

"A guy named Scott," Hasmed said. "Sal Macellaio's kid."

✸　✸　✸

Scott's mom wasn't Sal's wife. She'd waited tables in Idaho, where Sal had passed through exactly twice. Scott had been one error in judgment, among many, but it had turned out for the best. When Sal passed through Idaho again ten years later, he saw a kid hanging out at the same restaurant. A kid who looked like him.

Cute kid—soft faced, he was doodling robots and giraffes on his school notebook. Quiet. Sweet. And the resemblance was pretty damn profound.

Sal took it slow, but he remembered the mom, remembered his other trip to Idaho, and when he was sure the kid was his, he did the right thing. A lot of right things, actually. Made arrangements. In Idaho, it wasn't hard. Got the kid money for college, clothes, paid for a tutor when the kid wanted to learn how to use an airbrush. Nothing big, except to Scott.

Sal didn't see Scott all that often, really. Scott thought Sal was a kindly, distant uncle. But something about Scott made Sal feel all right. The kid was an artist. Smart. His mom had gotten married, and they lived in an okay neigh-

borhood, a place with block parties, a place where neighbors lent one another power tools and looked out for each other's kids.

It was normal, and knowing that there was something normal somewhere—that his *son* was being normal, somewhere—that made a lot of heavy stuff all right for Sal. Sal did bad things. He killed a stoolie with a power drill, he shot bank guards, he strangled a PI who got too uppity, he scammed a lot of money from a retirement fund for widowed teachers, but that was okay. That was the life. When he felt bad about it, knowing that his son Scott would never do those things put them in perspective.

That was why it was such a shock when Scott was threatened, and that was why he'd sprung the dough to send the kid to art school in France for a semester. Sal figured he'd have "Mr. Fortune" settled by the time Scott got back, and finding one American student in all of Europe... that wouldn't be possible, right?

❖ ❖ ❖

Things were hot. Johnny Bronco died two days after Harvey flew the coop. Sal, Cohn and Steel Pete all agreed it was best not to tell the *soldati* until things were settled.

Pudoto was getting bolder. Blood was being shed on both sides, mobsters zipping between the two cities in trains, planes, cars and busses, carrying guns and grenades and cash. Both sides were ratting each other out with ferocious speed, and the cops were loving it. It was warfare, fought with fire and stealth and treachery. Sal Macellaio was in the thick of it.

Sal found a cassette tape in his mailbox at home. He'd been out all night bickering with Steel Pete, making tough choices about who to send where and do what. Who could risk prison. Who they could trust in New York and Boston and Philadelphia.

When he got home, there was a tape, and it was labeled "Scott."

As soon as he saw it, he felt dread. He wanted to go to sleep, he was exhausted, but he knew he'd listen. He knew he had to listen.

With a deep, uneven breath, he went back out to the Cadillac and put it in the tape deck. He didn't want to hear it in his home.

There was a rumble, a hiss of audio blankness, and then abruptly Ciullo's voice.

"—didn't even know he was your dad?"

"Salvatore Macellaio is my uncle. You… you guys are all turned around."

"He's your dad, kid. Shit, you're not real smart, are you?"

Sal winced. Scott was a gentle soul, he wasn't used to insults.

"Before you die, kid, you're going to curse your dad's name."

"I told you—"

There was a meaty, smacking sound, and Sal winced again.

"Let's do this thing without a lot of back-chat. Sal's your dad, not your uncle."

"Hey, unless he's your dad *and* your uncle." This was a new voice, unpleasant, one Sal didn't know. "That would be pretty hot."

"Look, who… whoever you guys are, whatever you want, I, I can…" Scott's voice was uneven. He was trying to be brave. For the first time in eight years, a tear ran down Sal's cheek.

"I'll tell you what I *want*," Ciullo said. "I want Sal to suffer. I want him to suffer like I've suffered."

"I'm sorry that you… but look, it's not… I'm…"

"Physical pain." Ciullo said it with a philosophical chill. Then again. "*Physical* pain."

"Ah… ah… *Ahhhiiiiieeee!*"

"Pretty bad, huh kid?" Scott was sobbing in the background as Harvey spoke. "But it's really only meat. It stops, eventually, y'know?"

"Oh please… please…"

"Now you want real torment? Real torment is knowing that someone you love is going to die, and that you can't save them."

"Oh *God*…"

"Sal killed my sister, you know. My half-sister, really, but she was a good woman who never did shit to nobody, and your *dad* killed her for no reason besides he was pissed at me."

"My dad… my *uncle*… he's, he imports specialty foods! He sells olives and cheeses! He never killed anyone!"

"Do you ever read the goddamn newspapers? Never heard of Sal Macellaio, the alleged hijacker and robber, suspected member of the Vuoto crime family? No? Stuck to the comics pages, eh?"

"None of that... I'm from Idaho, there isn't..."

"Idaho, huh? Funny."

There was another scream, high and long and full of despair.

"I want you to say you hate your dad."

"No."

Another sound of pain, this one softer, more like a gasp.

"I want you to say you hate Sal Macellaio."

"No!"

"Say it," Sal whispered, knowing it was too late, knowing his son must be dead, but stupidly still hoping.

"That's another torment, you see. When you *love* someone and you give everything for them and make sacrifices they can't even understand, but they *hate* you. That's pretty bad."

"Go to hell."

That got thick laughs from both men. Not nasty snickers intended to intimidate, but real, honest belly laughs.

"Kid, you got no idea. Hey, you wanna see something? Watch this."

"Nnnnn... nnnnnnooooo!"

"Yeah, that's pretty bad huh? Hurts like a motherfucker, yeah? But, well, once they're crushed, that's it, right? Right?"

Scott's answer was high-pitched sobs.

"Wrong. Abracadabra. Alakazam, you poor bastard." The tape caught a peculiar hissing sound, then Ciullo's voice again. "Good as new. Ready to be crushed all over again."

"Applied with malice, the healing gift can be the cruelest of all." This was the second voice, Harvey's unknown friend. He sounded so happy it was almost hysteria. "See, we're not gangsters. We're not some petty crooks, breaking human laws. Should we show him, Has—" There was an abrupt skip in the tape, a few seconds' worth of rumbling, and then Scott's voice again.

"Oh... oh no. No. Please no."

"THE SINS OF THE FATHER ARE VISITED ON THE SON." The voice was... unearthly, loud and beautiful and terrifying.

Each word was like the climactic note of some unworldly symphony, something grand and awe-inspiring. Even the flat, imperfect recording made Sal's bones thrill within him. "FOR HIS CRUELTY AND CRIME, YOU SHALL BE CONDEMNED INTO THE MAW OF THE DEMON DUKE VO—" Again, that click and rumble, something missing before the voice continued. "—SUFFER IN ETERNITY FOR YOUR FATHER'S BOLDNESS! NOW, WITH YOUR DYING BREATH: CONDEMN THE MAN WHO DOOMED YOU TO THIS AGONY! HATE YOUR FATHER! DAMN THE NAME SAL MARCHELLEO!"

"IT'S MACELLAIO," said a second voice—a voice like a rumble of thunder, or like the hiss of hail striking down ripe crops. "COME ON, SCOTT. YOU KNOW THIS IS HIS FAULT. GET EVEN. GIVE HIM SOMETHING TO REMEMBER YOU BY."

"Oh God, oh God…"

"THE ONE ABOVE WON'T HELP YOU NOW, SCOTT. HE WON'T. HE CAN'T. IF YOU WOULD PRAY, PRAY TO YOUR NEW MASTER, V—" Again, the skip. What was getting edited out?

When the tape resumed, it was Scott speaking. If the tape had started at that point, Sal wouldn't have recognized the voice. It was his son, but transformed by physical pain and deep, deep fear. He'd only been listening for, what, four minutes? The longest four minutes of his life. Four minutes in which Scott's kind, soft, intelligent voice had been transformed into this broken whine, this whimper, every word groaning under a load of suffering and terror.

"God, please kill me. Please God, please let me die. Please. Please God…"

Ciullo's cold snicker drowned out Scott's pleas. "That," he said, "Is the one prayer God always grants. Eventually."

There was a wet sound, like when a gristly joint of meat gets separated from a cooked animal, and then silence.

"He died believing, Sal." It was Ciullo's voice again, full of cold purpose. "Just like you will."

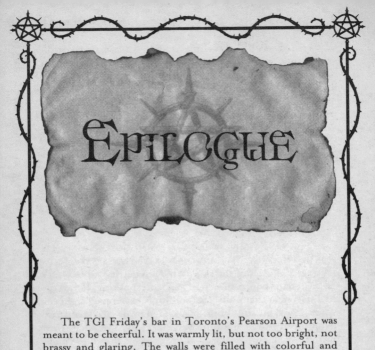

EPILOGUE

The TGI Friday's bar in Toronto's Pearson Airport was meant to be cheerful. It was warmly lit, but not too bright, not brassy and glaring. The walls were filled with colorful and charming mementos of good times gone by. Expert designers had plotted every inch of surface to make the place chipper and upbeat. Consultants had gotten handsome fees for cleverly naming the drinks the bar served. Even the selection of music in the jukebox had been focus-grouped for maximum fun appeal.

But while Sal Macellaio was listening to the sounds of his son's death, the bar was gripped by gloom.

This had nothing to do with Sal or Scott or Hasmed and Rabbadün. Instead, the gloom was focused on a short, hairless black man sitting at the end of the bar nursing a whimsically named drink.

The black man was wearing jeans, a polo shirt and penny loafers. He didn't look out of place, except for an ugly mark on the back of a mangled hand. But the drinker kept that hand in his lap, out of sight. Nevertheless, as he slumped forward and drank, he seemed to radiate a bleak sense of mortality and depression. It rolled off him like bad breath. It infected the bartender, who frowned as he restocked the lime slices and

garlic-stuffed olives. A waitress walking by was suddenly reminded of an ex-lover, a man who was now just a memory, and
a sad memory at that. She furrowed her brow, and for just a
moment all the trinkets and buttons she was required to wear
made her feel fragile and disposable. With slumped shoulders,
she asked a licensed Xerox repair representative and his lunch
date (who was the comptroller at a regional Foot Locker
warehouse), if they needed another drink. They decided, on
the spur of the moment, to just get the check and leave.

Scattered throughout the bar, people lost interest in the
hockey game currently on television, started suddenly talking
about their regrets and missed opportunities, or had minor
quarrels that baffled them once they got as far as the parking lot.

In short, while the bar had aimed for Buddy Holly singing
Little Sheila, its tone had somehow landed on Little Milton
and *Stormy Monday*.

A man with sparkling green eyes and thick red hair entered
and made a beeline for the source of the malaise.

Although the short black killjoy's back was to door, he
stiffened and turned, glaring. When the pair locked eyes, the
bartender dropped a glass of Molson Canadian. The waitress's
Bic ballpoint also cracked and leaked black ink on her fingers
as she handed it to the copier repairman, but he had problems
of his own as he'd just stabbed himself in the gums with a plastic
cocktail sword while sucking off the olives from his mahrtooni.
(It wasn't a martini: It was a specialty drink called a
"mahrtooni.") As for the Foot Locker comptroller, she had
suddenly started choking on a piece of bone from her supposedly boneless chicken tenders.

"What you drinkin'?" the redhead asked, cheerfully. The
black man glared.

"I believe it's called a 'Juicy Lucy,'" he said. His voice was
sour as pickle brine.

"Ah. Wasn't she the one who did the Watusi in a rockin' pair
of blue suede shoes?" He turned to the barman and said, "Another Juicy Floozie for my companion here and... hm, I'll have a
shot of Absolut Peppar with a Fosters back." He looked at the bald
man and asked, "Should we split an order of buffalo wings?"

"I'm not going to break bread with you, stranger."

"No one's talking about the breaking of the bread."

The black man scowled but said nothing.

"So," the redhead said. "That's a very interesting ring
you have."

"You want a closer look?" He said it the way he might have said, "You want me to shove your bloodless corpse into a wood chipper?"

"The last guy I saw with a ring like that was named Max Hirniesen." He nodded as the bartender served their drinks. "Thanks."

The black man's eyes widened. "So *you're* the one."

The green-eyed man smiled and modestly pressed his hands to his chest. "Guilty," he sang out coyly. Then he winked. "You can thank me by getting the next round."

"Who are you?"

"Max thought I was a woman named Penelope, but he was wrong. You guess."

"Guessing names is perilous for our kind. Every wrong name calls attention."

"I'll give you hints, then. Who would put a weapon of such power in the hands of someone so despised by his fellows? Someone formerly of the malhim, Heaven's most feared warriors? Someone almost guaranteed to turn its power against Hell's other inmates?"

"I would have guessed a servant of the Allmaker, but I know you're nothing of the sort."

The redhead looked serious for the first time since he'd walked in. He opened his mouth, but instead of speaking, he downed his shot of vodka.

"I've been following your troubles with Vassago. Most interesting."

The black man drew in a sharp breath. The redhead waved a hand negligently. "Your fiendish foe won't track *me* from that single utterance. Trust me."

"I'd rather trust a snake to nurse a kitten."

"Mm, I probably deserve that," the redhead said, sipping his beer. "But that doesn't change some essential facts. You've made a powerful enemy—one you aren't ready to fight... yet. You've hurt him, but he's on guard, and a forewarned Neberu is a dangerous foe indeed." Another sip. "Especially one who's corrupted a servant of Heaven."

"What do you know of that?"

"The question is, what do *you* know?"

The bald man looked down, ran one hand's fingers over the nubs where others had been burned off. "I know the Allmaker has not forgiven me."

"Hah. Of all the lessons you could have learned, that's one of the worst. What you *should* have learned is that the sides aren't as cleanly divided as you've always believed." He shrugged. "Though, I suppose someone who wasn't convinced by condemnation to Hell wouldn't knuckle under, even to obvious evidence."

"*Who are you?*" His tone and volume got nervous looks from the bartender and the waitress. Most of the other patrons had quietly settled up and found reasons to leave without dawdling.

"I—like you—am the enemy of the mad denizens of the Abyss. I'm an enemy of those demons who lurk like cancers in the sweet skin of Earth. I can guide you to great monsters when they are weakest, and I can teach you how best to steal their strength to use against their cousins in filth."

The black man backed off his barstool and stood, alert.

"I am your ally and patron, and I am the only of our ilk who will help you. I have been named Most Glorious, and Prince of This World, and Adversary. I am called Lightbringer and Morningstar and Lord of Lies."

"Lucifer."

The red-haired man grinned without mirth and tapped his own nose. "Exactly right, Usiel. And we have much work to do."

about
the author

In the course of his life, Greg Stolze has been a secretary, a librarian, a groundskeeper, a novelist, a full-time parent and a telephone solicitor. He has worked for a bank, a credit union, a college and two different real estate companies. He has written classified ads, answered phones and done data entry. Writing is, by far, the easiest job he's done so far. Parenting is the hardest.

СОДЕРЖАНИЕ

IMPRIMÉ EN CEE
le 01-03-1995
B/95BK02 – Dépôt légal, mars 1995
ISBN : 2871714-269-8